The Tyrant's Daughter

Legends of Pangaea: Book One

I.D. Marie

ISBN Paperback: 979-8-9896472-0-0
ISBN Hardcover: 979-8-9896472-1-7

Book by I.D. Marie

Illustrations by Lunaris Falcon Studios

Second Edition: March 2024

www.idmarie-author.com

To my Nana,
I used to write every word with you.
Now I write every word for you.

Content Warning

The Legends of Pangaea Series is an Adult-rated series. This means there will be content unfit for some readers including:

Trauma around death of a loved one

Drug and alcohol abuse

Domestic abuse

Graphic violence

Cursing

Depictions of PTSD, depression, and anxiety

Human trafficking

Adult sexual content (not included in this book but will be in later parts)

[[Mission Files]]
Major Arianne Ortiz: United Colonies of Pacific, Year 2550

[[For context of the following report :: list of known operatives experienced on mission]]

[[United Colonies of Pacific]]

Capital City: Citadel Island, 36° 28'44" N, 24° 46'16" E
　　Ruler: Caesar Ortiz
　　Objective: Create a democratic republic in defiance of Pangaea's monarchy. Pacificans believe people should have options for government instead of being forced to adhere to one single global empire.

Known Operatives:

Caesar Ortiz (status: ALIVE) - Pacifican President - Former Spanish Elite within the Pangaean Empire, defected and founded the Pacifican rebellion. Graduate of the Paris University of Pangaea. Legal descendent: Arianne Ortiz

　　Jaleel Leroy (status: DECEASED) - Pacifican Vice President - Former French Elite within the Pangaean Empire, defected and co-founded the United Colonies of Pacific. Last seen in Mende, France, during an enemy attack. Wife and two children were also pronounced dead. Graduate of the Paris University of Pangaea. Known descendents: ???

Bradley Shaw (status: ALIVE) – Pacific Vice President -The late Vice President Leroy highly recommended him to become Pacific's second Vice President. He has a background in commerce.

Orion Kalfas (status: ALIVE) - Pacifican General - Background ???

Arianne Ortiz (status: CLASSIFIED) - Pacifican Major - Background CLASSIFIED

Jaya Bahri (status: ALIVE) - Pacifican Lieutenant - Pangaean Empire refugee. *Fera* mutation positive: skin and hair color manipulation, advanced abilities, and wall climbing. Citadel Academy graduate. Known relative: Kalinda Bahri

Kalinda Bahri (status: ALIVE) - Pacifican Field Medic First Class - Pangaean Empire refugee. Known relative: Jaya Bahri

Adam Williams_ Codename: RHINO (status: ALIVE) - Pacifican Lieutenant - *Fera* mutation positive: gray coloring, bullet resistant skin, advanced strength. Citadel Academy graduate.

Yina Lyn (status: ALIVE) - Pacifican Strike Force Captain - Detailed background of two decades of service for Pacific. Specialty: Vice President protection and extraction.

Carter Cadmilus (status: ALIVE) - Pacifican Strike Force Captain - Detailed background of two decades of service for Pacific. Specialty: President protection. Known descendant: Haris Cadmilus.

Haris Cadmilus (status: ALIVE) - Research and Development Corps Officer - Top island engineer, specialty: coding and electrical mechanics. *Fera* mutation positive: quill hair, quill projectiles, advanced abilities. Citadel Academy graduate.

Treena Helvig (status: ALIVE) - Forensic Scientist - Background ??? Known relative: Tyrell Helvig

Tyrell Helvig (status: ALIVE) - Forensic Scientist - Background ??? Known relative: Treena Helvig

Ignatius Ike (status: ALIVE) - Pacific Physician - Medical degree earned in Pangaea, Cambridge University.

[[The Empire of Pangaea, European Continent]]

Capital City: Leonueva, 46° 46'43" N, 25° 24'2" E
   Ruler: Leon Murray
   Objective: Pangaea is made up of six continents: Europe, Asia, Africa, Australia, North America, and South America. Each continent is ruled by one Commander. The Empire strives to create global peace and order after the chaos of the Great Disaster and Last War. A world united under the rule of six Commanders is the best way to maintain global homeostasis.

Known Operatives:

Leon Murray (status: ALIVE) - Pangaean Commander, Europe - Reagent of Europe, controls all of the continent's armies and citizens. Serum-enhanced psyche: every bit of Pangaean knowledge has been directly downloaded into his brain. Graduate of the Paris University of Pangaea. Known descendent: Andre Murray.

   Andre Murray (status: ALIVE) - Pangean Heir Apparent - son of the European Commander, next in line for the Commandership of Europe. Currently general of the Ward Squadron: the royal family elite military division. Graduate of the Paris University of Pangaea, Leonueva extension.

   Josephina Valentino Murray (status: ALIVE) - First Mother of Europe - Wife of Leon Murray, former Spanish Elite from Madrid. Graduate of the Paris University of Pangaea. Known descendent: Andre Murray

   Hera Richards (status: ALIVE) - European General of Scientific Warfare - Patriarch of the Richards family, reagent of the United Kingdom. Graduate of the Paris University of Pangaea. Known descendant: Pandora Richards.

   Pandora Richards (status: ALIVE) - Heir to Richards Family Title - Undercover operative for Murray family. Graduate of the Paris University of Pangaea, Leonueva extension. **Approach with caution****

   Blue Krait (status: ALIVE) - property of the Richards family - Apprehended six years ago, this servant's objective is to operate as an agent for Hera and Pandora Richards. *Fera* mutation positive: neurotoxic venom, advanced abilities, extreme flexibility **Approach with caution****

[[European Cartel]]

Capital City: UNKNOWN
Ruler: Imani Azikawe_ Codename: ACE

Objective: operates in the criminal underground of Europe. Specializes in drug and human trafficking. Made up of continent-wide casinos and undercover bases. An elite division of trained agents known as Jokers operates the organization under their boss's recommendations. Jokers can be identified by an Ace of Spades tattooed onto their dominant wrist.

Known Operatives:

Imani Azikiwe_ Codename: ACE (status: ALIVE)—Queen of the Underground—former Pangaean citizen on the continent of Africa. After an attack on her hometown, Ace was left with nothing to spare her ambition and hatred. Crawling to the top, Ace took over the European underground at a young age. She currently rules her organization with a manicured fist.

Blackjack (status: UNKNOWN) - Right Hand of Cartel - Background ???

Jamie Ramirez (status: ALIVE) - Joker trainee - former Pangaean citizen in the continent of North America.

Carol (status: ALIVE) - property of Ace - bought from her father at the age of eight, the household servant for Ace and her guests. *Fera* mutation positive: clawed fingers, increased agility, tail for balance.

Eleven Years Ago

S he did not remember who she was.

The past was a black chasm without even a hint of a light. Deep down, she knew something lingered there, but all she felt when she looked into the abyss was blood-chilling fear. She was everything. She was nothing. She was the warmth of the sun, the chill of the invisible wind, and all that rested in between.

Above the confusion and the atmosphere buffeting against her chilled face, there was one word driving her forward into the unknown: *survive.*

So she flew on her golden wings, still speckled with down, rocketing towards the horizon that bursted with vibrant color. The world was a beautiful expanse below, forests of green and mountains of purple sweeping past at dizzying speeds.

Despite all of the majesty before her, something malignant lingered beneath the surface. The girl didn't remember what, but she held onto the pressing feeling that she needed to continue onwards. So she soared through the sky, powerful wings beating against the pull of gravity. The movement was natural, freeing, and her very soul sang at the sensation. In her heart, she knew she belonged in those skies.

That's why she continued onward. Maybe she didn't remember what she was running from, but she knew that entity had fought to keep her bound to the earth from the moment her gifts had been brought into the world.

Then a novel sensation blossomed in her newborn mind: pain. The feeling was icy and burning all at once. It was violent and all-encompassing, beginning in her wing and radiating throughout her body. The world, once bright with color and promise, faded to gray as her very strength fell from her like rain from a cloud. For the first time in her short memory, the girl cried out in agony.

She fought to continue forward. *Survive, survive, survive.* Eyes focused on that beautiful horizon, she was convinced that if she could make it to that far-off place, everything would be okay.

But everything was far from okay. To her right, her once beautiful golden wing was covered in sickly crimson red. She didn't have to remember her life before her flight to know that she was in danger.

The sea rippled below her. She had a moment to take in the sparkling blue of the water before black spots blinded her vision. Her breathing grew short and irregular, and her head felt lighter than the clouds drifting around her. She tilted, her body losing its balance. The wind, once her friend as it carried her, turned against her. Her wings were useless, flopping behind her as she was sent into a downward spiral.

She fell, the water rushing up towards her at deadly velocity. But the winged girl was too disoriented to feel anything. In one thundering clap, her limp body hit the surface of the water. The impact was as hard as concrete. Unconscious, she sunk into the crystalline depths.

Chapter 1

She Came From the Sea and Sky

Caesar Ortiz was not watching for an angel to fall from the heavens. He had a suffocating need for fresh air to calm his racing thoughts.

The hull of his warship directly outside of his office cleared his head but didn't take much weight off his heart. The President of the small nation of Pacific leaned heavily on the railing of the ship, his clouded eyes assessing the waters of the Aegean Sea in deep consideration. For a fleeting moment, he was desperate enough to hope that the waves would provide him with a solution to his troubles. But all he saw was the distorted reflection of his face: severe, frowning, and weathered by years of leadership and cold wars.

Forty-five years. When had he gotten so old?

Their warship had been too late. Another colony had been attacked. Another failure. Another loss. More people, more *friends*, dead. There'd been no preventing the attack, but failure weighed heavy on his shoulders, regardless. As did the responsibility for every life lost.

A splash sounded, as loud as a crack of thunder, yanking him from his thoughts. Head snapping up from his melancholy reflection, he scanned the surrounding sea. At first, he only saw calm waves amongst the expanse of bright blue. Then his eyes caught something strange: a golden speck floating a few hundred yards away. He almost missed it as it began to sink.

Caesar turned, craning to see if someone else had witnessed the crash. Was he going crazy, or had a figure fallen from the sky? Before he could shout, alarms sounded across the ship.

Heavy boots pounded on the deck, followed by their screeching halt and a breathless question. "Are you all right?"

Caesar turned to the familiar sound of his friend: General Orion Kalfas.

"Something fell into the water," the President responded distantly, turning back towards the sea.

Kalfas shook his head as he joined his friend's side. "From where? There's water for miles in every direction!"

They were silent as the ship drew closer to the landing site of the mysterious object. A group of sailors took a raft to investigate. There was a collective gasp of shock as the rescuers pulled what looked like a body from the waves. The President shook his head as a million possibilities stirred inside of him. Was this newcomer a threat? How did they get there?

Caesar and Kalfas pushed through the crowd gathering at the ship's hull as the raft was pulled up from the sea. Concern was tangible amidst the crew, and Caesar wanted to be the first to intercept the phenomena.

The sailors hoisted a gurney onto the deck. A body was sprawled on top of it. Caesar stepped forward with a gasp. "It's a girl."

The small child was unconscious. Caesar would've believed that she was dead if he hadn't noticed the soft rise and fall of her chest. Her delicate round face was pale from the cold water and her dirty blonde hair stuck to her skin as she shivered in her sleep. She was covered in feathers, water, and blood.

"How is she still alive?" Kalfas wondered as he squatted down and checked her pulse.

Caesar was stunned into silence; she couldn't have been older than ten. A golden necklace of an angel with sapphire eyes glistening at her collarbone caught his attention. But the rest of the crew had their eyes fixed on something else. On both sides of the girl's neck were exactly five slits, evenly spaced between her ears and her shoulder line. The holes gaped open and closed as they searched for water like a fish caught on a line.

"She has gills," Caesar realized. Even as he spoke, the gills began to close and the girl's mouth opened in shallow breaths.

Someone spoke up in alarm, "She's bleeding, sir!"

Carefully, Kalfas searched her body for any wounds that could warrant so much blood. The General lifted the girl up to investigate her back to reveal another incredible abnormality. She had a set of golden-brown wings the color of her hair. And those golden wings were glossy with blood.

The General's searching stopped as his eyes widened. "Someone shot her," he hissed in alarm.

Caesar finally lunged forward. The sight of her back was nauseating. Kalfas was right, an ugly hole was torn through the girl's right wing leaving flesh, feathers, and sinew torn to bits. And blood was still flowing.

It was fresh.

"Someone call Dr. Ike!" Kalfas ordered.

"Already done, sir," responded one of the sailors.

"I've never seen a *Fera* like this before," Caesar said quietly. "Two distinct mutations. How did she get here? We're in the middle of the sea." He gathered her in his arms as Kalfas sprung up to search for the summoned doctor. He hardly noticed the gore ruining his military uniform as he held her tighter to counteract her shivering. "She's just a kid," he whispered in a trance.

The boat turned toward their home just south of Greece. Caesar didn't let the little girl out of his arms until they arrived on the island of Citadel: his tiny nation's capital city.

A day later, unable to concentrate on his work, Caesar found himself at the hospital. The only thing on his mind was the shivering winged girl who had seemingly fallen from the sky. Caesar didn't know what had come over him. A President who'd just lost an entire colony, worrying over a girl they'd found in the sea. Maybe he needed a distraction from all the death, maybe he just needed to see that there could be a happy ending for *someone*.

Dr. Ike greeted Caesar at the door as if he'd expected the President to show up. They fell into step together. "How is she?"

The doctor fixed his glasses and looked at the tablet in his hands. "She'll live, but her physical condition is troubling." They boarded the elevator. "She's extremely malnourished. We ran x-rays and her bones are hollow—like a bird—but even with that considered, she's still underweight."

The elevator dinged at their floor, the doors sliding open. Caesar gritted his teeth. "What the hell happened to her?"

Nothing was adding up. A *Fera* child was found half-dead in the middle of the sea, miles away from any land. The girl had been suffering from a bullet wound with blood loss that should have killed her. And now, obvious signs of neglect. Even considering her two mutations, she was an utter anomaly.

Dr. Ike pursed his lips as he pulled up a file on his tablet. "That's not even the worst of it," he sighed. "Have a look at this."

Caesar gazed at the images on the screen. "Are those . . .?"

"Whip marks, yes," Dr. Ike responded gravely. Angry ragged lines ran across her back, some even snaking into her wings. Dr. Ike, despite his many years of work, seemed unnerved. "Most have turned to scar tissue, but others cannot be more than a couple weeks old."

"They tortured her," Caesar growled. "They tortured a little girl."

"Thank God she was a mutant then," Dr. Ike said. "A normal child would not have survived this type of abuse."

"She's from Pangaea. She was abused *because* she was a *Fera*."

"How do you know?"

Caesar looked down. "We've all seen the worst Pangaea has to offer, Ike."

They'd been tearing the world apart for centuries. The worst crimes were against the emerging population of mutants that scientists had taken to calling *Homo feras*. Pangaea saw them all as subhuman and treated them as such.

That girl, whoever she'd run from, hadn't been saved from prejudice even as a child.

The doctor was quiet as he led Caesar down an uncharacteristically vacant corridor. Once alone, the doctor sighed. "I'm sorry, but we couldn't have her near the other patients in case there was any, ah, *commotion*."

Caesar knew what the doctor meant. It wasn't the safety of the girl he was worried about when he moved her into a private wing—the concern was for the other patients. There were plenty of stories that warned of *Feras* who'd been treated like animals turning into animals themselves.

Caesar nodded. "I checked in with the other outposts, and no such girl is missing from any of them. She's definitely from Pangaea."

"Who's going to take care of her?" Dr. Ike asked in a whisper as he opened the door to the girl's hospital room. "Pacific takes in any refugee from Pangaea, but we've never gotten an unaccompanied *Fera* child."

Dr. Ike did not say what both were thinking: *Who would take in someone like her?*

Caesar felt drawn to the girl as he sat down at her bedside. She was so young, tiny, and delicate. But at the same time, she was a strong little thing—she'd run away from *something* and survived. Under her pale skin, almost drained of life, she had a heart and a fighting spirit.

His eyes tracked the mutant girl's slow and even breathing. She'd fought every moment to make it to that island and beat every odd to survive. Without even formally meeting her, Caesar respected her. Blinking, he suddenly realized what he was meant to do. He wasn't religious, not many people were anymore, but he had a feeling that her arrival was a sign from some god—if any still existed.

"I'll take care of her," Caesar announced. With his duties as President and founding his country, his life had gotten in the way, and before he knew it, the hope of having a family of his own had long passed. Maybe, something, somewhere, had decided to give him another chance.

Dr. Ike smiled. "President Ortiz," he said, "your charity continues to amaze me even after years of working together." With a respectful nod, he stepped out.

Caesar sat with her for a while as nurses came in and out: checking her pulse, reading vitals, and finally removing her I.V. lines. He read documents and articles from his tablet as he patiently waited. Even after just a few hours at her side, Caesar felt at home with his decision. He only hoped she would wake up and agree.

At around dinnertime, when Dr. Ike came in with a couple of nurses to examine the girl, she finally woke up. Her large eyes, the color of the ocean on a cloudy day, widened as she took in her surroundings. Pupils narrowing to pinpoints, she screamed. Without warning, she leaped out of bed and shot towards the door. It took the combined strength of two nurses to catch her and hold her back.

Caesar stumbled in shock at the child's frantic reaction. *Feras,* though simply mutated forms of humans, could be pushed to become something very inhuman if left to fester. The phenomenon was termed going feral. Such a dangerous state had been rumored to give the mutant the capability to wipe out everyone in their path.

Even such a small girl had the strength to take out that entire room.

But, as Caesar watched the nurses hold the girl down, there was still a very human emotion glinting in her eyes: fear. The girl wasn't feral—not yet. She was a ten-year-old child, scared, far from home, and surrounded by strangers.

Caesar calmly asked the nurses and Ike to step out. Without her restraints, the girl sprinted to the corner of the room where she curled up against the safety of the wall. The President stood up slowly and cautiously advanced toward her. He raised his hands peacefully, hoping to show her that for most likely the first time in her life, someone didn't mean her harm. He frowned when he realized how forcefully the child shivered.

The girl let out a whimper as the President drew closer. It broke his heart. "It's okay, I'm not going to hurt you," Caesar said, kneeling to meet her eyes.

"Please don't send me back!" the girl cried out in Spanish. "*Por favor.*"

Caesar lowered to her level. She pressed herself further against the wall, and it pained him to see someone so young have so much fear.

Composing himself, Caesar replied in a language he hadn't spoken for almost twenty years, "I won't send you back," he said softly in Spanish. "I promise."

Her large eyes gazed fearfully into Caesar's but she didn't speak.

He offered a smile. "My name's Caesar, like the salad. What's your name?"

The girl hugged her knees tightly to her body, even though he'd spoken in Spanish, she seemed confused at his words. After a few seconds of consideration, a fog seemed to lift, and the girl blinked in realization. "Arianne," she whispered, "I think my name's Arianne. Please don't send me back."

To Caesar's amazement, Arianne now spoke perfect English.

He blinked. It was like she'd *forgotten* her own language like she'd forgotten her own name. He studied her desperate yet determined face. She was still fighting. He wanted to protect her and, sadly, he felt like he'd already failed. He reached out and offered a comforting hand. At first, the girl's caution prevented her from accepting his offer, but then she slowly gave in to the first promise of comfort, still shaking.

"Arianne, I want to help you as best as I can." Caesar squeezed her hand lightly. "But you need to tell me where 'back' is."

Arianne's gray-blue eyes filled with tears. "I hate him," she spat, turning her head away. "I'm never going back."

"Who is 'him,' my dear?'

"My Father," she hiccupped, "in Leonueva. He-he's probably searching for me right now." Tears streamed down her cheeks. "You can't escape him, you can never escape *him*. He told me that." She buried her face in her knees. "I shouldn't have run."

"Who's your father?"

Arianne's reddened eyes looked up. "Leon Murray," she said through trembling lips.

Caesar's eyes widened and he withdrew slowly from the little girl. Leon. Not Leon. He should have known, should've realized why he felt so connected to the girl. For longer than he could remember, he'd been connected to her father. Like two sides of a coin, Caesar and Leon had been rivals and opposites for most of their lives.

The features of both of her parents were engraved on Arianne's face. The blonde hair and gray eyes came from her father. But her determination ... that unmistakably came from her mother, Josephina Valentino. That explained where the Spanish had come from. Arianne hadn't just run from anyone. She'd run from one of the most powerful families in the world.

Arianne Murray was the daughter of one of the six great Commanders of Pangaea: the rulers of the six inhabited continents. Leon Murray was the reigning reagent of Europe itself. Years ago, Caesar had stepped away from Pangaea to found his own colony of free people in spite of Leon. Had Arianne been born a human and remained in Leonueva, Europe's capital city, she would've one day become Caesar's enemy when she Ascended to Commander.

But no. Caesar would raise her differently. He would raise her to be *better* than her Murray ancestors who had terrorized Europe for generations—and aided the other five continents in world domination.

"Arianne," Caesar began, "I am the President of the United Colonies of Pacific. You have a home here if you wish. We are independent of Pangaea. On my word, we will protect you."

Arianne was quiet. She raised her golden necklace to her mouth and held it lightly in her teeth for comfort. Then she nodded her head. "Okay."

"If you would like," Caesar continued, "you can stay with me." He quickly corrected, realizing what it might look like for another adult man to determine her life. "But we have other foster programs if you would prefer that."

The winged girl considered his words. Her piercing eyes claimed as much dominating power as her father's as she stared at him. Caesar almost buckled under that gaze. Yes, in another life, Arianne could have grown to become one hell of a Commander.

"Okay," she said again.

Caesar struggled to keep from shaking as he placed a reassuring hand on the girl's shoulder. "Okay." He smiled. "But, you need to promise me something first. No one must ever know where you came from. From this day on, you're Arianne Ortiz. My daughter. All right?"

Because if anyone found out who Arianne was, there would be hell to pay. The people of the island would shun her, sure. But Caesar's true fear was Leon. The European Commander would bring the entire might of his continent down on their little island and drown them all to get his daughter back.

Part I

A Beautiful Prison

Chapter 2

Arianne

T he alarm blared.

Arianne bolted awake on the morning of her last day. It had finally come. She jumped out of bed before the third ring as energy coursed through her veins. Her limbs were a hurricane of motion as she dressed herself in a perfectly pressed white tee shirt, brown military khakis, and shining black boots.

Her large wings of brown and speckled golden feathers extended and tracked behind her as she moved. Getting dressed with wings was not easy, but Arianne had twenty-one years of practice. Now, no matter what outfit, she could get dressed as quickly as most. Much like tucking her shoulders into a shirt, she held her wings close and let her shirt slide over them. Even with practice, the task got more complicated with each year. As the muscles of her wings filled out and the bones grew to carry her longer distances, her wings were growing larger. Arianne probably only had another year until it was impossible to keep her *Fera* genetics hidden in regular clothes.

While Pacific was *Fera*-friendly, Arianne enjoyed moving about the island without curious eyes following her. Besides, she didn't want her wings to be the main focus on such an important day.

That sunny morning marked the beginning of her last day at the Pacifican Military Academy. That following weekend, she would graduate as a Pacifican Officer: bachelor's degree and all. After years spent studying, training, and building her expertise, she would start her new life.

Finally, she would be somebody more than the destiny she ran from eleven years ago.

Arianne moved to run out her bedroom door when a glint caught her eye. Her golden angel necklace hung on her vanity, shining in the sunlight filtering in through her bedside window. She slowed, considering the necklace. That small item of jewelry was the last reminder of her life before the island. She almost considered putting it on.

Her hand went to her neck where a new necklace hung- her military dog tags. Setting her jaw, she turned away from the golden angel's sparkling sapphire eyes as a pointed reminder that she was officially leaving that part of her life behind. She was Arianne Ortiz now, a soon-to-be Academy graduate. As if to solidify her thoughts, she turned her dog tags around to look at the name etched into the reflective metal.

Yes, her past was behind her now. By finishing her degree, she would be a self-made female. She would build her future based on her merit, education, and *talent*. She wouldn't be *his* daughter. Ortiz, Ortiz, Ortiz. The name repeated itself over and over inside her head, drowning out the true name she had pushed down for over a decade.

"Get up, Arianne," she heard Him shout. *"Get up!"*

She turned back to the necklace, her father's voice seemingly echoing off the golden chains. Her lips parted, transfixed by the necklace. She leaned towards her vanity, reaching for the keepsake in a trance.

Leon Murray, the Commander of Europe, came through in whispers once again, *"Get up, Arianne!"*

"You're not real," Arianne hissed, her eyes squeezing shut.

"Get up, Arianne! You're going to be late for your last day! *Vamos!* "Caesar's voice came from downstairs, breaking her from her trance.

She pushed herself away from the necklace, spinning to run out her door before her father's ghostly hands wrapped themselves around her mind once again. In dismay, she glanced toward her alarm clock and realized she had been frozen for ten minutes. Part of her wanted to tell someone that her blackouts were getting worse, but she couldn't stand the questioning. She didn't know if she could handle someone reaching into her past and bringing it all back... she barely tolerated the few memories she'd retained. She didn't want more to be brought to the surface.

She didn't want to experience what would happen if the floodgates of her mind were allowed to open. Caesar tried to bring her to therapy when she was younger, but the sessions were too painful. After years of trying, Caesar had eventually given up. Arianne was resigned to keeping the past *in the past.*

The winged female broke out into a cold sweat as she reached the staircase down to the kitchen. She felt troubled and distant. Memories of her time in Pangaea always threatened to pull her down into a pool of madness. The memories were nothing more than fractured nightmares, but they still left her deeply unsettled.

"You're not there anymore," she steeled herself, "you're not there anymore."

It had been eleven years since her adopted father, Caesar Ortiz, rescued her. As the years slowly crept past, her memories of her original home seemed to fade with the breeze. But small and lingering glimpses of her time before Pacific managed to find their way through minuscule cracks in her subconscious at the worst times.

Like when she was supposed to be celebrating her last day before the rest of her life.

Arianne shook herself as she reached the bottom of the stairs, mastering an air of controlled calm. Caesar was in the kitchen, a steaming cup of coffee at his side despite the Mediterranean heat. The Pacific President was busy reading some files as Arianne approached the counter.

Caesar looked up, brows furrowing, "What were you doing up there?"

"My hair." she grinned, knowing full well all she had done was hastily throw the wild mane into a ponytail.

"Your hair," Caesar eyed his daughter in disbelief, "you mean the rat's nest on top of *tu cabeza*?"

"I like my hair like this," Arianne countered, grabbing an apple. "Besides, if I took the time to do it, I would ruin it while flying," the female said, sitting with her foraged fruit and two muffins.

"Arianne," Caesar scolded. "You don't have time to sit down- you're going to be late."

"*Quiete*, "Arianne shushed Caesar's fussing. "Everything's fine."

It wasn't like she was going to school, anyway.

With a quick goodbye, Arianne grabbed her bag and ran towards the balcony behind the kitchen. Straddling on the railing before the daunting drop down the cliff below, she mockingly saluted her father one last time. Caesar, used to her typical departure, simply rolled his eyes.

With a grin, Arianne leaned back and let gravity pull her downwards. Her stomach gave an exhilarating flop, and she let out a scream of excitement. The ground rushed upwards toward her: leaves and rocks blurring past her eyes as she gained speed. At the last moment, she let her wings unfurl behind her from the holes she had slit in the back of her shirt. She trusted in her wings' unwavering strength as they pulled her from the free fall and straightened her out to glide above the dirt road leading to her house just a few feet below.

Years of flying from her home had allowed her to calibrate that fall from the balcony down to a fraction of a second. Arianne formulated the perfect ratio of free fall and time to catch herself. Caesar hated every moment of it, including the months of practice it took to not face plant in the ground—like she'd managed to do multiple times. All failed attempts sent her to the hospital, where she earned wonderful lectures from both Caesar and Dr. Ike. She didn't listen though. Her *Fera* healing meant that whatever mistake she made would be gone in a few weeks or less.

She directed her flight down a familiar path toward the home of her closest friend. Much like the free fall, the path was a reflex for Arianne: she'd been flying it for almost as long as she'd been on the island. Fanning out her wings to slow her approach, she caught sight of a purple head waiting outside. Jaya Bahri, the queen of living by the books, was unsurprisingly punctual. Arianne altered the angle of her wings as she began her landing procedure. The wind stirred from her breaking tossed around dust and rustled Jaya's hair in silky violet strands.

Arianne slid in front of her friend, her dragging feet slowing her down like an anchor. Jaya didn't flinch as her friend stopped mere inches from her face and managed to sassily cross her arms once Arianne finally halted. "What did I tell you about speeding through the neighborhood?"

Arianne let out a breath, folding her wings behind her, "Come on, cut me some slack, Jay. I'm excited!"

Jaya frowned. "Are you sure about this?" she asked, slowly gesturing down to her wetsuit. "We could get into a lot of trouble."

"It looks like you already made a decision," Arianne chided, nodding at Jaya's purple wetsuit, the color perfectly matching her hair.

Like most, Arianne thought Jaya's purple hair was a cosmetic choice when she first met her. But the truth was far more complicated. Jaya, like Arianne, was a *Fera,* but her abilities were more cosmetic than most. Much like a chameleon, she could change the color of her hair and skin. Without any conscious interference, her hair was naturally the brightest shade of purple.

Jaya played with a strand of her famous hair, thinking, "Unlike a wetsuit, you can't change out of a write-up."

Arianne laughed; it had taken her weeks to convince her friend to join in on Senior ditch day. No graduate went to school on the last day—no graduate that knew how to have fun. Arianne ignored her friend's last-minute concerns as she started to change out of her uniform. Unlike Jaya, who lived with her sister, Arianne couldn't walk out of her house in a wetsuit on a school day, or the wrath of her father and the *President* would cripple her plans before she reached the door.

In the past, Caesar had even sent his daughter with a security escort when he thought she was up to something.

Arianne was so busy storing her uniform in her bag and retrieving her wetsuit that she didn't notice Jaya's awkward lack of a retort. Realizing what her friend was staring at, Arianne's packing slowed to a halt. Without her uniform, Arianne's back was exposed to the world. Most would notice the set of golden wings protruding from her lats. But, since the pair of best friends had grown up used to each other's abnormalities, Arianne knew her wings were not what her friend was fixated on. There was only one thing Arianne rarely let anyone see.

Her scars: the nasty collection of thin lines built up from years of living under her father.

Had Arianne not retained scars from her time with Leon, she wouldn't remember much about that specific realm of treatment. She decided a long time ago that she didn't want to explain her father's actions. Trying to rationalize everything that she remembered—and didn't—was a one-way ticket to insanity.

The whip markings and the bullet wound were painful fragments of her past she struggled to tolerate. Even as time healed her and feathers covered most of the scars on her wings, Arianne still knew where every scar sat—especially the bullet wound. Eleven years later and she could still feel ghostly throbbing like it was bleeding.

Arianne used to try and make herself look at the scars, but every attempt left her exhausted and foggy. She learned long ago that she was perfectly fine as long as she ignored those awful markings on her skin. But that fix wasn't bulletproof. Yes, she understood the irony. Sometimes, people caught a glimpse of what she had run from, and their reaction wasn't easy to ignore.

In the chaos of the morning, Arianne had forgotten to change in a way that kept her back concealed. And now Jaya was looking at her like *that*—like she was horrified and sorry all at once.

"I-um," Jaya attempted to speak to remove the tension in the air, "do you need help with your suit?"

Arianne quickly pulled the wetsuit over her back and expertly tucked her wings inside the flexible fabric. She focused on fixing her wetsuit to avoid the awkward air. She fought to ignore the heat of her friend's stare even though she could feel the melting gaze. She hated it when she could sense people feeling sorry for her. Moments like those reminded her that there were some things years of hard work could never change.

"I'm fine," the winged female said a little too bluntly.

Jaya knew enough not to press, she rarely did on subjects like Arianne's life before the island. The purple-haired *Fera* allowed a small smile to come to her face. "Okay, let's have some fun."

Arianne nodded, shaking the gloom away with a smile. Another learned reflex.

The pair waited for their ride at the edge of the stairs up to Jaya's house. A few minutes later, a topless car turned into the gravel drive. A *Fera* with brown quilled hair leaned out of the driver's seat, a broad smile coming to his face as he pulled down a pair of glinting sunglasses.

Arianne brightened, waving at the *Fera*, "Haris!" She greeted him.

Haris was like sunshine after a rainy day. No matter what mood Arianne found herself in, he was always able to pull her out of it. Something about his aloof, carefree happiness made her smile on the worst days. Even Jaya—who worried more than what was probably good for her blood pressure—brightened around Haris.

Haris lowered his glasses, "Mission senior skip day is a-go." He revved his engine. "Hop in, I'm getting old."

Jaya and Arianne barely got into the car before Haris turned up the volume on his speakers and pressed the gas. Arianne stuck her head out the side of the vehicle as Haris sped down the dirt road toward one of Pacific's famous beaches. She closed her eyes and let the wind blow through her hair. With her head hanging out the window and the warm island air buffeting her face, it felt like she was flying.

Well, nothing matched flying. But it was close.

The three danced and sang as Haris pulled up to the beach. About fifty more seniors were already waiting for them, surfboards, beach ball nets, umbrellas, speakers, and towels painting the beach in bright pops of color. Butterflies of excitement filled Arianne's stomach as she anticipated the day waiting ahead of her.

Arianne pulled her surfboard out of the back of Haris's car, "This is what I'm talking about!" She shouted, the smell of sunscreen filling the air.

"Look who finally decided to show up!" Bellowed Rhino as he tanned his umber skin to a slick bronze on a towel next to his girlfriend, Treena.

The fourth *Fera* in Arianne's friend group was Rhino, who'd earned his nickname well. He was easily one of the largest people on the island, with shoulders broad enough that he struggled to get through doors. Rhino's silver hair, shaved at the temples and kept long and spiked in the middle, worked hard to emulate his namesake.

Rhino nodded to Jaya, who was carrying over her surfboard, "I can't believe you got her to come." he smirked, which earned a slap from his girlfriend.

Jaya snarled at the larger *Fera*, "Well, I'm here, aren't I?"

"Alright! Who's surfing with me?" Arianne shouted.

With her memories deciding to be extra volatile lately, Arianne needed the day more than most. The last thing she wanted was her friends' bickering. And if she knew Jaya, the female knew how to bicker better than most. Rhino sprung up from his beach towel and grabbed his surfboard. Jaya shouted in agreement and joined the charge to the water.

Arianne sighed as the sea water surrounded her, the salty air filling her nose. Yes, there was a part of her born of the sky, but there was another part born of the sea as well. She felt her breathing transfer from her lungs to the gills that lined her neck. The transition, similar to a manual car, wasn't always perfect, but it had become normal for her. Time and practice from years spent surrounded by water allowed her basic control over the sometimes jerky transition.

She still wasn't perfect, though her issue had grown worse on land. Panic attacks were deadly. If Arianne got too panicked, her hyperventilation would get so intense that her gills would take over as her body searched for another way to get air.

Arianne dove under the waves, her surfboard attached to her leg dragging behind her. The waters were crystal blue, allowing for perfect visibility. Sunlight trickled through the rippling surface, bouncing and diffracting in soft patterns around her. Bubbles floated up from her neck as her gills took a deep breath of water, reminiscent of a satisfied sigh.

This was heaven.

Arianne surfed all morning with her classmates. With the water around her and music pounding from the shore, she felt alive. She could have lived every day like that. She stayed out with Jaya on the waves longer than most; the exhilaration of surfing to the shore kept them addicted to the refreshing Mediterranean waters. The friends caught the same crashing wave, and they raced, eyes set in determination as they taunted each other.

The part of Arianne born from water sang in satisfaction.

By midday, Arianne was playing beach ball with Haris and a couple of other engineering students. Haris was a prodigy in coding and technology; he was at the top of his class because of it. He was so impressive that he received a prestigious offer to start as an officer in the military research and development division after graduation.

"I got it!" Arianne shouted as she dove into the sand to save the ball.

When Arianne got up, she was covered with sand. Luckily, none of it got in her feathers. If it had, she would have been stuck cleaning them for days. And there was nothing that annoyed her more than sand in her bed at night. She told herself that keeping her wings clean was the only reason she still wore her wetsuit while others had changed into their bathing suits, but she knew she was lying to herself.

She wore that shirt to pretend, even just a little, that she was normal. She would never trade her ability to fly for the world, but sometimes, it was nice to feel like she was no different than everyone else around her. Her wings were not getting caught on everything when she moved—and no one saw her scars. With her back concealed, she could simply be Ari: the driven, energetic, and competitive Pacifican. No one saw the haunted Pangaean Princess underneath.

If she had her way, no one would ever see that side of her again.

As she played, students from the culinary department grilled on the shoreline. She paused as the teams rotated, breathing in deep and basking in the glow of the beautiful summer day. She couldn't think of a way to make it more perfect. But that was life on the Pacific island of Citadel: a beautiful oasis in the middle of the barren desert of Pangaean rule. She wasn't blind to the struggles of the rest of the world, but enjoying herself didn't make her evil. She deserved it after the hell she'd been put through.

The Citadel Academy Senior Class partied on that beach until the sun dropped below the waves they were surfing. Despite all the sunscreen that seemed to float in the air like a haze, everyone's skin turned some shade of pink or another. To Arianne, despite the sunburn complaints, it meant they all had a fun time. Nothing made her happier.

Once it got dark enough, bonfires sprung up and down the beach, tongues of flame reaching up to the night sky above. The seniors danced and sang loudly in the cooling sand as a student band called *The Black Sails* played their deafening music. Arianne twirled with her friends, her bare feet moving through the sand as its granules brushed across her skin satisfyingly.

The night wound down, and Arianne sat at the edge of the waves next to Jaya, Rhino, and Haris. Jaya rested her head on Arianne's shoulder, a deep sigh escaping as she smiled. The group sat in silence, all of them watching the moon slowly brighten above the indigo horizon.

"Are you ready?" Jaya asked, breaking the peaceful quiet.

Tomorrow, their lives would begin. Haris would become an engineer among the respected ranks of the Research and Development Corps. Jaya and Rhino, as top trainees, would become Lieutenants in the Air Force. And Arianne, as their valedictorian, would join the military as a Major.

Throughout their time at the academy, Jaya and Arianne spent countless nights dreaming of all the missions they would go on together as partners. And now that dream was right on the doorstep. She couldn't wait to see where her new life would take her. For the first time in her life, she could make a difference. She could join in on the fight against Pangaea.

Arianne smiled softly, chin pointed up towards the sky. "Am I ready to spend the rest of my life going on missions with you? Seeing the world? Saving the world?" She couldn't help but feel a jolt of glee shoot through her.

Rhino let out a deep, rumbling laugh. "We'll be heroes."

"That's what I've been waiting for my whole life," Arianne whispered.

A new start. She would leave behind her past as Leon Murray's daughter. She would fight the good fight with her friends by her side. She couldn't think of anything better. As the waves lapped peacefully in front of her, her eyes were pulled closed to their sound. Surrounded by the warmth of her friends against the chilling sea breeze, Arianne fell asleep as her mind raced with dreams of far-off lands.

Tomorrow, her life would begin. Tomorrow, she would become a hero.

Chapter 3
Blackjack

Blackjack couldn't remember the last time he'd felt the music.

Once, the whole world was a symphony inside of his head. He could create songs in seconds from the call of birds or the patter of feet. Instruments demanded to be played, and when he couldn't find one, his fingers would constantly move like he was in his own silent orchestra.

But as years went by, the melodies disappeared. The world, once bright with color, was only gray. Now, the only sounds he listened to were ones that kept him alive. The sole instrument he played was the trigger of a gun, its thundering power drowning out any hope of hearing something beautiful.

Once upon a time, he had been someone with hope, family, and dreams. Now, he was whatever his boss wanted him to be. When he was younger, he had a name given to him by the family he loved. Now, the people who feared him called him Blackjack.

"Where is he?" Jack droned as he marched down the dilapidated and gloomy corridor. Jack was in Budapest, Hungary, on a *housecleaning* mission. His job took him to many places—one of the few upsides.

"Right this way," the man next to him muttered.

Jack smiled. The man next to him was twice his age, and yet Jack was the one with the power. He decided he liked doing business in Budapest; they showed him the respect he deserved there—unlike back at home.

Jack was led into a dimly lit room where ten men sat at a long table. As soon as he entered the cramped space, all of their eyes turned to him. He knew what they were thinking: the infamous Blackjack, coming to visit them. But he wasn't concerned with underground grunts. His only focus was on the man sitting at the head of the table: Istvan Zoltan.

His target.

Jack ignored the chair one of the grunts pulled out for him. Instead, he hopped onto the long gray table, grinning like a cat when his landing sent a reverberating clang throughout the room. The people seated at the table flinched, and Jack felt a momentary feeling of satisfaction. They *feared* him.

His reputation preceded him, then.

Jack sauntered down the table towards Istvan, the sound of his boots echoing in the terrified silence. Unlike his companions, Istvan seemed unamused as the newcomer approached. Once Jack reached the end of the table, he crouched down in front of the man. "Ace wants to know why the hell you've been screwing her over."

Ace was the head of Cartel, an Underground organization that stretched across Old Europe. Any black-market deal, from drugs to organs to weapons and even slaves, was on the table. Ace had her well-manicured fingers in every black-market pie in Europe. And Blackjack was her enforcer, bounty hunter, and right hand.

Istvan frowned as he returned Jack's stare, "I have no idea what you mean." He looked at the other men at the table, muttered something in Hungarian, and laughed nervously with the rest of the room.

The bounty hunter felt a wave of annoyance surge inside him, but he pushed it down, opting for a more *professional* glare. With a powerful thrust, he threw a folder down on the table. "Do you want me to open this, or can we save some time?"

Istvan's eyes drifted to the folder as he raised his upper lip in a scowl, "screw you.

Jack rubbed his hands together eagerly. "Great, I love it when people say that."

The bounty hunter raised his pistol and fired two shots. The room around him jumped back at the sudden sound. Jack was so used to the ear-splitting explosion that he hardly batted an eye. The bullet hit home, and Istvan's body shot backward with the close-range shot. Blood, fresh and bright red, splattered on the wall behind the former head of the Budapest branch. The vibrant splash of blood could almost be called artistic in the way it brought a fresh pop of color to the ugly gray concrete.

He grinned, allowing himself a few moments to bask in the aftershock. He loved it when he left people speechless.

Jack dropped his pistol on the table, resulting in a jarring clang in the silence. Pivoting to look at the rest of the room, he frowned, "How many times do I have to tell you guys not to fuck with Ace? This is the second time I've been here this year. Not cool, guys, not cool." Jack pointed to the man sitting to the right of Istvan's body. "You," the man made eye contact with him and began to shake, "You're in charge."

The man nodded frantically. "Yes, Mr. Blackjack. Thank you, Mr. Blackjack."

Jack waved the man off as he hopped off the table and walked out of the dimly lit room, "Whatever, just clean that mess up." He looked down at his watch. "I'll see you in six months." He grinned.

Once Jack closed the doors behind him, he let his façade drop. He knew he needed to keep up his guise of apathy and fearlessness in front of others, but that didn't mean maintaining a specific reputation wasn't tiring. Even Blackjack needed a moment or two to breathe without the judgment of others. He took a moment to remind himself that his reputation was his survival, that leaving no cracks to find weaknesses kept him above ground. Still, behind closed doors, he was just another man happy to survive another day. Another day, another mission complete, another paycheck—things never guaranteed in his line of work.

"Hey, you're Blackjack, right?" Someone asked behind him.

Jack turned around with a scowl of annoyance. "What is it?"

A younger boy with sunken eyes stood behind him. "We were wondering if you could look at the captured *Feras* while you were here. Istvan didn't watch over 'em well."

Feras were a subspecies of humans: animalistic mutants growing in population throughout Pangaea. They were stronger and faster and carried stunning traits similar to certain species of animals—those traits unique and varying from *Fera* to *Fera*. Sometimes, their inherited abilities left them too different to exist comfortably in society. Jack's mother used to describe the phenomenon as having one foot in the forest and one foot in civilization.

Since the founding of Pangaea, thousands of tribes have sprouted up on the edges of the Empire around the world. The nomad groups, which existed outside of the laws of Pangaea, had become popular homes for *Feras*. As Pangaea grew increasingly hostile towards the mutants, more *Feras* escaped to the wilds. This made the ratio of *Feras* to normal humans higher in tribes than in civilization. Existing as independent groups in the wilds of the world without any protective laws made the tribes perfect grounds for hunting slaves.

The Asian section of Pangaea had been doing it long before Europe, but once Cartel had its hold over Europe, Ace hadn't hesitated to bring the highly lucrative *Fera* trafficking market across the continent. Ten million units per slave was the average selling price.

Jack turned to the grunt who had spoken to him, "I don't work with *Feras*," he asserted.

Jack would do almost anything Ace said, but slavery was his line.

The grunt shook under Jack's stare. He couldn't have been older than sixteen. For a moment, the bounty hunter wanted to yell at the boy to get the hell out of that disgusting business before it was too late. Sometimes, Jack wished someone had given him another option at that age.

"Well," the boy pressed, "I don't think anyone else here has the expertise to deal with this problem. One of the female *Feras* have gone feral, sir."

Adult *Feras* preferred to be called male and female, not man and woman. Jack always thought it was ass-backward that people were eager to take *Fera's* rights away, but they were respectful of their customs.

Jack stopped walking and turned to the boy. Going feral was an interesting and dangerous side effect of being pushed to the breaking point. Mutants became much stronger than their sane counterparts, but the tradeoff made them volatile—insane. The theory was that loss of the mind led to a loss of control that held a mutant's full potential back. And that potential was devastating to anyone and anything unfortunate enough to be in their path.

"Take me to her." Jack sighed in annoyance.

He hated seeing the slaves. It triggered the last part of him that had any sort of moral compass. At least when he was killing and tormenting Ace's goons, the goons usually deserved it. Often, anyone Jack bothered had it coming long before he showed up. But slaves? They were innocent *Feras* with no say in who or what they were born as.

The Hungarian boy led Jack deeper into the compound and down three levels. The only positive of the basement he was taken to was that the moist air was refreshing compared to the insufferable heat a few flights above.

Then Jack heard them, cells upon cells of captured *Feras*.

They cried out in dozens of languages, most of which Jack couldn't understand. *Feras* were cramped in dark cells, shackled and collared. He could barely look at their helpless faces covered with grime and tears. He winced away. How could people do that to other people?

That was Ace's business—and, by extension, his. Even if Jack didn't work with slaves exclusively, his work to keep Cartel running meant he ultimately participated in keeping the European slave trade booming. Jack worked for a woman who profited off of that level of suffering. If he still cared about the state of his soul, he might have retched on the spot.

"Where is the feral mutant," Jack demanded, unable to lift his head.

"Through here," the boy responded, his thin hand reaching hesitantly to unlock the prison door at the end of the hall.

Before Jack reached the door handle, he could hear the guttural growls of the *Fera* beyond the metal door. The roars were so low and ancient that chills snaked up his spine. He wasn't quite sure if he *wanted* to see what awaited him on the other side. Unfortunately, looking like a frightened child in front of Cartel goons wouldn't be the best thing for his reputation.

Slowly, Jack opened the door. A singular *Fera* was kneeling on the ground. With her head down, he couldn't make out many features except her scaled skin, bald head, and two slits in her skull where earlobes should have been. Claw marks ran up and down the walls around the female like fateful warnings of what would happen if he accidentally got too close. The *Fera's* slightly clawed hands, the culprit of the marks, were chained up at the wrists.

Jack closed the door behind him, wincing at how the clang sounded like a dinner bell. The female looked up, and he could finally see her eyes. Black and depthless pits stared through his soul, and he was certain that nothing human remained there—only a caged animal.

Jack held out his hands, "It's okay, I'm here to help you," he said soothingly. "Help," he repeated in French, the only other language he knew besides English.

He knew before even trying that any of his attempts were useless. Once a *Fera* went feral there was no returning their sanity. Not entirely, at least.

A growl rose in the *Fera's* throat, and Jack did his best not to move. He knew from years of dealing with *Feras* in their many forms that he couldn't let the creature sense an ounce of weakness in him. For a moment, the female seemed subdued; then, she lashed out against her chains as claws extended from her bony fingers.

Despite all of his training, despite all the years he had spent seeing the worst the world had to offer, Jack still flinched. He jumped back and hugged himself as tightly to the door as possible as a startled shout escaped him. The female didn't make it far from her chained spot, but she got close enough to make him nearly wet himself.

She was so much more haunting up close.

The female's clothes were torn to shreds, leaving little to the imagination. But then again, what was modesty when her mind was in tatters? Jack slid across the wall slowly, fighting to calm his breathing as he analyzed the monster that paced in front of him. A monster his people created. That was the fate of any *Fera* pushed too far—any *Fera* that lost connection with their humanity. He had never seen anything more terrifying.

Jack threw open the door behind him, "What the hell have you been doing here?" He demanded of the boy waiting on the other side.

The boy looked at the *Fera* behind Jack with wide eyes, "Nothing, sir. We just—we just… well, some *Feras* take being trapped here a lot better than others."

"Is she the first one?"

The boy gritted his teeth. "There have been others; none of 'em have lived this long. Usually, they kill themselves before we can get a hold of 'em."

Jack looked longingly at the female behind him, "I want you to report to Ace's headquarters in Leonueva if you get any more. You can't help them here, and they'll just hurt more people if you keep them chained up like this."

Chained up like animals.

Jack frowned at the female behind him, who was flashing her sharpened teeth at him and raking her clawed fingernails back and forth through the concrete. The noise of the *Fera's* nails pierced his ears, and he covered them to block out the sound. Jack winced at the female. "Help," he tried to reassure her again.

The only response he received was a deep growl.

Before he lost his wits, he threw open the doors and dashed to the safety of the dungeon beyond. "I'll take this one back to Leonueva with me and speak with Ace," Jack instructed breathlessly. What was he going to say to his boss? He wasn't quite sure yet. "Until then, tell your superiors to make the conditions down here better. We can't have slaves going feral. It's a hazard."

The boy nodded quickly, "I'll tell 'em."

Jack hastily made for the exit. Before climbing up to the relief of being above-ground, he stopped at the bottom of the stairs and turned to the boy, "And kid? Get the hell out of here. I know there aren't many options, but go work on a farm, do something. Just get out of here before it's too late."

A couple of days later, Jack found himself in Ace's main casino in Leonueva: the current capital of Old Europe. He had been waiting for the past hour to get a meeting with Ace, not that he cared. He had plenty of games to keep him distracted.

Jack pushed his chestnut hair out of his face as he glanced at his cards and moved all his chips to the center of the table. "I'm all in." He smirked.

The rest of the table in the gloom roared in annoyance as the dealer flipped over the last card. Jack had won again. A larger man with long sleeves of tattoos on his arms threw his cards to the ground with a bark of annoyance. With a warning glare, the man stood up and stormed off. Jack let an empty grin come to his face: he'd been in Budapest for two days, and he needed to remind people in that casino who was the best gambler around. No one left the table with more Units than him, spare Ace, but even Jack was certain he could give the Cartel Boss a run for her money.

A teenage boy stumbled over. He was thin, with long black hair and tan skin. The boy snapped at the tattooed man as he passed. "Hey," he slurred, "don't hate the player. Hate the game."

"Jamie," Jack warned slowly as the dealer recorded his points, "I'm not in the mood to save your ass tonight."

"Well, I hope you are in the mood to make our asses some money tonight, *amigo*."

Jack's amber eyes looked up in the gloom of the room, "I'm not making us any money tonight," he grumbled as he scanned his hand on the table to save his winnings and moved away from the pressing younger boy.

Jack had minimal patience at reasonable times. Jamie cut whatever patience he had in half. Yet, he could never let the brat get killed.

Jamie bit his lip for a second before he ran to catch up to Jack, who was pushing his way through the crowd, "Come on," Jamie pressed. "It would be like old times! We win a bit and then take some people back to my place." He paused, "or someone else's place," he added more quietly with a suggestive raise of his eyebrows.

"I'm not in the mood," Jack hissed.

Jamie sighed. "Okay, I admit I promised a couple o' people that we would be stopping by. Well, most importantly, you. They wanted to meet the famous Blackjack. Just come with me? *Por favor*? We won't even stay out too late."

A girl winked at Jack as he walked beside Jamie, but he was too tired to wink back.

Jack rolled his eyes. "Don't you have Boy's Night tonight?" He asked Jamie, "I think that's a little more important."

Jamie groaned. "It's not fun without you there," he said. "Seeing as you're too important to show up now. Come on! The new recruits aren't scared of us anymore!"

"You know, when I saved your ass from Boy's Nights, I didn't expect to get an annoying fucking shadow following me around," Jack hissed, flicking the aforementioned annoyance off.

"Come by and show them how it's done!"

Jack continued moving. He'd spent years in grueling Joker training. He saw no need to go back again. Jokers were Ace's elite enforcers who protected her and executed her most critical missions. Boy's Night is an integral part of the Joker trainee culture, and its brutality created the hardened forces Ace relied so heavily on.

One special night a month, all of the Joker trainees would go out on the city and beat the living shit out of a predetermined trainee who was slacking off. The activity did a surprising job of bringing the trainees together, and it provided the unique opportunity to scare underperformers shitless. Boy's Night simultaneously sharpened trainees and saved them from a much worse punishment by their remorseless trainers in the future.

Before Jack had left the Jokers, he had been the ringleader of such sacred nights.

During his earlier days in Cartel, Jamie had been the unfortunate benefactor of most Boy's Nights. For some reason, the annoying American found a soft spot inside Jack, and he had taken the boy under his wing and made him into a half-decent trainee. Despite the odds, Jamie was now the top of his squadron and destined to be minted as a Joker any time now.

"Jamie, go do your damn job and knock some sense into the new guys." Jack poked the American. "Stop drinking like a dumbass."

Jamie mockingly saluted his former benefactor, "Ya' got it, all-mighty Blackjack." He rolled his eyes. "Not all of us have your legendary tolerance." The bounty hunter shrugged Jamie off. He wasn't about to get into his drinking habits—or lack thereof—with the annoying trainee.

Before Jack was inclined to respond to Jamie, a guard dressed in white techwear elbowed his way through the crowd. The man stepped in front of him and frowned, "Ace is ready for you," the guard grumbled. He briefly looked at Jamie in annoyance, "Your follower stays down here."

Jack barely had a chance to hear Jamie bark at the guard in frustration before he followed the white-clad man off the casino floor lined with Pangaea's wealthiest gamblers. While Jack wasn't the biggest fan of his boss, he had to appreciate the crime lord's brilliance. Ace had created a black-market monopoly in nightlife and casinos.

Jack couldn't hide his disgust at all the lavishly dressed members of the aristocracy milling about him. There was a regular admission casino down the stairs, but if Ace wanted the business of the elusive Pangaean Elite, she had to segregate the classes. A Pangaean snob wouldn't be caught dead next to a lower-class citizen, even in a shady casino.

He rolled his eyes at the thought: *arrogant pricks.* Granted, those arrogant pricks made up eighty percent of Ace's profits, including whatever minimal *earnings* he received. Not that he even saw a fraction of those earnings, he thought with another eye roll.

The guard opened two black oak doors, starkly contrasting with the casino's pristine white, and nodded for Jack to enter. Ace's office was white, like the upper-class casino, with green ferns to decorate it. The kingpin herself was seated behind her glass desk, her feet adorned in the tallest red heels propped in front of her to display the picture of comfort. The curvy and muscled woman was inspecting a burnt piece of wood, her rich skin almost matching the color of its charred surface.

Ace's dark eyes lifted from her inspection, "How much of my money did you take from me on the floor tonight?"

The condescending way Ace talked to Jack made his skin crawl. Ace was the only person he knew who deigned to speak to him like that, and yet, he couldn't object. Not if he wanted to keep the use of all of his fingers.

Jack grinned. "Only a thousand Units. You caught me before I could warm up."

Ace laughed, the sound deeply feminine and flirtatious. "I still don't know why I let you into my casino," she crooned.

"Maybe it's because you never give me my winnings," Jack smiled charmingly.

The two guards by Ace's desk stiffened, but the Boss didn't seem phased. She never did, even when Jack was the most dangerous person to come out of her training program. At the end of the day, he was her lap dog, and she was awfully aware of it. Anything Ace asked, he did, and they both knew he didn't have any choice in the matter. Jack was chained to Ace, and even if the chain was made of pure gold and adorned with diamonds, it was still a chain.

"I told you." Ace waved Jack off with hands decorated with pointed ruby red nails, "I have your winnings kept safely in an account. Besides, what is a twenty-three-year-old boy like you going to do with all of that money? I have you perfectly taken care of here." Her smile became feline, "You have everything you could ever need."

Jack's fists clenched. Ace knew precisely what he wanted to do with that money. Unfortunately, since his boss liked being an ass, he knew she would never let him see that money.

At one point, Jack had dreamed of leaving Ace's organization, but that dream had long since disappeared. He was loyal to Ace, even if it was because it was his only chance at making a living. He was in debt to the same woman that he was trying to run away from. A debt of life: Ace had been the one to find him dying on the streets of Paris as a child and raised him to become the revered Blackjack he was that day. Some would say such an upbringing was priceless. Well, Ace certainly found a price—a copious one.

Either way, he had nowhere to run. It was one hell of a life he'd made for himself.

"I couldn't just let you keep sending that money off to who knows where." Ace's black eyes gleamed, "They're most likely dead anyway—didn't you tell me something similar?"

Jack gritted his teeth to prevent himself from leaping at the Crime Lord. "You have no right to determine where my money goes."

Ace leaned forward. She was so close that Jack could see every intricate detail of the tattoo inked across the right half of her face. The symbol was her calling card: the ace of spades, a wildcard, and the deadliest of the four suits. That same symbol was inked onto his right wrist: the brand for all of Cartel's closest confidantes. When he became a Joker, he'd earned the right to wear his boss's symbol. Debt aside, he was pretty sure that brand meant he would always be Cartel's property. Jack couldn't leave, not with his head at least.

"That's where you're wrong." Ace scowled, the movement wrinkling her tattoo. "That's my money because you're *mine*. Don't get your head full of childish fantasies. Where would you go? Pangaea's just as awful. And Pacific is months away from being wiped off the map."

One of Ace's *Fera* slaves standing behind her shivered, the pitcher of wine in his hands splashing. The male was stunningly handsome—Ace's personal servants were always the most beautiful of her traded *Feras*. Ace loved beauty, and she surrounded herself with it no matter what. Jack quickly averted his gaze from the male. Ace had made it clear to him that he would become just like that servant if he lost his usefulness as a bounty hunter. Because of that, Jack couldn't look his potential fate in the eye.

Ace leaned back, eyes tracking to the slave next to her desk, "Are you sure that you would hate having such a comfortable job?" She gave a casual wave of her hand as if she wasn't talking about Jack's freedom. "You would be safe, protected by me. Expensive clothes, hours of lounging, and every beauty routine that you need to stay looking so—" her eyes roved up and down Jack with an assessing gaze that made him shiver—"*delicious*. You really have grown into a fine specimen, my Blackjack."

He stilled. Luxury... affluence... but the cost of all of that would be whatever tiny shred of freedom that he still had. Ace's advances had only increased in the past few years, and he knew her offers were becoming too good to pass up. She already owned his every thought, hope, and dream, so he couldn't—*wouldn't*—let her own his body too.

His predicament left millions of thoughts swirling around in his head. They grew in energy and size as they started crashing together. Soon, a storm of anger and annoyance was ready to break in his head. Jack was running out of time before he made a comment that got him locked in solitary confinement for two days.

The bounty hunter ground his teeth together. "Can we discuss what I came here to talk about?"

Ace's eyes lit up with amusement, and she looked to her male servants with a laugh, "I love how his eyes seem to glow when he gets mad. Have you noticed that?" The Underground queen looked back at Jack with a condescending smile, "I noticed it the first time I picked his skinny ass off the streets of Paris nine years ago."

"You're wasting my time," Jack spat.

The amusement died from Ace's eyes as she held up the wood slate, "Do you know where this is from? Did I ever tell you the story?" He was too annoyed to shake his head, but the kingpin continued, "You know my family is from a small town in Old Nigeria, correct? Had I not gone into the city with my grandmother one day, this piece of wood would be all that was left of me. My town was burned to the ground by Pangaea simply because we sympathized with some rebellious tribes in the area," she spat.

"I'm sorry to hear that," Jack said calmly.

But I have something more important to talk about.

Ace yawned. "You look like you're in a rush. Am I boring you, my Blackjack?"

"Not at all, but I came to discuss Budapest. Istvan has been taken care of, and a new man has been put in charge. I give it six months until I have to go back," he added with a slight chuckle. "But I got to see the *Fera* conditions there, and they are less than desirable."

The Cartel boss picked absently at her fingernails, "Why do I care? This is a business I'm running; I can't afford to have five-star accommodations for my products."

"Because the conditions have already turned multiple products feral. They've killed a couple dozen workers, including themselves," Jack shot back. "I brought a feral female back; we have better facilities to take care of her, and maybe we can see if there's anything we can learn from her."

Ace shook her head in bewilderment, "Take care of her? She's damaged goods. Why did you waste your time? Go be a doll and put her down for me."

Put her down. The words made bile rise in his throat. The *Fera* was still a human being—a human sent through the wringer because of Cartel. She didn't deserve to be euthanized like a rabid fox, and she certainly didn't deserve to rot in that pit in Budapest, either.

"No," Jack said. Ace looked up curiously at her investment, a predatory grin coming to her face. He held his ground despite knowing what that smile meant, "We can find a use for her. Maybe a scientist might be interested in her for a study, or you could use her as protection—I don't know."

Ace's ringed fingers pounded like drums on her desk, "Since you seem to have taken an interest in the slaves, I have another job for you. I have a little event coming up that I want you to oversee."

"What is this event?" Jack questioned.

"My trade partners from London have managed to send me a new shipment of freshly captured *Feras* ready to be auctioned off." Ace's smile told him she knew precisely how much he would dislike the plan. "Your mission is to ensure nothing happens to my investment, my little Blackjack."

"Who would interfere?" Jack snuck a glance at the slave holding the wine. The male looked down, though he didn't speak; his white-knuckled grip on the pitcher told Jack exactly how he felt about Ace's investment. "I told you I would help with anything but that," Jack snarled, venom clear in his tone.

Ace ignored him. "Slavery is still illegal in Old Europe," she continued. "We also don't want those Pacific nuisances sticking their noses into our business." Ace cracked her knuckles. "There have been reports of... someone interfering with slave trades in France. That someone is a rumor, but I want you to keep an eye out, regardless."

Jack looked down. This was a different mission than what he was used to. Usually, he was given a name, and he hunted them down. He never failed one of those missions. This, though, was a mission with too many variables. He wasn't trained in babysitting business deals; he was a fighter.

"And if I can't do it?" Jack asked. The entire mission sounded like he was being set up for failure. Then again, he also knew he didn't have a choice in the matter. Wherever Ace sent him, he went—without question.

Ace didn't look up. "I'll take your casino winnings as compensation. I hope you know, though, this last job will get you out of debt—if you do it right."

His eyes shot up. He'd been counting down the Units until he was free of what he owed her. If he saw this job through, he could stop owing money and start making a living. He could be worth something, he could go places... and he could avoid eventually being forced to accept a deal into Ace's bed.

Jack nodded without making eye contact. He understood completely: this job was for his freedom—whatever shred that was left of his honor code be damned. He hoped he could complete the mission, but his practical side was screaming and warning him that the task wouldn't be as easy as it sounded.

"I'm glad we have an understanding. Your flight to France leaves in the morning."

The bounty hunter gave a baleful smile. "Anything for you, Ace." The words tasted rancid in his mouth.

Jack couldn't leave the room fast enough. As the guards opened the door to let him out, Ace got one last word in. "Jack, for your sake, don't go off-mission. You stay in Brest, France, until the trade is finished. Then you come home. I don't need you getting distracted elsewhere."

His heart sank at the reminder that he couldn't even afford a visit to his old home, buried somewhere beneath the rubble of a forgotten town in France. Despite his disappointment, he kept walking to avoid a reprimand that would leave him with broken fingers. With a deep sigh, Jack headed to his room. He was going to need a good night's sleep.

Chapter 4

Arianne

"Arianne! Get downstairs!" Caesar called, as per their usual morning routine.

Arianne leaped out of bed. Exhaustion from the long graduation weekend made her sleep longer than she wanted. She quickly dressed, eyes avoiding her golden necklace as she rushed out of her bedroom door. She didn't have time for an existential crisis that morning: it was her first day in the military.

"Being late to school might fly with you, but you will *not* be late on your first day of work," Caesar muttered, half of his focus on a bagel he was balancing on a knee. "General Kalfas stuck his neck out for you to work underneath him. You need to prove he didn't make the wrong decision," he continued to scold as he typed notes on his tablet.

Arianne waved her father off. "Luckily, everything flies with me," she responded snidely with a fluff of her wings. "Besides, Kalfas loves me."

Her father pointed threateningly at her, his eyes rising from his notes to glare, "*Mira,*" he began with a sigh. "You need to start seeing General Kalfas as your superior when you have that uniform on." He shook his head, "I know he was like a coach to you, but he's your boss now."

Arianne still looked back fondly on her training sessions with Kalfas. She knew that she had been a handful with her overwhelming amount of nervous energy. Most *Fera* children tended to be chaotic, but it didn't help that she had quite the history to cope with. Caesar, being of the more even-tempered variety, struggled to fan the flames of her energy. But Kalfas—the force of nature that he was—was unfazed.

Together, Caesar and Kalfas practically raised her. And she couldn't be more thankful to either of them.

"I know, I know." Arianne mocked Caesar's presidential tone, "'he's General Orion Kalfas, a founder of Pacific, and you need to be treating him with more respect, *hija.*'"

"Arianne," the President sighed.

Unfortunately, Arianne wasn't in the mood to listen to another one of Caesar's lectures. Her excitement for her first day was beginning to override her focus. She hadn't left the island since the first day she'd arrived. For a while, it made sense: to protect her from the ever-present eyes of her biological father. Now, she was ready to leave and see the world—she *knew* she was. She wondered what other lands looked like: places where forests didn't end or where mountains stretched higher than the horizon.

The curiosity sometimes drove her crazy. Some days, when the call to adventure became too loud, she would sit on the edge of the island, watching out across the gorgeous sea and dreaming about what it would feel like to fly beyond. And now, years of dreaming would become a reality. That day would mark the beginning of a life spent exploring wherever her wings—or jet—could take her.

"I'll be at the Capitol building late today," Caesar continued. "I need you to stop at the farmer's market after work and get things for dinner. We're low on food."

The words went in one ear and out the other.

"*Adios*, Dad! *Te amo!*" Arianne chirped as she grabbed her backpack, hugged her father, and sprinted towards the back porch.

She pushed the windowed doors open, letting in the balmy island breeze. Picking up speed, she leaped over the balcony railing. The wind whipped past her ears as she began to free fall down the rocky slope off the side of her house. Then her wings expanded wide, and she caught the warm summer updrafts with a satisfying *whoosh*. As she rose higher into the sky, Arianne watched the islanders below her begin their morning routines: cars below buzzed on the small roads, and children started emerging from their houses to play on the warm summer day.

Nothing beat flying: not only was it faster than driving, but it made her feel alive. While she got along just fine walking on the ground, something about flying felt right. Arianne was *born* to be in the air.

She coasted in the dry Mediterranean winds until the island's military base came into sight: Angel's Camp. The stunning combination of modern engineering and classic Greek architecture made the hulking building as beautiful as it was practical. The main building was built on the edge of a cliff that dropped into the sea below, with large windows built to take full advantage of the picturesque view. Angel's Camp served as the island's armory, post office, airport, and research center. It was the heart of all of Pacific's military operations and, most importantly, the connection between the numerous outposts and colonies scattered across the globe.

A jet runway ran along the side of Angel's Camp that ended at the cliff. Growing up, Arianne and her friends would watch from the beach as jets rocketed toward that deadly drop before climbing into the air at the last moment. Now, the runway served as the last step of her commute to work. As she approached the tarmac, she willed her wings wide to fly down the runway like an airplane landing from a flight across the sea.

"Major Ortiz!" Kalfas yelled from the garage. "You're late. I expected better from you!"

Winded, Arianne ran up to General Kalfas and saluted, "Good morning, sir, is that a new haircut? It looks very slimming."

Kalfas didn't budge as he crossed his massive arms, "I'm not in the mood, Arianne. Put your hair up like everyone else." Then, his stern glare faded, and she saw the flash of her old coach. "Unless you would like me to cut it off."

The young Major quickly tied her long hair into a bun when Kalfas whipped out his military knife. With the dress code enforced, he turned around and walked into the enormous airplane hangar.

"So, where am I off to today?" Arianne inquired as Kalfas led the winged female into his office. "I heard there was a skirmish in Africa earlier this morning, or maybe to North America? Aren't we sending extra reinforcements to our San Francisco outpost since the North American Commander's health is deteriorating?"

Anywhere, come on, just send me anywhere.

The graying General sat at his desk, "Yes to all of that." Kalfas glanced at her from over his glasses. "But you aren't going to be attending."

She bounced on the balls of her feet with excitement. "Come on, Kalfas. Just tell me!"

Maybe she would finally see the famous Eiffel Tower or one of those deserts that looked like oceans made of orange sands. Perhaps she would fly to the grasslands of Africa or see Spain—her mother's homeland...

Kalfas looked up at Arianne and sighed. "Arianne, you're not getting a mission off-island."

Her heart dropped to her stomach. "What?

Kalfas frowned. He stood up and carefully closed his office door. "It's for your safety," he continued in a hushed tone. "We cannot risk you getting caught by Pangaea."

Her shoulders slumped, and her eyes darted back and forth as she fought to make sense of the news. There must be some other way around that crushing reality. She refused to believe that her dreams could be so quickly demolished like water over a flame. Then her lips parted in disappointed realization. "Caesar put you up to this, didn't he?"

"It is not whether or not *President Ortiz* did anything," Kalfas corrected Arianne, reminding her that—in the military—Caesar was her President, not her family. "Your orders are for on this island. No questions."

"Kalfas," Arianne began, disheartened. "Y-you know how long I've been waiting for this." She clenched her fists. "I've worked for this—I've worked *so* hard—in the classroom and with you. I'm one of the strongest fighters you've got, you told me this, and I was the top of my class. Tell me that counts for something. Tell me that I'm not going to waste my life here because you and Caesar think I need protecting?"

Kalfas didn't meet her eyes. "My word is final, Arianne—*Major Ortiz*." He handed her a manila folder. "You are to oversee the Research and Development Corps and report back to me. It is my understanding that you were competent in STEM in school. You will be well suited for the task."

The winged female grumbled and took the folder, ignoring proper military manners as she left the room. The young Major was livid as she stormed from the General's office to the research labs. Her friends were being sent around the world for the day, and she was stuck on the island. She frowned; everything she had achieved hadn't been enough to prove to Caesar that she was ready, that she could *protect herself*. Her life yawed before her: trapped on the island like a prisoner, never able to leave and grow to her full potential. All because Caesar thought she needed to be protected. All because she had to be the daughter of Leon Murray.

Hell, if she had been born normal, she would have lived a life of traveling around the world as heir to the Commandership of Europe.

Now, she would spend the rest of her life trapped on an island with her wings all but physically clipped.

The logical side of her suspected that Caesar was right—there was no way to guarantee her safety from her biological father. But she didn't care. That small risk was better than feeling like she did then. Who said she had to go hunting for the hidden capital city of Leonueva? Who said she couldn't fight and make a difference elsewhere?

She was born with wings for a reason. She was meant to be *free.*

The Research and Development Corps labs were on the top floor of Angel's Camp's massive main building. The headquarters came with the best technology Pacific could afford—spare the hospital.

Annoyed, Arianne brushed over the file Kalfas had provided her. She was to report to the head Engineer of the Research and Development Corps, learn the organization's specific schedules, observe for security issues, and then design a patrol route that she would execute Monday through Friday with detailed instructions for a weekend shift officer. She huffed. She was just an overqualified, lethal manager. Who was she protecting? Pacific was hidden from Pangaea by a scrambling system that blocked their detection like a cloud of fog. No one would be attacking the base.

I'm going to die of boredom working a goddamn fluff job.

A crumpled ball of paper flew towards her head, and she effortlessly swatted it away with the reflexes she had hoped to use in the field. "Hey!" Arianne hissed, hardly in the mood to be messed with.

"You've been sulking around for the past hour." The *Fera* who threw the paper frowned. "Want to talk about it?"

Arianne turned to see Haris leaning out from behind his newly assigned desk. She'd forgotten her friend started work that day as well.

"Hey, Haris." She sighed.

The quill-haired male fixed his glasses. "I'm sorry today hasn't gone as planned. I know you've been talking about it for a while." He gave an apologetic smile.

Arianne sighed and looked at her friend's handsome face as she sat on his desk. "I've wanted this for so long, and the day comes, and I'm stuck on research duty."

"Hey, research isn't all *that* bad! We're making some cool breakthroughs." Her friend fumbled around for his tablet. "I just left this meeting where I learned about how we found a potential way to breach Pangaea's mainframe; give us a few months, and we could have access to everything."

Arianne tried her best to look interested. "That's what *you* enjoy, Haris." she slumped, "I want to be out there." She swiveled to look out the windows of the lab and at the bright blue sky beyond. "I want to save lives, risk mine, and fight for something. I want to be moving. I want to be scared I might not survive. I want adrenaline rushing through my veins. Not *this*. This can't be the life I was meant to live."

Haris's quilled eyebrows furrowed. "I know what being out there means to you. I also know how much it means to Jaya for you to be out there with her. I know this is crazy, but did you try to talk to Kalfas and Caesar?"

Arianne shook her head as her eyes burned. "There were protocols I didn't consider," she spat in annoyance.

Like the protocol that stated it was too dangerous to let children of their sworn enemies leave the safety of the island.

The young Engineer glanced at his tablet and typed down a quick code before looking at Arianne. "I don't understand why they're doing this to you. You're the person I would expect to be the safest." He paused, considering. "For lack of a better way to say this: you're the one most likely to come back."

Arianne wished she could tell Haris why there was so much fear. Fear that her father would find her. Fear that she would be taken back to Pangea and subjected to the same horrors, the history of which was preserved on her back. She was scared of all of that too, but that couldn't mean she was *trapped*.

She shook her head, shutting out the desire to confide in her friend. No matter how close she was to Haris, he could never know her heritage. She had promised Caesar years ago that no one could ever know where she came from—which made sense. The fact that she was a Commander's daughter might cause a few problems.

"I think Caesar is just scared," she reasoned. "Plus, as his daughter, they could use me as a bargaining chip if I got caught—since he's the President."

Haris laughed. "I am fully aware. Jaya and I almost got arrested when we came over at midnight. And that was just in the last couple of months."

"I'm telling you, you need to call ahead so that doesn't keep happening."

The Porcupine went back to his work with a smile. "I've been arrested twice, Arianne. You have no idea how hard that was explaining to my parents."

Arianne smiled back at her friend as she stood. "I love you, Haris Cadmilus," she said fondly, even as dread haunted her.

As Arianne left the lab for her hourly patrol, her mind was distant, and she lost herself in the long hallways of the base. She felt herself shrink. Was this what her life was going to be? She had lived so long with one goal in mind; now, that goal was painfully out of reach. For the first time in years, she was uncertain where her life would take her—which was more exhausting than a fitness test at the Academy.

Above it all, she couldn't fight the sense that she was trapped in that beautiful prison she had chosen for herself.

Chapter 5
Blackjack

T he winds blew off the Celtic Sea, cooling the sweltering night.

Jack pulled down a mask over his face, the breeze making the mask just barely manageable. No matter his discomfort, he couldn't risk his face being noticeable, not at a slavery deal. Slavery was as black-market as it got.

He sighed as he looked out from the ancient ruins he was hiding in and down toward the courtyard below. Jack had only been to the small city of Brest, France, once before, during a day trip with his father. Even though he had been just a little kid, he still remembered the visit clearly. The fond memory was almost enough to make him smile.

Then, he was reminded why he'd returned, and the ghost of a grin that had come to his face quickly faded.

Jack watched keenly from his perch as hooded figures arrived in the courtyard. It was almost dusk, making it hard to see the captured mutants in chains behind the shadowed merchants. The bounty hunter drew a sniper from his back and lined it up perfectly with the hooded man in the center. If there were to be an attacker, they would go for the frontman first.

A couple of Ace's goons dressed in black techwear stepped out from the shadows and shook hands with the London traders. Jack made sure he was out of sight of the trade deal. Ace had told no one else that he would attend the trade to minimize the chance of him being compromised. The last thing Jack needed was one of Ace's men to spot him and start a not-so-friendly-fire fight.

He watched as Ace's men handed a briefcase to the London representative, his face hidden under the hood of his cloak. He sighed, shoulders tense. *So far, so good.*

The hooded man inspected the briefcase and turned to leave. A half an hour later, he returned with ten more chained *Feras*. There were now fifteen up for auction. Dusk had turned to an oppressive twilight, but the figures below carried enough lanterns to illuminate the space.

Soon, more people began to arrive, their faces covered in masks, bandanas, or shielded by hoods. As more customers appeared, the hooded traders shifted to the back to observe the selling of their wares. By midnight, the auction had begun. One of Ace's men led the sale as he described the *Feras* up for trade in French, his voice just loud enough to echo off the ruins' walls. Jack's stomach churned in disgust. He hated the sight of what was happening below. Those *Feras* could have been anyone. They could have been everyday citizens, harmless savages... now they were being sold into a life of servitude.

It almost made him sick.

Jack cringed at how the auctioneer described the slaves to the French customers. He called them *strong* and *obedient*— like the mutants were cattle. It was disgusting. If it weren't for his own freedom riding on everything going well, he would have wished for someone to disrupt the event.

At around one o'clock, the crowd began to disperse. All fifteen *Feras* had been bought. That wasn't a surprise, considering mutant slaves were few and far between in Europe. The rarity of slaves in Europe made them a natural commodity. As a member of the Pangaean upper class—the Pangaean Elite, as they called themselves—owning a mutant was an impressive sign of wealth and connection.

As the new owners and their purchases proceeded to the exit, smoke bombs went off with a startling bang. Jack jumped, his system suddenly pumped with adrenaline. He reached for his sniper and quickly began to search the courtyard with his scope for the source of the disturbance. To his confusion, no unknown figure could be found. People started screaming. Jack ran for his rope, tied it down the side of the fort, and jumped. As he descended into the courtyard below, he prepared himself for a fight.

"It's never fucking easy," he hissed as he expertly landed from his jump.

He could barely see anything in the smoke. Two more blasts went off, and it was all he could do to keep standing. The customers and the *Feras* retreated to the far wall that faced the sea. The British Traders and Ace's men opened fire toward the entrance, but Jack's gaze was on the prominent figure stalking across the courtyard in the shadows.

The figure was like a monster made of mist. The beast was tall with dominating shoulders and long arms that extended into sharpened claws. Whoever had joined the auction was certainly not someone Jack knew.

Jack flung his sniper over his back and retrieved his handgun: better for close range. Through the smoke, he crept over toward the figure. Slowly, he got in between the monstrous newcomer and the customers. It didn't matter if he hated everything happening that night, he would *not* let the mission go south.

The bounty hunter raised his gun and pointed it bravely at the concealing mists. "Stop where you are. Hands up," he commanded in French. As Jack cornered the hostile, he could hear responding gunfire behind him. He tightened his grip on his handgun—the mysterious newcomer had friends.

The figure didn't slow its walk towards Jack. The dark mass grew ever larger until Jack was looking upwards at the shadow in the mist. A towering *Fera* with a mane of unruly golden red hair and a scruffy beard appeared in the dispersed lantern light. Despite the male's seemingly mild continence, his demanding stature was enough to make Jack take a step back.

For the first time in a while, Jack felt utterly outmatched.

The *Fera* spoke, revealing pointed canines, "Get out of the way, Young One," he responded in English.

"I'll only ask you one more time to stop," Jack commanded in a weaker tone than he wanted to. He allowed a bullet to slide into his handgun's chamber.

Before Jack could fire, the *Fera* leaped at him. His right arm was broken on impact. Before he could think, he was flipped onto the ground, crying out in pain and wheezing as the air was knocked out of him. Jack's eyes widened. So *that* was the might of a full-grown *Fera*. He'd dealt with *Feras* before, but never one as mature in their power as this... Lion.

A new voice called, its owner obscured in the swirling smoke. "You and your people take the *Feras*," the voice offered. "But Pacific wants the bounty hunter."

The lion-like *Fera's* response came out in a low growl. "I agree to this trade. Knock some sense into him, Islander."

Jack was still lying breathless on the ground. His lungs struggled for air as he tried to make sense of the exchange happening above him. Other people arrived through the mist, surrounding the Lion and his capture. Faster than a bullet, the *Fera's* fist came down on his face, and his world turned to black.

Chapter 6

Arianne

Her painfully long first day finally drew to a close. Arianne let out a breath of disappointment as she stretched her stiff joints, sore from hours of immobility. She hated feeling like she'd wasted an *entire* day in that artificial air-conditioned bubble.

Alternatively, Haris seemed energized from his first day. "Let's go see what Jaya's up to!" he exclaimed. "She and Rhino should be back by now."

Arianne tried to hide her annoyance as she followed her enthusiastic friend out of the lab and down the stairs to the airplane hangar. The two friends spotted Jaya's purple head against the gray backdrop instantly. Jaya climbed out of a jet to where a silver-haired *Fera,* Rhino, was waiting for her in olive green flying gear.

"Ari! Haris!" Jaya exclaimed as she watched her friends come down the stairs. "How was your first day?"

Arianne looked down, unwilling to respond. Luckily, Haris was excited enough to speak for both of them. Haris detailed his first day of having access to all of the Research Corps' new projects. Even training and introductory meetings seemed like dreams come true from his account.

Arianne simply rolled her eyes.

"Jaya and I were partnered up," Rhino replied. "As a warmup, we followed a reconnaissance mission to Africa to observe the aftermath of a ground skirmish from yesterday."

Jaya's purple-green eyes were bright. "It was absolutely thrilling!" She gasped, her English accent thickening in excitement. "I never knew how *flat* a place could be! And the Sahara was so cool to fly over!"

Arianne looked at her two friends, bitterness making her insides recoil. The winged *Fera* tried to smile, but she couldn't. She and Jaya had talked about their first day for years: *she* was supposed to travel the world with Jaya... not Rhino.

Arianne was so caught up in her own thoughts that she didn't notice that Rhino had spoken to her. She looked up, realizing that all eyes were on her. "What?" She asked.

"I asked, how was your day?" The large male repeated.

"Fine." Arianne rolled her eyes, knowing she couldn't hide her disappointment forever. "I love it when Caesar and Kalfas decide what's best for me."

Jaya put her arm around her friend's shoulders. "I'm sorry to hear about what happened—I was as disappointed as you were about not being able to be your partner." At Rhino's objection, Jaya turned, "Not that you're a bad replacement." she smiled.

"Do you guys want to stop by Shipwreck before we head in for the night? The whole crew will be there in celebration of our first day," Haris suggested.

Even though Arianne was in no mood to be surrounded by hundreds of people, she wouldn't let her bad mood ruin her friends' first day. Shipwreck was an island hotspot popular with the younger members of the military. Ever since they began their senior year, her friends had started to frequent the place to meet for music, dancing, and food.

Arianne shrugged, fighting off her dark cloud of self-pity. "I'll stop by. How about you, Jay?"

Jaya paused for a moment, considering. "Kal might be expecting me home soon."

Kalinda Bahri, Jaya's older sister, was hardly the type to enforce a curfew, especially as her military field nurse hours were often sporadic. If one of the sisters had a specific time to return home, it was typically Jaya. Because of this, Arianne knew she could press the matter a little more.

"Come on. Join us for a few minutes?" Arianne pleaded. She was afraid that Shipwreck would be unbearable without her best friend.

Jaya pursed her lips. "I guess," she trailed off.

Shipwreck was built within the ruins of an old wooden vessel that resembled a pirate ship. Just about a mile from Angels Camp, the bar was a perfect place for military personnel to gather after work. Resting in the water just offshore, patrons had to walk down a floating dock to reach the ship.

Troves of people walked the dock as Arianne, Haris, Jaya, and Rhino approached the ship. Shipwreck was near many other attractions that made up the long expanse of public beach, so the area was always a popular place to be around at night.

The four flashed their brand new military I.D.s at the door and were ushered inside. Arianne remembered the excitement of her first time there: a newly minted senior in the Academy, filled with dreams of what the next year would bring. In one day, those dreams had been crushed. Well, everyone else's dreams had come to fruition. Only she had been left behind. She sagged at the thought.

A hostess welcomed them in as they piled into the darkness of the ship. The low-light ambiance never bothered Arianne, though. With her raptor's eyesight, she could see perfectly in the dark. At the hull of the boat sat a large stage where The Black Sails stood, playing their newest album.

Music... It was a relatively *Pacifican* concept. From her memory of Pangaea, most entertainment had been wiped out spare for the rare upper-class events. Even in her sperm-donor's household, entertainment had been a foreign concept. Arianne's eyebrows furrowed, trying to once again piece together the fractured parts of her memory. Leon had always seen entertainment as a waste: a frivolous activity that wasted time better spent elsewhere.

"Hey, over here!" Shouted Rhino's girlfriend, a woman with short rust-colored hair. "Where have you guys been?"

Rhino smiled and planted a kiss on her head. "Sorry, Treena. Got out of work late."

Treena was the first half of the Helvig twins. Tyrell was the second of the pair, seated across from his sister. The two were new to the island, having arrived from the Pacific outpost in Norway six months ago. Both were interested in forensics and were brought to help with autopsies and investigations.

"So, Rhino and I are meant to join a squad tomorrow to pick up Bradley Shaw from London," Jaya began, sparking interest from the group.

Arianne tried her best to hide her jealousy. Bradley Shaw, the current vice president of Pacific, was known to travel a lot when the Senate was not in session on the island. Shaw played the role of a wealthy Pangaean Elite who facilitated trade from Pangaea to Pacific. If Jaya and Rhino were put on that team, they would be given a prestigious opportunity—and get to travel the globe as Shaw's private security.

Arianne clenched her fists tightly. She wanted to curl up and die.

It didn't matter how much Shaw annoyed her. She was still jealous. She disliked the portly man for small reasons, like how he always seemed too eager to please Caesar. Arianne couldn't see how a fragile people-pleaser could run the country in her father's absence. Still, watch duty for Shaw would have been a great honor.

An honor that should have been hers.

She had heard stories of the Vice President's predecessor, Jaleel Leroy. He seemed like he had been the perfect yin to Caesar's yang. Caesar was kind but firm—an idealist who didn't know when to quit. Jaleel had been a realist who loyally supported his friend but knew when to call out potential issues. Jaleel—alongside Caesar and Kalfas—had helped found Pacific. For almost fifteen years, the three of them acted as pillars that held Pacific up: president, vice president, and general.

And then Jaleel was killed.

The former vice president had a family in the Pacific outpost in France and would often work from his home office there. Then, one day—a couple of weeks after Arianne had arrived in Pacific—the town's coordinates were betrayed, and it was destroyed. No one had survived, not even Caesar's dear friend, Jaleel.

Bradley Shaw, as the Vice President's executive assistant, had been highly recommended by Jaleel to be his successor in the event that he retired to be with his family. Even though Caesar was not a huge fan of Shaw, he felt a responsibility to follow his friend's wishes. So, in the next election, Pacific elected Shaw out of loyalty to their late vice president.

"Ari? Are you awake?" Tyrell's freckled face came into view. "Jaya said you were put in charge of the security for the entire Research and Development Corps—that's a huge honor!"

"Oh, don't worry about her," Jaya chided, used to Arianne's volatile moods. "She's just annoyed. She'll get over it."

Treena shook her rust-colored head. "I'm sorry, Ari. I knew how much you were looking forward to getting out into the field." Treena proceeded to play with one of her various piercings. "I happen to enjoy not having to leave this place, though. I would much rather stay here than go out there just to get killed by a Pangaean."

Arianne nodded slowly, trying to understand what Treena was saying. The twins both had a strange accent, but she could never pinpoint where it came from.

"Well, that's the point of going out there!" Rhino bellowed. "So we can kick some Pangaean ass!" He grinned, his olive skin looking almost brown in the dim light.

Arianne wanted to laugh with the rest of the table, but then, out of nowhere, her vision began to spin. She didn't know what triggered it. Maybe it was the flashing lights and pounding music. Maybe it was a combination of her disappointment and stress from the day. But as Rhino spoke, she didn't picture him fighting a Pangaean. She pictured herself shrinking in Leon's shadow. Her heart rate sped up, and she was forced to focus on the table in front of her so she wouldn't vomit.

Like a broken record, she knew what was coming next. Arianne started to struggle to breathe. "I'm sorry, guys," she hissed, the music and lights becoming suffocating. "I need to go."

Quicker than normal, Arianne arose from her seat and stumbled outside. She squeezed past groups of people as they danced, their cries of happiness and excitement sounding asinine to her. The world began to rock, nausea blooming, and a headache blossoming in her temples. She lunged for the dock railing, desperately needing fresh air before she passed out. She blanched, head spinning as she stared at the waves lapping against the dock's support beams. She felt like she was about to throw up. Her senses were overloading—too many smells, too much color...

It was all *too much*.

Sometimes, her *Fera* gifts were a curse.

Arianne tried to focus her senses like she had been taught. *Focus on one thing. Let the world fade.* She coached herself. But, as her heart rate continued to climb, she couldn't concentrate on anything aside from the thundering in her chest.

Her lungs closed, her gills automatically trying to accommodate the lack of air. Past and present zipped by her concussively. The whispers of a couple walking up the dock sounded like screaming. The salty scent of the sea smelled like blood, dripping down her back. Her scars began to throb. Then, hands curled around her shoulders, and she cried out. She could have sworn those long fingers were curling around her neck.

Her skin crawled as adrenaline flooded her system. Her mind screamed at her to run, and she almost flew away in a panicked flurry. But Leon's painful vice grip melted away, and Arianne quickly realized that those were friendly hands steadying her. Her eyes widened as she recognized Jaya behind her. Her breath came back in long gasps as she turned and gripped her friend's shoulders to steady herself.

"Shh," Jaya whispered as she pulled Arianne into her. "It's okay, love," she continued soothingly. "You're here now. You're here now. I'm here."

Arianne winced, feeling the glares of confused passersby and their judging whispers. She knew she must have looked utterly insane. She felt herself wilt in shame. *It happened again,* she thought in disgust. *You caused a scene* again.

Arianne let Jaya hold her as her friend stroked her hair. "You're okay," Jaya sighed. "It's all over."

"I'm sorry, I'm sorry," Arianne whimpered. "I couldn't stop the images this time. I'm sorry." Jaya led Arianne down the dock and towards the quiet of the beach. "It's getting worse," she whispered in terror.

Why is it getting worse now? What's wrong with me?

Jaya helped Arianne sit down on a bench, fluorite eyes painted with concern. "Do you want to talk about it?" She asked. "Talking about it can help you stop seeing these things."

"No," Arianne spat. "I don't want to talk about it." She looked down, ashamed of her cowardice. "I can't talk about it."

Jaya looked sad as she sat down at Arianne's side. "Maybe if you told me what happened to you back then, I could help you. Keeping all of this anger and fear locked up inside is hurting you, and it's only going to get worse."

"I'm fine now," Arianne responded in a steel tone. "I think all the noise and stuff just stressed me out."

Jaya frowned in disapproval. "Ari, that's not good—don't push me away. Don't push your feelings away like they're nothing."

Arianne stood up so quickly that she swayed with dizziness. "I'm fine, Jay. It won't happen again. Trust me."

"That's the fifth time this month," Jaya scolded with a tilt of her head.

"I don't want to talk about it," Arianne hissed, the finality in her tone warning that the conversation was over. "Go back to Shipwreck and tell everyone I wasn't feeling well."

"That's an understatement." Jaya sighed.

"I'm just going home." Arianne shook her head and put her face in her hands—a painful headache racking her temples.

Jaya watched her winged friend gravely, "You need to do something about this, Ari." She crossed her arms. "But, fine, have it your way."

Arianne felt a pang of guilt as Jaya turned around and walked away. She wished talking about it was that easy. She wished more than anything that she could tell Jaya everything.

When she finally walked through the second-floor porch door of her house, her head was low. The living room was dark and silent. Arianne sighed in relief. She wouldn't have to interact with anyone. She could just go to bed and forget about her awful day. Fortunately, in the quiet darkness, her headache was finally fettering out.

"Where have you been?"

Arianne looked up and noticed Caesar sitting at the kitchen island in the gloom. "Oh." Her voice was tired. "I was just out at Shipwreck with the usual people." She did her best to hide the catch in her tone.

"What did I tell you?" The older man demanded, and Arianne felt her back prickle at the warnings of a fight. Annoyance flickered inside her gut—she wasn't in the mood, especially now. "I told you to come back early tonight, didn't I?"

Her eyes went to the set kitchen island; plates, utensils, and napkins were carefully arranged on placemats. She sulked, hoping dearly to avoid a fight with her father. "Well, you didn't have to wait for me to make yourself dinner, Dad. I already had mine."

That was a lie. Arianne was going to eat a Shipwreck, but now she felt too sick to her stomach to even think about food.

Caesar crossed his arms. "Yes, I did."

"No, honestly, you didn't," she replied curtly, desperately hoping that Caesar would just let her go to bed.

Caesar stood up. "I had nothing to cook with Arianne! I told you to go pick up food at the market because I would be out late! That didn't mean I wasn't coming home."

"Why didn't you pick up some food then?" Arianne asked a little too harshly, but her temper was already short from the long day. She knew she should be trying to avoid a fight, but she was already in a foul mood.

"The market was *closed* by the time I was out of work. "Caesar pinched the bridge of his nose. "But that is not the point," he continued coolly. "You have no sense of responsibility or maturity. I give you simple instructions: come home early and pick up some groceries, yet you still cannot manage to do that."

Arianne shook her head, "Me? Not mature and responsible? I just graduated from Citadel Academy at the top of my class!"

She gritted her teeth: Caesar didn't know what the *hell* he was talking about. He had no idea what she dealt with every day. A small voice at the back of her head spoke up, *well maybe if you talked to him...*

No, she steeled her resolve, *not happening.*

"Yes, you." Caesar pointed. "The same girl that ditched school to climb up Devil's Cliff with your wings tied closed on a dare—don't act like I didn't get a call about that little fiasco!"

"I climbed that cliff in record time!" Arianne countered. "And anyway, I did it during lunch break. I didn't ditch anything," she added defensively, crossing her arms.

"You skipped the last day of school," Caesar added.

Arianne threw her hands out. "Come on! Everyone was doing that!"

"That's not the point," the President said. "The point is that you need to grow up and stop thinking about just yourself. You need to learn that there is a bigger picture. I thought you would already know that—you've seen what this world has to offer from the beginning. Sometimes I see it in you," Caesar paused. "I really do, but I need more than glimpses. I need to see that you are more than just a kid. You're twenty-one, for God's sake."

"I have a right to act like a child when you treat me like one!" Arianne fought back, her frustration from the day coming to the surface, "I worked my ass off for years! For what? For *nothing.*"

Caesar deflated, "Arianne, I'm sorry. You know full well why you need to stay on this island." His tone was even. "You're not safe out there. He could find you."

"We always have this conversation." Arianne rolled her eyes. "And my mind hasn't changed. I'm ready for this, Caesar. I don't want to live my life trapped on this island."

Caesar stepped away from his barstool and placed his hands firmly on his daughter's shoulders. "But it's a life, isn't it? At least you're *alive* here. I can't guarantee that as soon as you step foot on the mainland."

"I'm an adult, Caesar!" Arianne protested. "I don't need to be protected anymore. I should be allowed to take that risk." And then she looked at the man who had given her everything. She hated having fights about her freedom because she knew she sounded ungrateful, but the words needed to be said. "I know you mean well, but a life like this is not a life worth living."

Her father's hands remained on her shoulders. "I know how much this means to you, but everything is much more complicated than just doing what you want all the time."

Arianne pushed herself away, annoyance burning like a fire in the pit of her stomach, "You obviously don't know what this means to me if you're grounding me like this!"

"*Hija*, "Caesar breathed, "come on, don't be unreasonable!"

Arianne shook her head, storming up the stairs. She had nothing left to say.

Chapter 7

Jaya

Jaya tried to smile as Rhino landed in the seat next to her. Ever since their graduation, Rhino had become her partner on most of their missions. Rhino leaned back in his seat with a sigh, buckling up for the flight ahead. The cabin of the freight plane was filling up as older operatives began to sit in the remaining ten seats. Jaya scanned the group with growing excitement: this would be her and Rhino's first mission as official members of Bradley Shaw's private security force.

The mission had been delayed by two days. Bradley Shaw was supposed to be picked up in Moscow on Monday, but he'd extended his visit. Obviously, it was not the brightest idea, but no one in the military was going to tell the Vice President what to do.

Jaya tilted her head upward to rest her neck on the headrest as a deep sigh escaped her. She knew she should have been honored that she was selected to be a part of such an elite unit. There she was living her dream with some of the most elite operatives in Pacific. She was being trained by the best of the best, she was important.

She should be happy. But she wasn't.

This had never been her dream alone. Whenever she pictured herself here, she always imagined Arianne sitting beside her. It was possible Jaya was a little too hard on Rhino, but she could never hide her disappointment when he arrived as her partner. He wasn't her best friend. Rhino just represented a daily reminder that her best friend's dreams had not come true.

Jaya hoped Rhino didn't feel her disappointment. She hoped he didn't realize how much she wished Arianne was the one sitting down next to her. Unfortunately, she sucked at hiding her emotions, and it wasn't just because they changed her skin color.

Rhino's gray eyebrows furrowed in concern. "What's wrong?" His large arm wrapped around his partner and pulled her in tight. "Come on, let it out," he cooed.

Jaya frowned in annoyance. "It's nothing," she mumbled.

She pushed herself away from the large *Fera*. While she loved Rhino with all of her heart, he was too much for her sometimes. He was loud, *way* too touchy, and enjoyed joking around a little too much. They were *professionals,* and sometimes she feared Rhino was just around for the fun of it.

"Personal space," Jaya hissed, scooting one seat over.

"Oh, sorry." Rhino looked down in embarrassment.

"I'm worried about Ari," Jaya finally admitted once the plane had taken off.

It wasn't the whole truth, but the fact still bothered her. As Arianne's oldest friend, Jaya knew that missing the opportunity to be a part of the team would be eating her away inside, and the last thing Arianne needed was another thing to worry about.

"Oh?"

"She worked her ass off to earn a spot on this team, and now she's stuck on the island. It can't be good for her."

No, Arianne didn't need more stress in her life. Jaya began to chew on her lip. Arianne, much like Rhino, had way too much energy. She needed to expend that energy, or she would burn up from the inside. And when that happened, things started to get bad. Unfortunately, Arianne only let Jaya see when things got really bad.

It was always terrible to watch. First, Arianne would go deadly silent, her eyes fixating on some far-off place. Next came the shakes. Sometimes, those spells would only last a minute, while other times, they would feel like an eternity. In the worst cases, it would progress into a panic attack.

Jaya knew Arianne was reliving something awful from her past, but that was all she'd been able to discern. Arianne had never shared the details of her childhood before Pacific with anyone. Jaya had been a *Fera* from Pangaea as well, and she certainly didn't have good memories, but they didn't affect her as much as Arianne's did. The Chameleon shivered; she couldn't imagine what her friend had been through.

Unfortunately, those panic attacks had been growing more frequent.

"Whenever things got hard," Jaya began slowly, careful not to say something that would betray Arianne's trust. "Ari always looked to this to cheer herself up. She saw every challenge as getting her one step closer to making a difference." The purple-haired *Fera* wrung out her hands, the tips of her fingers turning green in concern. "And now she doesn't have that."

Rhino's gray eyes lit with understanding. Though he didn't mention it, Jaya knew that he noticed Arianne's moods as well. The larger *Fera* pursed his lips. "We'll figure it out," he said in an oddly severe tone. "She deserves this more than anyone."

By the time the plane landed in Moscow, Jaya had practically chewed her lip raw. She knew she shouldn't allow her stress to get to her before the mission, but she couldn't fight the guilt inside her gut. *Arianne should be here,* she kept thinking. *I shouldn't have my dreams come true while hers don't.*

She shook her head, trying to focus herself as the plane slowed to a stop. She needed to clear her mind. The first rule of a mission: keep emotions under control. Worrying about Arianne was only sending her emotions into chaos—a chaos that could compromise her teammates. But she couldn't help herself. Arianne was like a second sister to her. Technically, Jaya had a couple of other sisters, but Kalinda and Arianne were the only ones who mattered to her.

The team Captain, Lyn, stood up in the front of the cabin. She was a middle-aged woman with short brown hair and slightly uplifted eyes. Jaya remembered attending Captain Lyn's classes at the Academy and wanting to be her. Well, there was her chance if she could just focus long enough to take it.

Even if it was without Arianne.

"Marshall, Sanchez, and Stewart—you will survey the area from above. I want trained snipers in every direction and an alarm if you see a shadow move too close to Shaw," Captain Lyn's voice boomed.

Three uniformed soldiers nodded, strapped on their helmets, grabbed their guns, and marched out of the hangar. Naturally, the team's uniforms were unmarked. Each person wore a custom suit with Kevlar vests built in underneath. Their mission was simple in context: get in and out of Pangaean territory without being noticed.

Captain Lyn continued to give the rest of the team instructions until she finally turned to Jaya and Rhino. "Rookies, you're with me." Jaya couldn't help but perk up at that. Rhino, at her side, did the same. The Captain analyzed Jaya's hair, "You're going to have to do something about that, Bahri. We need to hide as many

Fera traits as possible." She eyed Rhino's pure size, "let's just hope they think you drank too much milk as a kid."

Jaya quickly nodded, willing her purple hair into a nondescript dark brown.

The Captain watched Jaya's transformation. If she was shocked, she didn't show it. Once satisfied with Jaya's appearance, Captain Lyn marched off the plane ramp and continued onto the tarmac. Lyn moved at a firm pace that even the two *Feras* struggled to keep up with. As Jaya and Rhino exited the plane, they instinctively surrounded their leader, automatic rifles prepared for a moment's notice.

Used to traveling in enemy territory, Captain Lyn seemed unfazed as she moved toward the airport. "If this mission goes without a hitch, I think the two of you have a bright future with this team," she said.

Jaya nodded. She tried not to think about what happened to free up two new spots. They were a team that routinely went into the heart of Pangaean territory and were sworn to protect Bradley Shaw with their lives. Jaya steeled herself; she had known the risks when she signed up.

"Remember the rules," Captain Lyn ordered. "Stay inside the areas we've covered, keep your guns visible at all times, and let me do the talking."

Shaw, as vice president, had the responsibility of running the trade into and out of Pacific under the guise of a private company. Pacific's economy relied on Shaw's private business to trade goods between the empire and the rebel force. While no one enjoyed working with Pangaea, Pacific needed to trade with *someone* to survive.

Due to Shaw's constructed identity as a wealthy businessman, no one batted an eye when he carried a private security team. That was the ruse Jaya and Rhino would have to learn to uphold: private hands. The law in Pangaea specifically stated that hired hands were legal, but their weapons had to be visible at all times.

Jaya didn't have a problem with that.

She stiffly surveyed the private airport and followed Captain Lyn into the terminal. There, Bradley Shaw would be waiting with the other two members of the team who had remained with him while he was away. Jaya sulked; she knew Arianne would have loved every minute of it. Maybe she could find a way to convince Caesar to change his mind once she returned. She was pulled from her thoughts when she heard Captain Lyn's order to stand at attention. Jaya and Rhino saluted as Bradley Shaw and his two guards appeared from inside the airport.

Jaya would have recognized Shaw anywhere. While far from attractive, Shaw had a distinctive look to him. He was a round man with a sharp nose and a balding head of fiery red hair. Her hands clenched. She could tell that Shaw lacked much of a spine from the way he cowered behind his guards. Despite being her first official day, she carried herself with more dignity than the man who had been elected to be put into dangerous situations. She just hoped Shaw made up for it by being a competent businessman. Pacific's economy was doing well, and she hadn't noticed a supply shortage for a while.

Still, she tightened the grip on her gun. Shaw seemed *too* jumpy. What had frightened the man?

Rhino, also noticing the Vice President's caution, raised his gun. "Probably just saw a bird," he laughed. "Scary little creatures."

Jaya let out a huff in response. She may not like Shaw, but he was her vice president—even if he won the election on kindness and Jaleel Leroy's blessing alone. Either way, her job was to protect him. Orders were orders.

Captain Lyn approached with Shaw at her side and the two remaining team members behind her. "Sir," she began, gesturing to Rhino and Jaya. "I would like you to meet our two rookies."

Bradley Shaw looked over the pair quickly. "The *Feras*?"

Jaya felt her gut clench. She hated being characterized like that. She wished people could see past the purple hair and acknowledge her for her accomplishments—not her differences. She had tried to will her hair to remain a normal color for a few weeks, but the physical strain and concentration it took to keep it a normal shade all day was more trouble than it was worth. Dyeing her hair never worked either. The dye never stuck.

Rhino's eyes dropped as well. His *Fera* traits were more challenging to conceal, being the size that he was. At least for situations like that, she could stay hidden for a few hours. Bradley Shaw must have gotten the report on their new assignment before they arrived. She feared that he disapproved.

Captain Lyn pursed her lips, standing up straighter. "They're two of the best graduates in their class." She pointedly ignored the word *Fera*. Jaya decided that she liked the Captain. "Now, let's get on the plane before our day gets exciting."

Rhino laughed deep and hearty as if he had been hoping for just that. Once behind the Vice President and Captain, Jaya elbowed her friend. Lesson two: a bored guard was a happy guard. The *Fera* partners remained behind on the tarmac as Captain Lyn and Shaw boarded the plane. They raised their guns, readily watching the perimeter until they were ordered on board.

A shadow fleeted across the hangar wall and then the runway. Almost too quick for anyone to notice. *Almost.* Jaya gritted her teeth, tracking the path of the shadow before it disappeared. It didn't move like an animal and was too large for a bird. The hair on the back of her neck rose.

Rhino, still facing the plane, gave her a light shove with his shoulder. "Don't get all jumpy like our fearless leader over there."

"I saw something," Jaya whispered back.

That earned a backward glance from Rhino. His trained eyes scanned the runway, and then he shrugged. "Just a trick of the light."

Jaya didn't budge as the other nine team members marched past them in a unified fashion. "It's never 'just a trick of the light,'" she shot back.

In the field, any chance of a threat had to be considered as a complete possibility.

"I looked, there was noth—"

"There it is again!" Jaya barked, skin turning a shade of orange in anticipation as the human-shaped shadow crossed another wall. Closer this time.

Rhino's breath quickened—finally noticing the shadow. Real urgency lit in his eyes. "Shaw and the rest of the team are secure on the plane. Let's go before your shadow becomes a problem."

They heard a discreet chuckle as they began to retreat backward. The laughter was too quiet to be heard by anything other than *Fera* ears. The sound was haunting, and it sent a chill up her spine. Rhino slowed, his lips parting in confusion. Someone else was certainly there. *Watching* them. Enjoying their fear.

Something was seriously off.

Neither Rhino nor Jaya turned their backs to the tarmac as the airplane door began to close behind them. She remained alert, scanning the airport and hoping that it was all just her beginner's nerves playing tricks on her.

Just as the door was about to close, she could have sworn she saw a flash of bleach-blonde hair as it shimmered in the sunlight. Luckily, the plane took off before their follower got any closer. Both Jaya and Rhino let out a collective breath of relief.

"It's never just a trick of the light," Rhino repeated under his breath.

Chapter 8
Blackjack

A pinch on his arm had his eyes bolting open. Jack gasped, his body subconsciously preparing for a fight. His last memory was the Lion-like *Fera* lunging for him in the darkness. And now—he focused his senses, willing his confusion to clear so he could observe his surroundings.

White walls and the nose-burning smell of antiseptic. Nurses in medical scrubs looking over him. His head swiveled, taking in as much information as he could. He quickly realized that he was in a hospital room. A window to his right was filtering in the orange light of sunset.

Instantly, his mind put a plan together: escape through the window and disappear under the cover of night. Before the people around him could react to his consciousness, he lunged. But something held him down. His right arm burned as shackles pulled him back down to the bed. *Shit*, Jack thought, straining, *shit, shit, shit!* He began to breathe faster as he took in his injuries. His right arm was in a cast, broken, and he could feel a bandage around his forehead.

Well, that explains the headache, he thought. A concussion must have been what knocked him out.

"He's awake," someone whispered.

Jack wanted to scream. He couldn't be in a *hospital.* His biologics would be put in the Pangaean system. Someone might find him. *Oh god, I'm in deep shit.*

"What am I doing here," Jack growled, tensing against the shackles.

A tall, gray-haired doctor walked up. "Why do I always deal with patients like this?" He sighed, fixing his glasses. "Hello, sir, you're in the hospital. You were severely injured in Brest, France. Do you remember anything?"

Jack forced his heart to slow as he fought against the fogginess of his mind. What *had* he been doing in Brest? His eyes narrowed, thinking. Slowly, the events of the night before came back to him, and he remembered the mission Ace had tasked him with. The mission he had *failed*.

Ace would take everything he had, including his chance of freedom. Jack tried to focus on calming down. He couldn't panic, not if he wanted to get out alive. He let himself relax a little, knowing he needed to take control of the situation—or he was doomed.

Control meant knowledge. He needed to know more about what was going on if he wanted a chance of escaping. Jack turned and realized that he was surrounded by sophisticated medical equipment: no random citizen of Pangaea would be admitted to such a nice hospital. No, services as nice as the one that hospital offered would have been reserved for the Pangaean Elite.

"Who are you," Jack asked. "You don't work for Pangaea, I know that."

The doctor nodded, not breaking Jack's furious stare. "Of course, no one told you." He sighed, "You've been taken into the custody of the Pacifican army for healing and questioning."

Jack shook his head in denial. He couldn't be under arrest—Ace wouldn't allow him to be questioned by *anyone*. Ace never let anyone say anything about her business. The best he could do was stay quiet and hope the Boss's men didn't find him. She killed people for less than just being captured.

"What are you going to do to me?" The bounty hunter asked warily. Jack had been trained to withstand most questioning tactics, but even he didn't know the extent of torture he was about to go through.

The gray-haired doctor shrugged. "You're only here for healing. After that, you'll be in the military's hands. I'm sorry, I'm just a doctor. I don't know much."

"No," Jack said as he squeezed himself against the bed frame. He couldn't imagine what Ace would do to him if she found out. He shrunk as an uncharacteristic sadness came from him. "Just kill me now," he muttered.

Nothing. Jack was *nothing* now. He ruined his *one* chance at freedom. It was just his luck that his first failed mission would be the one he needed the most. Now, he was captured by Pacific. His life had just become one giant fucking mess.

The doctor took a step forward and held out his hand cordially. "We have no intention of harming you." He smiled. "Everyone calls me Dr. Ike."

Jack rolled his eyes; he didn't give a shit what the Pacificans did to him. It was Ace he was worried about. He ignored Dr. Ike's hand as he glared blankly at the man. "I'm telling you—you'll have to kill me because I'm not doing anything for any of you."

Dr. Ike drew closer. Jack watched the older man for any openings. Maybe there was a chance that he could stun the doctor and make a run for it. Jack tried to move as the man leaned over him, but even such a slight adjustment of his weight sent pain shooting up his body.

"Don't try any sudden movements. Your stitches could rip open," Dr. Ike warned, "You've already lost a lot of blood. Now, Nurse Morgan is going to come in here and help you to your room. But first, I have a couple of questions for you."

Jack knew exactly what those questions were, but he knew there was no point in denying anything to the doctor. "Go ahead," he sighed.

"I have seen a number of people come through this hospital with your... condition. I have made it a policy to ask if you would like me to keep such information confidential or if you would care if it showed up on your hospital record."

For a moment, Jack was at a loss for words. No one had considered his privacy for the nine years he had been in Cartel. Dr. Ike must have been giving him some sort of test. Still, Jack felt himself sigh. "Keep it a secret," he ground out.

He knew that the doctor was full of shit, but it couldn't hurt to try.

Moments later, a shorter woman walked in with a handful of clothes. "Will do." Dr. Ike gestured at the woman. "This is Nurse Morgan. She will show you to your room." The doctor then turned away and left.

"Now, I want you to stand up nice and slowly. Any sudden movements might rip your stitches," the nurse said.

Jack took the nurse in. Though tiny, the woman had a stern look on her face, and her body was lean with muscle. The nurse unlocked his shackles. As he stood up and walked beside the woman, he looked down to notice that she had a slight limp—a limp he intended to exploit.

He was not staying in that hospital for another day.

Though moving was painful, he slowly got into a rhythm of deep breaths that helped keep the sensation at bay. Jack kept glancing at the nurse dressed in blue scrubs in front of him. The limp—he needed to target it. But first, he had to make sure he could move as fast as he wanted.

As he followed the nurse onto the elevator, he realized that no matter how much pain he was in, his best chance to escape would be before he was put into a cell. The elevator door closed, he counted to three in his head, and then he moved. But the nurse was quicker. As Jack lunged at her, she brought out a taser, and

Jack was forced to the ground as his body convulsed with the electric current. He gritted his teeth as he tried to maintain consciousness despite the pain. *Idiot,* he thought, how did he not notice the nurse had been carrying a taser?

He was dangerously off his game. Fucking concussion.

Nurse Morgan leaned down over him as the world began to grow fuzzy. "Did you really think I didn't expect you to do that?" She chided.

The nurse's face was the last thing he remembered before his vision grew blurry, his head rolled back, and he passed out.

Jack woke up in a concrete room, his bed parallel to the back wall. One window looked out towards the water and what looked like an airport. A bathroom door was left open to the right of a stainless-steel table with two chairs. Jack looked at the door, but it was barred up and solid concrete—there was no way he was getting past that thing.

As his drowsiness faded, the constant throbbing from his concussion and his broken arm slowly returned. For a moment, he wished he was still connected to an I.V. delivering him pain medication. He was in *deep* shit. His eyes traced the concrete walls above him, wondering what he could do next.

He lost track of how long he sat in that bed, his only focus on willing the ache in his arm to fade. At some point, the metal door to his side swung open, and a man with dark skin, close-cropped hair, and a finely pressed suit walked into the room. Composure radiated off of the man in waves. Jack could only assume that he was looking at the man in charge. He should have been cautious, yet something about the man's coffee-brown eyes displayed kindness.

Jack hadn't looked at someone so seemingly even-keeled for years.

Behind the man was a bulky officer in a military uniform adorned with medals. Jack almost rolled his eyes. He should have known it was only a matter of time before the muscle came along. The larger man had buzzed gray hair and green eyes that made his stern stare piercing.

The first of the two men nodded to Jack and sat at the metal table on the other side of the room. With a dip of his head, he offered for Jack to join him. The bounty hunter glanced at the open door waiting behind the military man, and he locked eyes with him. The larger man crossed his arms. His message was clear: *don't try it, boy.*

Jack got up from his bed, doing his best to hide the nausea that came up at the quick movement. Escape or not, he was in rough shape. He might be forced to wait in that cell for a few weeks to let his body recover. Careful not to use his right arm, Jack pulled the second chair out and sat across from the stately man waiting for him.

The man reached out with his left hand. Jack blinked, realizing the man's consideration of his injury. His shock at the man's kindness quickly made him suspicious, and he narrowed his eyes, refusing to offer his hand. *Who are you?* He seemed to ask with his untrusting glare.

"Good afternoon," the man began, his accent oddly similar to a Spaniard's. "My name is Caesar Ortiz. I am the President of the United Colonies of Pacific."

Jack's upper lip twitched in a snarl. "Oh, wonderful."

Caesar didn't seem deterred by Jack's annoyance. "We have a unique opportunity before us, don't we? You can help me, yes, but more importantly, I can help you."

Jack highly doubted that. "Oh really?" He asked, far from amused.

President Caesar Ortiz leaned forward. "Of course. All I need from you is the truth."

Chapter 9

Arianne

Arianne took a halfhearted bite out of her bagel as she tried to open her sleepy eyes. A cool breeze swept in from the porch, and the smell of salt filled the room. She yawned as she fought the urge to fall asleep on her heaping plate of eggs. A stack of papers dropped in front of her, making her jump. Caesar was looking at his daughter from across the kitchen bar with a frown, and she straightened as she prepared for the worst. She eyed her father cautiously as he began nonchalantly tying his tie.

Arianne had to admit that her attitude from the night before had not been the best. Yet, she still wasn't quite ready to apologize. Was he still mad at her?

"I want you to look these over," the President said as he picked up a cup of coffee.

Arianne shook her head, watching Caesar. It always amazed her how easily the man got up in the morning. Even when Caesar worked late nights at the Capitol building, he was always fresh the following day: perfectly dressed, face well-shaven, and hair neatly trimmed. Though Caesar was not a mutant, it seemed he had his own superhuman abilities when it came to early mornings.

She picked up the folder gingerly. "What are they?" she asked. The words on the sheets seemed blurry through her half-closed eyes.

Taking a sip of his coffee, Caesar shrugged, "A follower of the Pangaean Crime Lord, Ace, was apprehended two days ago in France. I spoke to him yesterday—he doesn't seem too willing to cooperate. I thought you would be interested in helping with the interrogations."

Arianne looked at her dad with a questioning face of disbelief. First, he grounded her, and now he wanted her on interrogation duty. She didn't care about some grunt working for Cartel. Her interest was in Pangaea. Her interest was in *fighting*.

Caesar looked ready to give Arianne another one of his fatherly scoldings. "You'll do it, and there will be no arguing."

"Why?" She questioned, opening the folder and flipping through the few pages inside.

She stopped at the photo of the man who called himself Blackjack. He was young, just on the cusp of adulthood. The younger grunt had tousled chestnut brown hair, light brown skin, and a defined nose that looked like it had been broken one too many times. He would have been handsome if not for his eyes.

For so young, Blackjack's amber eyes were devoid of every emotion as he blankly stared forward for the file's photo. Arianne paused in recognition. She knew that gaze all too well. When she was a child under Leon Murray, she'd looked just like that.

Arianne set the folder down, shaking her head. "You're better off killing him," she said dismissively. "You're just wasting your time."

She knew what she had been like as a child. She also knew that Blackjack was in the same headspace. There was no way anyone on that island would break him. He was already too broken.

Caesar nodded in understanding. "We got to you, didn't we?"

"I was ten, and I didn't remember anything. This is a full-grown weapon." She locked eyes with Caesar. "The longer you keep him here, the more dangerous he'll become."

She shivered, knowing what she had been capable of as a brainwashed ten-year-old with combat skills. This Blackjack, whoever he was, was far more dangerous as an adult with years of training and his full memory.

"He's not just some grunt," Caesar said. He flipped through Blackjack's medical reports to a photo of his right wrist, bearing a tattoo of the ace of spades. "That's Ace's symbol. Only important members of her organization have it. He's close to Ace. This is an opportunity we can't pass up."

"Why?"

Caesar looked to the side, uncomfortable for a moment. "We've never been able to find someone from Leonueva who can locate it on a map. Most in the military that we can find are ignorant. But someone from Cartel who's used to sneaking into places he doesn't belong? He'll have information."

Arianne had come from Leonueva, but her memories of her escape were blurry. Over the years, Kalfas and Caesar had tried to get any clue from her, but she'd never been able to remember anything aside from the thousands of miles of green forest flashing below her in her fear-induced flight. It had been a point of frustration for her for years.

But with this Blackjack, there was a chance.

Arianne perked up. "You think Blackjack can lead us to Leonueva?"

Leonueva was the capital of Old Europe, the headquarters of Leon Murray. Before Arianne's father became Commander, the capital of Old Europe had been Paris. Once the current Leon took office, he began construction of the most ambitious project of the century: a hidden capital. Leon had created Leonueva to be a sanctuary for the wealthy and upper military from the impoverished regions of Pangaea.

Now, as Pacific got closer to full-out war with Europe, Caesar was getting desperate. How could Pacific defeat a monster if they didn't know where its head was?

Caesar shook his head. "I don't know, but he's the best chance we've had in a while."

Arianne frowned. "And you want me to listen in?" She shook her head. "I won't be able to tell you if he's lying; I don't remember much about Leonueva."

"I know," Caesar sighed.

"You just want to keep me occupied with work on the island," Arianne realized. "You want me to feel important."

She jumped up from her seat at the kitchen island, suddenly wide awake. Caesar didn't need her help; he needed her distracted. He needed her to think that she was doing important work so she wouldn't think about being grounded from missions.

He sighed. "I just wanted you to see that you can do important things without leaving the island. You have a unique perspective, Arianne. Maybe you'll see something I can't."

Arianne sighed and looked at the papers. "You have got to be kidding me," she mumbled in annoyance. "I told you what I think. He's better off dead."

Caesar, while soft-spoken, was not easily pushed around. The President straightened, looking down at his daughter with a commanding air she rarely had to feel. He pushed the folder towards her again. "You are to be at the medical facility at seven hundred hours. And dress nice!"

The President was gone before he could see the obscene gestures his daughter was making at him behind his back.

An hour later, Arianne was waiting at the hospital for Caesar and Kalfas to arrive. She didn't want to be there, but there was no saying no to her father—especially since he was technically her boss. Annoyed, she dragged her feet over to the windows that overlooked the island to her right. Despite her foul mood, the spot always made her heart clench: it was the same view she had stared at when she'd first met Caesar. That view represented the first time she'd ever seen her home. The feeling the sight gave her was always bittersweet.

Noticing her reflection in the window, she quickly looked away and sat down. Her reflection had a way of reminding her of Leon, and she certainly didn't need a waking nightmare that early in the morning.

Instead of thinking about anything that could ruin her composure, Arianne busied herself with fixing her hair. Arms cramping, she braided her hair into a French braid. She pulled the dirty blonde strands tightly against her scalp, and once the braid reached the base of her neck, she bound the rest of her hair into the military standard bun. The movements made her jacket scratch uncomfortably against her neck, but then again, the uniform was not prepared for comfort.

The uniform tailors had designed her outfit with her wings in mind but neglected to build in extra room for her breasts. Feeling too restricted, she unbuttoned her navy jacket and sighed in relief at the extended range of motion. Now, with her light blue collared shirt exposed below, she got to work fixing it to ensure it was properly tucked into her matching uniform pants and belt. Completing her check, she lifted her foot onto a chair and examined her black boots to check if they were properly shined. Satisfied, she straightened and placed her uniform beret on her head, carefully ensuring that the Pacific symbol—the blue and gold emblem of a stag—was facing forward.

The first lesson every student at the Pacifican Academy learned was how to wear their uniforms properly. The lesson, ingrained in her over four years, was instinct now.

The elevator behind her dinged, and Caesar stepped out with Kalfas following closely behind him. Most people would have been intimidated at the sight: the President and a General of Pacific in the same room as her. But she had lost any sense of discomfort at their combined presence a long time ago.

General Kalfas eyed her with a half-amused grin. "Major Ortiz," he greeted, "shouldn't I see a salute from you?"

Arianne tensed, quickly saluting her General and President. "Apologies, General Kalfas."

"Quit torturing her," Caesar elbowed his friend, "at ease, Arianne."

She let out a breath, waiting for her father and Kalfas to walk past before falling into step behind them. She had already been detailed on her role that morning: shut up and listen. Unfortunately, everyone in that group knew she wasn't particularly good at either.

The sound of a thundering jet engine stole her attention. Her eyes swept back to the window, a longing feeling filling her chest as she watched a grouping of three jets disappear into a mountain of orange-tinted clouds. She hated that she wondered if her friends were out there. She wondered where her friends would be off to that day. All the while, she would be stuck in a sterilized hospital.

"Major, we need you here." Caesar's voice pulled Arianne from her wallowing.

She turned and quickly followed Caesar and Kalfas into one of the concrete holding cells the hospital kept for prisoners or captives who needed medical treatment. The doors clanged shut behind her, and she moved to the back corner of the room, content to observe.

"One of these is not like the others," came a half-amused purr.

His eyes came up to her in a flash, and Arianne was surprised by their rage. She had scanned the man's file before arriving, but even his photos hadn't done him justice. He did have amber eyes, but they were laced with a striking bright green. Somehow, despite the casual way he sat in his chair, Blackjack commanded the room that he was trapped in.

And now, that commanding stare had landed on her. He was reading her, assessing her like a caged predator. But Arianne didn't wilt under his pressure. She grinned as she returned his challenge, squaring her shoulders. She wasn't in the business of being dominated—especially by a man in chains.

She caught the quick flash of acknowledgment on Blackjack's face before it disappeared.

"Don't mind her," Caesar waved Arianne off and sat down. "Just some extra security so General Kalfas can focus on our conversation."

Kalfas nodded, opting to lean on the concrete wall closest to the middle of the table. His face was unreadable.

"Let's continue where we left off," Caesar continued patiently. "I am Caesar Ortiz, and this is General Orion Kalfas. Your name is Blackjack, correct?"

"Just Jack," he grumbled, eyes going back to Arianne and pointing. "And what's your name?"

Arianne scowled, her insides tingling with annoyance at the prisoner's gall to point a finger at her. "Classified," she replied blankly, not even wanting to be in that damn room.

She wasn't technically lying. Her real name was as classified as it came: Arianne Josephina Murray-Ortiz. A potential heir denied her chance to compete for the honor of being crowned the Commander of Europe.

Well... there was one other heir, but she did her best not to think about him. Andre Murray: her older brother and newly minted Heir Apparent to the Commandership of Europe. She didn't have bad memories of her brother, and that's what made thinking about him so hard. Whenever she thought about their nights spent playing hide and seek, or the countless hours he dedicated to cleaning her wounds, she would feel a deep aching sense of hurt. She'd abandoned him, left him behind to suffer Leon alone.

Arianne looked to the side, her teeth clenching with discomfort. She shook her head to free herself from the dangerous downward spiral of thoughts. She shouldn't be thinking about her brother. She needed to be a *professional* in front of that asshole. Looking up, she noticed his eyes were still on her, his deeply penetrating gaze unapologetically directed wholly at her. She narrowed her eyes in warning, and her upper lip curled in a scowl.

Yes, it was decided: Blackjack—or Jack—was an asshole.

Jack sat back, impressed. "Wow, I got classified security. Lucky me." Arianne realized that he spoke with the remnants of a French accent, and she tucked that kernel of information away for later.

"I was hoping we could get back to talking about my proposal," Caesar said. "You assist us in finding Leonueva, and we work on getting you full Pacifican citizenship: complete protection, amnesty from past crimes, and a program to get you integrated on the island of Citadel."

Jack chuckled. "I'll tell you what I told you yesterday: if you think you're going to get that location out of me, you're completely insane."

"Jack, we're offering you protection. Imani Azikiwe can't find you here." Imani was Ace's real name, though most were too scared to even attempt to utter it. Caesar pressed, "All you have to do is help us, and your life with her is behind you."

Arianne watched Jack. She analyzed how he looked down for a fraction of a second. If someone hadn't been looking for the reaction, they never would have found it. But Arianne knew Jack hated every bone in Ace's body for turning him into the person that he was. No one could love someone whose treatment turned them so utterly apathetic. She knew because she hated Leon just as much—it was a potent mix of idolizing your oppressor mixed with the duality of knowing that the same oppressor was the heart of every ounce of pain you felt.

Unfortunately, that level of hatred sparked loyalty that a simple bribe couldn't sway. To Jack, Ace was a goddess: the beginning and end. Escape was only possible if Ace allowed it. Arianne's wing ached right where the scar from her bullet wound sat. To that day, she still didn't understand how she had escaped Leonueva, nor where she had found the will to do it.

Seeing as she could never leave Citadel, it seemed like she had only traded one prison for another. Her jaw tightened as she fought the urge to scream at Caesar in front of their prisoner. But she quickly reminded herself of how unprofessional that would be and promptly told herself to shut the fuck up.

Jack steeled himself. "I enjoy keeping my head."

"We can remove it if you want," Arianne couldn't help but growl.

A lazy grin grew on Jack's face. "Now someone's playing my game."

Caesar and Kalfas turned to Arianne, both of them giving her a warning glare. She rolled her eyes but didn't retort.

Jack leaned forward in his seat, topaz eyes bored as his left hand casually traced down his cast. "I'll tell you what I told you yesterday: I would rather that bitch cut my head off than endure whatever convoluted hell Ace will put me through if I so much as betray an ounce of her information." Caesar moved to speak, but Jack raised a hand, "and that includes hidden Cartel passageways into Leonueva or Leonueva in general. Ace makes too much money on that city to risk having it get attacked by a ton of rebels."

"Citadel is just as hidden as Leonueva," Kalfas objected. "We have our own methods of remaining off the map. Ace won't touch you here."

Arianne almost spoke up again. She nearly warned Jack of the secret catch. Sure, the island of Citadel was hidden and offered safety, but there was no leaving—not for people in hiding.

Jack considered Kalfas's words, his lips pursing in thought. After a few moments, he shrugged. "Maybe I just don't feel like helping you assholes."

Arianne lunged forward, ready to pull his tongue out through his nose. But Caesar raised a hand, halting her. He turned back to Jack. "And why don't you want to help us? Pacific is fighting the good fight. We're working to make a home for people who are sick of Pangaea's tyranny. We're trying to bring back history, democracy, and a world filled with many different nations, rather than a single empire."

Jack scoffed, "And how well is that working out for you? Want to tell me how Mende, France, worked out?"

Caesar shrunk back, his eyes widening. Arianne's mouth parted in shock. Even Kalfas, unmoving as stone, managed a slight hitch in his breath. Mende, France, was the location of the Pacific outpost Jaleel Leroy and his family had once lived in.

The same outpost that had its location betrayed. The same outpost that got bombed by Pangaea. No survivors.

"So, you've done your research on us," Caesar managed.

Jack laughed, "I'm from France; we all know about your group's colossal mistake. So no, I won't fight for the losing side, no matter how virtuous you are."

"We're done for today," Kalfas announced, tapping Caesar on the shoulder.

Arianne looked at her father. He'd tried his best, but it was obvious the thought of Jaleel was haunting him. Jaleel had been Caesar's closest friend—they had founded Pacific together. Arianne knew Caesar still blamed himself for his friend's death.

She waited as Caesar and Kalfas left the room, watching Jack's reaction. She narrowed her eyes, reading the prisoner's intent with a hint of satisfaction. She recognized what he'd done because she'd done it plenty of times when a subject got too personal to talk about. Jack had gone nuclear. He'd brought up a subject so painful that the conversation was forced to end. The strategy saved him from talking about a subject too close to home. If she could only figure out why Pacific was such a painful subject to him, she could find a way into his psyche.

Realizing someone was still in the room, Jack rolled his head toward Arianne with a sigh, "And what do you want, Princess?"

Arianne had to hide her clenched hands in her pockets, "Don't call me princess." He couldn't possibly know how close that name hit home.

"Question still stands."

Arianne bit her lip, considering, "Why do you really not want to help us?"

It made no sense. She had seen people in far better positions be bought off by far less: local farmers paid for silence over a new colony or Pangaean army refugees offering up troop movements. Jack—branded like cattle and forced to be a bounty hunter for Cartel—was offered protection in a tropical paradise.

Why pass that up?

Jack's eyes widened for a second, his only admission of surprise at Arianne's ability to read him. As soon as the emotion surfaced, a look of passive boredom drowned it, "What did you say your name was again?"

"Classified," Arianne growled, "the question still stands."

Jack's mouth ticked upwards in a baleful smile, "Alright, Princess."

"I said, don't call me that."

"If you won't give me a name, I'm sticking with Princess," Jack's sneer showed just how insufferable he knew he was being.

Arianne was seconds away from lunging at the prisoner, "You're dodging the question."

"It's a long story." Jack stared forward, challenging whose stubbornness would break first.

"I have all the time in the world," Arianne shot back. "Just say the word, and I'll free up my schedule." Not that she had much of a schedule, but she wasn't about to tell him that.

Jack crossed his arms. "Maybe I just don't feel like telling it."

She shrugged and turned to leave, unwilling to waste her time in that cell waiting for him to talk. Still, the idea of having the last word certainly appealed to her.

Arianne paused in the cell's doorway, "Well, Jack, when you feel like telling me, I'll be right here to listen. We can have a good old-fashioned tea party with some of those small pastries and ridiculous hats," she winked. "I feel like those pastel colors would just make your skin pop."

Jack was about to discover Arianne could be just as insufferable as him.

Chapter 10

Jaya

"We need a small group to extract Bradley Shaw from Moscow." Captain Lyn instructed.

Moscow? Again? Jaya's purple eyebrows furrowed. Shaw had been stupid enough to return to the same place in the same month? Keeping him safe the first time was tough. Any bad attention they had captured during the previous mission could still be there waiting to strike.

Jaya and Rhino exchanged a glance in their debriefing room at Angel's Camp. Something in Lyn's tone seemed off. Even after so little time spent working underneath the Captain, Jaya could read her. There was something different about Lyn's voice and body language—it was like she was waiting until they were en route to tell her team something. Jaya didn't like that one bit.

Yes, everything seemed rushed. The team had been summoned at four that morning without a warning. Jaya yawned, still half-asleep. Now, without even fifteen minutes of debriefing, they were boarding a jet to Moscow. The sun hadn't even gotten a chance to rise.

Jaya threw her helmet on as the plane took off, her green eyes drifting to Captain Lyn. The woman looked troubled—or as troubled as a stiff-lipped Captain could look. Jaya frowned and elbowed Rhino. The larger Fera seemed bothered as well, but she couldn't find any words to comfort him. Neither of them had forgotten the haunting laughter they'd heard the week before. And now they were unceremoniously flying back into a less-than-optimal situation.

Before her stress gave her a headache, Jaya forced herself to close her eyes and catch up on her missed sleep. Even though her concerns should have kept her awake, she knew her exhaustion would only make whatever mission she was walking into worse. It seemed like the four other operatives had the same idea, and the flight passed silently as they all settled into a restless sleep.

An uncomfortable flight of half-wakefulness and half-sleep later, Jaya felt her stomach drop as the plane began to land. As she stirred awake, she heard Lyn walking around the cabin and waking the team: "Alright, take some caffeine tablets, ladies! I need you all bright-eyed and bushy-tailed in five minutes!"

Lyn didn't pause to update the team. Once the plane landed, she rushed the groggy officers into a silver car parked on the tarmac outside of their plane. By the time the team reached the city proper, the caffeine tablets had done their job, and the team was buzzing with nervous energy. Being *Feras,* Rhino and Jaya needed two times the number of tablets as the rest of the team thanks to their faster metabolism. Eventually, the copious amount of tablets did their trick on the mutants. Heart racing from her anticipation and caffeine coursing through her blood, Jaya tried to watch the city of Moscow go past to calm her racing thoughts. She was disappointed when the sight of the city sweeping past her vision only aided in growing her rising tide of anxiety.

After half an hour, the car slowed to a stop.

"I will go ahead with Sanchez to get Shaw. Bahri and Adams, you will wait at the car and cover us as we leave the hotel." Lyn readied herself to exit the car.

"Where's Shaw's other guards?" Jaya asked as she loaded her gun.

Lyn's tan face was grim. "Both were found dead this morning. No wounds, spare two pinhole-like bite marks on their arms."

No wonder they were called to Moscow at the last minute. And no wonder Lyn hadn't updated her team. There was no use terrifying them with stories of vampires. The mission was still the same: get Shaw out alive.

"Where they snake bites?" Rhino leaned forward and asked.

Jaya searched through her memories from her field survival classes. "There are venomous vipers native to Russia."

"No snake is going to slither up and bite two of my best men. *Especially* ten levels off the ground inside a hotel," Lyn said, tone troubled. "A *Fera* attacked them."

"Then why didn't they kill Shaw," Sanchez questioned.

"They want to draw us out," Lyn answered, checking her ammunition. "Whoever it is, they're not after Shaw. They're after Pacific. So, we get Shaw out discreetly and ensure we lose whoever might be following us before we get on that plane."

Jaya nodded, her pulse slowing as the mission settled over her. *This is what you signed up for*, she reminded herself. Sometimes, the job meant you didn't make it out alive.

Jaya and Rhino followed Lyn and Sanchez out of the car, the two rookies surveying the street with their *Fera* eyes in an attempt to find anything that Lyn hadn't noticed. To Jaya's disappointment, everything seemed normal.

Too normal.

Unsettled, the Chameleon took up her post with Rhino outside the Moscow hotel. Rifles resting in their arms, they waited. Each passerby had her nerves on edge.

"This doesn't feel right," Rhino grunted.

"Why did he come back here?" Jaya hissed out of the side of her mouth.

"I don't know," the large *Fera* responded with the same spark of annoyance.

Jaya huffed and checked to ensure her hair was still an unremarkable brown, "Did you hear? They captured a member of Ace's Cartel," she whispered, hoping to find something to talk about to lessen the tension.

"If he gives us information, there goes our chance at a long weekend," Rhino joked, keeping his eyes on the front door to the hotel.

"You think they would send us?"

Rhino didn't respond; his gray eyes searched the hotel lobby with concern. "Something's up." He gritted through clenched teeth. "They should be outside by now."

Jaya cursed. She was so focused on her anxiety that she hadn't been counting the seconds. Rookie mistake. She looked down at her watch—Lyn was running thirty seconds behind schedule.

She raised her gun. "Go check inside. I'll cover the car."

"Me?" Rhino's voice displayed the first sign of fear.

"I'm not the one with bullet-resistant skin," she hissed under her breath.

Rhino took a step forward just as the hotel doors were thrown open with a crash. Lyn and Sanchez were flanking Shaw as they sprinted down the lobby steps and towards them. "Get in the car!" Lyn shouted. "We have company!"

Rhino lurched forward, his bullet-resistant skin a human shield for Shaw as they hopped into the back seat. Jaya covered as the rest of the squadron dove into the car. Her heart thundered in her chest. *Faster, faster, faster,* she willed her teammates. Finally, with the car secured, she climbed inside.

Sanchez slammed his foot on the gas before Jaya was entirely inside. Gunfire popped behind them, making her duck below the window, her body somehow already drenched in sweat. Next to her, Shaw looked deathly pale, like the ghosts of the officers who'd died that morning were still haunting him.

"What the hell happened?" Rhino shouted in surprise.

Lyn, characteristically calm, let out a sigh as she watched out of the side mirror. "My hunch was right," she huffed. "Two pursuers, both female. I couldn't identify who they were working for."

The hostiles were either Pangaean or Cartel. Ever since Pacific had apprehended Blackjack, every offshore team had been briefed that Cartel could very well retaliate against Pacific for capturing one of their own. Sure, Blackjack had been captured under some shady circumstances, but it was safer to assume Cartel could somehow find out about Pacific's involvement than be blindsided. Naturally, knowing who their pursuers were would be extremely important. If Cartel were chasing them, there would be places where they couldn't engage in an attack. And if Pangaea was chasing them... Well, they were in a lot of trouble.

Jaya turned frantically to her shivering vice president. "Any important information, sir?" She demanded a little too sarcastically. She hissed at herself inwardly—she shouldn't be talking to her superior like that. No matter how stupid he was.

Bradley Shaw's lips were purple. "No clue. I knew something was up yesterday. That's when I sent the encoded message to Captain Lyn."

"When did you realize that? Before or after Marshall and Stewart were killed," Sanchez barked, eyes leaving the road to glare at Shaw in the rearview mirror.

Jaya never considered how much their two teammates' deaths were weighing on the veteran. Marshall, Sanchez, and Stewart—along with Lyn—were the oldest members of their squadron. Jaya couldn't imagine what losing old teammates would feel like.

"Car heavy on our tail. Five o'clock," Rhino declared, lowering his window to watch traffic and stick the head of his rifle outside.

Sanchez slammed his foot on the gas, the car jolting forward. Jaya turned her head around and rolled down her window. Her heart lurched when she spied their first pursuer swerving through traffic behind them: a young woman with bleach-blonde hair.

"That's her!" Jaya gaped in horror. "That's the woman I saw the last time we were here."

Captain Lyn reached into her jacket pocket. "Bahri!" She shouted as she extended a hand behind her and passed Jaya a vial filled with bright red blood. "Take this!" The rookie frowned at the bottle as Lyn explained, "We had just enough time to get two vials worth of Marshall's blood." Not even Lyn could hide the sorrow in her tone. "You have one, and I have the other. We need to get at least one back to the lab to see what manner of *Fera* we're dealing with."

Jaya didn't have to ask why that vial was so important: in case that *Fera* came around again to cause trouble.

"Captain? Didn't you say you had two pursuing us? There's only one behind us." Rhino turned from the window in concern. "Where's the other—"

Jaya heard the sound of the sniper, but it was already too late. Sanchez's head was shot to the side with neck-snapping force. Lyn cried out as her teammate was thrown into her and blood splattered the windshield.

Jaya screamed as the car swerved out of control. Rhino cursed as he wrapped himself around Bradley Shaw. There was a shuddering crash, and she was launched forward into the seat in front of her before she had a chance to brace. As their car was brought to a jolting halt, the startling deployment of the airbags sounded like gunfire. Her body was bruised from the impact, and her ears were ringing from the airbags. She was dangerously disoriented.

And now their primary source of escape was stuck in the middle of a multi-car pileup.

Lyn was furiously shoving the airbag out of her face. "We need to move. Now!" She shouted.

But Jaya barely heard her Captain. In the seconds following the crash, everything slowed to a dangerous halt. She was staring at Sanchez, his deathly still face resting on his airbag covered in scarlet blood. Her mouth gaped open in horror, but no words came out.

Sanchez had been alive moments before. *Talking* moments before.

"He's dead," Jaya's voice shook.

She froze as she took in her teammate's body. For a few heart-wrenching moments, she didn't know what to do. She lost herself to the ringing in her ears as she stared forward, nausea slowly creeping up her throat. Her hands at her sides began to turn red, matching the only thing her mind registered: Sanchez's blood.

"Rookie! No time to freeze now!" Lyn shouted through Jaya's daze.

Jaya barely registered Rhino frantically shaking her out of her trance. Numbly, she exited the car. Her vision blurred, the sun suddenly becoming too bright.

Reality hit her harder than she had ever calculated. She could *die*. She had just stepped into the kill box.

Focus. You need to focus.

Sanchez's wound was on the left side of his body. That meant the shooter was coming from the building on the left side of the car. Which also suggested that the right side of the vehicle would be safest for the Vice President. Raising her gun, Jaya's mind cleared, and she guided Shaw to hide behind the right side of the car with Lyn and Rhino.

Squatting down with her back to the car, Jaya tried to calm her racing heart as she turned to her Captain. "What do we do now?"

Lyn took a calming breath as her sharp brown eyes analyzed the stopped traffic around them. "We survive." She gritted, "I sent a message to the backup squad on the jet, but they're twenty minutes out. We have no idea what we are dealing with—possibly two *Feras* and whoever they're working with."

And they were stuck in the middle of a road. Fish in a barrel waiting to be shot. Shaw was shaking in between Rhino and Jaya. "I'm sorry," he mumbled, "I-I had no idea."

Jaya had to force herself not to give the man a look of disgust.

Rhino peeked his silver head over the trunk of the car. He stiffly aimed his gun toward the shooter's building. A shot was fired, and he ducked behind the car again. "We're stuck," he breathed in confirmation.

Jaya looked down, not surprised to see that the red tint in her fingers had traveled up to her arms. Extreme emotion made it hard for her to regulate the colors of her skin. She wouldn't be surprised if her entire body turned blood red with fear. By how Shaw looked at her in shock, she assumed that was already the case.

"Someone's coming," Jaya whispered, the ringing in her sensitive ears fading just enough to hear the ever-so-soft footfalls coming down the road. It was a miracle she could hear anything over the constant sound of car horns and her own racing heart.

Lyn nodded to the car next to them. "We are going to pull that man out of his car. Once in, we will have just enough room to try to push through the wreckage." Everyone nodded. On Lyn's count, they moved.

The sniper fired a couple of times. Jaya used the wreckage of the other cars as cover as she dove into the vehicle. Lyn pulled the driver from the car, taking the wheel. Rhino rushed to the back, giving it a push to get its wheels over the accident's debris before jumping inside. As soon as the team was shut in the car, Jaya felt a momentary sense of relief. One step closer to freedom: done. As Jaya allowed a deep breath to fill her lungs, Lyn floored the gas as she maneuvered through the traffic.

Behind them, the light blonde-haired woman appeared as she climbed on top of a stopped car. The woman fired a couple of shots of white-hot plasma from a strangely rounded firearm. Jaya was forced to duck as the beams of energy burned into their car's back window.

"Fuck, they have blasters!" Rhino barked.

Jaya hissed in frustration, "Not good!"

Blasters were relatively new technology in Pangaea. Being so novel, they were expensive and typically saved for the upper Pangaean military and the wealthy private guards of Elites. If their opponents had blasters, it meant they were dealing with someone important. Jaya watched as the woman pursuing them moved with elegant grace over and around the car wreckage. Even chasing a car, she was gaining on them.

Unfortunately, the traffic made it hard for Lyn to drive at full speed. "The radio was destroyed in the crash. I can't contact the backup squadron! We'll have to wait for them to get to us."

"Of course, it was," Rhino sighed, still eying their pursuer from the window.

"We're going to need to draw her out," Lyn instructed. "We can't board a plane being actively chased. There is an abandoned building coming up. I'll lead Shaw and Adams inside. Bahri, you hide at the entrance and wait for that woman. When she passes you, you ambush her."

The car slowed just enough for Jaya to jump out. She was already sprinting towards the building while the rest of her team drove off to the other side. Once inside, she quickly located some dense shadows and readied herself in the darkness. Using her lizard-like *Fera* abilities, Jaya crawled up the wall and toward the ceiling. Once situated, she willed her hair and skin to become as black as night.

Her pursuer wouldn't know she was there until it was too late.

From her lizard's eye-view, Jaya watched a wrecked vehicle pulled from the car accident creak onto the property. The car was barely operational—its front crushed like an accordion and its passenger side doors hanging on by a thread. Jaya clenched her teeth in anticipation as two women exited the car. She recognized the first: the ghostly blonde with a face set in terrible determination. The second pursuer was new to Jaya: an Eastern woman with short-cropped black hair and a remarkably slender build.

As the blonde advanced toward the building, the short-haired Eastern woman remained behind. "It's a setup," she sang mockingly.

The blonde waved the other woman off with a growl. "Do you think I don't know that? Let me have my fun." Her voice carried a slight English accent that Jaya recognized as far more proper than what she was used to hearing in her hometown.

The Eastern woman yawned. "Well, don't blame me if this whole thing goes up in smoke. I don't play with my food."

The blonde whirled. "Last time I checked, you don't talk to me like that." The slender woman, though taller, shrunk under the blonde's glare.

The blonde whirled away from her partner, creeping towards the building. She hadn't even passed the doorway before she opened fire on the first floor. Drywall and wood splintered to dust as the gunfire threatened to burst Jaya's sensitive ears.

The blonde skipped forward. "Awe, leaving so soon, Bradley?" She chuckled darkly. "Here, kitty kitty!"

Still gripping the wall, Jaya crawled after the woman. Even after years of practice, she hated the feeling of blood rushing to her head as she hung against gravity. Neck straining, she tried her best to keep her eyes on the woman even while upside down. Despite the adrenaline rushing through her veins, Jaya knew she could only be in that awkward position a little longer before the cramping of her limbs and back became unbearable to maintain.

The blonde snuck around a corner and shot a couple of times. "Don't worry, sweetie, we can still be friends. I forgive you," she cooed.

Every part of Jaya wanted to stay far away from the woman below. From her short interaction with her, Jaya knew the blonde was one of the most vile human beings she had ever come across. But as the woman slowed her pacing, she came to a spot directly below the Chameleon hanging in wait. The woman's eerie blue eyes lit up the gloom as she continued to scan the room in awful entertainment, oblivious of what was above her. The time to attack was now or never.

Jaya took a deep breath—relishing the last few moments of calm before she disturbed the hornet's nest—and then let herself drop.

Chapter 11

Blackjack

Jack banged his head against the window of his cell in a slow and steady rhythm. He was vaguely aware of planes taking off from somewhere beyond the view of the hospital and the sound of wind warning of an upcoming summer storm. He wasn't sure what was worse: having no entertainment or being tortured by the view of a tropical paradise just beyond three inches of bulletproof glass. So, he sat in a purgatory of boredom and avoidance, uncertain of the last time he had nothing to do with himself.

Half insane by the monotony of his new predicament, Jack finally fell back into his bed, fairly certain that a bruise had formed on his forehead from his incessant banging. It was there, staring up at the uninspired concrete ceiling, that he managed a spiteful laugh at himself. He knew that he was an idiot to pass up a deal to live on the island and prolong his suffering in that awful cell. But he hated Pacific. He'd given up believing in the country a long time ago.

Leaving his mind to wander, questions began stirring in his head. How many more people were on the island? Citadel was obviously their capital, and he knew outposts were hidden all over Europe, but surely the population of the island could help pinpoint the size of the rebel force. If he could figure that out, he could sell the information to Ace.

His head spun. If he could escape, he could get back to Leonueva and sell everything he knew. The amount of money might even be enough to pay off his debt. Jack paused, considering. *No*, he realized in disappointment that simple information wouldn't be worth much. He needed more. He needed *captives*.

Slowly, an idea began to form. Assuming he was on an island, the only way off was via boat or plane. Jack couldn't simply escape his cell; he would have to escape the island as well. And if he wanted to deliver people to Ace, then, well, he couldn't simply run away.

No, the Pacificans needed to think his departure was their idea.

His thoughts were interrupted by the door opening. Two armed security guards came into the room, followed by Dr. Ike. The stringy man was cautious as he stopped at the entrance of the room and gestured for the armed guards to handcuff Jack.

Jack, though rolling his eyes in annoyance, complied. Despite his desire to leave, he had no advantage in attacking the doctor. Even after a week spent in that hospital, he still wasn't in the best health. And he was smart enough to know that he needed to be healthy before he pulled anything.

Once security had cuffed Jack, Dr. Ike nodded to the pair. "I can take it from here."

"But—" the first guard objected.

Dr. Ike raised his chin. "I don't care who he is. He's my patient, and he deserves privacy."

With hesitant nods, both guards walked out as the door to the room shut.

"Good morning, Jack." Dr. Ike smiled, pulling on a pair of blue latex gloves. "How are you feeling today?"

"Fine," The patient commented flatly.

Dr. Ike fixed his glasses. "If you don't feel comfortable taking off your shirt, you can just unbutton the front. I need to inspect the bandages and make sure the stitches are healing properly."

Hesitantly, the bounty hunter unbuttoned the front of his shirt, and the doctor began to carefully cut away the gauze.

Dr. Ike nodded when he finally removed the last strip of the bandages. "That's what I thought."

Jack knew what he would see when he looked down. The claw marks from the Lion *Fera*, once angry, ragged gashes barely held together by stitches, were now light pink scratches. He winced, knowing that such an injury should have taken a few more weeks to heal. Then he remembered that he was in the hands of Pacific, and not Cartel, and he reminded himself that such a rapid recovery wouldn't be heavily questioned.

Jack remained quiet as the doctor got to work pulling out the stitches with tweezers. He tensed, expecting some pain, but quickly found that Dr. Ike had an expert hand. "How's Pangaea these days?" The doctor asked, attempting to make small talk.

The bounty hunter grimaced. He hated useless conversation almost as much as he hated Pangaea.

Unfortunately, Dr. Ike was the only person on that island he had to keep a good relationship with. "Same old pit." He paused, "Wait—why?"

Dr. Ike laughed, placing the last of Jack's stitches on his tray. "Pacific isn't even thirty years old. Most of us found our way here from Pangaea in some way or another."

"Oh," Jack said, looking down. He hadn't thought about it like that before.

The doctor removed his blue gloves. "Well, that looks about it. With how your stitches healed, I think I could take your cast off next week."

The patient nodded. "Perfect."

"Well, not *perfect*," the doctor abridged. "You'll probably need a brace for a few more weeks. Not to mention physical therapy..." He trailed off.

Jack didn't respond. He didn't care about a brace. A brace could be taken off. A brace meant nothing was truly broken anymore. The sooner he could make it back to Leonueva, the better.

"Another week then?" Jack asked.

Dr. Ike smiled. "Another week and you'll be well on your way to recovery."

Jack watched the doctor leave his cell and patiently waited for the armed guards to return and remove his handcuffs. As they worked, his eyes went to that window of bright blue sky, and the view of the island didn't feel so torturous anymore. One week and he would be free.

Perfect.

Jack didn't expect to be woken up in the middle of the night.

He'd fallen asleep alone—in fact, he'd been sure of it. When he arrived a week ago, he'd made it a point to search the entire room. No cameras and no prying eyes through tiny peepholes. By all of his accounts, he should have been left alone to sleep. So, naturally, he was confused when he felt eyes on him.

Jack jumped up, scanning the gloom to figure out who had disturbed him. He had trained himself to be a light sleeper, his body always partially primed to wake at the slightest noise. That meant whoever had arrived knew how to be virtually silent. His suspicions were confirmed when he spotted the ominous figure sitting at the table at the edge of his room.

"Good, you're awake," came a voice Jack could have sworn he recognized. "I guess I don't have to dump this water on you."

"Princess," Jack purred. "Hate to break it to you, but official hospital visiting hours start at seven."

"This isn't a visit."

An interrogation, then. Jack's eyes glowed with curiosity. What could the Pacifican Major want with him so late at night? Something told him that it wasn't a sanctioned visit. He grinned evilly, knowing he must have looked utterly terrifying with his broad smile and eyes the only things visible shining in the darkness, "You have questions you're not supposed to have," he sang.

The Major didn't hesitate, "You answer my questions, and I make your life easier."

"Oh?"

"Better food, maybe some more comfortable accommodations," the Major continued.

Jack leaned back in his bed. "Come on, you can do better than that." He'd grown up on the streets of Paris and then Leonueva. A bed with a roof over his head was a lot, considering his humble background. And his *own* room? In a temperature-controlled environment with guaranteed meals? Jack was sitting pretty. He had room to negotiate.

"Well, I have two whole buckets of water waiting right here," the Major said simply. "I could just dump them on you."

Jack sighed in annoyance. "What do you want to ask me?"

"Do you work with the European Royal family often?"

Jack perked up. "You mean the Murrays?"

"Yeah, them."

"Hell no," Jack almost wheezed. "Fuck that."

"Why not?"

He glanced at the Major, attempting to see her in the shadows. What game was she playing? Why did she care? Was this some kind of new interrogation tactic that they were employing? Maybe the location of Leonueva wasn't even Pacific's final goal. Maybe they wanted to infiltrate the Murray family themselves.

He decided to go along with it. Maybe there was a chance he could get information out of his new, young interrogator. "We don't work with Leon because he's untrustworthy," Jack began. "Ace and Leon have a specific business relationship where Leon lets Ace keep her operations, and Ace keeps the Underground in check. That's how it's been, and that's how it will remain."

"So, your loyalty is towards protecting the status quo," the Major questioned.

Jack jabbed at his chest, "My only loyalty is to me, got it?" He frowned, "that's the only way I've kept myself alive. Can I go back to sleep now?"

The Major chuckled, "What? Get grumpy if you don't get your eight hours?"

"I'm always grumpy."

"Apparently," the Major chided. "Fine. What do you know about the Murray family?"

The bounty hunter chewed on his fingernail, "What? Don't get out much?"

"N-no," she said, too defensively. "It's just a fair assumption that someone who has some unorthodox connections might know more about the Murrays than someone raised on a remote island."

Jack raised an eyebrow, "So you were born here?"

"Classified," the woman replied blankly.

He'd take that as a no. Jack grinned. Who had this woman been before Pacific? What brought her here? Maybe if he kept her talking, he could learn more. "Everything is classified with you," He said with a bored yawn. "Doesn't really make an interesting talk for me. How about this: a question for a question. Kind of like a game."

"Fine," the Major sighed in frustration. "What do you know about the Murrays?"

Jack shrugged. "Not much. Like most Pangaean Elites, they keep their family matters pretty private. It makes it harder for us regular folks to plot against them. Andre Murray was only recently made public as Leon's Heir Apparent. But we've all heard some interesting stories about him."

For some reason, Jack noticed the Major's breath catch, but she righted herself quickly. "What about Andre?"

"No," Jack tsked. "That's not how the game's played. What's your name?"

"Arianne," she ground out.

"Your *full* name."

Arianne bared her teeth, "Arianne Ortiz."

"Ortiz," the name rolled off of Jack's tongue. "Like Caesar Ortiz?"

Arianne frowned in confirmation, her gray eyes, like liquid pools of silver, darkening. Jack smiled. He wasn't just dealing with classified security. He was dealing with the top dog's daughter. He'd been right in his first mocking nickname of her: in every right, she was an island princess. He rolled his eyes. She'd most likely been *handed* that cushy job as an interrogation officer. The idea sickened him, but he couldn't let his annoyance at her position throw him off his game.

"Now, about Andre."

Jack shrugged, willing the picture of passive indifference to come onto his face. "Word on the street says the Prince is... volatile. A loose cannon of sorts. He's the Captain of the royal guard, a division called the Wards. Andre commands the Wards in a way that would make Leon proud: cold, efficient, and without mercy. Other criminal groups who've dealt with him claim that his attention is a death sentence. And he's not the type to simply kill you because it's his duty. He enjoys it."

Jack got his own kind of awful enjoyment from Arianne's gasped breath.

He waved a hand in the air. "Maybe consider what you're dealing with before you and your merry band of islanders decide to attack Leonueva. I'm a walk in the park compared to that."

"I assume I have to give you an answer now."

Jack snapped his fingers. "Now you're catching on. Where are you from?"

Jack never studied biology, but even he could point out that there was no way a blonde-haired, blue-eyed woman came from someone of Afro-Hispanic descent like Caesar. That meant she was adopted. But from who?

"Pangaea," she muttered. "Where are you from? Because you sound French, but you don't look... *French.*"

"Do you really want to waste your question on that?"

He could almost hear Arianne's eye roll. "Is Andre the only child of Leon?"

Jack sat up. "Now that's a good question." He realized that he didn't mind talking to the Pacifican Major. She gave him something interesting to think about while he sat in that cell waiting for his wounds to mend. And he wasn't giving her anything important, not really. Still, he wondered why she was so willing to bargain over Cartel gossip. And in the dead of night, at that.

"He's the only child that we know of," the bounty hunter replied thoughtfully, "but there have always been whisperings."

"Of what?"

"A *Fera* child."

The greatest bane of the *Fera* population was its unpredictability. Two completely average humans could be surprised with a *Fera* child if they carried the mutated genes. Having a mutant in the family, especially among the ranks of the Pangaean Elite, could be social suicide. Elite families having *Fera* children were not unheard of, but most did their best to hide it.

Such an unpredictable phenomena happening within a Commander's family was even more problematic. That *Fera* child could very well grow up to become Heir Apparent. And no one wanted an animalistic and savage *Fera* rising to carry that kind of power.

"A *Fera* child of Leon's wouldn't be impossible. His own brother was one," Jack continued. "Notice how I said, *was*. The Murrays have a history of disposing of their mutant relatives. If Leon had a *Fera* child, it's most likely dead. Some people even claim its death was what sent Andre over the edge. But everyone wants to come up with an excuse for crazy nowadays."

Arianne's breath caught. Jack registered the momentary hitch of breath from the Major and he wondered why she cared. Without warning, Arianne sprung up and made for the door.

"Hey!" He objected, "You still owe me a question!"

"I guess I do. Let's take a rain check," she breathed as the door clanged shut.

Chapter 12

Arianne

Arianne didn't sleep a wink the rest of that night. She cursed herself for messing with things left well enough alone. She struggled with two sides waging war inside of her: the side that knew her past was a part of her and the side that wanted to drown it all in the Mediterranean Sea. Either way, she knew that what she left behind, however foggy her recollection, was what made her who she was. That didn't make any of it less painful, though. She felt the healed scars of her past ripped wide open. And now she was hemorrhaging memories like blood spilling from a torn artery, and there was nothing she could do to stop it.

Distraught, she paced up and down the beach. The sand surrounding her bare feet and the calming sound of the waves were just enough to keep her grounded despite the swirling hurricane of guilt and sadness. Sure, she had somehow run away from her father, but she left the people she loved behind. Andre, her mother… she buried her face in her hands as more tears burned in her eyes.

She'd thought she'd moved on, but she'd taken the first opportunity she had gotten to learn about her family. And it had left her feeling raw and broken. She'd been foolish to think the simple bandage of forgetting the past would heal her; that it would somehow close the wound on her heart that no stitches could ever repair.

The pain came from loving the people she was supposed to hate. Like a fever, it burned and destroyed everything from the inside out.

Arianne didn't remember much about Andre or her mother, Josephina, but she still had that intimate feeling of love and warmth at the thought of them. She remembered sunlight in the darkness of her life with them around. And now Andre was turning into Leon because of her—because she *left* him.

What could she say for herself? How could she justify causing her brother so much grief? A brother who loved her? And Josephina? Her own mother? She hadn't even had the courage to ask Jack about her. Arianne sobbed again, dropping to sit on the cool sand of the beach. How did her mother feel, believing that her daughter was dead?

She bit down on a clenched fist to cover up a scream. She wanted to fix everything, but she couldn't. She could never go back to that awful place. At the end of the day, she was selfish.

And a coward.

Resting on the beach, watching the sky brighten into lighter purple, pink, and then orange, Arianne was exhausted. And yet, the morning came anyway. Removing her clothes down to her sports bra and underwear, she dove into the water, hoping the weightlessness would clear her head.

She swam further out to sea than most would say was safe, but she enjoyed staring at the sea floor dropping further and further down below her. Still so early in the morning, the water below her darkened quickly, but the mystery of the depths never scared her. The terrors of the hidden sea faded when one could breathe below the waves.

Arianne let herself float just below the surface, weightless. She allowed her rib cage to expand and shrink as her gills worked to bring oxygen to her body. She was a coward, yes, but she needed to run from her father. She could never go home, yes, but she could fight for Pacific. In her own way, she could pay back the universe for the sacrifice her mother and brother made on her behalf.

Her eyes opened. The water was glittering a bright turquoise now as the morning sun shimmered above. She must have finally fallen asleep, the dawn transitioning to morning while she rested. Arianne propelled herself upwards, her head breaking the surface as droplets fell around her in sparkling crystals. She looked out to where the sea stretched toward the horizon's edge—where shimmering blue met a cloud-filled orange sky, and took a moment to wonder what lands existed beyond that horizon—lands she had long since forgotten.

What would it be like to visit somewhere beyond her tiny island?

Maybe she still could. Maybe if she tried again, Caesar would see reason.

Swimming to shore, Arianne collected her clothes and jumped into the air, heading home. She needed to shower and change; she had a meeting with the President.

Later that morning, Arianne found herself climbing up the grand staircase of the Capitol building. Once inside, she rode the elevator to the top floor where Caesar's office resided. Checking her folder, she knocked and was let in by the floor's receptionist.

The woman smiled, "Good morning, Miss Arianne, you look lovely today."

Of course, I'm going to look good, she thought to herself. *I'm about to beg for my damn freedom.*

"Morn," Arianne tried to put on a smile, but she was utterly exhausted.

"Go right in. Caesar shouldn't be on a call," the receptionist waved.

Walking into the office was staggering. The grand room took up half the floor as the ceilings reached well above fifteen feet. A large desk rested in front of a towering window that overlooked the ocean. The left and right walls were covered in floor-to-ceiling bookshelves and impressively, those countless tomes were not decorations. Most were heavily worn from Caesar's studies. Grand couches and chairs with an elegant coffee table made a small living room setting in the middle of the room. The entire office was full of memories, creative touches, and a comforting feel.

Much like Caesar himself, the space felt warm.

Arianne could hear her boots squeaking on the polished granite as she walked over to her father's desk, "Caesar?" She asked, waiting for him to look up. He didn't.

"A man known by the name of Albert Einstein once said, 'Curiosity is more important than knowledge,'" Arianne's father stated, "But when your curiosity leads you to knowledge, that information is usually more impactful than you would have liked."

Arianne shook her head, questioning. "What do you mean?" Her lack of sleep had not put her in the headspace to ponder one of her father's philosophical preaching's. Looking for a way to rest her tired limbs, she leaned over the President's grand desk and placed her palms on it.

Caesar looked at his daughter with warm brown eyes. "Did you find what you were looking for last night?" Arianne remained silent as he continued, "About your family." He stood up, carrying a file he had been working on over to the bookshelf. After a few moments of searching, he turned back to his daughter, awaiting her response.

"Why did you never tell me about them?" She asked, her voice distant. "All these years... you never told me anything." For a while, she'd convinced herself that she was okay with knowing nothing. However, when the opportunity arose to learn more, she couldn't resist.

"I wanted to protect you," Caesar began, his eyes lowering. "I wanted to help you forget the past. But deep down, I knew it was only a matter of time before my reassurances wouldn't be enough for you." He shook his head, filled with regret. "I shouldn't have hidden their existence from you. But you need to understand that I was doing what I thought was best for you."

Arianne gritted her teeth. "That's not the only reason."

Her father hung his head in shame. "I felt terrible that I could never be the person your mother was to you, or share the same blood as your brother. But I always tried my best. I knew that someday my love for you wouldn't be enough, that you would begin to wonder what had become of your family. That you'd have questions. Though, I hoped against hope that this day would never come. Now, I see how naïve that thinking was. A part of you will always be drawn to them, even through your hatred. You've been searching for answers," he added. "Answers I cannot provide completely."

Arianne wanted to shout at Caesar, but she was too tired. "But all these years—I never knew what happened to any of them. You never told me how bad it got, Caesar." She shook her head, her voice trembling. "If I had known... if I had known what Leon was still doing to my family..." Her words trailed off.

I would have left a long time ago.

She witnessed the same dangerous thought flicker through Caesar's eyes. "I didn't want to lose you," he sighed. "I didn't want you to think about them, the people who hurt you so deeply, especially when you've been making progress. I hoped that, in time, you could heal and find happiness in the life you've built for yourself on this island."

But I'm not healing, Arianne wanted to scream. It would have been easy; she could have opened up to her father right then. She could have sought help. But at that moment, she believed there was only one path to recovery: leaving the island and experiencing the world she had been hidden from. She needed an opportunity to reclaim the life she had unceremoniously abandoned.

"Caesar, your love means more to me than I could ever express," Arianne looked away, her eyes welling with tears. "I just needed to know what I left behind. I needed to understand." She shook her head as her voice quivered. "Knowing the pain you've caused others, hurts. Remembering the pain others caused you, hurts. But I can't just keep feeling useless."

Arianne's departure had caused her mother and brother immense pain, and she couldn't bear the thought of it all being in vain. She couldn't accept that the sacrifices of her past had been made so she could wither away on that isolated island.

Caesar remained silent for several moments. In the quiet, Arianne took in a deep breath, letting the smell of leather and worn books fill her nose. The scent was familiar and comforting and she was reminded of how many hours she had spent accompanying her father in that majestic office. She was hit with a pang of ingratitude. Who was she to complain about wanting more when she had been given all of this?

Then her eyes drifted to the windows behind Caesar's desk. She saw the sky, deep tantalizing blue speckled with dotted clouds, and her very soul demanded that she explore it. The very thought of remaining in that office, detached from the winds, felt like an itch in the small of her back that she couldn't reach and scratch. That itch grew and grew until it was unbearable to ignore. She knew then that if she simply chose to accept her father's protection, she would go insane.

Even if it was the healthiest option.

Caesar was right; the second she stepped outside the island's protective wards and signal shielding, her life could be forfeited. But, somehow, that argument couldn't stack up as her longing eyes drifted to the window once more. She frowned as she realized that she didn't know what she would do if she was forced to stay. Could she defy Caesar? Could she go against the man who had protected and raised her as his own?

Arianne wasn't sure if she had the strength to break the heart of yet another loved one.

"I can't let you leave the island." Caesar finally admitted, anticipating the question his daughter was going to ask.

She stared blankly ahead, attempting to stop her tears. What options did she have? Break her father's heart? Disregard his warnings? No matter how painful it was, Caesar had far more experience than her. He'd built an entire nation from the ground up. She couldn't just ignore him.

Her gaze shifted to the side as she fought to keep the storm of emotions most likely playing across her face from her father's eyes. Regardless of how much she wished Caesar were wrong, she couldn't defy him. She just couldn't.

"My best friend left this island's protection," Caesar began quietly, "he went to raise his children closer to their mothers' home." Arianne looked up at her father as his voice caught. "I couldn't protect him out there and I lost him. I can't make that same mistake twice." She felt the heat of his stare, "I won't."

Arianne's lips parted as she felt the grief rippling off of her father. He was talking about Vice President Jaleel Leroy: founder, father, and... friend.

Hands shaking, Caesar opened a drawer in his desk and produced a picture frame, "I suppose you've never seen a photo of him," he said almost too quietly.

Arianne took the frame, a soft smile escaping her lips as she took in how well her father had taken care of the protective glass. There wasn't a smudge or speck of dust to be found, even after ten years of safekeeping. She turned her attention to the photo enshrined beneath and studied it curiously. In the picture, Caesar stood beside a lean man with wavy brown hair, dark skin, and striking green eyes. Both appeared younger than Caesar when he first met Arianne, and both wore bright smiles as they posed for the photo in front of the Capitol building construction site.

"Why did they attack Mende?" Arianne asked, her heart breaking for Pangaea's unending capacity to take.

She scrutinized Jaleel's face, which seemed familiar, although she couldn't pinpoint where she'd seen it before. This handsome man had once been Caesar's closest friend, and yet Pangaea had mercilessly taken his life and the lives of his family. She clenched her teeth; if Jaleel had suffered such a cruel fate, what chance did she have?

Were her only options truly between her freedom and her life?

"I still have no idea who betrayed their outpost," Caesar confessed, his shoulders slumping in defeat. "Not a day goes by that I don't think about how much I failed him. He gave up a safe life as a Pangaean Elite to build this country with me, and this is how I repaid him."

A pang of guilt surged within Arianne as she realized that she was asking to leave the island, knowing that Caesar would blame himself if she met the same fate as Jaleel. She looked back at her father, voice trembling, "If there were any survivors, Jaleel has to be one of them. Let me find him," she pleaded.

"*Hija*," Caesar sighed heavily, taking the photo back from her. "Remember what I told you. There isn't always a silver lining. Bad things happen for no good reason, and there's nothing you can do. It's been over a decade. I've long since accepted that Jaleel is dead." He looked longingly down at the photo, "but acceptance doesn't mean the pain goes away."

"Well, *I* haven't accepted it," Arianne responded stubbornly. "And I refuse to believe there are times when the only choice we have is to do nothing."

Chapter 13

Jaya

Jaya's stomach flopped as she fell from the ceiling. With a neck-jarring crash, she landed on the blonde below her and fought to hang on. The pair were brought to the ground under Jaya's downward momentum. Fortunately, Jaya remained on top. As they landed, the blonde's skin made an uncomfortable ripping sound as it glided across the dusty concrete floor. Jaya cringed for a moment, the sting of that sound promising an unpleasant scrape.

But the attack didn't slow the woman. It only enraged her. With an annoyed cry, the blonde twisted under Jaya's weight with unexpected strength. Leveraging what little weight Jaya had with her short stature, she held firm as they both rolled to the floor.

The commotion signaled Rhino from his hiding place behind the building's fortified staircase. The muscular *Fera* charged, his thunderous steps shaking the ground as he drew closer. Jaya timed her friend's sprint. At the last moment, she let go of the blonde and rolled away as Rhino ran past, hooking the blonde's black jumpsuit and pulling her with him. Still moving, Rhino flexed his meaty arm and threw the woman into the wall. Stunned, the woman was helpless as she shot backwards, her head hitting the wall with a surprisingly metallic thud. Jaya stood up behind Rhino, observing the woman as she slumped to the floor.

The fight should have been over.

But the Chameleon watched in horror as the woman's eyes burst open, glowing bright, unnatural, blue in the dimly lit building. Those eyes were far from human, she realized in an awful mix of curiosity and freight. Rhino was still watching the blonde in shock as she sprang from her resting spot on the ground at daunting speeds. When the woman struck at him, it was with enough force to push the powerful *Fera* backward.

Jaya's breath caught. Whoever that woman was, she definitely wasn't human, but she wasn't a mutant either.

Rhino squared his shoulders, recovering from the blow, and lunging to attack back. However, the blonde casually sidestepped him. Her blue eyes gleamed with amusement as if she were sparring with a child. In her moment of satisfaction, Rhino delivered a backswing that had her head snapping to the side from the blow.

Jaya gaped; the power Rhino just unleashed should have been enough to decapitate a human.

"Oh, good." The woman smiled, cracking her neck, "I was hoping for some entertainment."

Jaya, recovering, raised her gun. "Don't move."

Those haunting blue eyes finally focused on Jaya, "I'm not the one you should be worried about. Love the accent, by the way. I wonder if we were neighbors?"

Jaya's eyes widened; *the other woman!* But she didn't budge, not until whatever that creature was in front of her was under control.

Rhino inched forward as the woman raised her hands in what seemed like delighted surrender. He pulled handcuffs from his belt and secured the woman's hands behind her back, "Jaya, I've got her," he reassured his friend urgently, "You go check on Lyn and Shaw!"

Jaya turned and sprinted, panic squeezing her chest as she searched for her Captain and Vice President. She rounded the corner to what used to be a back office. Three figures waited there: Shaw... and Lyn hanging limply in the lithe woman's arms.

Her heart stopped in terror; Lyn was dead, and it was all her fault. She had completely forgotten about the second attacker, so focused on the blonde woman's power that she had neglected the second threat.

The slender woman turned as she heard Jaya's approach, and two yellow eyes with pupils slit like a snake's shone maliciously in the darkness. The glare almost paralyzed her. This woman—no—this *Fera* female, had killed Shaw's original guards. It was that female's venom that lurked in the vial Lyn had given her.

"Move, and they both die," the female warned, her forked tongue curling over her lips. "I only gave your Captain enough to paralyze her, but she has a day before it kills her. Any sudden movements, and I'll give her enough to kill an elephant."

Jaya tensed. She couldn't let that female come within biting range of her. She couldn't guarantee that her *Fera* capabilities wouldn't save her from the venom. She observed the female; two *Feras* locked in a standoff. *Feras* were tricky opponents due to their unpredictable and unique natures. Jaya was fast, but was she faster than the Snake?

It wasn't a bet she could afford to make.

Jaya was careful to keep perfectly still, "What do you want?"

Those piercing yellow eyes did not so much as blink. "We want the location of your people, of course." A smile revealed two pointed fangs, much like a vampire's. "Well, my owner wants the location of your people. I couldn't care less."

The Snake was a slave, then. Controlled by whatever owner had sent her on that mission. If Lyn weren't dying in the female's hands, Jaya would have felt sorry for her.

"Not going to happen."

"Well, that was the goal before you captured my partner. Here's the deal: I take my people, and you take yours. No one has to die today," the Snake bargained, her voice an awful whisper.

Sanchez's lifeless body flashed into Jaya's head, and anger welled up inside her, "Too late for that, Snake."

"People call me Blue Krait, but you can call me Blue. But let me rephrase that: no one *else* has to die today."

Jaya glanced back at Lyn's limp body and she felt the color fade rapidly from her face. Behind Lyn, Shaw crouched in the shadows. Her stomach churned. She was a rookie, she wasn't supposed to be making decisions of that caliber. What did the textbooks she studied in class tell her to do? Had she ever been told? What could she do? Trade Lyn's life for captives or bring those who remained alive home? Lyn was a good soldier and a better person. She couldn't let her Captain die, but captives would be essential.

"We can help you," Jaya hedged, trying to buy time. "With us, you can be free. You won't be a slave."

At that, Blue looked down as if considering. Jaya could almost describe her as stricken. Had anyone ever offered her a way out? The second of weakness passed, and Blue shook her head as if fighting to return clarity. "It's not that easy," her voice strained for a moment before returning to its original vigor. "Now, you take your people, and I'll take mine."

Behind them, Rhino dragged the blonde woman with him as she struggled in annoyance. Jaya looked back, realizing that Blue was offering a trade. She considered it again before saying, "Why would we trust you?"

"Because I'd rather not die today," Blue reasoned, giving a serpentine smile. The smile, paired with uplifted eyes and high cheekbones, did a stunning job of making her seem like all deadly angles. "Now, give me Pandora, and we will be on our way." The Snake's eyes shimmered as she looked down at Lyn in her arms. "We don't have all day; your friend will be going into shock soon."

"Jaya, don't let them get away," Rhino commanded, "We can't trust them."

Jaya didn't dare move. "She poisoned Lyn," she mumbled to Rhino. "No one else dies today."

Rhino frowned, examining his friend for a few long moments. Finally, he nodded. Ever so slowly, Rhino picked up Pandora and began to inch her towards Blue. The Snake did the same with Lyn.

"Now, Shaw," Rhino grumbled once Lyn was lying in his arms. The Captain looked so small compared to his hulking size.

To Pandora's obvious annoyance, Blue didn't release her, "I don't think so." The Snake flashed her teeth. "I said you could have your people. Shaw's ours. Now take your Captain home and be happy with your lives."

Rhino stiffened next to Jaya. From behind the pair of rookies, she heard the sound of trucks rolling to a halt. Dozens of boots stomped on the ground as reinforcements rushed into the building. She almost buckled in relief.

"Would you like to reconsider?" Jaya cooed.

Blue's eyes shifted from Shaw to Pandora. "Yes, I would; it seems like some variables have changed. Wouldn't you say so, Pandora?" She asked her partner smugly.

Pandora tried to spit in rage, but she'd been gagged by Rhino.

Blue saluted mockingly as she picked up her partner with *Fera* strength. "See you two around." Her smile was the stuff of nightmares.

Jaya was still trying to keep herself from breaking down into shakes as the back-up squad appeared behind her, their leader shouting to follow the two women. Jaya managed a bark in protest, "We need to get out of here. Lyn doesn't have much time."

She was exhausted. All she wanted to do was get on a Pacifican jet and pass out. Rhino, seeing her reaction, nodded as if to say he was ready to sleep for a week.

"What happened," the reinforcement squad Captain questioned.

"We were attacked by those two," Rhino responded. "It was an ambush. We lost Sergeant Sanchez, and our Captain was wounded."

"Is Shaw safe?" The reinforcement Captain questioned.

"I'm safe," the Vice President whimpered.

In under an hour, the group was off the ground and headed back home. Shaw was being briefed by the Captain, and Jaya and Rhino were left to catch their breath. "How did they know about Shaw?" Jaya asked, collapsing into the seat next to Rhino. Her hair, purple once more, was frayed as it fell out of her once pristine bun.

He shook his massive head, "Who the hell were they?"

"That snake girl, Blue Krait, was a slave," she breathed. "But when I offered to help her, she said that it wasn't that simple," she trailed off in confusion.

"You think she was owned by Cartel?" Rhino questioned.

Jaya shook her head, "I don't think so anymore." She ran her mind through her studies on the illusive underground organization, "They were using Blasters. Cartel doesn't like to waste money on them."

Rhino nodded, "Do you still have that vial?"

Her hands shot to her jacket pocket; she let out a sigh of relief as she felt the glass in her hand. "We need to take it to toxicology and figure out what the hell we are dealing with."

"Let's go to the twins' lab. At least with them, we can see the results."

Chapter 14
Blackjack

Arianne didn't join his interrogators this time.

Caesar and Kalfas entered the room, but they were alone. Jack took note of that with a grin. There must have been another reason why Arianne was initially allowed to join. Obviously, they hadn't needed her for extra security. Evidently, they found out about the young Major's special visit earlier that week.

Jack's concussion was gone, the scar was completely closed, and his cast had been switched to a brace—he was ready to leave. Sure, his arm was still technically broken, but a brace was something he could work with. He grinned in delight as Caesar sat down across from him for the third time. He was finally ready to play his hand. This discussion would be entertaining.

"Where's the Major?" Jack asked knowingly.

Caesar looked down and crossed his arms. Jack raised an eyebrow, reading the President like a book. Caesar continued slowly. "She has been reassigned," he said.

"You know her personally," the bounty hunter said with amusement. "Isn't that right, Mr. President?"

Caesar maintained a practiced calm, "I'm aware of your conversation the other day. None of that changes what you and I are talking about."

"If that's what you want to believe," Jack sat back. "In reality, you just became far more interesting to me *Señor* Ortiz. I'll offer a trade as I offered her: a question for a question."

And Arianne still owes me a question. He licked his lips; he would make that debt hurt.

Kalfas crossed his thick arms. Jack observed the older General with an ounce of respect. There was no way a man of his age remained that large without one of two things: steroids and a constant strength regimen.

"What kind of questions," Kalfas asked.

Jack sighed and looked up, "Well, I already know your questions," he began, "so let's think of something of the same caliber. You share the location of Citadel with me, and I'll give you the location of Leonueva. Fair trade."

It was common knowledge that Europe and Pacific had been at a stalemate for years since neither knew where the other's capital lay. Leonueva and Citadel remaining hidden from detection was the one thing keeping Europe and the small rebel colony from full-out war. The entire continent had been holding its breath for a while; everyone was wondering which one would strike first.

Sure, Leon and his forces had taken out some of Caesar's outposts, but they had never found the prize. Jack eyed the President in front of him. If he hadn't been so apathetic, he might have been awestruck. Sitting in front of him was the man who had successfully thwarted Leon Murray—the Lion of Europe—for the better part of thirty years. Caesar was a nameless legend, whispered about throughout Europe. But those meetings had shown Jack the truth: Caesar wasn't a legend. He was just another tired man who'd found a way to do the impossible.

"I'm sorry, I can't do that, Jack," Caesar breathed. "I'm not in a position to trade the lives of innocent people."

Jack gave a humorless laugh. Caesar and Kalfas and the entire island were made up of good men, idealistic men, and that was their problem.

"That's what's going to get you all killed," Jack whispered balefully, "being so *good*." Being good got people nowhere but six feet under. Jack had learned that the hard way. The fact was so deeply ingrained into his skull that Caesar's morality made him sick. "Ace and Leon wouldn't hesitate to make that trade," he continued, enjoying the disgust coming to Caesar's face, "that's why you'll lose."

An uncharacteristic darkness washed across Caesar's expression. "You have no idea what I've sacrificed, boy."

Jack was surprised that he recognized the pain in the President's eyes. It was an old and familiar pain, one that had lived in the mind so long that its ache was numb. He was reminded of his hometown and the very same tug of hurt and loss came back to him. Jack paused, wondering if the kind-hearted man in front of him had more demons in his heart than he let most believe.

For the first time since meeting Caesar, Jack was intrigued. "Then enlighten me," he purred, "and Leonueva is yours."

"You've only lived twenty-three short years," Caesar laced his fingers together, a glacial cold taking over his voice. "I've been President of this country for longer than you've been alive. And the things I endured in Pangaea before that are just as scarring." The President leaned forward, "You think you're so strong, using your pain as a weapon to hurt others. I've been through more suffering than you could comprehend, boy, and I've learned one thing: inflicting pain because you're in pain only makes you weak."

Jack's smile wavered. He had to lean away from Caesar as the weight of those words fell on him. His hands began to shake, and he was forced to hold them under the table to hide his shock. Who was this Caesar Ortiz? Where had he come from?

Maybe Jack had underestimated just how powerful Caesar, the only man outside of Ace to stand up to Leon Murray, truly was. Maybe it was time for Jack to get out of there before his toying earned him whatever threat Caesar was giving him with those burning brown eyes.

"Fine," Jack couldn't meet Caesar's gaze. "I'll help you."

Kalfas's grunt of annoyance was Jack's only sign to continue.

"You know the Artery, yes?" He began.

The Artery was a powerful Pangaean highway that went from London all the way to Tokyo. The highway also went south: through France, Spain, and into the heart of Africa. From the main Artery, thousands of other highways split off from it like the blood vessels of a planet-sized human. It was the essential highway that connected three of the six continents that made up the Empire of Pangaea: the most powerful three. Without the Artery, goods couldn't be so easily traded between the vast regions. Much like its namesake, the Artery kept Pangaea alive.

"Leon would have been insane not to build his city along the Artery," Jack continued. "It's the easiest route to give his city goods. The only question is: *where* along the highway?"

Naturally, the Artery was continents wide. Finding a city along its many veins would be like finding a needle in a haystack. A dangerous, enemy-riddled haystack.

"We've had this same theory," Caesar said, raising a hand to hold his chin in thought.

"Ace has a network underneath many of the Artery's routes. She also has a tunnel system out of Leonueva where she moves her products. With the security that city has, it's your only way in. With only Pangaean Elites and occupying forces allowed inside, the population and security are well-regulated."

Jack lowered his chin and watched Kalfas and Caesar exchange a glance. He could feel the pieces of his perfect puzzle fall into place. He set the bait. Now, all he needed was for them to take it. The crafty bounty hunter waited a few more moments, soaking in the tension like a sponge.

"We're running out of time," Kalfas said to Caesar slowly, "if we don't attack first, we'll lose our only chance at an advantage."

And then Jack moved for the final hook, "You'll need me to get you in." He raised his arm, flashing his ace of spades tattoo. "The tunnels will only open with this," he finished with a smile.

"That's what I was worried about," Kalfas muttered.

Chapter 15

Jaya

The forensics lab was only a short trip from Angel's Camp. With so much data from the Research and Development Corps and samples collected in the field, Angel's Camp used forensics for far more than just criminal cases. Jaya and Rhino slowed outside of the building, neither of them too sure what to do with the vial once they got inside. For a place with such a gruesome purpose, it certainly looked cheerful on the outside. The forensics lab entrance sat just across the street from the beach, and the many windows allowed bright light into the building.

Jaya held the vial of blood up to the sun and the crimson liquid shone ominously in the bright summer light.

"Can I help you?" A security guard waiting at the door inquired.

Jaya corrected herself, turning to the officer, "Um—yes, hello," she began with a smile, "my name's Lieutenant Jaya Bahri. We're here on business for the Vice President."

"Morning Larry!" Rhino greeted from behind her, walking up to shake the officer's hand, "We're here to bother my girlfriend."

The officer, Larry, grinned as he gladly shook Rhino's hand. "Of course!" Larry eyed Jaya, "Is she with you?"

Rhino looked over at his friend and partner, "Yeah, don't worry about her. She's a little stiff, but she's all right."

Jaya was too shocked to respond as Rhino led her into the building. They were greeted by a blast of air conditioning that was a relief after walking in the arid summer heat. The two Lieutenants continued down the brightly lit hallways, Rhino leading the way with certainty.

"You know that guy?" Jaya asked in shock.

"Yeah, I visit Treena a lot," Rhino said casually, "but—man, Jay, you gotta' relax. Acting like a stiff will make people act weird."

She paused in shock. "Act *weird*? I was following protocol!"

Rhino waved Jaya off, "People following protocol typically get everyone else in trouble."

Jaya rolled her eyes, running to follow behind Rhino's massive footsteps. The pair reached the lab and stilled, noticing that Treena and Tyrell were not the only people inside. The rust-haired twins wore matching lab coats and had their backs to the door. They were talking to a familiar dirty blonde *Fera*.

"Arianne?" Jaya asked in confusion.

Treena, Tyrell, and Arianne turned to greet the Lieutenants. Hidden behind Tyrell's frame was Haris. The engineer waved nervously. Jaya stiffened as she looked between Haris and Arianne. Years of friendship had taught her one thing: how to recognize when her friends were up to something.

"Hey Jay," Haris pursed his lips awkwardly.

Jaya raised a purple eyebrow, "What's going on?"

Arianne, who was seated on one of the metal-topped lab tables, swung her legs back and forth. "Top-secret official business." She puffed out her chest. "I couldn't possibly tell you."

"Arianne wanted to see if I could break into the President's interview files using the Forensics system," Haris blurted, face turning bright red as he covered his mouth.

Arianne hissed with a glare towards the quilled engineer. She turned and smiled innocently at Jaya and Rhino.

Jaya pinched her nose, "I thought you were working on the interrogation project with that Blackjack guy?"

"I kind of got kicked off the project," Arianne winced, looking down.

Treena raised her hands, "We were just trying to help," she began, "Arianne said it was a matter of island safety."

"It is!" Arianne objected with a scowl, "I don't trust that guy."

Jaya crossed her arms. She always felt like the babysitter when she was around her friends, "And why did you get kicked off the project, Arianne?"

"Reasons," the winged female mumbled.

"She snuck into the prisoner's cell after hours," Haris blurted again, earning a shove from Arianne.

"Jesus, Ari," Jaya gritted. "You're lucky you didn't get court-martialed." She looked around the room, "You're lucky all of you aren't getting court-martialed for this!"

Treena and Tyrell stiffened, faces going pale. Haris looked like he was about to throw up.

"Hey, remember our conversation?" Rhino whispered, "Be *chill*."

Jaya let out a long breath, "Treena, Tyrell? I'll forget about all of this if you could look at this sample," she held out the vial of blood. "This was from one of our teammates. We need to know what kind of venom killed them."

Tyrell buttoned up his lab coat, face darkening as he took the vial of blood, "You said venom?"

Jaya nodded. "Our Captain is currently in the hospital recovering. She was bit as well. Luckily, we were able to stabilize her system with dialysis and symptom treatment." She exchanged a wary glance with Rhino, "but next time, we might not be as lucky. We need to know what we're dealing with."

Treena pulled out a set of glass microscope slides, her face heavy with worry, "You're saying a *Fera* did this?"

Jaya nodded.

The Helvig twins exchanged a look of concern. The two quickly threw on a set of latex gloves and began preparing a couple of microscope slides with the sample. The entire room watched the pair work with curiosity. The twins added a small droplet of blood to each of their slides and then they slid the slide cover over the droplet to flatten it out across the glass. Next, they carefully placed the slide cover on top of the flattened layer of blood and hastily moved over to dual microscopes.

The room was quiet as Treena and Tyrell observed the blood samples, their hands moving the dials of their microscopes to correct the focus.

"Hmm," Tyrell said.

"Are you seeing what I'm seeing?" Treena asked.

"Yup. The blood cells are committing apoptosis: they're dying from the venom."

Arianne leaned forward, eyes wide with curiosity, "So a *Fera* poisoned one of your teammates?" She asked, "A *Fera* with snake-like traits?" Jaya and Rhino nodded, and Arianne's face grew troubled, "A *Fera* working for Pangaea?"

Treena sprung up. She ran over to a cabinet where she withdrew a vial labeled *Blue Krait Antivenin.* Treena and Tyrell exchanged a look of recognition. Tyrell nodded. Jaya's eyebrows furrowed in confusion. Why did the name *Blue Krait* sound so familiar?

Treena removed the slide cover on her glass and added a droplet of the antivenin. Her frown deepened as she watched through the microscope lens in front of her. "That's what I was afraid of," she sighed.

"What?" Rhino asked, arms crossed.

Treena clenched her jaw, "The venom in the sample clumped when we added the antivenin. It's a perfect match."

Jaya raised a hand, stomach dropping, "Wait, how did you know to use the blue krait antivenin?" She stilled, remembering, "That's the name the *Fera* went by."

Tyrell wiped a bead of sweat from his brow, "Back in Norway," he began slowly, eyes looking down in consideration. "We came across a *Fera* with venom just like this. Blue krait venom: the most powerful venom found in any snake. It's a neurotoxin that attacks the nervous system and shuts it down. Even with the antivenin, there is only a fifty percent chance at survival for a human delivered a lethal dose."

Jaya's skin and hair turned white with horror, "Captain Lyn," she whispered as she looked at Rhino.

Rhino shook his silver head, "That *Fera* said that she didn't give her enough to kill her."

Treena glanced at her twin brother. "She learned how to control the dosage," she muttered in terror.

Tyrell locked eyes with his sister. "Meaning she can selectively kill, paralyze, or incapacitate her targets at will."

Jaya shook her head, "How did you say you knew her again?"

"We came across her once," both twins responded in unison, only giving a half-convincing smile.

"Right," Jaya said, not buying it. "I'm getting a strange feeling you know more than you're saying."

Tyrell quickly turned to Haris and Arianne, "How about we get back to helping you guys out," he smiled.

Jaya gave Haris and Arianne a warning stare before turning back to the twins, "No, I think there's more we need to talk about here," she demanded.

Somehow, the twins knew about this *Fera* who called herself Blue Krait. Blue worked with a woman named Pandora who wasn't human but wasn't *Fera*. The two of them also knew that Bradley Shaw was connected to Pacific and were smart enough to use Shaw to draw Pacific forces out. Pandora and Blue together were powerful enough to take out a top Pacifican squad.

Everything about that sounded like an awful combination. And the twins were keeping something from her.

"How about you tell me who Pandora is," Jaya asked.

To Jaya's surprise, it was Arianne who stilled. The winged Major looked at her friend, eyes turning icy. "What did you just say?"

"Pandora?" Jaya said in confusion.

Arianne's eyes were foggy with confusion, "I knew that name," she said distantly, "Pandora," she trailed off again, "Yes, I remember hearing that name back in Pangaea. But... I can't remember how."

All eyes turned their focus it Arianne. It was no secret that Arianne was from Pangaea, but that was typically where her information ended. Jaya had her own awful memories from her childhood in Pangaea and if she was willing to talk about her past it only told her how awful her friend's past was in comparison.

No, Jaya never wanted to push. But, if Arianne's former life was somehow connected to her team's safety, she needed to know.

"What can you remember about her?" The purple-haired female pressed.

Arianne blinked. "Richards, her name was Pandora Richards."

"Richards?" Jaya asked, "Like the Pangaean Elite family, the Richards?"

The Richards were one of the wealthiest European Elite families. The family had spent generations close to the Murray family side. The current Matriarch of the family, Hera Richards, was known to have been betrothed to Leon Murray before Leon chose a different wife. Now, Hera used her wealth and scientific genius to become the foremost mind in the European Military in biotechnology and weaponry. She was an inventor and one of the most knowledgeable experts in *Fera* physiology.

The only reason Jaya knew so much about the Richards family was because they ruled over most of England, where she had grown up. Many Pangaean Elite families owned and governed ancient landmarks and castles across the globe, with some more prominent families governing major cities and regions under their respective Commanders.

"Hera," Arianne trailed off knowingly. Jaya watched as her friend flinched and jumped up, "Excuse me," she said, quickly moving to leave the lab.

"If Richards is deploying one of her own kin with an experienced *Fera* slave, it would make sense that they're working for Leon," Jaya continued with a sigh. "That can't be good."

The doors to the lab opened for Arianne to leave, but she bumped into a larger body on her way out. The group turned at Arianne's startled gasp as Kalfas entered the lab. "Yes, Jaya," Kalfas began. "Which is why we need to move quickly. Leon is gaining on us."

The group saluted the General, including Arianne, who had to recover from crashing into the muscular man. "General Kalfas?" She asked in confusion.

Kalfas fixed his sleeves, olive green eyes surveying the room, "Hate to eavesdrop. Captain Lyn said that you would be here," he nodded to Rhino and Jaya, "She's up and moving, but unfortunately, she won't have too much time to recover."

"What do you mean?" Jaya asked.

Kalfas shook his head, "Not here. Lieutenant Bahri and Lieutenant Adams, I need you to report to Angel's Camp for debriefing in one hour. Come with your bags packed."

William Adams was Rhino's real name, but he hadn't used it since before puberty. Not that he wasn't reminiscent of his namesake as a child. For as long as Jaya could remember, their gray-haired friend had always towered over his classmates.

Kalfas didn't wait to hear Rhino or Jaya's response as he turned to leave. Arianne turned to look at her best friend, shock visible on her face. Jaya didn't have time to ask her about what she knew before her friend turned and ran out of the lab to follow Kalfas.

Rhino pulled Treena into an embrace, his eyes closing as he hugged her, "I have to go," he sighed into her hair. "I love you."

"Be safe," Treena breathed.

Jaya stiffened, the tension in the air warning her that the mission waiting for them wasn't another routine pick-up.

To her surprise, Haris ran up to her, the smaller *Fera* wrapping his arms around her, "Good luck out there." He frowned and reached into his pocket and produced a rectangular device, "in case you get stuck."

Jaya took the prototype phone. "You fixed it?"

"I updated it to have location mapping," Haris perked up as he pulled out another device from his other pocket. "Now it's similar to one of the mobile phones some Pangaean Elites have." He opened up his prototype and pointed at a couple of buttons. "Press this to send a distress signal."

Jaya smiled at her friend, "Thanks, Haris."

Rhino turned to her. "Ready?" The large *Fera* breathed.

Jaya nodded to her friend as a brief moment of uncertainty passed between them. They'd barely survived their last mission. Were they ready to go out again? She willed her hands to return to their normal color, the conscious effort calming her mind. She would just have to wait and find out.

Chapter 16

Arianne

Caesar forced Blackjack to give up the location to Leonueva.

Arianne stared at her bedroom walls, torn between excitement and terror. Leonueva, the place she had fled from years ago… They were going back. If Pacific could attack the city, they could gain a significant advantage.

And then there was Leon. Arianne's stomach lurched at the thought. Her biological father could be killed, ending the waking nightmare that had haunted her life. She could finally be free.

"I'm going on that mission," she said, her hands clenched in determination.

Caesar couldn't refuse her now. She would be committed to finding the city more than anyone. If she could help Pacific get inside, she would do her part and prove herself worthy of the life she had gained by escaping. Arianne could destroy her father by unlocking the city and unleashing Pacific on him. The battle would likely kill him, and she would never have to look upon the face that caused her nightmares again.

Arianne jumped up from her bed, her thoughts racing. Caesar had kept the discovery from her. Kalfas had recruited Rhino and Jaya right in front of her while keeping her in the dark. That couldn't be a good sign, but she was ready. She knew she was.

The tentative knock at her door didn't surprise her. Caesar let himself into her bedroom, his eyes downcast. They both knew the conversation to come.

"Could you come to my office, please?" Caesar asked.

Arianne nodded, wordlessly following her father. In classic Caesar fashion, his office was well organized without a paper out of place. Heart pounding, Arianne took a seat in one of his leather chairs. Her father sat behind his desk, letting out a deep sigh before folding his hands in front of him. The room was filled with tense silence, each waiting for the other to speak first.

Finally, Caesar gave in. "Blackjack has offered to guide a small group of us to Leonueva, and I'm going to lead the expedition."

"What?" Arianne burst out.

Caesar's chin rested in his hands, his voice heavy as he continued, "A good leader doesn't hide behind the lines. This could give our country the edge it needs to end this war before it begins."

"But, Caesar—dad—you can't go," Arianne jumped from her chair. "No one's questioning if you're a good leader. We can't risk losing you." *I can't risk losing you.*

"It's been decided, Arianne," Caesar's tone was uncompromising. "Kalfas helped build this country, and he is more than equipped to lead in my absence. If this mission goes south, I'm the only one with the bargaining power to keep your father at bay."

"What do you mean?" Her voice trembled.

Caesar's gaze drifted away. "Your father and I have a... history," he admitted slowly. "I won't send my people on a mission that I wouldn't go on myself. If things go wrong, I—and only I—will be able to bargain for Pacific's safety." His face darkened. "I won't have any more blood on my hands."

The color drained from Arianne's face. "Let me come," she demanded.

Caesar raised her when she had no one else. She couldn't, no, *wouldn't* tolerate the man she loved most in the world subjecting himself to Leon's whims. She would go to the ends of the earth to protect him. Going on that mission was no longer a want; it was a need.

"You're staying here, Arianne."

"No."

"Yes," Caesar's voice was powerful as his eyes locked with his daughter. "You and I both know that you are the last person who will be going on this mission. If Leon finds out you're alive, it's over for all of us. He will tear this continent apart looking for you—that includes this island."

"Not if we get to him first," she pressed with determination.

Caesar shook his head. "We have no idea how you'll react to any of this," he admitted. "We have no idea how your memories will manifest during this trip. We can't have anyone in our party freezing, Arianne."

"I won't freeze."

"The labs beneath the Murray Monument," Caesar muttered with regret, "Hera's experimentations."

As she promised, she didn't freeze, but she would be lying if she said that she didn't hesitate. Just the mention of that cold and forbidding place below ground sent a chill running down her spine. Though other memories had faded, those were still clear as day. Scientists, like worshippers in a sect, walking around that lab like it was their temple as they carried lab notes like sacred texts. Tubes connected up and down her body, monitoring her as she ran tests for hours. And worst of all, a woman with platinum strawberry blonde hair recording her findings as she put her subject through countless horrors.

Picked, prodded, pulled apart.

Subject One is giving me wonderful results today, Hera Richards' voice echoed in its thick London accent.

Arianne managed to grab a hold of herself, fingers digging into the skin of her forearm to pull herself back to reality. "What the hell," she growled at Caesar, hating how quickly that reminder had soured her mood.

The president looked troubled. "And those were just words. What will you do when faced with the real thing? I'm sorry, Arianne. I can't let you come."

The hidden daughter's hands clenched and unclenched at her sides. "Have you considered that Jack's lying?"

"Unfortunately, that's not your concern," he replied. "You're not ready. This isn't training. When you're out there, it's real. Don't you see that? This isn't as easy as you think it will be."

Arianne leaned on Caesar's desk, pleading, "And you have to see this is more than just a goal. I've been training my whole life for this. I have been waiting, and I'm ready. Please don't take this away from me. Please don't lock me up like you've done for years. Please. I can learn! The only way I'll get better is by facing my fears."

Caesar didn't flinch. "Absolutely not. You're staying here." A heavy weight seemed to settle on his shoulders. "I promised you a long time ago that I would keep you safe. I won't throw you into the most dangerous mission this war has seen."

"I'm not a kid anymore," Arianne whispered, her rage growing. "I don't need your protection like I'm some helpless little girl!" Her eyes flared, her voice steadily rising.

Arianne was surprised when Caesar jumped from his chair. The President slammed his palms onto the desk, the sound making her jump, "I didn't want to do this to you, Arianne," he warned, voice dropping to a threateningly deep tone, "but as Commander and Chief of the Pacific Military: I hereby prevent—"

Arianne paused, she knew where those words were going. "No Dad," she pleaded, "please don't."

Caesar continued, no longer her father but the President of Pacific. "As Commander and Chief of the Pacific Military: I hereby prevent you from joining this mission. Failure to abide by these orders will result in your immediate discharge."

"No," the word escaped the winged female in a horrified whisper. "Y-you don't understand what this means to me," she said, mortified. "You're not protecting me. You're hurting me!"

"I do understand," Caesar grimaced like he had been punched in the gut, "you have no idea how much I understand. That's why you can't go."

Arianne hated that she was crying. "Fuck you, then," she spat, turning on her heel and exiting the office.

She regretted her outburst as soon as the office door slammed behind her, but she couldn't take it back now. Her anger escaped her in a long breath as she slid down the door, her wings aching to carry her far away from that fight. Her face fell into her hands, tears soaking her palms.

Everything felt like it was crumbling around her. She craned her neck to look behind her, as if her eyes could see through the wooden door into her father's office. On one hand, her relationship with the only family she had was being torn to shreds. On the other, her life's purpose was fading away into nothing.

To stay or go—the decision was easier than she would have liked.

Slowly rising, Arianne wiped her tears dry and ran to her room to pack a bag.

Chapter 17

Jaya

Arianne was nowhere to be seen the next morning as the new infiltration team prepared to board the jet at Angel's Camp. Others had arrived to see the squad off, including Haris, whose father had been appointed the Captain of the squadron assigned to protect Caesar.

Captain Carter Cadmilus hugged his son, and Jaya watched with a smile as Haris melted into his father's arms. She knew her friend was scared: his friends and father had been selected for a difficult mission. Her stomach dropped at the thought; there was no guarantee any of them were coming home.

Caesar appeared on the platform, his typical suit traded for an olive green military jumpsuit. Jaya gasped as she pieced the shocking details together. Captain Cadmilus was leading the mission and Caesar was in uniform. The President was joining them. Her stomach dropped as she realized the added weight to their already terrifying mission.

Rhino said his goodbyes to Treena. It seemed like none of his siblings or even his parents had come to see him off. Jaya frowned; the family most likely wouldn't even notice their son's absence.

Caesar certainly noticed his own daughter's lack of attendance in the crowd in the hangar. The President searched the small collection of people who had gathered to see the squadron off, his face filled with disappointment when he didn't see Arianne waiting. General Kalfas whispered something at his friend's side, and the President reluctantly nodded—it was time to go.

Haris ran up to Jaya and Rhino, the engineer offering his friends one last hug. "Be safe," he said, his voice thick with unshed tears.

"I'll protect her," Rhino promised Haris, leaning over to clap Jaya on the back. She hissed in annoyance, pushing the large *Fera* away.

Haris paled. "Just, um, look after my dad, okay?"

Jaya turned to watch Captain Cadmilus board the jet. She smiled at her friend and rubbed his shoulder affectionately. "Of course, Haris, we'll take good care of him."

"Am I late?"

Jaya wished that was Arianne's voice. But she would have recognized her sister's heavy English accent anywhere.

Kalinda Bahri was the eldest of the Bahri sisters, and before Jaya became an adult, Kalinda had been her legal guardian. With green and hazel eyes similar to hers and long, dark hair, Kalinda was a striking beauty.

She was also one of Pacific's best field medics.

Kalinda was dressed in military briefs with a red cross stitched to her breast. The elder Bahri sister smiled. "Don't think you're going on this mission alone."

"N-no," Jaya protested. "Not happening." She reached out to shove her sister.

Kalinda smirked, expertly blocking her sister's playful blow. "Remember who the rookie is," she sang. "I've run more missions than you."

Jaya sighed in annoyance, giving Haris one final goodbye before letting her sister usher her onto the jet. Kalinda had promised to meet Jaya at Angel's Landing before take-off; she hadn't mentioned that she would be joining.

Caesar, Captain Cadmilus, Rhino, and now Kalinda... Jaya sat down and buckled herself up. She had her work cut out for her. And if her previous missions warned her of anything, it was the lack of guarantees.

"Good morning," Captain Lyn announced as she boarded the jet. Jaya was surprised to see her in such high spirits. If her information was correct, the Captain had only left the hospital a handful of hours ago.

Captain Cadmilus followed Lyn onto the jet. Behind him stood a squad of five more soldiers. He nodded to Lyn. "Captain." He saluted.

Lyn's countenance faltered for a moment. "I don't deserve the name of Captain anymore," she announced with a glance at Rhino and Jaya. "They're the only two remaining on my team. I failed the rest. I'm just a Major reporting to you now."

Jaya and Rhino lowered their heads. With so much going on, no one on their team had gotten a moment to remember the people they'd lost on their last mission to protect Bradley Shaw.

"Major Lyn," Captain Cadmilus nodded. "We all lose people."

Not today, Jaya's eyes narrowed.

Caesar was one of the last to board the jet, his eyes hard. Arianne hadn't come. Her father must have waited for her for as long as possible. Jaya shook her head as annoyance sparked inside of her. She knew Arianne was frustrated that she couldn't join, but that didn't give her an excuse to be a bad friend *or* daughter.

All eyes went to the entrance to the jet as two more of Captain Cadmilus's men walked up the ramp. Between them was a younger man with bronze skin and brown hair that curled around his ears. His mouth was covered to prevent distress calls and his hands were cuffed behind his back, and while he wore olive military khakis, he was the only one on the jet without Pacifican badges.

Blackjack.

Jaya eyed the Cartel bounty hunter suspiciously. As if noticing her stare, Blackjack looked over at her, and she was startled by his sharp amber eyes. She flinched away from the malice she could feel lurking beneath the stunning irises. Blackjack raised his eyebrows in amusement for a moment before giving a bored flick of his head and continuing to his seat. Her lips parted, surprised at how desensitized he was to others' fear.

So young, yet so lost.

Sensing Rhino's bristling, she turned to her friend in concern. The large *Fera* was scowling at Blackjack, his shoulders tensed in resentment. Jaya could tell what her partner was thinking: their entire mission relied on the words of that creature Caesar had chained up before them.

"All right," Captain Cadmilus announced as Blackjack was buckled down behind him. "The name of the game: quick and clean! Reconnaissance only. Infiltrate the city, get the coordinates, and return to Citadel safe and sound." The Captain's blue eyes glanced over the group. "Do we have any questions?"

"And he's leading us to the city?" One of the officers asked with an incredulous frown.

Caesar glanced at Blackjack. "Yes," he said, all eyes snapping to their President. Caesar held up a tablet. From the glass screen, he projected a map of Europe. "Blackjack has information on supply tunnels that Cartel uses to get into and out of the city." He pointed to a red dot just west of the Black Sea. "He's going to grant us access to a tunnel system starting in Old Romania. From there, we'll be guided throughout these tunnel systems and the Pangaean Artery until we reach Leonueva."

Blackjack rolled his eyes and managed a scoff through his muzzle.

Jaya gritted her teeth. They all knew the incredibly high chance that Blackjack would betray them. She feared how desperate her country was if they were willing to take that bet. What was Pacific offering Blackjack that could guarantee his cooperation? Was there anything that increased their odds?

Kalinda, at Jaya's other side, shook her head. "What are you thinking about?" She whispered. "And don't say nothing; your fingers are turning purple."

Jaya cursed her abilities for betraying her. "I don't trust him as far as I can throw him," she muttered.

Luckily, Jaya wasn't expected to throw a human. That task was typically reserved for Rhino in combat. And he could throw a full-grown human pretty damn far.

Kalinda sat back in her seat, her purple-painted nails casually playing with her red cross badge. "Then don't lower your guard, rookie." She winked.

When the jet landed in Romania, Jaya's stomach dropped once more. She felt like such a major mission should have more ceremony than boarding a jet and getting out. But there she was, shouldering her rifle and getting into position next to Rhino as they prepared to file out of the jet. In the moments before moving, she turned and glanced rows behind her to where Kalinda was marching in the back. If everything went how she hoped, her sister wouldn't even have to see the outside of the jet.

The night was dark as Captain Cadmilus waved for his squadron to advance and secure the area. The only people who remained behind were Kalinda, Major Lyn, Caesar, and the two guards positioned around Blackjack. Jaya marched forward, her jaw tight as her boots landed on the foreign soil. Once in position in the surrounding undergrowth outside the jet, the Captain's squadron stilled and waited for their superior's signal.

One of the senior members of the squadron lifted his nose and sniffed the air. Jaya blinked in shock; another *Fera* was in their ranks. The male moved to stand at the Captain's side. "I can't sense anything," he whispered.

"All right," the Captain nodded. "Squadron, complete final weapons checks. We're ready to begin."

Blackjack was led out of the jet, followed by Caesar. Jaya and Rhino crouched low behind a set of bushes, hidden by design in case their squadron was ambushed by anyone who might come out of whatever tunnel to hell Blackjack opened. Naturally, a tunnel system owned by Cartel could only be considered as a tunnel to hell.

Unfortunately, Jaya knew what those tunnels had in store. She shook her head, quickly clearing her mind from the darkest moments of her life. She couldn't let her old fears get the best of her, not at a time like that.

Blackjack walked up to a nondescript oak tree and raised his wrists in a silent request. One of his guards moved to unlock his handcuffs while the other aimed a pistol at him. Jaya hoped Blackjack wouldn't be stupid enough to test his luck against an entire Pacific squadron.

Wrists free, Blackjack turned to the tree and removed the brace on his right forearm. For the first time, Jaya could see the bounty hunter's infamous Cartel tattoo on the inside of his wrist. The ace of spades' black sigil seemingly absorbed the little moonlight filtering into the clearing as their prisoner held his wrist up to the tree.

From the oak tree's bark, two blue beams of light focused on the tattoo and scanned it. There was a beep in recognition. Then, the trunk of the tree split in two, revealing a staircase going downwards into an underground tunnel.

"That's kind of cool," Rhino whispered.

"Rhino, they use that to traffic children," Jaya spat.

Her partner winced. "Right."

Blackjack bowed sarcastically at the entrance to the Cartel tunnel system, but he didn't have the chance to straighten before gunfire filled the night with its deadly thunder.

Chapter 18
Blackjack

Something wasn't right.

Sure, Jack had expected Cartel to retaliate as soon as his identification was announced in the system, but that wasn't the problem. The problem was that they weren't alone. Gunfire wasn't just coming from the tunnel; it was coming from behind the Pacific squadron.

There was another hostile force present.

More gunfire sounded, its piercing popping filling the once-quiet forest, and Jack rolled away from the entrance to the tunnel. He righted himself behind the cover of a tree, his eyes closing so he could listen to what was going on beyond his cover.

Three factions: Cartel, Pacific, and an unknown... Jack opened his eyes, thinking. He had a couple of choices there: he could risk himself in the fight, or he could run.

The choice was easy. He would let the three parties kill each other behind him.

Jumping to his feet, Jack broke into a sprint and ran as fast as his legs could carry him. He knew he was giving up millions of Units that he would have gained from delivering the squadron to Ace, but his life was worth far more to him than his debt. And his life was exactly what he would be gambling if he dumbly threw himself into that firefight.

Jack was a gambler at heart, but the only reason he'd survived as long as he had was because he knew when to fold and leave the game. A three-party battle didn't give him the odds of survival that he was willing to bet against.

His eyes strained as he ran faster through the thick Romanian undergrowth. He hoped he didn't trip on a stray root or fallen tree, he didn't have the time. He needed to get at least a mile out before he could relax. Even then, he wasn't safe: he needed to find a city to disappear into. Pacific had a couple of *Feras* with them, and they could track him like bloodhounds if they survived the firefight.

He hoped they all killed each other.

Jack was so focused on maintaining his balance that he didn't hear the savage battle cry until it was too late.

A figure barreled out of the darkness and tackled him to the ground. Jack realized that the shout was female as a shadowed mass landed on top of him. He raised his hands to protect his face as a fist cut downward in an attempt to connect with his temple. Collecting his bearings, Jack calculated his attacker's shift of weight above him and moved as soon as she reached backward to strike again.

Jack rolled out of the way. His legs twisted around his attacker's left thigh, and he used their combined weight against her as he spun. A small hint of satisfaction filled him, not just anyone could ambush him. This might be a fun fight for him. The attacker shouted in annoyance as Jack landed on top of her, and he didn't hesitate to move and wrap his hands around her neck. He grinned as he began to squeeze.

Pain, white-hot and burning, laced up his right arm before he could comprehend what was happening. Jack barked back in pain as he realized his attacker knew about his broken arm and she'd managed to deliver a deadly chop right on top of the fracture. His momentary recoil allowed the attacker a chance to free herself and recover to a defensive position a couple of yards away.

"Where do you think you're going?" The attacker growled.

Jack straightened. He recognized that voice. *Princess*, he thought. He would have quipped his response had his mouth not been covered by the muzzle.

There, crouched low to the ground and preparing for another attack, stood the Major from his interrogations: Arianne Ortiz. He grinned. Somehow, the President's daughter had followed them. And Jack couldn't be happier.

He was going to teach her why sheltered girls like her should stay hidden on their private little islands.

He would give Arianne a proper Pangaean welcome, and then he was going to deliver her to Ace to pay off every debt he owed. The daughter of the Pacifican President would be worth a fortune.

Jack didn't wait for another sly comment from the Major before he charged her. He was taller, stronger, and he had a longer reach. By all accounts, the fight would be over quickly. Jack's first punch was directed low, targeting Arianne's diaphragm: his favorite first attack. Knocking out someone's wind was debilitating and the target was soft enough to save his fist from damage. If done correctly, a fight could be over in seconds—much like a hit to the jaw—but without bruising his knuckles. Jack angled his fist. One moment, Arianne was there. And the next, she was gone. His fist hit the open air.

A millisecond too late, he recognized a boot in the low light swinging into his right periphery. Arianne's sideward kick connected with his shoulder with a deep bone-bruising ache. Jack stumbled to his left as he fought to regain his balance from the blow. Arianne hardly gave him a moment to correct himself, her leg lowering to deliver a sweeping kick to his ankles. Jack jumped, just barely missing the second attack and he gritted his teeth as he fell into a defensive position.

She's fast. Why is she fast?

Arianne advanced, her gray eyes dark in the low light, "You're lucky I can't kill you," she spat.

Jack managed a chuckle through his mask. There was no way the girl could kill him. He'd seen killers, and that pampered island princess certainly wasn't one of them.

Without warning, the pampered island princess attacked. Luckily, he'd already planned his counter. Arianne closed the range between them, her knee raising to connect with his stomach. Prepared, he slapped her leg away, and he adjusted his body to make himself a smaller target. As expected, Arianne had another attack lined up. She swung her elbow wide as she attempted to deliver a blow to his jaw. Jack stepped back, tracking her movements with mild interest.

The Major was fighting with Muay Thai. That explained her lower body heavy attacks.

Jack raised his left arm to intercept Arianne's next kick. He caught her leg, but he was surprised by the amount of power he had to absorb to block the attack. The two of them locked eyes, and he was almost ready to give her credit. The Pacifican had selected a fighting style that made it hard for him to take advantage of her shorter stature. She was battle-smart, he would give her that small ounce of credit.

Too bad being smart didn't determine who won in a battle in real time. Being experienced did that. Jack was willing to bet Arianne hadn't seen much more than her school's sparring gyms.

He waited until Arianne attempted another karate kick. Palm raised to deflect, he slowed her attack, and then dropped his elbow into the meat of her quadriceps. He felt her buckle as the muscle cramped from the blow and she lost her balance. Arianne leaned forward, and he head-butted her with enough force to make her stumble back in a daze. Finally on the offensive, he jumped at his stunned target, ready to end the fight once and for all.

Arianne recovered faster than expected. For a moment, Jack could have sworn her gray eyes pooled to black. He balled up his left fist, preparing for an uppercut, but he didn't get a chance to deliver on his plan. In one swift movement, she slapped his fist away and jumped into the air. With an ear-piercing cry, she kicked outward at his head, which was now level with her foot.

Jack saw the attack coming but his arms were still at his sides from her deflection. He had a moment of awful realization that his body was exposed and he was defenseless before her boot connected with his face. Jack dropped to the ground, a headache blossoming across his temples.

When he collected himself, the world still spinning around him, he realized that Arianne was above him with a Greek short sword extending from her left hand. Her eyes were hard, but they had returned from those demon-like black pools he had seen during their fight. Was he going crazy or had that been a trick of the lack of light? Either way, he shook his head to clear the fog from the corners of his vision.

Arianne raised a set of handcuffs in her right hand, "Put those on or you find out just how well I can use this thing," she warned with a pointed look at her blade.

Jack seethed, accepting the handcuffs in exchange for his life. He hated it: a couple of minutes of freedom only to lose to a sheltered brat. Once Jack was handcuffed, she pointed her sword at a tree to his left, and he begrudgingly moved to stand next to it. Looping a rope through his handcuffs, she quickly tied him up around the trunk of the tree.

He rolled his eyes in embarrassment and disbelief. He was Blackjack, for fuck's sake. And there he was, tied to a damned tree in the middle of the forest by an unseasoned Pacifican rebel. Jack turned to Arianne to see how much she was gloating over her lucky victory. But the woman was gone, her long braid swaying behind her as she ran back towards the gunfire.

Chapter 19

Arianne

Arianne's arms pumped as she sliced through the forest undergrowth. The sounds of gunfire were drawing nearer but also growing fainter. Her breath quickened as she ran, determined to make it in time. She couldn't afford to be late. She *wouldn't* be late.

She was grateful for her *Fera* night vision as she skillfully navigated through the trees and rocks at a sprint. She needed to reach the battle. Hours spent trying to keep up with the speeding jet and her clash with Jack had snapped her energy, but that was irrelevant now. Jaya, Rhino, and Caesar were out there, and she had to help.

Gunfire illuminated the forest in bursts of white light just ahead. Arianne channeled her emotions into her legs, now aching with pain. First, she channeled her regret and annoyance at being left behind. Then, she channeled her hurt and anger at Jack for betraying her people.

It was enough to deliver one last burst of speed.

She was unprepared for what she saw when she returned. Bodies, eerie and unmoving, were scattered in the clearing. Ace's thugs and Pacific's soldiers lay strewn on the ground, indiscriminate in their casualties. She winced at the metallic scent of blood and the unmistakable odor of fear.

The skirmish was over. She was too late.

Her breathing came in uneven gasps. "Jaya?" she shouted as she frantically scanned the dead and dying around her. "Rhino?" Arianne rushed from one body to the next. *"Caesar?"*

Her plea for her father was desperate. They couldn't be gone. They couldn't be *dead*.

Arianne's heart constricted as she continued to wade through the ugly aftermath, "Please," she whispered, "please be okay."

Fuck you. Arianne winced at her bile-filled last words to her father. She'd been so caught up in her own disappointment that she hadn't considered that conversation might have been her last with him.

"Oh my god," Her breath caught. "Oh my god, what did I do?"

The lifeless bodies, the dying moans, and the eerie silence of the forest beyond were unbearable. She continued searching, her throat constricting with every corpse she uncovered. Caesar... Jaya... Rhino... none of them were to be seen.

She began to shake, her legs refusing to cooperate as she fell to her knees. Relief had been momentary and now pure terror had taken over. Their bodies, dead or alive, were not there. But where were they? Where was her dad? Her nails dug into her skin in distress.

Gone.

Her best friends and the man who had raised her were gone.

And they hadn't escaped on the jet. Squinting through the forest underbrush, Arianne spotted it beyond the clearing in the darkness. No lights illuminated its interior to indicate anyone was still there.

Whoever hadn't perished in the forest clearing had been taken.

"I'm sorry," she whispered into her hands. "I'm sorry I was late."

Caesar had been right. She wasn't ready for this. So much death, so much loss, all in so little time. Despite her exhaustion, Arianne almost let her wings carry her home. She should report back to Kalfas, and get to safety before someone came for her too.

But then she halted her crying, her head snapping up in realization. A predatory anger surged within her as she realized who she still had trapped in the woods. The person responsible. The one who could lead her back to her family.

Blackjack.

She couldn't go home. Not yet. Not when Jack might be the key to finding her loved ones. Arianne jumped to her feet, renewed energy propelling her as she sprinted back to the tree where she'd left Jack waiting.

Arianne continued to sprint, her memory and increased scent guiding her back to her captive. She was grateful for her training, which had given her the stamina to retrace her steps despite her crippling fatigue. But when she laid eyes on Jack, gratitude was the farthest thing from her mind.

No, what Arianne felt was a lot closer to seething, white-hot rage.

Their eyes locked as she entered the clearing. "What did you do?" She bellowed, stepping up to violently rip the muzzle from Jack's mouth.

The bounty hunter's responding laugh made her blood boil. "They're all gone, aren't they?" He said.

Her stomach churned at his knowing tone. Without thinking, she backhanded him across the face, her anger building to a destructive level. "What did you do?" She repeated, each word slow and deliberate.

"I did what they asked me," he chuckled, seemingly unfazed by his split lip. "I showed them the tunnels."

Arianne bared her teeth. "Where did they go?" she demanded.

Jack shrugged. "I don't know. Things started to get a little crazy," he replied coolly. "Hence why I ran."

"You summoned Ace's goons. You must have signaled them or something. And then, on your signal, they ambushed the Pacificans and kidnapped them for Ace," Arianne spat.

She shook her head in confusion. Why would Jack do that? Caesar had promised him safety and a fresh start on the island. Why would he return to someone like Ace when offered paradise?

"Business is business," Jack replied, his tone glacial.

Arianne pulled out one of her short swords from her sheath and stepped toward Jack. Their breath mingled as she pressed the sword horizontally against his neck, just hard enough for the smooth metal to break his skin.

"Tell me where they're being taken," she demanded.

Jack managed a charming smile despite the blood trickling down his neck. "Leonueva, of course."

Arianne's upper lip curled. "Give me the location, or I'll cut your god-damned head off."

"I betray the location to you, and I'm no better off." He winked, "I would rather take the chance that you're bluffing."

Arianne leaned into her sword, the smell of her enemy's blood on her blade making a primal part of her sing. She could do it. It would be so easy to simply press downward. The smug, grinning bastard above her would be proven deliciously wrong as he paid for taking her loved ones away from her.

Arianne's eyes narrowed as she salivated over the possibility. It would be as easy as leaning forward. But... she leaned backward, her moment of blinding rage subsiding. Killing Jack might have made her feel better, but it wouldn't solve any of her problems.

Jack watched his captor's consideration with amusement, "So, make a decision yet?" He asked, too relaxed to be inches from death.

Arianne clenched her jaw, fighting back a stress headache that was building between her eyes. "While you deserve to bleed out hanging from this tree," she said, eyes rising to meet her prisoner's. "You've just given me a problem I'm going to have to fix. So I'll ask you one last time: where is Leonueva?"

Her voice had taken on an otherworldly calm. She was confident in what she needed to do and the only thing standing in her way was that bounty hunter. She would go into Ace's Compound and save Caesar and her friends. Caesar might not have thought she was ready, but they didn't have a choice anymore. Arianne certainly wasn't going to go back to Citadel to wait for Kalfas to appoint someone else for the job. This was her mission, and she didn't have time to wait for someone else to take it.

Jack looked down, a humorless laugh making his shoulders shake. "Let me clue you in on something, Princess. I like to play the odds, and working with you is not something I'm willing to do."

"I'll make sure to re-negotiate your amnesty deal with Pacific," she offered, "once you guide me to Leonueva, you'll be protected."

"Come on," Jack cooed, "you got to have something better than that."

Arianne stepped back, considering. What else could she offer the bounty hunter? He'd just made a trade with his boss to make him rich, and he didn't give a shit about Pacific. So what could she, a rookie breaking almost every military rule, have to offer him?

The realization came to her almost as quickly as she thought about the question. She was already in deep shit for everything she'd done that day. What was breaking one more rule? She wilted, even if breaking that rule made her the most selfish person in Pacific.

Maybe I am just a selfish Murray after all.

But she was also a female saving the lives of the people she loved. She could live with that.

And so Arianne decided to commit treason. With a deep breath to prepare herself for the weight of what she was about to say, she conceded. "You guide me to Leonueva and help me save the captured Pacificans and I will give you the location of Citadel."

Jack's smile became utterly feline as he considered her offer. "I'll need collateral," he sang.

"I'll give you an approximate location now and once the job is over you'll get the exact location of Citadel: a far more valuable piece of information," she bargained. "You will guide me north to Leonueva—no using Ace's tunnels or passages. We'll take the Pacifican jet."

"Absolutely not," Jack spat. "No one flies into Leonueva without specific approval: even Ace hasn't cracked that code. That jet has already gone as close to Leonueva's air space as I would be willing to risk. And without the tunnel and highway system, we're looking at weeks of hiking!"

Arianne smiled darkly. "Then we better start walking," she commanded. "I won't be taking any of your tunnels just so you can turn on me. You guide me north in this forest or I'll figure it out myself."

Jack groaned, struggling against his bonds once more before speaking again, "It's not just a simple hike through the woods," he protested. "There's a reason why Ace erected tunnel systems! The territory surrounding Leonueva has become a hot spot for slave hunting. If the slave hunters don't capture us, the savages will kill us thinking we're hunters. It's called the Darwin Zone for a reason. Ever heard about Darwin? Survival of the fittest?"

Her mouth dried out, but she fought to keep her fear from Jack. Slave hunters? Tribespeople? Arianne always heard that the tribespeople were mostly peaceful, especially to Pacificans. But hunters? If they got her in their custody, it would be game over. Could she survive weeks of being hunted by everything that lurked in those woods? She shook her head, she knew that she didn't have much of a choice.

"The offer still stands," she said stiffly.

Jack let out an exasperated sigh, "Get me out of these cuffs, Princess. We have a fucking deal." The bounty hunter looked down in annoyance. "Even if we die in the process," he muttered.

Arianne sheathed her sword and produced a card to unlock his cuffs. "Alright, Pangaea Boy." She frowned. "To Leonueva we go."

Jack shook his head at the pure absurdity of their predicament. "First, we have to survive the Darwin Zone."

Part II

Survival and Other Extreme Sports

Chapter 20

Jaya

"Good evening, ladies and gentlemen," came a delighted female voice. "Welcome to your non-stop flight to Leonueva. I hope you got some rest because you won't be sleeping for a while."

Jaya burst awake, her breathing rapid and ragged as she surged forward against her restraints. Gunshots, blood, people screaming in terror... and then nothing. She pulled against her restraints again, her hands bound behind her and her legs tied at the shins. She pulled at her handcuffs to test—two metal bands around her wrists connected by a steady stream of glowing blue light that allowed a slight range of motion but were impossibly strong. She hissed, lowering her hands. There was no way she was escaping.

But where was she? Once Jaya got her bearings, she started to look around. She was in the cabin of a jet very similar to the one her squadron had used to fly out to Old Romania. *Romania!* The mission returned as if a fog was being lifted from her memory.

Her breathing quickened as panic turned her insides cold. Her head whipped around, searching. Across from her, Captain Cadmilus and Major Lyn were knocked out, their hands and legs bound similar to hers. To her side, she noticed Rhino asleep as well. To her other side, one of Captain Cadmilus's men lay limply, his right shoulder bloodied from a grazed bullet, but otherwise, he seemed okay. Then she saw her sister, the only one not sleeping. The pair shared a glance in relief.

Kalinda was okay, and Jaya almost breathed a thanks to God.

Then she saw Caesar. The Pacifican President was on the floor with a pool of red blood surrounding him from a deep wound in his right leg. Once a rich shade of brown, the President's skin was ashen. The only reason Jaya knew the man was still alive was from the dangerously shallow rise and fall of his chest.

Jaya's breath caught in horror. They had arrived on that mission with just over twenty people in their party. Now, only seven of them remained.

"Oh look: one's awake," said the woman from before with an ounce of disappointment. "I thought your venom was going to kill all of them."

There was a grumble of annoyance. "I know what I'm doing."

Jaya turned and narrowed her eyes. She recognized the bleach-blonde hair instantly: Pandora Richards. Jaya could have gone her entire life without seeing that awful woman ever again.

Her heart dropped in her chest. Ace didn't capture them—they were prisoners of Pangaea. Any hope she had of negotiating with Ace and appealing to her infamous money-loving personality was out the window. There was no negotiating with Pangaea, there was only the hope of weathering whatever storm was coming their way.

"Medical neutrality," Jaya blurted, her eyes darting behind her to Kalinda before going back to Caesar.

Pandora spun around with fury, and Jaya clenched her teeth against the surge of terror that rose inside her. She fought to maintain her composure, stiffening her resolve and bracing for Pandora's wrath. In front of them, Caesar—her best friend's father and her president—was bleeding out. Jaya couldn't stand by and let him die.

"Excuse me?" Pandora seethed, her ghostly eyebrows arching in astonishment as if taken aback that a prisoner would have the gall to speak to her.

Jaya's breath quickened, and she suddenly felt horribly claustrophobic. "Medical neutrality," she repeated, her voice steady. "In war, specific rights are granted to both sides." She closed her eyes momentarily, recalling a quote from one of her textbooks. "'Regardless of political affiliation, medical professionals must be allowed to care for the sick and wounded.'"

Pandora blinked in disbelief, a twisted smile tugging at her lips. "Are you serious right now?" She leaned in closer to Jaya. "Do you think I give a shit about war rights?"

Jaya stole a glance at Kalinda who was shaking her head in a silent plea. Jaya met her sister's hazel-green eyes and frowned. They couldn't afford to let Caesar die.

Kalinda attempted to maintain her scolding glare, but Jaya looked away. From her little experience with Pandora, she knew the European Elite would take every opportunity she found to hurt the people around her. Jaya couldn't afford to let Pandora discover that she *loved* someone else in that crew—not if she didn't want that to be used against her. From then on, she knew that she needed to treat her sister with little more care than she did another one of her comrades in their captors' presence.

Jaya turned her attention back to Pandora. "You may not care, but the Pangaean Constitution does," she spat, "and I doubt you want to deal with all that paperwork."

Pangaea, as awful as it was, had a Constitution that the Commanders were obliged to follow. No matter how much she hoped the entire empire burned to the ground, she was grateful that in the aftermath of the Great Disaster and the subsequent Last War, Pangaea's six founders had crafted and implemented a Constitution. It outlined the rights of the empire's citizens and established rules to prevent devastating conflicts like the Last War—including provisions for medical neutrality.

Blue, who had entered from the cockpit, let out an exasperated groan. "Just let them treat him. It doesn't matter." She glanced casually at her black-painted nails.

Pandora hissed in annoyance as she approached Kalinda. "Fine," she conceded to the field medic, "but if you try anything, I'll ensure a bullet goes through his heart this time."

Pandora turned Kalinda around, raising a card to unlock her handcuffs connected by that strange blue light. The handcuffs let out a soft beep, and the blue light around Kalinda's wrists faded, freeing her hands. She repeated the process for Kalinda's shins, allowing the field medic to rush to Caesar's side.

Kalinda's silky black hair cascaded over her face as she removed her jacket and quickly fashioned a tourniquet to slow the blood still trickling from the wound. Jaya watched her sister work, praying that her efforts would be enough to save the president.

Pandora turned away from the scene, seemingly bored of witnessing someone save her captive's life. Meanwhile, Blue Krait reached into a cupboard near the cockpit and retrieved a first aid kit. The snake *Fera* knelt and handed the kit to Kalinda. Hands too bloodied to take the kit from the Snake's hands, the medic nodded in gratitude before returning to work. Blue didn't respond as she stood back up and quietly leaned on the metallic wall next to Pandora, yellow eyes assessing.

"Die, Cartel bastards!" Suddenly, Rhino jolted awake at Jaya's side, the larger *Fera's* powerful jump against his restraints sending him rocketing back into the wall behind him. The cabin shook with his effort. "What the hell is going on?" He demanded, fighting against his handcuffs. "What—"

"Pangaea captured us," Jaya muttered before Rhino could shout in her ear again. "Not Cartel."

He stiffened. "We're on a jet?"

"Yup."

"We're in trouble, aren't we?"

Jaya nodded. "Most definitely."

"Interesting," Blue mumbled. "And I gave him the most venom." She took out a notebook and jotted down her observations.

Pandora chimed in with interest: " I guess your *Fera* theory was correct. They can handle more toxins and metabolize them faster."

Jaya watched their exchange with disgust. "So poisoning people is just a game to you?"

Blue Krait's yellow eyes flared as her snake-like pupils narrowed to slits. "Balancing on the edge of life and death is never a game," she hissed, her forked tongue flickering. "It's an art I've been perfecting for twenty years."

"Do you have Second Blood?" Kalinda interrupted, looking between Pandora and Blue. "He's lost a significant amount of blood—he won't make it much longer."

Jaya glanced up as Blue and Pandora exchanged glances. Second Blood was a costly Pangaean invention beyond the reach of most Pacificans. Fortunately, many Pangaean officers were known to carry a backup supply. Second Blood was a lab-engineered substitute for real blood, capable of sustaining the wounded until they could reach a proper medical facility.

Blue wordlessly retrieved a labeled package filled with ruby-red liquid from her military bag. The Snake handed the bag to Kalinda, who now wore blue latex gloves. Connected to the package by a tube was a separate bag with a sterile needle inside. Kalinda expertly cleaned her hands with alcohol, removed the needle from the pouch, and inserted it into Caesar's forearm.

Pandora rumbled, watching the procedure. "So we're wasting resources on prisoners now?" she sighed. "This is getting boring; I'll go wake up the others."

Like a puppy looking for stimulation, Pandora walked around to the rest of the squad and began kicking them until they woke. The unnamed soldier winced as he awoke, bound hands going to his grazed shoulder. Major Lyn jumped awake, eyes as wild as Jaya's had been. But Captain Cadmilus woke up slowly, stunning blue eyes glazing over as he took in the room.

The Captain's head dropped. He'd lost all but one from his original squad, and now his president, the man he had been sworn to protect, was down as well. Defeat settled like a heavy rainstorm over the entire cabin.

"Oh, quit your pouting," Pandora tsked. "All this depression is ruining my fun."

Major Lyn glared at Pandora but didn't bring up her obvious resentment. Instead, she turned to the Captain and whispered to him, most likely attempting to align on some plan. Pandora resumed her explanation, a tone of annoyance in her voice. "All right, I only want to explain this once. You are now in the custody of the European Military—"

Rhino, however, couldn't contain himself. "I remember you now! You're that bitch from Moscow!"

Jaya elbowed her friend, "*idiot.*"

Pandora rubbed her temples impatiently. "Yes," she replied, her glowing eyes fixed on Rhino. "An astute observation."

Rhino struggled against his restraints as if he might miraculously break free. "How did you find us? I'm going to kill you once I get out of these things!"

Pandora exchanged an incredulous glance with Blue before returning her attention to the large *Fera*. "Knock yourself out," she retorted through gritted teeth. She began pacing, her annoyance palpable. "You know what? Looks like I only have a minute. Let's make this quick."

Blue checked her watch and reported, "We're still fifteen minutes away. You have time."

"No!" she exclaimed, turning to her partner. "I meant their attention spans."

"Ah." Blue breathed, nodding in understanding as she glanced at Rhino.

Pandora took a deep breath to calm herself. "Yes, we were in Moscow. Did you really think we didn't know Pacific was using stolen Pangaean jets? After that, it wasn't too hard to activate an alarm that tells me when a missing jet's serial number appears on the radar. Typically, it took me some time to find you guys, but you would imagine my surprise when you flew right into my backyard."

Jaya lowered her gaze and sensed the rest of the team losing what little morale they had left. Even if Blackjack had initially planned to betray their squadron to

Ace, he had inadvertently made them perfect prey for Pangaea by bringing them so close to Europe's capital.

Pandora seemed to relish in her victory. "Well, you heard the Snake. You've got fifteen minutes to rest up," she declared before returning to the cockpit.

Jaya stared blankly out of the expansive windows of the jet. The forest passed below, trees standing like dark sentinels against the night sky. The moon was full, and the stars, so far away from any civilization, shone as numerous as specs of sand on a beach. She would have thought the view was beautiful had she not been riding to her impending doom.

Instead, Jaya couldn't help but see it all as painfully ironic. There she was, traveling to the most exquisite city she might ever see as a war prisoner and rebel accused of treason against the empire.

Ten minutes later, the scenery began to glitch like a malfunctioning computer. The forest image stretched and distorted, pixelating before the illusion shattered completely. In its place, a grand city sprawled beneath them—towering buildings reaching skyward as if they could touch the stars. The city was aglow with lights, like the night sky had fallen to the earth.

Leonueva: the youngest and wealthiest city in all of Pangaea. The city was truly an achievement of science and modern marvels. Despite her predicament, Jaya heard her breath catch in awe. The city was magnificent, hidden in plain sight through the same advanced technology that made it such a world power.

The jet continued its course over the city, heading toward its center. Directly in their path, a black tower rose above the rest of the city, its obsidian windows absorbing the surrounding light. The tower thrummed with power, and Jaya's small hope for mercy shattered as the jet flew directly towards it.

Even though Jaya had never set foot in Leonueva, she'd heard whispers about the black tower: the Murray Monument, home to Leon Murray himself.

Chapter 21

Blackjack

Jack's plans to turn Arianne into Ace for a large prize weren't personal. Well, at least they hadn't started that way.

Then Jack hiked with her for two days straight, and his plan very quickly became personal. The woman was painfully naïve. It was obvious she had never been in forests like those before because of her lack of ability to navigate or understand her surroundings. He could've ignored that pesky annoyance had it not been the reason to slow them down. Arianne insisted on being in charge, which meant she made every decision. Their typical decision-making process went as follows: Jack would make a suggestion, Arianne would argue with him about it, and after they'd both yelled themselves hoarse at each other, Arianne would agree to go with his original plan.

Annoying didn't even begin to describe her.

Fortunately, Jack had retrieved his personal items from the jet before they began their hike. Everything he had with him when Pacific captured him had been returned to him as a sign of good faith before the mission. Ultimately, the gesture was lost on him. Good faith was why the Pacificans were captured and why he had another chance at repaying his debt.

Ace favored a device called a Simulator—a technology that usually filled an entire room and connected to the minds of those within it. The Simulator could extract memories from anyone in the system, allowing subjects to relive those memories as if they were happening in real-time. Ace mainly used it for training her Jokers, but it could also be employed for interrogation if the memory was recent enough.

Upon completing his Joker training, Ace had gifted Jack a smaller version of the Simulator. It came in the form of two wireless earbuds. While not as potent as Ace's larger device, the earbuds allowed Jack to immerse himself in memories, including those of the vinyl music records he had found during his travels. Music had become scarce in Pangaea, mostly reserved for the Elite. If he channeled the memories of music from his record player, he had a constant stream of music playing through his headphones. He didn't talk about it, but music was the only thing that reminded him of his family anymore.

With the nature of the Darwin Zone, Jack didn't trust losing the ability to hear the environment around him, so he kept one ear open. This solution, unfortunately, left an opportunity for Arianne to be heard.

"Hey, I think there's a rash on my right leg," Arianne complained. "Should I be concerned? I can't stop itching."

Jack rolled his eyes. It was the third time that day she'd mentioned her rash, and he couldn't ignore her any longer. "It's poison ivy," he grumbled. "Stop itching it or it will spread."

Poison ivy, he recalled, was best treated with witch hazel—a lesson from his grandfather. Crush the leaves of the plant to extract the juices and apply them to the affected area. Jack quickly pushed away the memory. Thinking of his grandfather and their cabin made his stomach churn.

Besides, if Arianne was foolish enough to step into poison ivy, she could handle it like an adult.

"I hope you know that I hate you and you're a fucking bastard, but walking in silence is going to drive me insane," Arianne huffed as she climbed over a boulder after Jack. "Can we at least find a subject that doesn't make us want to kill each other so we can break up this fucking monotony? How about your favorite color? Okay, I'll start: I like mint green."

Jack sighed, fortifying his patience. "I like to hike in silence." He wanted to say *rot in hell, you psycho bitch,* but that would have sparked a shouting contest he didn't have the energy for.

"Your preferences are duly noted," Arianne continued, "but I do have some questions."

Jack removed his second earbud, the sound of bass and guitar fading as he pocketed it. "Let's get this over with."

"Okay, I still don't understand this. Tribespeople are peaceful—why can't we go to one of their groups and ask for safe passage?"

Jack halted, pointing a finger at her. "Alright, I know what you're thinking, and you're going to stop right now."

Arianne paused, her hands clenched at her sides. "I don't know what you mean. I learned about the tribes as a kid. They're *good*. Protectors of the forest and the people who live in it. I get they're not nice to Pangaeans, but Pacificans—like me—are on their side!"

"That's exactly what I'm talking about," Jack retorted. "You're just another kid who grew up on those legends of Strix and Cervi—worshiping them like gods. But let me tell you the reality: those Legends are gone. What remains are horror stories told to Pangaean children to keep them out of the woods."

Arianne's eyes burned. "Don't talk about Strix like that. She was my hero when I had no one. She's real. I don't give a shit what you say."

Jack blinked in surprise; he'd grown up on the legends of Strix. She'd been his favorite, too. He was surprised that Arianne would choose Strix as her favorite of the powerful Champions of the famous Selvian Tribe. There had been Cervi, the Selvian leader with antlers like a prized buck. And then there was Cavalier, a Champion with skin so thick that he never lost in battle.

The tribespeople were fabled to be protectors of nature across the world, living outside of Pangaean rule and cultivating lives seemingly torn out of ancient European fantasy stories. Over generations, more and more mutants abandoned civilization to live a life more in tune with their abilities and hidden away from prejudice. Now, the tribes were concentrated homes for *Feras*. But most stories surrounded the fabled protectors of the tribes: Champions. The Champions were rare warriors who honed their mutant abilities to legendary levels. Arianne and Jack's childhood hero, Strix, had been the most famous of modern Champions: a *Fera* with hair the brightest of silvers and speckled white wings the color of freshly fallen snow. The warrior was once called *The Silent Death* due to her virtually silent flight.

"The Selvian Tribe is gone," Jack repeated, "Leon Murray saw to that just over twenty years ago."

Arianne looked down, "The Selvian War."

Jack wasn't certain of the details, but eventually, the Selvian Tribe became too great of a nuisance for Leon. The tribespeople were not Pangaean, but some tribes participated in Pangaean politics. The Selvian Tribe had been the most outspoken against the treatment of the *Feras*. Eventually, their protests and border raids had worried Leon enough for him to escalate the growing tensions. Most people called the skirmish between the Selvians and Europe a war, but Jack knew the truth: it was a massacre. Leon's forces destroyed what was left of the once-great tribe. After the war, other tribes throughout the world went into hiding out of fear.

The massacre practically declared open season on *Fera* hunting in Europe. After that, the tribes were never welcoming forest-loving people again. Every tribe—whether twenty people in size or two thousand—kept to their own. Especially in the Darwin Zone.

"We can tell them that we mean no harm," Arianne protested, "because we don't," she said with a glare.

"You want to know why I call them savages?" Jack countered, "Because out here in the Darwin Zone, that's what they are. You won't even make it within eyeshot of camp before they pump you full of arrows. Like I said, in the territory surrounding Leonueva, it's kill or be killed. And these savages—they fucking kill."

Arianne frowned, the reality of the hostility of those forests settling on her. "Because your people are taking their friends—their family—like they're animals," she spat as her eyes darkened.

Jack didn't enjoy the punch to the gut he felt at the reminder that he was intimately involved in such an awful industry. He ignored Arianne's piercing glare, moving to continue the hike, "doesn't change that we are staying clear of the savages."

"Why don't they leave?" Arianne asked, voice small.

Jack's shoulders slumped. For a question seemingly so complicated, he knew the answer better than anyone. "Because they have nowhere else to go," he said too softly.

Why had he worked for Ace all those years? Why hadn't he run before he accrued so much debt to the most powerful kingpin in Europe? The answer was the same as the tribespeople in the Darwin Zone: he had nowhere to go. His home was destroyed and his family torn apart. Maybe he wasn't too different from those savages after all.

A deep sadness—which he preferred to stuff down underneath years of indifference—threatened to come to the surface again. Jack physically stumbled at the brief debilitating feeling of emptiness that washed over him. Clenching his teeth, he locked those feelings as far down as he could shove them. He'd learned long ago that it was better to feel nothing than crumble under the weight of everything he lost.

I am Blackjack. I am the feared right hand of Ace. I am not that scared boy anymore. I am Blackjack. I am Blackjack.

"Are you okay?" Arianne asked with genuine concern.

Jack leaned against a tree, regaining his composure. "No more talking," he snapped.

They hiked north for the remainder of the day. Jack focused his energy on studying the sun's path to ensure they remained on the right trail to Leonueva. If his memory served him correctly, the tunnel systems that began where they'd landed two days ago were directly south of the city, with branches extending throughout the Darwin Zone. The tunnels had been built primarily so Ace's representatives could visit hunters in their respective camps and trade for the captured *Feras*. If Jack kept his eyes peeled for landmarks—like identifiable peaks in mountains or a fork in a large river—he had a basic idea of where he was.

If his approximations were accurate, they were still ten days or more worth of hiking away.

As the sun set, Jack made it through another day with little concern. They had passed some tribal trail markers made of painted feathers and carved bone, but he made sure to steer clear of any paths that looked too worn to be natural.

Dusk settled over the forest, and Jack decided to set up camp on the mossy ground underneath a sprawling maple tree. The moss would make for comfortable sleeping, and the broad leaves of the tree would ward off the coming showers the dripping humidity was warning of.

After some brief time spent hunting for firewood and food, Arianne and Jack returned to the camp. There, Jack began to light a fire as Arianne got to work skinning a rabbit she'd caught. He watched the woman out of the corner of his eye while trying to light the tinder he'd collected. For someone who lived a sheltered life on a tropical island, she certainly wasn't squeamish when it came to blood.

Or expertly throwing daggers at forest animals.

The pair worked in silence. Jack could sense Arianne's annoyance from across the camp, but he couldn't get himself to care. It wasn't his problem whether she liked him or not. All he was concerned about was surviving until they reached Leonueva.

The fire finally caught after minutes spent building the wood around the tinder to start the flame. Jack managed to smile as the camp was lit in orange light and let himself relax as his vision returned.

Arianne, on the other hand, seemed unsettled by the flames. "Can you keep that thing small? I thought we didn't want to attract attention."

Jack pointed at his measly fire in disbelief. "No one's going to see any smoke in such a dense forest at night, especially with a cloudy sky." He looked at the woman and noticed with delight that she seemed uneasy as the flames flickered across her face. "Don't tell me, are you afraid of fire?"

The woman shook her head, eyes snapping back to Jack. "It's not my favorite," she admitted with a scowl. "A fire burnt down my first house with Caesar on the island."

Jack grinned, tucking that small tidbit of information in his head for later.

Once the two of them had eaten, he followed the usual procedure Arianne laid out for him: she pointed to a tree behind him and promptly tied him up. He wanted to object, but an objection was hard with a rifle pointed in his face. He understood why she was overly cautious. The woman had shown a supernatural ability to read him from their first series of encounters and had obviously discerned he was unpredictable. Even if Jack had collateral, there was no guarantee that he wouldn't change his mind about their deal at any point. Honestly, the Pacifican's strange insight into his personality was right: even he didn't know if or when he would get bored and decide to say fuck it to that entire operation.

That still didn't make his sleeping arrangements any more enjoyable.

Once her guide was secure, Arianne doused the fire, curled up, and fell asleep without another word. Sleep didn't find Jack as easily. Naturally, something was unsettling about falling asleep in a forest full of things that wanted to kill him while tied to a tree, which made escape impossible. Not that he was much of a night sleeper before. Years spent in Cartel had made him a night owl—he liked the hours of darkness when the rest of the world was asleep. There, he could exist in silence, protected by the thick veil of night.

After years of fighting against the crushing realities of the world alone, the night had grown to be his only trusted companion. Unlike most things in his life, the night was predictable. Even on days when Ace chose to be specifically volatile or when it was uncertain if he would ever wake up without pain lacing his limbs, the night always came. No matter how terrible his day was, the moon would rise eventually, and the world would go to sleep.

And he would be left blissfully alone in the company of darkness.

Jack didn't know how long he had lied awake listening to the soft patter of rain on the leaves above when he noticed Arianne had begun to shift. The Pacifican's eyebrows creased with worry as her hands began to clench and unclench. Jack watched with mild concern as the woman's thrashings grew more volatile. She started to mumble in distress. Summer thunder crashed overhead, and still, Arianne wasn't pulled from sleep.

"He can't hurt you, too," the woman mumbled. "He can't hurt you, too," she repeated between deep gasps.

He watched Arianne curiously. She was having a nightmare, but about what? He almost threw a rock at her to wake her but stopped himself. Who was *he* to save her from her nightmares? They all had shit to deal with. At least *her* terrors only came to her when she slept.

Then, his attention was pulled elsewhere. Beyond their camp, he could hear rustling in the undergrowth. His jaw clenched. With the storm, all the animals in the forest would be hiding. Someone else was coming.

Jack turned back to his hiking companion. It seemed he would need to wake her after all.

Chapter 22

Arianne

Arianne's fractured memories had been coming back as dreams for a few nights now. Perhaps her unconscious knew she was heading back home, and perhaps the added stress of the past few days was weakening the veil that kept the horrors from her childhood from ruining her sanity.

Her dreams were scrambled nightmares of sterilized labs and a dark room of concrete that loomed with despair. Every flash of horror left her shaking, wishing desperately it would be enough to wake her. But with each memory, she was dragged down deeper and away from the surface.

As a *Fera* with gills, Arianne never thought she would know what drowning felt like.

And then her descent stabilized, and she realized she was in a room, *her* room. The small space, barely large enough for a bed and dresser, felt familiar and comforting even if she hardly remembered it. She had a somewhat pieced-together memory of the labs of the Murray Monument and the training rooms she practiced in with her father, but the places where she felt true peace seemed to slip away from her consciousness faster.

She was hiding underneath the white sheets of her bed and shaking. Her ears hunted for every sound they could detect. Any shift in weight on the floorboards or creak of an opening door could be her father. Arianne's muscles ached from her earlier testing, and the ripped skin on her back stung. She couldn't handle more pain.

Not tonight.

Then, a cautious knock came to her door. At first, she was terrified that her father had decided on a visit but quickly remembered that Leon Murray never knocked. Leon was the most powerful man in all of Europe. In his mind, he deserved to be in whatever room he felt like entering.

"Come in." Arianne's voice was small.

Her brother opened the door as wide as his nerves would allow. The young prince was careful as he squeezed into his sister's room and closed the door quietly behind him, cautious not to make any noise. He carried a tray in his hands shielded by a maroon tablecloth. At four years, her senior, Andre Murray, was slowly growing into his lanky shoulders and awkwardly large feet. As the son of the towering European Commander, he was expected to be just as tall and domineering as Leon was.

Andre placed the tray on Arianne's nightstand before sitting on the edge of her bed. "How are you doing?" He asked softly.

"It hurts," she admitted, "but if I don't move, it's not so bad."

Andre carefully guided his sister into a sitting position, frowning as he saw her bedsheets. A rock settled in her stomach at the sight. "Am I bleeding again?"

She knew she had been sticking to the sheets all night but had been too afraid to admit to herself what that meant. If her wounds weren't healing, it told her that she was at risk for infection.

Andre leaned forward and touched his forehead to hers. "Hey, hey, it's okay," he said soothingly. "I brought bandages and medicine Mom gave me."

Arianne was quiet for a few minutes as her brother helped pull off her nightshirt and cleaned up the lash marks lining her spine and around her downy wings. Though her golden brown plumage had mostly grown in, soft gray down from when she was a baby was still speckled around the mature feathers.

As Andre finished applying bandages, Arianne finally built up the courage to ask, "Am I going to be okay?"

"Yes," her brother replied, removing the tablecloth from his tray to reveal sealed-off leftovers from dinner. He opened the container and offered it to his sister. "You're very brave."

But Arianne only shook her head. "Won't you get punished for this?" She asked.

Hera and Leon were running another one of their studies on her. They wanted to track her physical performance over time without food. She hadn't eaten in three days—she wasn't sure if she wanted to risk the consequences her brother would get because of her.

"It's fine," he reassured her, lifting a cookie. "Look, I brought your favorite: oatmeal raisin."

Andre was the only person in the world who knew her favorite food. The two of them had learned to keep what they enjoyed a secret at a young age. If Leon knew what brought them joy, it simply became another thing he could take away.

Andre's offering almost tempted Arianne, but she quickly righted herself. "He can't hurt you, too," she said, pushing the cookie away.

"You're hungry," the young prince objected, his hazel eyes—so much like their mother's—lowering in sadness. "Just eat something for me. I can handle whatever happens."

Arianne didn't have the willpower to object again. She devoured the food, even when her stomach ached after days of staying empty. Once full, and with the stinging in her back subsided, she felt exhaustion begin to pull at her consciousness. With a yawn, she curled up beside her brother as her eyelids grew heavy.

"Andre?" She asked amidst another yawn.

"Yes?"

"Will you stay with me until I fall asleep?"

Andre smiled softly, and he kissed her on the head. "I'll stay here all night if you need me to."

"Arianne!" Someone called.

Arianne's eyes widened, but when she looked up at her brother, he hadn't been the one to shout. She looked around in confusion, disturbed that her brother hadn't heard the call. Andre was focused on packing the medical kit at her side, his eyes fiercely concentrated as he rolled up the unwound gauze.

Was she the only one able to hear that sound?

"Arianne!"

Like being pulled from the water, the dream rushed away from her. She fought the pull for a moment, desperately wishing to remain curled up in the warmth of her brother's arms.

Abruptly, she was lying on damp moss in a camp that smelt of embers and rain. Disoriented, she shook her head—the haze of her dream threatening to pull her back under.

Jack was shouting. "Arianne!" He barked, "untie me! We have to go!"

She heard it then: the sound of feet running through the undergrowth just outside of their camp. "Shit," she cursed. Someone was coming, and fast. "We might have a slight problem."

"*A slight problem*?" Jack wheezed, "Cut me out of here!"

Arianne felt like she was moving through molasses as she stood to free Jack with a quick swing from her sword. As Jack scrambled to get up and move, she jumped on the balls of her feet to clear away the final remnants of drowsiness. As she listened to the forest beyond, she realized the attackers were practically on top of them. Like it or not, there was no time to run—she needed to prepare for a fight.

"Give me a gun!" Jack demanded, coming to the same conclusion.

"Not a chance."

Jack bared his teeth. "You'll need me to fight!"

"If they're tribespeople, a gun won't do you any good," Arianne argued.

There was a reason Leon trained Arianne in the art of sword fighting. Laser guns or old-fashioned semi-automatics were the modern solution to combat, but they were only effective against humans. *Feras* needed a lot more than a bullet wound to slow down. In many cases, a mutant shot and dying would go feral and take their enemies out with them. And a feral *Fera* felt *nothing*. The only guaranteed way to stop a *Fera* was to physically remove the body part they wanted to use.

Guns didn't guarantee that. Sharp weapons did.

"I'm not arguing with you right now," Jack replied as he knelt and relit the fire pit at his side. Soon, the small camp was aglow with orange light.

The feet trampling the forest grew closer. Arianne did her best to assess the situation before their new guests arrived. She could pick out at least six sets of feet if she concentrated. She was also willing to assume the attackers were mutants because humans couldn't see at night. All those factors added up to a not-so-optimal conclusion: a fight against six mutant attackers did not give her a good chance.

With an eye roll over her unfortunate predicament, she tossed Jack the rifle next to her bag, "Guns won't do much against *Feras*."

The bounty hunter cocked the gun with a devilish grin and hid behind a tree. "They do if you know how to aim."

With a crash, the ambush trampled the undergrowth surrounding their camp. Their attackers rushed forward with various cries of outrage and excitement. As the first three tribespeople ran into the camp, arrows rained down from the darkness behind them as cover. Arianne let out a sharp hiss as the projectiles sunk deeply into the bark of the tree she'd hidden behind, happy she had elected to take cover instead of rushing the initial wave.

Arianne slowed her breathing, and her academy training returned to her as she surveyed the clearing. As she'd guessed, a party of six tribespeople were invading her camp: two with bows and four with weapons fashioned from staffs sharpened to deadly points.

She had never seen tribespeople before. She wasn't sure what she expected, but from Jack's description, she hadn't expected martial-like sophistication. They wore well-fitting hunting leathers and moved with tactical efficiency. Arianne watched from behind her tree as they surveyed the camp, most of their faces obscured by bone masks or paint. She could tell at least two tribesmen were *Feras* from one's deep blue skin and the other's scaled tail.

Without warning, Jack whirled from around the trunk of his tree, his eyes glowing with a deadly light as he aimed and fired. The first archer fell to the ground, a single trail of blood dripping down his forehead. Another loud pop shook the clearing, and the second archer fell with an identical bullet wound.

Arianne didn't have time to be stunned. The remaining four tribesmen were running at her one-way ticket to Leonueva. Jack fired again, but the attackers were moving too fast for him to aim properly. Arianne lunged, tackling the frontmost *Fera* and pulling her away from Jack's path.

She shouted in shock as the pair of them tumbled through the bushes. The female threw herself off of Arianne and across the grass. Rolling to a stop, Arianne collected herself. Pulling a dagger from her boot, the female bared her sharp teeth, just barely visible underneath an eerie deer skull mask. Arianne pulled her second sword from its sheath and smiled back despite every inch of her body screaming at her to run.

Before Arianne could attack, a male arrived at the female's side. The male *Fera* outstretched a staff decorated with feathers and beads and pointed it threateningly towards her. Reassessing her odds, Arianne took a step back into a defensive position. A glance to the side showed Jack had killed the third attacker and was now wrestling with a fourth. She wouldn't be getting any help from him.

Two against one—she'd dealt with worse odds in gym class. Granted, gym class wasn't against two full-grown *Feras* who just had their tribemates murdered in front of them.

"Can we talk this out?" Arianne smiled.

The pair looked at each other and exchanged a few words in a language she didn't recognize. Then the male stepped forward, face furious. "Domesticated," he growled.

That was a word Arianne recognized. Her smile faded. *Domesticated* was an insult the tribespeople saved for *Feras* who grew up in civilization. It was a term used to mock those who tried to pass as human by hiding their true nature. That meant the *Feras* in front of Arianne could smell that she was a mutant—she couldn't let them make a comment that would tip off her lovely travel partner.

"All right," Arianne sighed. "I tried."

Then she jumped.

The male reacted first with a raise of his staff to block Arianne's short swords in the center of her swing. The reverberation of his block stung down to her bones, and she was forced to land and step out of the way to recover. As the male corrected himself, the female picked up the slack and rushed at Arianne with a dagger. If Arianne's swords had been any longer, she wouldn't have been able to intercept the female's close-range attacks; luckily, she had trained for that specific situation. Watching the female's swings, she managed a deep slice into the female's dominant arm, which stunned her enough to disarm her. With a scream, the female lunged out of her reach, and Arianne was left alone with the male.

The male swung his staff downward, and she crossed her blades to block the attack. Forcing the staff away from her with an upward shove, she took advantage of the male caught off balance and advanced. The male attempted to recover with a defensive blow, but Arianne expertly dipped her sword below the path of the staff. The move provided an opening for a killing blow to the abdomen.

But Arianne didn't take the opportunity. She'd never killed before, and she didn't want to start that night. Instead, she took advantage of her close proximity to the male, stepped around his backside, and delivered a deep swipe across his hamstrings. The male cried out in pain as his legs buckled underneath his weight, and he fell.

For the second time in that fight, Arianne was painfully aware that the final kill was open for her to take. She stared down at the male writhing in pain, but she couldn't force herself to finish the fight. It was like there was a block deeply ingrained in her soul. She couldn't just kill people trying to protect their home...

Her hesitation cost her. The female had recovered her dagger, now in her lesser hand, and took advantage of her opponent's pause. Before Arianne could dodge, the tribeswoman's dagger landed a well-placed slice across her chest, just centimeters below her golden angel pendant. Arianne barely had the reaction time to dodge backward to avoid a deadlier wound. Had she been slower—had she been human—that slice would have easily cut through her sternum. Arianne's eyes widened as her breathing hitched.

Blood, *her* blood, dripped down her sliced military jumpsuit. Somehow, until that moment, that entire mission hadn't felt real. Now, with the stinging pain reminding her of her reality, the crushing weight of her predicament fell down on her. She was alone with a bounty hunter who wanted to sell her in a forest full of monsters that wanted to kill her.

"Shit," Arianne breathed.

The female moved to attack again. But a strange calm settled over Arianne—a calm Leon pounded into her as a child. So what if that tribeswoman wanted her dead? Her own father had wanted her dead her entire life, and that hadn't stopped her. She had *survived* before. She would survive again.

Oddly enough, the reality of just how dire her situation was focused her. Arianne moved her feet quickly, using the longer reach of her swords to her advantage. Whenever the female lunged, Arianne chopped downwards to block her with a wall of metal. Soon, the female tired, and Arianne grinned as she went on the offensive. The fight was hardly a place for smiling, but she was excited that she had not forgotten who the hell she was.

I'm a Murray, like it or not, and I won't be scared.

"You want to kill me?" Arianne challenged. "Get your ass in line!"

The tribal *Fera* howled in response, jumping with cat-like grace. She was fast, much faster than Arianne, but Arianne had skill. Swipe. Dodge. Perry. Swipe. Dodge. Perry. The Pacifican fell into a rhythm, her gray eyes tracking the pattern of the female's movements. When she lunged in an attempt to clip Arianne's shoulder, Arianne saw her opening. The female was off balance and exposed.

With a broad stroke of her right hand, Arianne slashed the female's fingers, and the tribeswoman dropped her dagger with a cry. To the female's surprise, Arianne advanced and forced her to the ground. Arianne raised her sword to the female's throat and stepped on her chest in victory.

"Yield," Arianne warned the female.

A gunshot rang out across the camp. The female gasped in shock before falling limp.

Arianne jumped at the sound, turning in horror to face Jack—holding a still-smoking gun. Though his face was bruised and his arms had a few gashes, he looked like he had avoided any significant injuries from the fight. Despite that, his face was one of unending annoyance.

"Hey!" Arianne spat, "she was going to yield!"

Jack looked at the female he'd shot. "No, she wasn't. Next time, don't mess around."

Arianne whirled on her travel partner, "Why the hell did you shoot her? She was unarmed!"

Jack took a step forward as he leaned towards Arianne's face with a scowl, "I saw you fighting them. You could've killed both of them in the first few attacks of the battle. You made a different call." He shouldered past her, eyes going to the male she'd left wounded. "I'm not going to let you get both of us killed because you have a soft spot for your forest friends."

Arianne looked away as Jack aimed his gun at the injured male and fired. The sound of the gun left her ears ringing, and then they were met with awful silence. Jack killed all six of those attackers without so much as an ounce of hesitation.

"Turn around," Jack ordered.

Arianne shook her head. She'd spent her childhood exposed to such cold calculation and refused to be a part of it ever again. She gritted her teeth, "Don't tell me what to do."

"Turn around," Jack demanded again, pointing to the bodies of the male and female Arianne had been fighting just minutes before. "This," Jack spat, "is Pangaea. *This* is what you need to make peace with if you want to survive. Got it, Princess?"

Arianne's gray eyes turned glacial as she met Jack's molten amber gaze. "You're an asshole," she spit out every syllable.

Jack collected his things without an ounce of notification that her words had offended him. "Let's get moving," he muttered. "We need to get away from here. We made too much noise."

Arianne got one last look at the tribespeople Jack had left massacred on the forest floor before marching behind her guide. Bile rose in her throat at the sight: the bodies looked so similar to the ones left behind after the Pacifican firefight. She understood why Jack had done it—she understood that it was to hunt or be hunted—but she couldn't escape the dark cloud that settled over her in the presence of so much unnecessary death.

To make it worse, she had a suspicion the bodies would keep piling up. She didn't know if she had the power to stop it. Like watching oncoming traffic, she could see the collision coming but could do nothing but brace for the impending disaster.

Chapter 23

Jaya

Jaya hadn't seen her sister in two days. The chameleon-like *Fera* paced back and forth in her cell, stress making her feel like she was ready to explode. Kalinda had always been by her side through everything. Now, at their most dire, they were torn apart. Blue had taken Kalinda to the medical bay within the Murray Monument, claiming that once Caesar came out of surgery, one of his own would take care of him.

Even the mighty empire of Pangaea didn't want to waste valuable resources on rebels.

But that was two days ago. Jaya's fingers turned bright green with worry. The more she paced, the more that green tint traveled up her bronze skin. What was happening to her sister? Were Kalinda and Caesar okay?"

"Rookie, you're going to wear tracks into the floor," Major Lyn retorted from the cell across from her. "Sit down before you waste all of your energy."

Jaya's breathing slowed as she realized how worked up she'd become. She looked around; everyone in the prison block was on edge. Two days of being locked in their cells. Two days away from their President. Two days of not knowing who was coming for them next.

Rhino patted the concrete floor next to him with a look of understanding. "She'll be okay," he reassured Jaya.

Jaya sighed as she slid down the wall next to her friend, saying, "I don't know what I'll do if she's not."

"It helps to talk it out," Rhino offered. "You can have my undivided attention, but I can't guarantee how long it will be before I get distracted."

Jaya looked up above her, her green eyes scanning the ceiling as if she could come up with some brilliant way to escape the most secure building in all of Europe. She never talked about her life before Pacific. Most people didn't. Jaya's memories from England were not the happiest, but Kalinda had always been there for her. No matter what. Jaya was the reason Kalinda left their home in England, and now she couldn't help but feel like she was the reason her sister was trapped in Leonueva.

"I was the youngest of six siblings," she began, "and the only *Fera*. I think my parents tried to love me, but they didn't know what to do with me. We were from a small town and I was probably the only *Fera* who lived there—or just the only one dumb enough to stick around," she finished wryly.

Rhino frowned. As a *Fera* himself, he most likely knew a version of that sob story all too well, despite being born on the island of Citadel like Haris.

"I-I didn't have as much control over my color changes back then," Jaya continued. "My parents kept me locked in the house for my own good. But I was young and curious. I snuck out of the house one day." She shook her head in frustration, "I just wanted to *see* what the world was like out there—I even stole my mother's *dupatta* to cover my purple hair."

"And you got caught." Rhino closed his eyes with a frown.

Jaya nodded. "Most people in Pangaea don't have a lot of money. And we weren't far from an infamous *Fera* trading site in London called The Block. It didn't take long for them to capture me and bring me there."

She shivered at the memory. She was just a little girl, and those monsters had sold her like cattle.

She could still remember her days spent in those *Fera* holding cells hidden deep underground. What stuck with her most was the despair. She'd never been around other *Feras* before, and she certainly didn't know how to act like one, but she quickly learned. To be a *Fera* in Pangaea was to be hopeless. Crammed in those small cells, smelling of mold and urine, she realized just how hopeless someone could be. Sickness made her hug her knees and squeeze tighter against Rhino. The more she thought about it, the more the cell she was in began to feel like the one she'd been trapped in as a child. Her lips began to quiver, and that hopeless feeling came back to her with the crushing weight of the world.

"Kal used her life savings to bribe a few of the guards before I was put to auction," Jaya whispered. "The rest of my family gave up, but not her. Not her."

She closed her eyes for a moment. Kalinda claimed she'd used money every time she told the story. But Jaya knew the truth: no one from her hometown had the kind of money to free a slave. Whether or not Kalinda suspected that Jaya knew she had sold her body, the sisters never spoke of it. Either way, that detail of the story was not Jaya's to tell.

"Do you hate your family?" Rhino asked slowly.

Jaya closed her eyes, thinking. She knew she should despise her parents for giving up on her, but the feeling never came. All she remembered were the good things: her mother's sweet dumplings on Holi and watching her brothers and father dance Bhangra in their backyard. Those memories told her the truth. Her family was like most in the lower classes of Pangaea. They were just people trying to get through the week. They knew accepting loss was easier than fighting it.

"No. They didn't know any other way. Pangaea takes and takes," Jaya explained. "For my family, there weren't any options. But Kalinda has always been a little bit more headstrong," she laughed. "She knew I couldn't stay. She heard rumors of Pacific growing in the south and set out to find them."

Rhino and most of Jaya's friends knew the rest. The Bahri sisters were brought to Citadel's shores and Kalinda worked hard to gain citizenship and custody over Jaya. She then put herself through training to become a field medic and they never looked back. Jaya's eyes began to water. Kalinda had sacrificed everything to give her a better life in a new home. And now it felt like it was all for nothing.

Her first tear had barely slid down her cheek before the doors to the prison block opened with a startling snap. Pandora, looking as volatile as ever, strolled inside followed by a taller man whose very air seemed to make the entire room turn its head. The door clanged shut behind the two newcomers and the pair paused outside of the first set of cells.

Jaya finally got a good look at the second Pangaean. The man was more than just tall, he towered a head and a half over Pandora with a height that might only be rivaled by Rhino. He wore a black uniform with red trim, badges marking high rank decorating his right breast. A black mask covered the lower part of his face, shielding his nose, lips, and chin, but Jaya could make out his eyes: a hazel that burned so brightly that she could see the green and gold specs from where she sat.

"And when is he supposed to be back," Pandora asked the man. "Don't you think this capture is rather *important?*"

The man tapped his right temple and the mask disappeared with a sharp *click* to reveal handsome full lips and healthy caramel skin. "Commander Murray is currently at a Leadership Summit in Beijing," his voice was low and impatient. "Or would you like to tell the other five Commanders that your time is more important than theirs?"

Pandora bared her teeth, clenching and unclenching her hands impatiently. "Of course not," she seethed.

"Commander Murray has sent me in his stead," the man continued, turning to look at the rest of the cells with a mild look of interest. Jaya realized the man was young, no older than thirty. "I would hope you wouldn't scoff at my presence," he snarled.

"Of course not, princeling," Pandora bowed mockingly.

Jaya's blood went cold. Leon was coming. They were going to be presented to *Leon*. And if that representative for Leon was just called princeling, there was only one person he could be. Andre Murray, the Heir Apparent to Leon Murray's throne.

"*Ten cuidado,*" Andre hissed in Spanish. "You will address me as *Your Highness.*" His hazel eyes burned.

Jaya was surprised that Pandora didn't flinch away from the Heir. Instead, the ghostly woman gave him a baleful smile. "If my mother had married Leon Murray, *you* would be the one addressing *me* as Your Highness."

"But she didn't," Andre growled.

Pandora grinned. "No, he married your commoner mother instead."

"Careful with how you speak about the Mother of Europe," Andre warned. "Commoner or not, Josephina Valentino Murray owned every citizen of Europe when she married Leon. Like it or not, that includes *you*. Or did you not read the Constitution?"

With a frown, Pandora turned and left the prison block without another word. Jaya watched the interaction between the two in silence. Pandora must have been high up in the rankings of Europe if she was willing to address the future Commander with so much disdain. Jaya smiled. She was starting to wonder if there was an advantage to being trapped inside Leonueva's heart.

Politics could be just as deadly as weapons if used correctly.

"No," Rhino warned, "I know that look. Stop it. Stop it right now."

Jaya raised her hand to the wall behind her, concentrating hard as she willed her skin to turn the color of the rugged concrete. Slowly, an idea formed in her head. "We could learn a lot here," she began slowly. "It would be a shame if I accidentally broke out."

Chapter 24

Blackjack

In the hours following the tribal attack, Jack relied on his Simulator to stay awake. The heavy crash of drums and electric vocals from his memories kept him alert as his eyes threatened to close. His legs moved on autopilot, their tired muscles carrying him step after step through the slowly brightening forest. Once the sun rose above the trees, Jack would be comfortable enough to stop and rest for a few hours. But with the disadvantage of darkness, he wanted to stay on his feet and keep moving.

A break in the trees appeared up ahead, and he quickened his pace to reach it. It led to an outcropping with a view of the valley below, marking the end of a small range of low mountains they'd been traversing and the beginning of a valley. The sun creeping above the horizon illuminated the landscape with the first signs of soft morning light.

If Jack hadn't been so tired, he would have marveled at the view. Dense emerald foliage stretched as far as his eyes could see, occasionally interrupted by a river to the west, cutting through the land like a scar. In the distance, taller mountains with rocky peaks tipped in white reached towards the heavens. Beyond those mountains lay the Artery, the route they'd follow to reach Leonueva.

Jack hated that he could see where he needed to go, all the while knowing he was still so far away.

Arianne appeared at his side. "Wow," she gasped, her gray eyes examining the expanse of forest. "I had no idea the world was so large."

Wind buffeted Jack's face as he looked at the Pacifican in disbelief, wondering how long it had been since he felt that same sense of wonder. A part of him wanted to feel it again. He quickly shook off the thought, allowing his irritation with his travel partner's naiveté to show. "Yeah, well, maybe you should educate yourself," he muttered.

"I have a bachelor's degree in battle strategy. I've educated myself plenty, shit stain."

Jack rolled his eyes. "And I've got a street degree in keeping my ass above ground. Maybe we can compare notes."

Though Jack's words were cutting, he wasn't quite certain which degree he would have preferred. It wasn't like higher education had ever been available for someone like him.

He could feel Arianne's vulgar gesture in his direction as he turned around and began to set up camp. Hopefully, tribal hunting parties would be less daring in the approaching daylight. The outcropping provided decent cover, allowing them to focus on guarding their front instead of worrying about their backs.

"Instead of plotting how to kill me, maybe we should get a few hours of rest," Jack suggested slyly to Arianne's middle finger.

"Cool," she sang. "You can go ahead and tie yourself up then."

His lip curled in amusement. "I've been meaning to talk to you about that," he began, knowing he was starting a fight. "No more tying me up. I'm not interested in participating in your fantasies anymore."

Joke or not, being tied up had made Jack incapable of defending himself when they were about to be ambushed. If he hadn't woken Arianne up in time, both of them would have been dead long before they could argue about who was right.

A bright red blush blossomed across Arianne's cheeks. The Pacifican quickly replaced the blush with a red face of outrage. "What? No! The only thing I fantasize about is making it to the fucking city!"

Jack leaned back against a tree. "I'll be honest with you," he replied evenly, "if I screw you over right now, I screw myself over. I stand a better chance of betraying you once we reach Leonueva."

Arianne's eyes widened with rage, her mouth puckering like she'd eaten a whole lemon. Jack found the gesture more adorable than terrifying. "You're really making me want to tie you up now," she warned.

Jack crossed his ankles and folded his hands behind his head, the picture of leisure. "Aw, Princess, if you wanted me to fuck you, all you had to do was ask."

"Ugh," Arianne protested, turning to stomp off. "You're the worst!"

"I know," Jack hummed, closing his eyes. "I do it on purpose."

The next few days passed without any significant issues.

After the ambush from the tribal hunting party, neither Jack nor Arianne were confident that they could make it through those forests alone. No matter how unsavory, they needed each other, and that brought on a level of trust even Jack was surprised to give.

It seemed all it took was a life-or-death situation to force him to *almost* enjoy someone's company.

Arianne continued to talk incessantly during their waking hours while Jack drowned her out with the music droning in his ears. Hiking through the forests proved peaceful, and he remembered how much he loved the scent of rain-soaked leaves and moss. If it weren't for the fact that they were in the Darwin Zone, he could have convinced himself he was on vacation.

The sun began the final hours of its descent in the sky as the pair crested a large hill, almost ambitious enough to be considered a mountain. Jack scanned the path before him, his eyes tracking the sun's direction as it descended toward the western horizon. They still had a few hours' worth of hiking before they needed to set up camp, but as long as they kept the sun to the left of them, they would keep heading north toward the capital.

Not that he was planning on telling Arianne exactly where they were heading.

"*Merde,*" Jack cursed under his breath as he spotted smoke rising above the trees below.

Arianne joined him, frowning. "It's going to take hours to go around. No way we're setting up camp anywhere near that."

Jack nodded, impressed. Arianne might have been relatively clueless when it came to surviving in central Europe a few days ago, but she'd learned quickly. By simply following him, she picked up on how to calculate travel times by looking at distances. While she still annoyed the shit out of him, he had to admit that she wasn't completely useless.

Jack scanned the smoke, pondering whether it was a tribal camp or a hunters' village. Then, he noticed a faint dirt road through the thick foliage. Dirt roads meant trucks, and trucks meant hunters. He breathed out a sigh of relief. As long as they kept an eye out for traps, they were far better off with hunters. Hunters were far less aware of their surroundings than tribespeople were. Tribespeople had been raised in those forests and many had superhuman *Fera* abilities: they could practically sense a twig out of place. Hunters were just an obnoxious and clumsy invasive species.

"Hunters," Jack muttered, thinking he should clue Arianne in on the situation.

The notion of sharing his thoughts was a strange one. He wasn't used to voicing what was going on inside of his head. Sometimes, he had to force himself to speak to his travel partner because it certainly didn't come naturally. Unfortunately, for his own sake, Arianne needed to know his plans every once in a while.

Arianne bared her teeth, and Jack knew that if she'd been a cat, her hackles would have risen, "What are we going to do about them?"

Jack considered for a moment, thinking about his ever-lightening bag. Even with rationing and hunting, they were running low on supplies. Even though they both had come to Romania with some basic supplies, neither had been prepared for a hike. And that had been a week ago, whatever sparse supplies they had were close to gone. Last he checked, he was down to his last match, and they were in dire need of other goods like blankets, canned food, and more weapons. Their fight with the tribal hunting party had drained him of half of his rounds.

"We're going to steal some of their stuff," Jack decided.

Arianne grinned wickedly as she drew one of her razor-sharp swords. "Are we going in swinging or in disguise? I'd prefer to teach a few of them a lesson."

Jack had to restrain a chuckle. "Preferably neither," he replied. Then he shook his head, reminding himself not to get too close to her. Arianne was a means to an end, a trade he would make to Ace for his freedom. Jack couldn't start seeing her as more than that. He raised his chin and reminded himself how irritating she was. "We're going to sneak in after dark, steal supplies, and keep going. Got it?"

The Pacifican Major slouched. "You're no fun."

"I'm not trying to be fun."

By twilight, the pair had made it to the outside of the small hunters' village. The settlement wasn't much: a few rows of hastily constructed cabins with a bonfire in the middle. Beyond the housing cabins, Jack could make out cages where he assumed the captured *Feras* were being kept for trade. But he didn't care about any of that. Instead, he kept scanning for the supply sheds, but they were hard to see beyond the rows of cabins.

The pair watched and waited as the band of hunters occupying the village celebrated and drank by the bonfire. From the sounds of excitement, Jack suspected they had a successful hunting day. He suppressed his disgust, they were celebrating capturing *people*.

"Okay, so tell me again why we can't just go in there and act like hunters?" Arianne asked.

Jack rolled his eyes. "Catching slaves is complicated. Stealing slaves from other hunters is easier. Hunting parties are extremely tight-knit groups and are very untrusting of newcomers," he explained. "We walk into that camp and one of two things will happen: they'll shoot us thinking we're rivals or lock us up assuming we're mutants."

Arianne stiffened, "But we're not *Feras*," she muttered.

"Yeah well," Jack sighed. "Hunters are the type to try and sell you anyways, just in case."

They waited until the revelry in the camp died down and the drunken hunters stumbled off to bed. Jack kept an eye on the three hunters who remained awake to keep watch. While they were armed, they were also heavily intoxicated. If he was quiet enough, he was certain that he could get around them easily.

"I'll search right, you search left," Jack ordered before ducking low and running into the dark village on almost silent feet.

Jack had spent his teenage years mastering the art of hiding in the shadows. By fifteen, he'd been an accomplished thief, breaking into Elites' homes and stealing their valuables. Those homes had security. This camp had log cabins. Stealing enough goods to survive the next week or so would be a breeze.

Jack heard the stumbling footsteps of the guard before he saw the man's shadow. With expert grace, he snuck around the side of one of the cabins and crouched low. He waited, controlling his breathing as the guard walked right past him. A grin came to his face. *Piece of cake.*

Beyond the row of housing cabins, Jack spotted a hastily built shed, too small to be a residential structure. Checking to make sure the coast was clear, he jumped out of the shadows, crossed the worn dirt path, and approached the lopsided shed door. Taking one last cautious look, Jack snuck into the shed, quickly closing the door behind him.

He was thankful for the sliver of silver light from the moon as he searched his travel pack for his final match. Soon the small shed was washed in the dim orange glow of a small flame. Jack smiled as he observed his surroundings, he'd found the supply cabin.

Hastily, he began to search the shed. He found a shelf full of canned corn, beef, and green beans first. Jack gladly filled half of his bag with the food, cautious not to let it get too heavy. They still had hiking to do. Next, he came across a tarp and a lighter, both of which he gladly stuffed into his bag. His search was complete when he found rope, a hunting knife, and more matches.

While he knew he might find more if he stuck around and searched, he also knew he shouldn't push his luck. Extinguishing the flame, Jack slowly opened the shed door and sprinted into the cover of the woods. Once he was hidden within the thick undergrowth, he managed a sigh of relief that was rare in his line of work.

Now he just hoped Arianne had found some weapons and ammunition and they could get out of there.

He waited for a few minutes in the calm of the night, listening to the peaceful chirps of crickets. He was almost lulled into believing that he would have an uneventful night. Naturally, his wishes were premature. The bounty hunter winced when he heard sounds of shouting followed by gunfire. He knew instantly, with a hot prick of annoyance, that it wasn't the ammunition Arianne had found.

"Fucking idiot," he cursed, springing into action.

Chapter 25

Arianne

Arianne knew she was about to disobey Jack's very short list of orders, and she also knew it would be far easier to simply do as she was told. However, there were *Feras* in that camp about to be sold into slavery, and there was no way in hell she would simply abandon them.

Even if that meant Jack was going to rip her head off.

Fuck him, he can try.

She waited in the bushes, surveying the walking path in front of her like a predator watching for her prey. A hunter lumbered past, and Arianne sprang into action. He didn't even see her coming as she leaped from the forest on *Fera*-fast feet. She made quick work of the hunter, knocking him out before he had time to react. Her eyes narrowed as she backed away from the man. If she ignored his slight breathing, she could pretend that he was dead. Hell, the hunter deserved to die, but she couldn't bring herself to kill him. Somehow, there was a mental block inside of her that activated whenever she stood on the verge of ending someone else's life. She couldn't describe the feeling, but she wasn't about to figure it out just then. The last place she wanted to go soul-searching was in a forest full of people who wanted her dead.

After stealing the guard's rifle, she continued down the village dirt path toward the cages she had spied on earlier. If she was quiet enough, she could release the *Feras* and still have enough time to look for supplies, as Jack had instructed.

The captured tribespeople were silent as she approached. A deep sadness settled over her when she saw the looks of utter despair on their faces in the darkness. There were four in total, huddled in the corners of their cages in an effort to hold each others' hands for a small ounce of comfort. Arianne's heart stopped when she noticed the smallest of the group.

The little girl couldn't have been older than six.

One of the older *Feras* raised her head when she heard Arianne approach. The female's eyes shone in the darkness, a sign that signified night vision—not every mutant had it, but it was a common trait. Arianne watched as the female's eyes widened in recognition.

Solemnly, the female bobbed her head in recognition.

Arianne ran up to the cages and shook them to test their strength. "I'm going to get you out," she whispered in a tone low enough that only a *Fera's* sensitive ears could hear.

"Get out before they get you too," a male from one of the other cages said in heavily accented English.

"Not an option," Arianne gritted out, scanning the cages for a way inside.

The tribal male shook his head, crossing arms that looked sleek like a reptile's. "Keys are in that cabin," he muttered, realizing Arianne wasn't going to leave.

Arianne turned to the nearest cabin. Lights were still on inside. Whoever had the keys was still awake. She cursed. She had come too far to give up now. She couldn't give up on them, not after seeing their faces.

"Get your friends ready to run," Arianne instructed the male.

In response, the male turned and said a few words to the other three. She could have sworn they were speaking some form of Latin, but that wasn't possible. Latin was a dead language.

Before she had a chance to consider how crazy her plan was, she snuck up to the nearest cabin and peered inside. A man and a woman were seated at a worn wooden table. The woman was already passed out drunk, and the man, with his head slowly slumping over, was not long off. Pulling a rope from her bag, Arianne readied herself.

Adrenaline had her heart racing as she slowly opened the cabin door. At first, she opened it only a fraction of an inch to test the hunters' reactions. She paused as the door made a slight creak, but as she'd hoped, the hunters were too intoxicated and half-asleep to notice. Wincing, she opened the door an inch further. Then another. Then another.

Once the door was just wide enough, she snuck inside. She hissed as the door caught on her back. While her uniform covered her wings enough to pass as a normal human, there was still a sizable increase in her back that made it harder to squeeze through things than she would have liked.

The door shifted, and its hinges groaned in displeasure. The man seated directly in the line of sight of the door opened his heavy eyes. Arianne's stomach flopped. She attacked before he could react. The hunter barked, lurching from his chair and waking the woman. Fortunately, the quick movement had the man's chair sliding out from under him, and he stumbled. It was all she needed. The man hit the ground, and she delivered a swift kick to his temple to knock him out.

But there was still the woman, and Arianne hadn't had the time to knock her out.

Her eardrums cracked as a shotgun fired. Milliseconds later, a sharp pain blossomed in her hip as a bullet grazed her side. Arianne cried out, and for a moment, blackness crowded her vision.

Ignore the pain, something inside her demanded. *Attack now.*

She didn't hesitate to listen to that little voice.

Before her wound had time to slow her down, she jumped at the woman. Arianne was two steps away when the hunter pumped her shotgun. One step. *Bang.* Her breath caught at the sound, but she'd reached the gun in time, her open palm thrusting upwards into the barrel. The bullet careened into the roof. The winged *Fera* winced as her hand began to burn like she'd just placed it on a hot stove, and she realized that the gunfire had turned the metal of the barrel oven-hot.

"Idiot," Arianne hissed inwardly as she squeezed her hand against the terrible sting of burnt flesh. Before the hunter could reload, Arianne swept her right leg low and took her assailant out at the ankles. Once the hunter was on the ground, Arianne wrenched the woman's right arm behind her. There, she pulled until the shoulder was about to dislocate.

"Keys, now," Arianne growled.

"Fuck off," the hunter slurred.

Arianne didn't hesitate as she pulled hard on the woman's arm. She felt a satisfying pop, and the woman screamed out in agony. Her face darkened; she wouldn't kill these people, but that didn't mean she was beyond punishing them. The woman began to whimper, and her sounds of agony were enough to make the pain in Arianne's own wounds disappear.

The winged *Fera's* upper lip curled as she pulled on the wounded shoulder, making the woman retch below her. "Keys, now!"

"Inside the safe!" The hunter cried out. "The code is 0422!"

Once she had the information she needed, she stood and kicked the woman in the temple like she'd done to the man before. Arianne watched in displeasure as the hunter passed out, wishing she could have kept the woman awake longer to feel every ounce of pain that she deserved. But Arianne knew she couldn't keep an active threat conscious, even for her own sick pleasure. She quickly straightened and blinked away the ugly rage that had taken over and made her *desire* someone else's suffering. For a moment, she stood frozen over her work, shocked and horrified at how quickly her mind had gone to such a dark place.

Her hesitation took her out of her battle haze and the pain in her side doubled. She almost threw up. She focused her thoughts on the captives outside, channeling her anger towards moving forward, step by step. She made quick work of the safe, grabbing the keys and running to the door. She realized too late that the gunfire had attracted guests and only had a second to dive to the side as bullets flew toward her head. People were shouting, and more gunfire sounded.

Above the chaos, Arianne heard something different: the sound of a rumbling motor and wheels whirring over mud. She risked a glance around the edge of the cabin she was hiding behind. Bright white lights lit up the night as a jet-black pickup truck barreled toward the hunters. They cried out for the driver to slow down, but the vehicle only sped up, sending them sprawling in different directions as it ran through their small crowd.

Arianne sagged in relief as Jack rolled down the passenger seat window. "In the goddamn truck. Now!" He barked.

"But the captives," Arianne argued.

"Truck," Jack said, his tone uncompromising. "Now."

Arianne's eyes tracked more hunters running down the small dirt road. Their guns popped as their bullets bounced off of the walls of the truck. She nodded to the new group of pursuers snidely. "It looks like you have more people to run over."

And then she ran.

Arianne didn't hear Jack's retort as she sprinted towards the cages. The *Feras* were watching with wide eyes, the youngest two jumping in excitement. Twenty more yards. The pain in her side intensified, and she sucked in a breath. Ten yards. Arianne stumbled, suddenly growing dizzy. Five yards—

She wasn't going to make it.

Arianne tripped and fell on her hands and knees, her freshly burnt palm scraping the dirt. Nausea made her head spin. As a last-ditch resort, she propped herself up and threw the keys the remaining distance.

Arianne barely managed to keep her head from hitting the dirt long enough to see the first *Fera* escape. Once certain she'd done all that she could, her energy left her in one final whoosh. Head spinning, her face dropped forward as exhaustion claimed her.

Chapter 26

Jaya

"We have an escaped captive!" A Ward cried out. "Cell five is missing one of its members!"

Much like Prince Andre, Wards wore black uniforms with red trim and hard metallic masks that could be deployed or deactivated by a structure behind their right ear. At first, seeing the Wards, Jaya had to admit they were impressive: strong, domineering, and professional. But after days of watching them, she knew one thing: they were still human.

And all humans could be tricked.

Rhino played his part well as two Wards raided their cell. The large *Fera* was passive as the first Ward shouted at him to stand against the wall. The second was busy looking around the cell for weaknesses in the bars or places where Jaya could have broken out.

The funny part was Jaya hadn't escaped yet.

There, waiting in the back corner—and embarrassingly naked—she stood. After a couple of days of practice, she had perfected the replication of the texture and color of the cement walls that lined their cell. She knew her disguise wasn't perfect, but that didn't matter. All she needed to do was fool whatever passing Ward came through long enough to make them come inside the cell.

And leave the door open behind them.

Jaya and Rhino locked eyes for a moment, moving on to phase two.

Rhino threw his cuffed hands up as the first Ward began searching him. "Come on, man!" He protested loud enough to get the second Ward's attention. "Even my girlfriend doesn't touch me like that!"

The first Ward scoffed. "Where did your cellmate go?"

A sly grin crossed Rhino's face, "I could have sworn I just saw her a minute ago," he trailed off.

Jaya waited patiently as the first guard patted down Rhino's heavily muscled shoulders. Right as the Ward's face was in kicking range, Rhino moved. Swinging his knee up, he hit the first guard in the nose. The stunned man stumbled back in annoyance, a gloved hand reaching up to check his bleeding nose. Jaya almost laughed. The man should've been thankful Rhino hadn't put any force into the attack.

When both Wards lunged to pin Rhino down, Jaya moved.

Her hands were still bound, but that would be a problem for a later time. Sliding out of the cell, she closed the doors behind her and ran to throw her clothes back on. Rhino was still holding the Wards' attention when she was fully clothed and heading towards the prison block entrance.

Major Lyn, who'd watched the exchange in silence, nodded her head. "Quick recon only," she instructed. "Figure out where Kalinda and the President are being kept. We can't leave without them."

"You got it," Jaya nodded.

Jaya's eyes quickly moved to Captain Cadmilus. Haris's father hadn't shifted from his corner of the cell. The Captain's head was still bowed low. Even at the chance of Jaya finding a way out, he hadn't moved. Losing most of his party had shaken the him to his core.

Major Lyn noticed her hesitation. "Don't worry about him!" She ordered. "The best way to get morale back is to find Caesar."

"Right," Jaya managed, turning to run out of the cell block.

Rhino was still wrestling with the Wards when the door leading out of the prison block closed behind her. A Ward was waiting outside. The woman called out in surprise, a hand going to her right ear to raise her mask back over her face. Jaya had expected the third Ward, and she didn't slow as the woman raised her gun.

Taking advantage of her *Fera* speed, Jaya closed the distance between herself and the Ward in a near fraction of a second. The Ward didn't get a chance to fire. Jaya ducked under the gun, stepped behind the woman, and used the binding, solid stream of blue light between her cuffs to choke her. Jaya braced, her biceps straining as the Ward struggled, fighting for breath. She passed out a few moments later, and Jaya carefully lowered her to the ground.

Killing the Ward might have been easier, but Jaya wanted to avoid as much punishment as possible in the very likely event she got captured.

Frisking the Ward's utility belt, Jaya found the card she'd seen Pandora use to take off Kalinda's handcuffs. Swiping the card over the metal sensor on her left wrist, the blue light connecting the cuffs faded. The Chameleon let out a breath as she rolled her shoulders, basking in her newly granted range of motion. Next, she stole the Ward's uniform. Seeing as she was trapped behind enemy lines, she didn't have the mental capacity to care about modesty.

Jaya stood in the black suit, slowly getting used to the fabric. The thick polyester armor in front of her chest, over her shoulders, and around her legs was surprisingly flexible. She patted her body down, looking for weak points, extra supplies, and—there! She pulled out a key card and swiped it across the next door. To her satisfaction, they opened to the outside hallway.

Willing her hair into a forgettable shade of brown, Jaya crept out into the corridor beyond. She frowned at the sight around her. For a building so grand, the Commander hadn't wasted much time decorating. The hallways were a crisp white, with light emanating from the floor rather than the ceiling above. Jaya looked around her, hoping to find any indication of what floor she was on and how far away the exit was.

A small part of her wanted to take the freedom she'd gained and run from that building as fast as she could. But the intrusive thought disappeared as quickly as it came. She couldn't leave her squad or her sister. Besides, she knew she was working on limited time. If she ran, she wouldn't make it far.

Jaya continued down the hallway, finding an elevator just barely outlined against the seamless walls. Cautiously scanning her key card, a map of the building appeared in front of the door. She did her best to memorize the blueprint: they were on the first basement level, and the Murray private quarters were on the top two floors. There were almost one hundred floors between herself and the Murray penthouse. Another floor caught her eye, an unmarked level right below her.

Jaya heard footsteps approaching. She tensed, aware she was running out of time to do research. She frantically scanned the map until she found a floor listed as *Medical Bay*, selected the option, and ducked inside.

Blood pounded in her ears as the elevator slowly ticked upward. What would she do if Kalinda or Caesar weren't there? What would she do if they were dead? She quickly shook her head, pushing the awful thoughts away. She needed to focus.

The elevator slowed, and she clenched her teeth, preparing for whatever was waiting on the other side. The doors opened, and beyond was a small hospital. Doctors and nurses in scrubs walked past, paying her no mind. Jaya had to force her skin to stay a regular human shade as the stress inside of her built. Too much was going on in front of her, making her exposed and uncertain.

"Jay?" Kalinda hissed.

Jaya looked to her side, relief rolling off of her in waves at the sight of her beautiful sister. Kalinda was almost unrecognizable in Pangaean scrubs. She would have passed for another nurse if it wasn't for the black control collar strapped around her neck.

Kalinda pulled Jaya towards a hospital bed and closed the curtains behind them.

"You're alive," she gasped, pulling her into a tight hug. "You're alive," she repeated, her voice heavy with relief.

Jaya breathed in Kalinda's familiar scent of sandalwood and orange, melting into her sister's arms. For those fleeting moments, everything seemed okay. Tears threatened to come to her eyes. As long as she had Kalinda, everything was always okay.

"What are you doing here?" Kalinda demanded, her relief quickly turning into protective worry. "You shouldn't be here!"

Jaya nodded, taking a step away from her sister to compose herself. "I snuck out," she admitted. "I needed to know you and Caesar were okay."

Kalinda snuck a quick glance from behind the curtains. "You should've run," she scolded her sister.

The Chameleon reached for Kalinda's wrists. "Not without you," she frowned. "Not without everyone else."

The field medic stole another quick hug from her sister before opening the curtains slightly to point at a hospital bed a few rows down. There, Jaya recognized Caesar, who was still sleeping.

Jaya's lips parted. "Has he woken up?" she asked breathlessly.

"Yes, but only briefly," Kalinda's face darkened. "He lost a lot of blood, Jay. We didn't know if he was going to make it for a while."

Jaya's feet carried her out from behind the curtains. She went to sit by Caesar, a hand cautiously going to wrap around his. His skin was cold and clammy, giving him a ghostly pallor. She frowned. The man at her side was a far cry from the warm presence that used to envelop her in hugs whenever she came over to visit.

Her heart lurched as she realized that Caesar was the closest thing she ever had to a father in Pacific.

No wonder she had risked everything to come to this floor. Her family was up here, and she could never abandon her family.

"Does he know that he's here?" Jaya asked softly, her thumb faintly brushing against Caesar's rich brown skin.

Kalinda shook her head. "He wasn't awake for long," she admitted. "And if we want him to get better, we need to eliminate as much stress as possible."

Jaya followed her sister's gaze to Caesar's right leg. Or, rather, the space where his right leg should have been. She recognized the outline of his left leg underneath his blanket, but the sheet settled flatly on the mattress on Caesar's right side. Her stomach flopped. His right leg was gone from the hip down.

"H-his leg," Jaya stuttered in horror.

Kalinda's jaw ticked as she clenched her teeth. "The femur was shattered, and the exit wound was too large to close up," she admitted. "Prosthetics have advanced to the point in Pangaea where it makes more sense to amputate. He stands a better chance at surviving and walking again that way."

Jaya mourned Caesar's lost leg. When her president woke up, he would be a prisoner behind enemy lines with an integral part of his own freedom missing. She knew they would all most likely be dead in a few weeks, but seeing someone she cared about lose something so personal struck home harder than she thought.

When was Pangaea ever going to stop taking from them?

Kalinda steadied her younger sister with a soft hand on her lower back. "Jay, you need to get out of here," she warned.

"I know," Jaya sighed, hating the idea of leaving her sister to the unknown once more.

"You two are just adorable," someone hissed from behind the sisters.

From the way Kalinda's face drained of color, Jaya knew that she was in trouble. She didn't hesitate. Without even a breath to prepare, Jaya jumped up from her seat and ran.

Something razor sharp and pointed embedded itself deep into the back of her leg. Jaya shouted as her hamstring seized up. Pain shot like electricity up her leg until she suddenly couldn't bear to put weight down on it. The sudden loss of mobility stunned her, and she tripped onto the sterile white hospital floor.

Through a wince, Jaya saw Blue lunge towards her. She gasped and forced her injured leg to move at the last moment and push herself out of the Snake's path. Blue's yellow eyes flashed as she drew another ninja star, twin to the one in Jaya's leg. Jaya forced herself to her feet, and her eyes landed on a medical dolly. Fumbling, she reached for the cart and started to search for anything she could use as a weapon. She gritted her teeth when the only tool of any use to her was a scalpel.

Nurses and doctors screamed. Some of the braver medical professionals moved to get their patients away from the fight. Blue Krait smiled, and Jaya caught a glimpse of her fangs dripping with venom. Venom meant for her. Before the Snake could throw her second star, Jaya sprung forward and took the offensive. Blue bent backward underneath Jaya's lunging attack. For a moment, the Pacifican was frozen mid-swing. Blue had flawlessly vaulted away from her on impossibly flexible limbs.

While Blue was still moving backward, Jaya attempted another attack. Her plans were effortlessly thwarted again by Blue's flexibility. Jaya's momentum threw her forward, but she caught herself quickly enough to steady herself. She put her arms up in defense but, to her surprise, Blue wasn't initiating another attack. Instead, the Snake was analyzing her, a grin coming to her navy blue painted lips.

"What?" Jaya snarled, palming her scalpel.

Blue Krait smirked. "You're pretty slow for a *Fera*."

"Excuse me?" Jaya gaped.

The Snake shrugged. "It's what happens when you're domesticated. Can't expect much from a mutant who thinks she's a human."

The Chameleon's jaw dropped open at the insult, "I know exactly who I am," she replied a little too defensively.

Blue sidestepped Jaya's attack like she was dodging a ten-year-old in karate class. "I don't know, it seems like you forgot you were my prisoner."

Jaya shook her head in confusion, "but you're trapped here too?"

Something changed in Blue's eyes. The entertainment the Snake once had in the fight faded, replaced with glacial contempt. Jaya neared Blue, but that time the enslaved *Fera* didn't hold back. One moment, the Pacifican was swinging for the Snake's throat, and the next, she was on the ground, the air drained from her lungs thanks to a well-placed kick to her chest.

As Jaya lay gasping for air, Blue approached slowly like a predator closing in on their dying prey. The Snake's navy blue upper lip curled in a scowl as she planted a heeled leather boot on top of her chest. "I never forget what I am to them," she hissed, her slit pupils so thin that it looked like her eyes were made of pure yellow.

"Then leave," Jaya wheezed as her body began to tingle from the wound in her leg.

The Snake tapped a black-painted fingernail on the black collar, similar to Kalinda's, wrapped around her neck. "Even if I didn't have this—" Her angular face dropped. "No, you wouldn't understand.

"Help us," Jaya tried, "and we can help you."

Blue's eyes clouded for a moment. Her pause was almost long enough to make Jaya believe she was genuinely considering her offer. But clarity, and damning resolve, snapped the Snake out of her confusion and she pressed down harder on Jaya's chest with her foot. "It's not that simple," she replied. "Now, we're going back to your cell. You're lucky Pandora didn't find you first."

Jaya blinked. "That's it? No punishment?"

Blue Krait eyed Jaya. "I don't enjoy hurting fellow *Feras*," she said. "But next time I won't have a choice. Stay in your cell unless you want to give Pandora an excuse to have a field day with you." The Snake shivered. "And one *Fera* to another: don't use your abilities again. You don't want to end up in Hera's lab."

"Hera?" Jaya's stomach dropped, recognizing the name of the matriarch of the Richards family. "W-what would she do?"

Blue grinned. "That venom should be kicking in any moment now."

Jaya realized in horror that the tingling she felt wasn't simply from the ninja star lodged in her leg. Her symptoms were from what had been *coated* on the star. Her body started to shake as blue krait venom seeped into her nervous system. Even with her increased metabolism, Jaya couldn't fight venom from pulling her down, down, down. Fear gripped her bones as she recognized the awful pull to unconsciousness.

"W-wait!" Jaya protested even as her body slowly prepared to shut down. "What do you mean about Hera's lab?"

"Goodnight, little Chameleon," Blue waved, yellow eyes sparkling in a mischievous light. "I don't envy the headache you're going to have when you wake up."

Chapter 27

Arianne

Arianne woke up to the sound of singing.

The voice was soft and careful, like it was afraid to be heard, yet enchanting and smooth. For a moment, she almost believed she was hearing an angel's call, summoning her to the afterlife.

Arianne's eyes fluttered as she slowly woke. She was deep within the forest, the smell of rain-soaked leaves filling her nose. Then, the events leading up to her eventual unconsciousness came back to her. The hunters' village, her side tearing and bleeding as she ran against the sickly pain of the bullet wound towards the *Feras*. The *Feras!* Were they alive? Were they safe?

She jumped up, a gasp of pain escaping her as her injured side screamed in protest. Then she looked around, trying her best to piece together why she was no longer bleeding out in that village. Her heaving breaths slowed as she took in the massive olive green tarp above her head attached to the trunk of a black pickup truck and a nearby tree. She was resting on the grassy ground, a tasseled blanket the only indication her resting spot was meant to be a bed.

She glanced at her burnt hand, now carefully wrapped in woven white cloth. She froze when she realized a bandage was wrapped around her midsection. Whoever treated her had seen her wings.

The singing stopped.

"Relax, I didn't touch you," Jack's familiar annoyance had an oddly soothing effect on her.

The truck shook as Jack jumped down from his perch on the roof. Arianne watched his shadow near as he climbed down from the trunk and ducked underneath the tarp's canopy. Jack's chestnut brown hair was damp with water droplets, and she realized a soft rain was falling outside.

"The captives," Arianne asked breathlessly.

Jack rolled his eyes as he sat down on the dry grass beneath the makeshift tent. "They're safe," he reassured her, pointing through the trees to a barely visible camp. "Good thing, too," he added, "I don't treat stupid."

Arianne curled her upper lip at Jack. "Why aren't we in the camp? Did they already realize how insufferable you are?"

Jack grumbled as he stood back up. "How about a thank you for saving your life?" He pressed, "And no—we're not staying there. The last thing we need is to be in the heart of a savage camp when they realize we killed some of their own. For all we know, they could be the same tribe."

"*You* killed those tribespeople," Arianne corrected. She hated it when he called them savages.

His grin was insufferable. "*They* won't make that distinction."

Arianne glanced away from the bounty hunter, regretting the feeling of relief she'd felt in his presence just moments before. She really was in tough shape if he was the person she felt safest around. That considered, why had he gone through the trouble of saving her? She risked a quick glance back at him.

Jack must have noticed her assessing glare. "You're worth more to me alive than dead, Princess. Don't think it's more than it is."

"You're a real charmer," Arianne grumbled.

"What?" Jack pressed.

She turned, her temper rising. "You heard me," she shot back. "You're an asshole."

Jack raised an eyebrow, his entertainment at her frustration making her impossibly more annoyed. "You're going to have to be more creative with the insults to get the reaction out of me you're so desperately searching for."

Arianne's nostrils flared. She was tired, she was injured, and she was stuck with that apathetic asshole who insisted on reminding her at every turn how little he cared. For a fleeting moment, she imagined he actually felt something beyond indifference around her—only to be blissfully reminded the infamous Blackjack didn't care about anyone but himself.

Despite her burns, Arianne's fist balled up at the warning signs of conflict. "And what reaction am I begging for?"

Jack bared his teeth. "You want a fight," he seethed. "Look at you. Do you know how to do anything beyond pissing people off?"

The possibility excited Arianne. She wanted nothing more than to tackle the man sitting in front of her and wipe every inch of that scowl off of his face. Her rage was icy cold, "what happened to you to make you so awful to be around?"

The bounty hunter smiled, but it was far from a pretty sight. The look was dripping with bile and poison and every nasty thing in between. With that one flash of teeth, Arianne got a glimpse of the rot Pangaea had left inside of him to fester. She wondered how long it had been since he'd stopped fighting it and let it metastasize. Was it too late? Could anyone cut out all of that hatred? Or was it just a toxic wall erected to scare everyone off before they found a way inside? She analyzed the bounty hunter harder, hoping to see a glimpse of the truth, but even she couldn't read minds.

She'd have to pull the truth out of him.

"Who says I want people around me?" Jack asked.

There. Arianne sensed the weight of the question. He was probing her—analyzing to see how much she suspected. If she was right and there was someone else hiding underneath, all she needed to do was keep pushing. If Jack really didn't care, her prodding would be little more than an annoyance he would ignore.

But if something was underneath, she would eventually hit a pressure point. Much like Arianne liked to do when her insecurities were in danger, Jack would go nuclear. In that second, she prepared for the eventuality that he would go for her emotional jugular. She wasn't sure if she was ready, but if they wanted a chance at surviving, she needed to know if she was traveling with the demon Blackjack made the world believe he was or if there was a chance she could pull out someone else underneath.

Arianne grinned, "you're right. I piss people off because I got a lot of shit I haven't figured out," she admitted. "Something tells me you're the same."

Jack's amber eyes narrowed, "don't go roping me in with your bullshit," he warned.

"What bullshit?" Arianne pressed, "The bullshit where you make it your mission to make sure everyone knows you're the biggest asshole in the room? The bullshit where *good people* offered you a new home and a new life, and you fucking sold them like livestock?" She wasn't prepared for the real anger she felt at admitting that all out loud. "My fucking family!" She exploded, her voice rising with every word, "you sold my goddamn fucking family!"

"Oh boo-hoo," Jack mocked, making anger blaze in Arianne's stomach, "you act like you're the first person in the world to lose your family. Get the fuck in line."

Arianne stood up and held her hands out, welcoming the conflict. "You want to have a childhood trauma competition? I'll take you any day in that category, so you better back the fuck down. And from my personal experience, I know all of this is an act to protect the injured little boy hiding underneath. A boy too caught up in what Pangaea has taken from him to recognize when people want to help."

Jack did the opposite of back down. The bounty hunter stood and glared down at Arianne in defiance. "Thanks for the psychology lesson," he growled as the air cracked with tension. "How about we do you next?"

Ire sparked in Arianne's eyes, "Oh, I'm dying to hear what you got," she rumbled, and the temperature in the tent seemingly dropped ten degrees.

There it was—Arianne could see Jack's hands hovering over the trigger. The fire blazing in his molten eyes told her he was ready to go nuclear. Curiosity aside, she was so furious with the man that she hoped he would finally set off the explosion that had been building between them for weeks. Jack jabbed a finger at Arianne's sternum, making her anger burn even brighter. He was close enough that she could see the emerald specks in his irises. He was also close enough to punch, but she held back on the impulsive thought.

"You're a fuckup," Jack whispered the words, knowing how much they would hurt her. "You don't belong," he continued, his haunting smile growing in awful excitement. "Everything you do is a mistake, and you hurt everyone around you because of it."

The air around them disappeared. Arianne felt like time was slowed to a halt. The rustling of the trees faded, and her lungs refused to take in air. "You're a fuckup," Arianne started to sway as those words reverberated in her head.

Her father used to say something similar.

"*You're a mistake,*" Leon would growl down at her. "*You never should have happened. Murrays are Commanders! Not creatures like you.*"

A tear fell down her cheek before she could stop it. Arianne didn't break Jack's gaze as she furiously wiped the traitorous drop away. Her lips trembled. "At least I don't ruin lives because I'm miserable," she murmured.

Jack didn't get a chance to retort before Arianne was too overwhelmed to stay in that tent. She suddenly felt awfully claustrophobic. She pushed past the tarp canopy, feeling the pressure in her chest lift once she reached the open air. She would have run if she weren't terrified of reopening her stitches. Instead, she had to settle for a brisk walk.

Unfortunately, walking didn't have the same dramatic effect as running.

Arianne ensured she was out of Jack's earshot before she let the sobs take over. She felt hopeless and so utterly alone. Jack was right, she was a fuckup. If she hadn't arrived late, Caesar and her friends wouldn't have been captured. If she had just listened to Jack, she wouldn't have been wounded and slowing them down. Just with recent events considered, Jack's words rang true.

And that didn't include the years before.

Now, she was in the middle of the Darwin Zone with a man who couldn't even stand to be around her, looking for a hidden city built to be impossible to find. She was tired, lost, and hopelessly out of her depth. Caesar was right, Jack was right, everyone was right. Arianne wasn't ready for any of it.

Through her tear-soaked vision, she waded in distress through the trees until she heard the promising babbling of a river lodged into a small ravine up ahead. She stumbled towards the rippling waters, her body craving the feeling of being immersed under the surface. Slowly, she pulled off her boots and military khakis. Her head swiveled, checking for onlookers before she revealed her exposed back. Arianne removed the last of her clothing and bandages caked in clotted blood before quickly diving beneath the surface.

Relief washed over her like the current as her body touched the cooling waters. She let herself sink into the brown sediment of the riverbed, her gills opening and bringing a new rush of oxygen through her bloodstream. Slowly, her head cleared.

The water was cold, but the chill running up her spine quickly cooled her anger and distress and replaced it with calming satisfaction. In the underwater gloom, Arianne let herself spread her wings wide. Pins and needles shot to the tips of her wings, but she stretched wider, bringing pure euphoria. The sensation of the long-needed freedom of her wings was enough to clear her mind from Jack's awful words and her own despair.

She sighed, or whatever the equivalent of a sigh was with gills. Stretching her wings out while suspended in the water felt as relieving as a warm cup of tea after a cold day of surfing. So close to Leonueva's airspace, she hadn't dared risk a flight while Jack was sleeping, and she certainly wasn't going to risk letting her wings out during the day. But under the water, Arianne had a rare chance to be herself.

Whatever needle-thin truce Jack and Arianne had would be thrown out the window if he knew that she was a mutant. She closed her eyes in frustration. It didn't matter if Jack claimed he wasn't a part of the slave trade—she knew how intimately connected he was with his boss. And that connection meant Jack was trained to have a particular distaste for mutants.

Arianne didn't know how long she lingered in that river. Slowly, the awful thoughts faded until she was left with blissful emptiness. The sensation was amazing, and she could have remained in that river for the rest of her life. Unfortunately, she knew she needed to face reality at some point. She eventually worked up the will to pull herself from the water. Before revealing more than her head, she cautiously watched the shore to make certain no one was watching. Once positive she was alone, she climbed to the surface and changed into her dry clothes.

Squeezing her wings to her back once more was a struggle. Arianne knew it would be hours before her back dried off. The feeling wasn't the best, but she'd grown used to the discomfort over the years. Over time, she equated the sensation to that of letting soaking wet hair rest on a dry shirt: annoying but tolerable. Maybe, at some point, she could sneak out of camp again to let them dry.

Jack was lounging by the truck when Arianne returned. His eyes were closed, and he had his strange headphones placed in his ears. The bounty hunter looked almost peaceful as he hummed and tapped his feet, most likely listening to some form of music. She didn't know much about the headphones except that Jack used them to block her out. Wordlessly, she plopped down on her blankets and tried to forget about her soaking wet back.

Jack's amber eyes opened. Even with the music blaring in his ears, he was intimately aware of his surroundings. Arianne didn't blame him—if she'd grown up in an organization like Cartel, her spatial awareness would be like a sixth sense, too.

"You're back," he murmured, removing his headphones from his ears.

Arianne was too emotionally exhausted to start another fight. "Don't have anywhere else to go." Her head slumped.

A painful silence settled between the pair. Jack's words hurt her more than he would ever know, but she wasn't going to waste her time trying to catch him up on that.

"The only reason I called you a fuckup was because I'm a fuckup too," Jack sighed.

Arianne blinked in shock. She waited for more. She waited for another sarcastic quip or deprecating comment—none came. The winged female looked over at her reluctant companion, lips parting in surprise when she noticed genuine sincerity in his eyes.

Maybe her nuclear plan had worked. Maybe she'd succeeded in pulling out the man hiding underneath. Granted, she was still too pissed at him to be excited at the prospect. Coping mechanisms or not, Jack'd still done some despicable things.

His admission that he was a fuckup didn't change that he did, in fact, fuck up. Multiple times.

Jack looked up at the tarp above him as if he could see the rain-cloud sky. "Look at me," he continued weakly, "twenty-three years old, and I've already thrown my life away. I'm wanted in every region of Europe, I'm utterly alone," his jaw ticked, "and owned like a slave."

Arianne's eyes went to the ace of spades tattoo on his inner wrist once more. No, Jack wasn't just indebted—Ace branded his very skin. A claim over his entire life. Arianne's back began to ache as though she could feel each individual scar her father had given her. Like Jack's brand, those scars were Leon's way of claiming ownership over her.

Was Arianne really that different from Jack?

"I understand," Arianne whispered.

Jack tilted his head in confusion. "*You*? Understand?" He looked down, the waves of his hair shadowing his face, "No, I don't think you do."

Arianne swallowed hard. She was walking on fragile territory, but their fight from earlier had drained her of all the angry energy she had. What was left were just words and a hope that maybe they could exist in some form of mutual peace.

Arianne never liked to talk about her past life in Pangaea, but somehow, with Jack, it felt right. For once, she felt like she was talking to someone who'd lived with similar pain and understood the beast that it was instead of only feeling bad for her.

"My father—the one back in Pangaea—thought he owned me too," she admitted slowly. "Eleven years ago, I escaped and found Pacific." Arianne's hands clenched tightly, "I never left the island because they were trying to protect me—not because I was spoiled."

Jack nodded slowly, "And I called you naïve," he frowned.

Arianne sighed deeply, "You're not wrong," the admission was painful, "but you're still an asshole." The words weren't charged like they once were. She even felt a smile tug at her lips.

"All right," Jack held up his hands in defeat, "let's be fuckups together then. We can call it even."

Arianne blinked in surprise. Was that a smile? She searched for words to respond, but failed. Arianne knew Jack had always been *conventionally* attractive, but that smile... for some reason, she couldn't think straight. Dimples, he had dimples. She froze. Those dimples mixed with those distracting lips made an utterly devastating image. It took all of her willpower to pull her gaze away.

He betrayed your friends. Arianne reminded herself. *He betrayed your dad! A cute smile will not be your breaking point. You were raised better than this.*

"We'll call it even then," Arianne grumbled.

Jack stood up, and he walked over to her carrying a bowl smelling strongly of herbs. Cautiously, he extended it to her. "Here, I made this while you were out. It should help with the pain in your hand and hip. I can make more tomorrow."

Arianne paused, examining the bowl, "You made this?" She questioned in disbelief.

Jack shrugged. "My grandfather was the healer in my hometown. He taught me a few things when I was a kid."

Arianne looked at the bowl again. In astonishment, she realized the salve was his olive branch—a way to offer a truce. She didn't blame him, she admittedly struggled with apologies as well. Stunned, Arianne managed a nod before accepting the bowl. She unwrapped her hand first. The burned and blistering skin of her palm was tender as she applied the herbal medicine. She hissed as the pressure on her palm started to sting but soon sighed in relief as the salve began to cool the burning flesh.

"I guess I didn't poison you then," Jack chuckled. "Damn it, I must have used the wrong recipe."

Arianne gaped and shoved him softly. "Prick," she hissed. Then a laugh escaped her lips as Jack fell over as easily as a stack of books. "Was that a joke coming from the infamous Blackjack?" She asked.

Jack, still on his side, managed a shrug, "I guess it was. How'd it go? I'm kind of out of practice."

Arianne analyzed the bounty hunter with a smirk. When he lightened up, he wasn't the worst person to exist around. But she wasn't going to let him off so easily—not yet, at least. Arianne pursed her lips, pretending to think, "Pretty terrible, but you have potential."

Jack gave her a thumbs up from the ground, "I'll take it."

Arianne looked down at her hip as if she could see the wound buried under her clothes and bandages. She winced as she realized her stupidity had cost them a few days as she waited for her wounds to mend. The female frowned. "I guess it can't hurt to be nicer to each other," she began slowly. "You know, so we're not miserable for the next week we're forced to be together."

Jack sat back up. "You know? That's the smartest thing you've said, Princess."

Arianne extended her hand, "All right, Pangaea Boy." She grinned. "For the next seven days, we don't try to kill each other. Got it?"

Jack reached forward and shook her hand. "Desperate times call for desperate measures," he replied.

"My thoughts exactly," Arianne agreed.

Chapter 28

Blackjack

By the following day, Arianne's wounds had closed enough for her to travel again. Jack decided to leave the truck behind for the tribe to deal with when they finally packed up to leave. While the idea of traveling with the truck enticed him, it couldn't offer them enough of an advantage. The terrain was too overgrown for a motor vehicle, and he didn't want to risk making too much noise. Even if they had opted to drive on the road, there was no guarantee that he could find Leonueva while traveling down the Artery. To make matters worse, the Artery had security checks—neither he nor Arianne would pass any of those.

So, traveling by foot, it was.

Their conversation from the night before weighed on him while they hiked. He tried to turn up the volume of his music to drown out his thoughts, but the emotions brought by the powerful guitar, thundering drums, and moving vocals only made him think even more.

Usually, blasting the old genre of rock and roll protected Jack from his emotions and memories. Now, his beloved music was betraying him, bringing his painful emotions back to the surface. A sigh escaped him. When did it all go so wrong?

Jack found himself asking that question more and more throughout the day. And the more he thought about it, the harder it became to pinpoint the event that sent him down his spiraling path to hell. Was it when his hometown was destroyed? Maybe it was when he finally decided to work for Ace. But neither of those answers seemed right.

Maybe it wasn't one fateful event but a succession of incidents, each one dooming him to his fate more and more.

Jack didn't want to be like that. He wanted to be happy. That word was foreign to him: happy. The idea of such a feeling was fading faster than his sister's face in his memory. His sister. His family. Jack frowned. He'd been happy once. Once upon a time, he'd had everything he could have ever wanted. Honestly, it made perfect sense he found a way to lose all of that and end up where he was. Hopeless—that's what he was.

A warm memory surfaced, one of those fleeting thoughts Jack refused to let himself have. He didn't deserve those memories anymore. He turned up his music to deafening levels in an effort to push the recollection away. Unfortunately, it came all the same.

To make matters worse, the movie that played in his head almost forced a smile onto his face.

The rock ballad slowed, and a powerful verse began to play. Just like that, Jack was sitting next to his mother at their family piano in his former living room. He couldn't remember his mother's face anymore, but the one thing he never could forget was her beautiful voice. His mother sang an enchanting melody as his much smaller hands expertly played the piano beside her. Behind them, a toddler with a mess of fiery red curls danced on the carpet.

Happy... I was so happy...

Jack's thoughts betrayed him as he stole a glance at Arianne behind him. His stomach twisted. He could be happy again. If he finished this mission, if he sold Arianne to Ace, he could have his freedom. He could run away.

He could find what was left of his family.

Jack clenched his teeth. Just days ago, there hadn't been a question in his head. He would sell the Pacifican squad and Arianne to Ace, and he would be debt-free. But it wasn't that simple anymore. Was it?

Jack was so distracted he almost tripped over a root.

Hands gripped his shoulders and steadied him before he rolled an ankle. Jack turned to Arianne in shock, and she offered him a soft smile, "We can't have more injuries slowing us down now, can we?"

He was distracted by the way Arianne's gray eyes seemed to turn green in the shade of the forest. For a moment, words escaped him as he stared at the woman, hating himself for even entertaining the idea of selling her. Sure, she was loud and didn't have a self-preserving bone in her body, but he didn't hate her. The realization shocked him. How long had it been since he felt anything outside of indifference about someone?

"I don't think you're allowed to dictate the injury budget," Jack managed, glancing at Arianne's hip.

She quickly let go of his shoulders, "Am I allowed to dictate break time? Good lord, it's hot out today."

Jack wiped a bead of sweat from his brow. He had been so focused on his own inner turmoil that he managed to block out everything else outside of hiking the next few miles. He took a deep breath, realizing how awfully thick the air was with humidity. The midday heat had come with little remorse, and even the canopy of the trees couldn't protect them from the suffocating heat.

"I think a break would be a good idea," he admitted, pointing through the trees, "there's a river up ahead."

Arianne and Jack hiked down a ridge formed by the rushing water cutting through the valley. At the bottom lay a river pooling into a small pond before a waterfall that cascaded down the rocky slopes of the mountain. The pond was clear, thanks to the rocky riverbed and shore. Jack's knees weakened at the thought of how amazing the crystalline waters would feel.

Arianne quickly unlaced her boots and rolled up her khakis. The Pacifican let out an audible sigh of relief as she let herself wade knee-deep into the water. Jack didn't hesitate to join her. The rippling pond reminded him of how hot he was, and he couldn't resist a smile as he splashed some water on his face.

"Oh look, Pangaea Boy is smiling," Arianne chided, "it must be the end of the world."

Without warning, Jack sent a wave crashing towards her. Water cascaded down on Arianne, soaking her shirt and turning her dirty blonde hair a dark brown. He couldn't stop a laugh from bubbling up inside of him at the look of utter shock on her dripping face. He blinked when he realized her soaked shirt outlined every curve on the front of her body. He couldn't look away as his eyes scanned down the curves of her breasts and toned stomach.

Jack was shaken from his trance as a wall of water cascaded down on him. He attempted to put his hands up at the last second, but it was too late. He was soaked to the bone. He turned to Arianne—betrayed—and realized she was laughing. And not just a simple laugh, but full-body shaking cackles.

Arianne's eyes were closed, her mouth wide as she pointed at Jack in delight, "That was the most satisfying thing I've done all day!" She cried out, "You should see your face! Oh, how the mighty Blackjack has fallen!"

Jack should have been annoyed. But he wasn't. Watching Arianne laugh and smile brought a lightness to his chest that he hadn't felt in a long time. He stood frozen in time as he watched the woman double over with laughter. She was drenched, her hair caked to her neck, and whatever wheezes were coming from her chest were far from pretty. But Jack suddenly couldn't stop thinking about what those peach-colored lips tasted like.

The desire hit him before he could stop the bullet train of emotion. He was hardly in control of himself as he quickly closed the distance between them. Something changed on Arianne's face, and lightning seemed to crack as Jack closed the last few feet of space. Then Arianne was in front of him, her breasts brushing against his chest and sending his head spinning.

"Princess, am I mistaken, or are you actually having fun?"

"Don't call me Princess," Arianne sighed, but all the fight in her voice was gone.

Arianne tilted her chin up towards Jack as her storm gray eyes closed. Jack's heart thundered through his veins, delivering blood that should have been in his brain somewhere *else*. She leaned into him, the touch sending a jolt through his body. That jolt also brought back a momentary sense of awareness.

What are you doing? Something shouted from the back of his mind.

Jack's eyes shot open. Without hesitation, he gripped Arianne's shoulders and threw her sideways into the water. He used his vital few moments before all hell broke loose to move out of swinging range.

"Fucking asshole!" Arianne bellowed as she erupted from the river. She would have been terrifying had her hair not covered most of her face.

Jack grinned, falling back on half-amused boredom to keep him composed, "Lesson twenty-two of survival," he chuckled, "*no distractions.*"

Steam practically billowed from Arianne's ears, "Oh, I'll teach you a god-damned lesson!"

Jack sidestepped her attack, lunging to get out of the water before she could pull him under as well. Despite himself, he was laughing maniacally. When was the last time he had this much fun? Jack ran out of the water and onto the shore, breathing heavily as he finally saved himself from Arianne's attack. As the excitement faded, white-hot mortification settled over him. He'd lost control. He almost got *attached* to his mission.

Jack shook his head to bring back clarity to his thoughts.

He quickly tied on his boots and strapped his bag to his back. He called out to Arianne, saying he would scout ahead for a camp. The rainclouds he saw coming in over the river looked ominous. Most of all, he needed some alone time to clear his head.

After years of Ace ingraining survival instincts into his very senses, was he really going to let some woman take that all away? No, he needed to focus. He needed to get his freedom by any means necessary, which meant he needed to recalibrate his priorities.

What was one more bad deed?

At least I don't ruin other people's lives just because I'm miserable, Arianne's cutting words came back to him. Jack's breathing hitched. Was he really just going to prove her right in the end? He clenched his jaw and continued to walk. Was it really that simple?

If Jack never bought his freedom, the cycle would perpetuate. If not Arianne, then someone else. More lives would be taken, more families would be separated, and more people would be sold. With that perspective, wouldn't it make more sense to simply trade Arianne in?

The small part of him that still had a fraction of a conscience recoiled. He knew her. That made things different, and he knew it.

Jack's hands rose to his head, digging his nails stressfully into his skull. What about his home? What about the people he left behind? Was anyone still left? With his freedom, he could start piecing back the shattered remnants of his past.

"Genevieve," Jack whispered his sister's name like a prayer.

It had been months—maybe even years—since he'd let himself mutter her name. Genevieve. His younger sister, whom he promised to protect. A promise he shattered almost a decade ago.

"Did I miss the memo for a brooding session?" Arianne pressed, pushing her way through the undergrowth to join him.

Jack frowned, more confused than ever. He looked around him and pointed to an outcropping of rocks leading to the mountain they needed to transverse tomorrow. If storms weren't coming in, he would have recommended that they reach the other side by nightfall, but even he didn't think he was immortal when it came to lightning.

"I'm thinking that we hang the tarps here," Jack pointed as the prophesied rumblings of thunder came in the distance. "We should get some firewood and food ready before the storm hits."

Arianne nodded, but she struggled to meet his eyes. At least he wasn't the only one overthinking earlier. That gave him an ounce of relief.

The two of them didn't speak as they divided tasks. Arianne set up camp, hanging their tarps over the rocks and clearing the space underneath of excess brush. Jack took off into the woods, hunting for firewood and tinder as the skies above him darkened. He made it back to the safety of their makeshift tent as the first flash of lightning hit the sky.

Jack didn't start a fire. They had plenty of canned food and heat from the humidity to last the night without a blaze. But, he had collected the wood anyway, just in case the storms cooled down the night enough where a fire could be helpful in warming their rain-chilled bones. The wind picked up outside, and the tarp began to flap above them. For a moment, he was worried the tree-rocking gusts might carry their protective roof away from them. But as he examined the expert knots Arianne had tied to secure the tarps, his worry faded.

Arianne grew more competent with forest survival with each passing day. He allowed a short moment of impressed recognition. Then—realizing where his mind was going—he quickly reached to his side and grabbed a piece of wood to whittle and distract himself.

The rain started its rapid patter, accompanied by the deep rumblings of thunder. As it intensified, the forest filled with the lovely smell of petrichor. Arianne, lying on her blankets across from Jack, was slowly lulled to sleep by the calming sounds of the storm. Alone, he focused on his whittling as a flute slowly shaped in his hands.

Jack's mother had taught him how to make instruments from wood. She claimed she'd been young when she learned how to do it and wanted the same for him. Music had always lived at the center of her heart, and she passed that passion down to her children.

Maybe it was the peaceful storm raging outside or his second thoughts during the trip that weakened him enough to think about his mother. He wasn't sure. Either way, it had been a while. His shoulders slumped—his mother would have been so disappointed if she saw the life he currently led.

And how little he allowed music to touch his soul.

Jack jumped as a flash of lightning lit the sky. Thunder rolled across the clouds above him, seemingly dragging along for miles. The sound almost pulled him from whatever trance he'd found himself in from fashioning that flute. What was he doing? Music brought emotions and heart and, well, if Jack let those things in, he wouldn't be able to stop the pain.

Jack allowed the songs inside of him to go silent years ago. Music made him feel the depths of every emotion, and after losing his home and his family and being forced to become Blackjack for Ace, he couldn't bear to handle it all. It was better to stop feeling. It was better to push it all down and forget.

Despite that, as Jack finished his flute, he realized how much he missed that deep-rooted connection to music. By the time he neared the completion of his flute, he realized how dark it had grown. Taking a minute break, Jack started a low fire to bring light to the small camp. Once he could see again, he started fashioning a reed for the flute.

Thunder crashed loudly overhead—the storm was on top of them now. The rumble shook the ground and woke Arianne up from her sleep. The woman was startled, jumping up as her eyes scanned the camp around her. Jack wished he didn't notice how much she relaxed when she saw him. It meant there was something there—something more than just neutrality.

And Jack didn't know if he could give that to her.

"Another nightmare?" Jack asked absently. After a week together, he'd grown used to Arianne's fitful sleeping.

The woman nodded distantly as if she was still sorting out what was real and a dream. He frowned at her. He knew what nightmares like that were like. He didn't have any shortage of memories that could fuel sleepless nights.

Arianne's eyes settled on Jack as he tuned his flute, "Did you make that?" She asked, blatantly changing the subject.

"Yeah. Didn't have much else to do."

The Pacifican raised an eyebrow, "So you fashioned a fully functional flute?"

"You wouldn't get it." Jack shook his head, feeling his walls go back up as he realized how ridiculous carving an old-fashioned flute was.

"I do," Arianne responded quietly, "Caesar gave me a Spanish guitar as a kid. My mother was from Spain. He hoped it would give me a small taste of home." Her head lowered, and her hair cascaded around her to shield her face, "I loved that guitar. A fire burnt down our first house, and I lost it to the blaze. I don't know—I couldn't get myself to pick one up again." Her eyes were rimmed with tears, "I just lose everything I care about—you know?"

And he had caused some of that, he realized in horror. He succeeded in getting her father captured and sent to Pangaea. Her despair made him want to snap his dumb flute in half.

"I-I'm sorry," Jack could hardly believe the words left his lips.

Arianne's head snapped up, "Do you mean it?" She asked, her jaw setting. "Do you *actually* mean that, or are you just saying it to shut me up?"

"I wouldn't have wasted my breath if I didn't."

Arianne nodded, clenching her teeth against more tears. "Can you play anything on that?"

Jack looked down at the flute, his hands starting to shake. Of course, he could. At least he used to be able to. Making the flute had been one thing, but actually playing it—letting himself make music—was entirely different.

Memories began to flow. Nights spent after dinner in his family's living room, when his father would play piano and his mother would sing. Jack let out a long sigh as he remembered how beautiful they'd sounded together. Once, he'd been on the road to be just as talented as both of them.

But now?

He was terrified to search inside and take stock of how much he had lost. But he was also terrified of what would happen if he never let music back into his life again. So, Jack thought long and hard as he considered what he wanted to play.

Your music must tell a story, his mother used to say.

What story did Jack want to tell tonight?

"This is an old song," he began tentatively, listening to the sound of the rain. "A song and a story about the beginning of the tribes. My mother used to sing it to me when I was young." Jack began to bang slowly on one of the pots to his side, "Hundreds of years ago, when the world began anew, and Pangaea was still young, there were six *Feras*."

The drumbeat began to quicken as an otherworldly trance settled over the camp.

"Oh, I've heard this one before," Arianne cut in, excitement shining in her eyes.

"Just let me tell the story." Jack rolled his eyes, "You haven't heard it this way, I promise."

No, only Jack's mother could sing the hymns and play the mythical music of the tribes with such serene talent.

"When the world began anew," Jack repeated, "there were six *Feras*—and they were in mourning. The seventh among them had died in the war. Though their names have been lost to history, who they were together has stood the test of time. They were called the *Filii Luna*. The Children of the Moon. For the moon was a symbol of Artemis, the goddess of beasts, and they were the most powerful beasts to ever walk this earth."

Thunder rumbled ominously, as though the forest itself wanted the legend remembered.

"Their leader was dead," Jack continued to bang on the pot like a second heartbeat. "She sacrificed her life to end the Last War. Their new leader—a *Fera* with antlers of a stag—created the tribes as a home for more who fled from the newborn Pangaea. The tribes promised their people a life free of civilization: a life full of wonder and freedom."

As Jack spoke, his words weaved around the small camp. They were mesmerizing, carrying him and Arianne back in time to where it all began. Arianne's eyes filled with wonder as he crafted the tale. In those moments, he was just like his mother: a storyteller, a carrier of mysteries and history.

"The *Filii Luna* dispersed among these first tribes, never to be seen whole again. But their descendants reign in the tribes of the world today as protectors of nature and Champions of freedom. This is the story of their battles and the civilization they made through blood and loss."

Jack's lips went to his flute, and he began to play. At first, he was unsure of the correct notes, but as the tune started, his fingers remembered. After all those years his muscle memory hadn't failed him. The song was savage, sad, and even frightening. Yet, despite that, it never felt foreign. The melody sang to his ears. It didn't feel stolen from an alien culture, it felt like his own. It felt like home—a part of him.

The song depicted battle, suffering, and loss, but it also sang of victory and freedom. It sang of mystery and curiosity. Jack's mother once called it *the Song of the Feras*. It was a song of a people who fascinated the world but never let it understand them.

It was written as a beautiful tragedy, but it was more than that. Jack could hear it now: the tones of beauty and happiness tangled together to breathe life into the long-lost legend. Even in the darkness of the storm, the melody took Jack beyond the blackness around him. He was delivered to a frost-covered forest where he found himself walking through powdery white snow.

Jack's mother once told him that anyone who truly *heard* that song would be delivered somewhere. For a moment, he risked a glance at Arianne and wondered if she was seeing some other world as well. Maybe she saw the open blue skies above a golden meadow. That vision came to Jack only once before when he played the song after his parents passed. In the vision, his mother had been standing on a hill covered with golden grass and next to a young birch tree, her hair blowing in the wind.

Something told Jack that Arianne would love the feeling of an open sky above her.

The flute continued to weave its horribly beautiful story. Jack closed his eyes, and he was delivered back to that forest. He felt no pain in these moments, no loss, only wonder. The sun sparkled through frozen trees, reflecting off of the ice that coated the branches. He found a path of footprints that led toward the sound of music up ahead. He wanted to move closer, look closer. He wanted to *see*.

Inhuman eyes watched from behind evergreens as Jack walked down that path, but he wasn't afraid. He felt safe under those mystical stares. It was like being watched by forest nymphs given human form.

People were singing up ahead, flutes and drums pounding, and above it all, the ancient sound of a choir.

Where am I?

"Home," a woman whispered from behind him. Jack turned and saw his mother standing in the snow-covered woods, a green scarf covering her head. She was as beautiful as he remembered. "You're home now. Welcome back."

Warmness filled Jack's heart as he stepped towards his mother. As soon as he touched her hand, he was transported into the heart of a camp. Jack stood before a place born of legends. Large fires kissed the night sky, and *Feras* danced with the energy of a thousand suns. It was a land of beauty and peace, like long-forgotten lands of magic in ancient mythology.

The shadows surrounding the fires grew as the song rose to a crescendo, sending a chill over the camp. Then Jack was alone, the pits that once held fires sending only smoke into the air.

The beauty of the melody faded as an eerie stillness took over the song. Discomfort crept up his spine. As a child, he'd always been terrified of that part of the song. The part that served as a warning for those from the outside. The tribes were peaceful until they were not. They were people who'd lost everything and would fight to keep what they had left. Champions—trained in the ways of their forefathers—could be reapers of death if provoked.

The tribes were people of high power—both good and deadly.

The song slowly moved towards a close, the crescendo and crashing of war fading with a melody beautifully written to sound like a soft summer breeze.

Arianne swayed, listening to the song's last few breaths as a tranquil calm settled over her.

"You're right," she said quietly as Jack lowered his flute, "I've never heard it that way before."

Jack analyzed the woman, "What did you feel?"

Arianne blinked, her eyes tracking over the ground, "this is going to sound crazy, but," she paused, "I felt like I was home."

Jack raised an eyebrow, intrigued. So she *had* felt something. He was torn between pressing for more and giving her space. As exhaustion began to make his eyelids heavy, he settled for the latter. "Hopefully, no more nightmares, then," he smiled, "and we should both get some rest."

As the thunderstorm faded, the pair fell asleep with a strange sense of peace, as if his song had summoned the spirits whispered of in his melody to protect them.

In his dreams, he watched a girl with wild red hair run across a rolling green hillside speckled with yellow and white flowers. Her green dress blew in the wind as her laugh of delight echoed across the meadow. Jack felt his heart crack. He knew who the girl was.

"Genevieve! "He called out, but the more he yelled, the further his sister drifted away. "Gen! Please! Come back! Gen, it's me!"

Jack fought to follow his sister, but he couldn't move. Genevieve continued to run but no matter how much he struggled, he couldn't follow. Then he looked down, he realized his feet were sinking into the mud. When looked back up, his sister had disappeared over the hillside. Panic made his heart pound. He couldn't lose her.

Not again.

"Gen! Gen, please!" He shrieked.

His knees weakened. He'd abandoned his sister—he couldn't blame her if she did the same.

Then he saw that fire-red hair peek out from over the crest of the hill, "Jack?"

He felt warmth flood through him: the warmth of home and family.

"Jack!" Genevieve called again.

He freed himself from the mud at his sister's cry. He ran to his sister, tears threatening to come to his eyes. He called out to her again, his voice catching. Genevieve called back, running toward him. And then she was in front of him and Jack remembered that face face like he'd only lost her yesterday. She had round cheeks smattered with freckles and a face outlined by that unruly mop of curling hair. His heart became an aching weight in his chest.

But he stopped himself from reaching out to her. Genevieve had never known him as Jack. His head dropped at the painful realization that he was in a dream.

"Jack! Wake up!" Genevieve cried, "Jack! We need to go—I hear them! They're coming!" His eyes blinked open in a daze. Genevieve's face faded, and a woman replaced it.

He was shaken awake by strong hands around his shoulders, but he was still trapped in the tendrils of the dream. "Genevieve," he whispered.

"Jack," Arianne screamed, "We need to go!"

"We have to get Genevieve," he insisted.

Arianne was frantic as she fought to pull him to his feet, "I don't care about Genevieve! We have to go! Now!"

Arianne finally succeeded in pulling Jack to his feet, and he stumbled as his limbs acclimated to wakefulness. He shook away his exhaustion and grasped her shoulders to steady himself. Jack didn't have long to wake before Arianne slung his backpack over his arm. The last bit of his drowsiness faded when he saw the pure terror in her expression.

"We need to run," she said sincerely.

Chapter 29

Jaya

Defeat hung in the air, as heavy and stale as a suffocating, humid day. No one dared move, they couldn't muster the energy. Even days after her altercation with Blue Krait, Jaya was still recovering from the effects of the poison and the multiple bruised ribs she'd sustained.

She didn't know what hurt more: the ache of her injuries or the sting of her idiotic failure.

Jaya had gotten a chance at freedom, and she'd squandered it. And for what? Confirmation that her sister and the President were alive? She clenched her teeth and looked down. They'd all be dead soon anyway.

Leon still hadn't returned from the Commander's summit, but Jaya and everyone else in that prison block knew it was only a matter of time before they faced his wrath. Leon, the infamously ruthless Commander of Europe, never tolerated rebellions.

The Selvian Tribe had learned that lesson the hard way.

"Repeat the building map, Bahri," Major Lyn commanded from her cell.

Jaya looked up at the Major with sunken green eyes. She'd reported her findings multiple times to the meager team. There was no point in speaking again, but she knew the Major was trying to keep up some semblance of hope.

"The Commander's private quarters are on the tower's top two floors," she sighed. "We're below ground. There is only one unmarked level below us. We're two levels from the main floor and exit. The elevator is in the hallway beyond the next room."

"Good work," Major Lyn's jaw tightened. "We can use that, Lieutenant. Don't forget that."

Lyn's words fell flat in the cement space. Jaya knew that the Major was trying her best, but she didn't have the heart anymore to listen.

"Up for a round of rock, paper, scissors?" Rhino asked with a sideward glance at Jaya. "The suspense of who's going to win round two hundred and three is killing me."

Even the large *Fera* didn't have the heart to put humor into his jokes anymore.

The doors to the prison block slid into the walls with a sharp clang. All heads turned as the very air in the room seemed to disappear. Jaya couldn't help but scowl as Andre Murray strode inside, his Ward's mask disappearing with a jarring snap to reveal a look of deep distaste. Just as she remembered, the prince carried an expression of pure apathy as he surveyed the Pacificans with sweeping eyes. Andre frowned, folding his hands behind his back as he gestured with a flick of his head for the Wards behind him to follow.

"I believe these are yours," Andre grumbled in boredom.

Kalinda was dragged into the prison block, still wearing her Pangaean scrubs. The field medic was furious as she glared up at the prince, who easily stood two heads taller than her. Despite Andre's intimidating air, Kalinda managed a scowl. "He needs another three days in the hospital," she spat.

Andre waved at a Ward to open one of the empty cells. "Let me inform you on how things work around here, nurse." Andre's glare could have frozen molten lava as he whirled on Kalinda. "There is only one person on this planet who can give me commands," he leaned threateningly close to her as his upper lip curled, "and you're not him."

Jaya's heart stopped, and she gripped the prison bar in front of her as hard as she could in an effort to hold her tongue. She strained like she could make some psychic link to yell at her sister to be quiet. Fear made her shake—if Andre wanted Kalinda dead, he could do it with no more than a flick of his hand. That was the power the Murrays carried.

Fortunately, Andre had never dealt with Kalinda. Jaya's beautifully brave sister met the prince's hazel eyes with her own and didn't flinch. "I don't observe Pangaean rankings," she scowled, "not anymore."

Andre's face reddened with rage, and he raised his hand, preparing to backhand the medic. Jaya was practically pushing herself through the prison bars in any attempt to get to her sister. *She* deserved punishment for escaping—not Kalinda. She was about to speak up when someone was wheeled into the prison block.

"If you're going to strike someone, strike the person she's causing trouble for." Caesar's voice was unwavering and powerful as it echoed across the cramped space.

All eyes in the room turned to the Pacifican President. Caesar was cuffed to a wheelchair, his three remaining limbs tied down as a Ward pushed him into the prison block. But despite his fatal wound and losing his ability to walk, Caesar looked as formidable as ever.

Andre turned, his thick eyebrows furrowing as he locked eyes with the President. The room seemed to drop ten degrees as the two leaders stared each other down. And despite Andre's intimidating air and the way he towered over everyone around him, Caesar—wounded in a wheelchair—overpowered the prince. Andre's anger seemed to bounce off Caesar's steady and confident energy like water off a rain jacket.

Andre took an intimidating step towards Caesar, and the President didn't so much as flinch. Andre didn't scare him. And the energy of the room grew.

Rhino jumped up from his seat. His meaty hands wrapped around the cell's bars as he cackled, "Why don't you pick on someone your own size, shithead?"

Rhino was probably the only one in that room who could rival Andre in height. But he easily had a hundred pounds on the lean prince. Jaya managed a grin despite her sister's potential danger. The thought of Rhino going a round against Andre was enough to lighten her heart—if only for a moment.

Andre clenched his teeth hard enough that Jaya wondered what kind of dental plan the Commanding family of Europe received. She hoped that it was around-the-clock service from the look of the prince.

"Put him in his cell," Andre growled, "and keep the nurse with him in case there are any problems." The prince swung his head towards Kalinda, his expression loathing, "Does that work for you, nurse?"

Kalinda didn't shy away from the prince's shadow as Caesar was rolled into their cell, "This nurse has a name," she spat.

"I don't waste my time learning the names of the dead," Andre said before walking off, reeking of anger and annoyance.

Rhino sagged in relief as soon as the cell block doors slammed shut. "Well, isn't he a prince charming," he muttered.

Caesar was as alert as ever as he examined the walls around him. The President's oak brown eyes turned to the commanding officers in their cells, "Carter, Yina," he began, "report." Captain Cadmilus and Major Lyn both stood and saluted the Pacifican President.

Cadmilus was the first to speak, bowing his head. "For my failure as Captain and member of the Pacifican military, I formally resign my role. I cannot continue to serve this nation with honor after failing to protect you, President Ortiz. Please accept my resignation, and I will willingly endure whatever punishment you see fit."

Caesar looked down at his leg, a shadow crossing his eyes for a moment, "We've all been punished enough, Carter," he said slowly, "and if we're going to make it home to our families, I'm going to need you."

Captain Cadmilus nodded, "At least let me step down as Captain," he abridged, "Major Yina Lyn has proved her mettle as a leader these past few days." Haris's father turned to Major Lyn and gave her a deep bow of respect, "If anyone can get us back to our loved ones, it's her."

A deep moment of silence fell over the group. Jaya looked over to her sister as she thought about the people they'd left behind in Citadel. She knew Kalinda was thankful she was there instead of at home worrying about whether Jaya was alive or dead. The sentiment was shared.

Caesar looked between Yina and Carter. "Captain Lyn, welcome back." He turned his attention to Jaya, "All right, here's the plan. Lieutenant Bahri," Caesar began, "I'm aware that Haris Cadmilus gave you one of his prototype phones."

Jaya winced, worried that her friend might be in trouble, "Yes, sir," she reported.

"Good," Caesar smiled at Major Cadmilus, "your son is a talented young engineer. If I recall from Arianne's copy of the device, it has location tracking. Is that correct?"

Jaya perked up. "Yes."

"Perfect." Caesar continued, "Once we escape, the next step will be to find where the Wards of this facility are housing our personal items. All we need is one person to find that phone and bring it to the communications center—which should be located somewhere in this tower. Connecting that phone to the system should let us bypass the city's communications defenses."

Captain Lyn began to smile, "and send Pacific right to us."

"Precisely," Caesar said. "If General Kalfas has half a mind, he would have tracked that phone's signal and created a radius of its location before it disappeared behind the city's signal blockers. Hopefully—and I mean *hopefully*—Pacific shouldn't be too far away."

"That could work," Rhino perked up as an evil grin grew on his face.

"Major Cadmilus, we'll make sure we get you back home to your son," Caesar promised as the energy in the room grew.

"I'll get back to my wife, Linda," Captain Lyn smiled.

Major Cadmilus's last soldier, a gruff man who called himself Gunner, nodded his head, "I'll see my brothers again."

"Treena and Tyrell," Rhino whispered, his gray eyes softening.

Haris. Jaya's heart constricted thinking about one of her best friends. She hoped he and Arianne were together and keeping each other safe.

Even if Arianne didn't have the maturity to see all of them off.

For some reason, that memory stung more as she looked at Caesar in the cell next to her. Arianne had stood both of them up—now it would take nothing shy of a miracle before she saw either of them ever again.

"Arianne," Caesar's response was so quiet that most in the room missed it.

Jaya paused, locking eyes with the President. Did he really mean that? Arianne's annoyance and jealousy led to her ignoring her adopted father before he left on the most dangerous mission of the war. Something sharp prickled up her spine as annoyance took over her. Arianne was an ungrateful child. Caesar was an amazing father—he worked hard to give her everything she could have asked for, and she repaid him by fighting and ignoring him.

If Caesar had adopted Jaya, she would've spent every day thankful for having such a confident and kind father figure. Jaya blinked, straightening. If she'd been adopted by Caesar...

She quickly looked away from the man who'd been there for almost her entire life. She remembered days when Caesar picked her and Arianne up from school as kids, and the beautiful beach days their small families had spent together. Jaya frowned, remembering morning pancakes after sleepovers with her friends and celebratory dinners after each successful semester at the Academy. She put the pieces together, her heart constricting. How long had she seen Caesar as a father figure?

Jaya stole another quick glance at him. The President was talking in hushed tones to Kalinda as she patiently helped him stand and walk over to his meager cot. Her stomach flipped when she realized how much she loved Caesar like her own father. No wonder she'd been so desperate to know if he and her sister had lived or died. It wasn't because of some overpowering sense of duty.

It was because Caesar and Kalinda were the only parents she had.

Stunned, Jaya numbly walked over to the corner of the cell and leaned on the wall she shared with her sister. Slowly, she let herself slide to the floor. Hugging her knees, she began to shake. How long had she been angry at Arianne for squandering her relationship with Caesar? How long had she secretly wished she could have taken her friend's place? Jaya frowned. What if things had been different? What if Caesar had found her and her sister before he ever found Arianne?

"How are you holding up, kid?"

Jaya blinked tears out of her eyes as she turned to Caesar, lying on the cot beside her. *Kid.* Caesar had called her kid since the first play date she'd had with Arianne. Her lips wobbled as she nodded to the President, "I-I've been better," she managed.

"I heard what you did a couple of days ago," Caesar's eyes were warm like hot chocolate. "Thanks for checking in on me. I'm sorry you and your sister got roped into this." He looked down. "You're too young."

Jaya suddenly couldn't meet the man's eyes, "I'm glad at least one of us is here with you."

They could both hear the name that went unsaid. *Arianne.*

Caesar let out a long sigh, "I wish we left on better terms," he replied, his head leaning back to hit the wall behind him. "I was only trying to protect her. The world's already taken too much from her," his eyes clouded for a moment, "I hate that this mission took so much more."

Jaya sulked. Despite her annoyance, Arianne was still her closest friend. Deep down, she was glad that Arianne was safe at home. "I'm sorry," was all she could manage, looking at Caesar's leg, "and I'm sorry about what happened," she winced.

Caesar frowned, looking at his leg again. "This certainly isn't easy," he began, his voice heavy, "but to lose hope right now is to sign our death certificate early." The words seemed to help Caesar correct himself, and he nodded with renewed vigor. "I was never much of a fighter anyways," he pointed to his temple. "As long as I have this—I'm unstoppable."

Jaya managed a half smile, "Thank you for giving us some hope."

Caesar's grin seemed forced as he looked up toward the ceiling of the cell. "I promise you, no matter what, I'll make sure you all leave this city alive."

Jaya turned in surprise, but Caesar had already closed his eyes. Her lips parted in concern. He'd promised everyone else would leave alive. But what about him?

Chapter 30

Arianne

Pushing through the undergrowth, Arianne ran like hell. The night was dark, but with her *Fera* vision, she could see through the underbrush and logs without much trouble. Something had tried to sneak up on their camp. She was just lucky that one of her nightmares woke her before their pursuers did.

Now that adrenaline had taken over, the nightmare was a blur. One moment, she was heaving awake in a cold sweat, and the next, her *Fera* ears picked up on the ever-so-soft sound of footsteps prodding quietly across leaves.

"Arianne?" Jack asked groggily as he fought to keep up with her. "What's happening?"

"I don't know," she replied between breaths, "I think our tribal followers have finally caught up." Arianne clenched her teeth in shame. "They probably met up with the tribe we stayed with, and they pointed them in our direction."

Arianne heard Jack crash to the ground behind her. She slowed and helped him scramble up, grabbing his hand. "I'll guide you. Just follow straight behind me," she instructed calmly.

Jack nodded and gave her hand a trusting squeeze. "We need to find a river," he reported, "They'll lose our scent if we cross water."

Arianne's memory sparked. "The river from earlier," she recalled. "It's not far."

Guiding Jack through the darkness, she realized the risk she was taking in revealing her *Fera* abilities, but the alternative was far worse. The distant barking of dogs and the ominous pounding of approaching feet sent shivers down her spine. Their pursuers had reached their camp—the same camp they'd been forced to abandon. Arianne knew they had mere moments before their enemies realized it was empty and resumed their pursuit.

"How did you hear them?" Jack asked, his hand tightening around hers.

"I was lucky enough to be awake," Arianne said evenly.

Jack didn't need to know that her *Fera* hearing was why they were still alive. Her heart almost stopped when she heard the dogs barking cease. They'd locked onto their new scent trail.

She picked up her pace. "We need to move faster."

Jack resisted. "We're too far from the water. We need to stop!"

"We can make it. Just run faster!"

Jack dug in his heels, bringing them to a sudden stop that yanked at her shoulder. Arianne tried to pull him forward, anxiety surging through her, but Jack wouldn't budge. "I'm slowing us down," he confessed, "If we stop now, we might ambush them when they catch up."

Arianne recoiled, "We need to move!"

Her unspoken fear gnawed at her. She dreaded another confrontation and the death that would follow. Worst of all, she wasn't sure if she could fight with her injuries.

"They have better endurance," Jack reasoned, "and most are adult mutants—they're faster than us. If they strike first, we don't stand a chance."

Arianne tugged on Jack again. "We can reach the river in time," she insisted.

"Will you just listen to me for once?" Jack demanded, startling Arianne, "You're why we're in this mess."

Arianne's jaw dropped. "Excuse me?"

He . "I have your attention. Good. We're running out of time. I'm going to climb that tree and set up my rifle. You're going to hide in the undergrowth and set up a perimeter with the fire starter fluid. When they reach the camp, I want you to light it. Hopefully, they'll be fish in a barrel, and I can take them out."

Arianne's stomach bottomed out, "I'm not lighting a fire that big," her eyes widened as she remembered the smell of smoke and the licking tongues of flames coming to claim her when her house burned down, "We're doing something else."

Jack's eyes darted to where the rustling in the woods was getting louder. The attackers weren't even trying to hide their presence anymore. He quickly looked back at her and cupped her face in his hands. Arianne blinked in shock at how easily his touch steadied her.

Slowly, the two of them shared a few vital, calming breaths. "We don't have a choice, Princess," Jack said, leaning his forehead against hers.

Arianne nodded, her resolve solidifying. "This plan better work, Pangaea Boy."

Their roles established, Arianne spread fire starter fluid in a circle around the forest floor while Jack climbed into position. As the distant sounds of their pursuers grew louder, her heart raced. She held a lighter and a match, ready to ignite the fiery trap. When the attackers reached their position, she had a precious few moments to give Jack the light he needed. She shook at the idea of being engulfed in flames, but she pushed it down.

Arianne needed to survive the night if she wanted to save her loved ones. Caesar. Jaya. Kalinda. Rhino. Carter Cadmilus. She repeated their names, her resolve building. She imagined what they must all feel—trapped and alone in Leonueva. She was going to survive the Darwin Zone and save all of them. If she focused on that mission, she could steady herself.

Suddenly, the ravenous claws of two dogs trampled the line of trees in front of her. The canines were followed by what sounded like dozens of feet. Arianne clenched her teeth as she lit the match in her hand and dropped it into the circle of lighter fluid. Bright orange flames burst through the dark forest, bringing the night to life as the tribespeople cried out in alarm.

"How's that for the element of surprise?" Arianne taunted, her eyes maniacally reflecting the flames.

"Less puns, more guns!" Jack barked as he opened fire, taking down their pursuers one by one. Arianne watched in awe as he eliminated target after target, the firelight dancing in his determined eyes. The shadows cast by the trees added to the eerie atmosphere, intensifying the chaos below.

Arianne's comment attracted the attention of the two hunting dogs. The canines gnashed their fangs, saliva rolling from their ravenous mouths. Arianne paled. She'd never fought animals before. Unsheathing her blades, she lowered into a defensive crouch and willed herself to calm down. She took a long breath that filled even the deepest points of her lungs. That fight was no different than training with Kalfas. If she focused on that, she could win.

The fire was warm at her back as the dogs lunged at her. She sidestepped the first one, extending a sword to intercept the second. It howled in pain as metal pierced its ribcage. Arianne winced at the ear-splitting sound and her delay cost her. Snarling, the second dog leaped into the air, aiming for her exposed back. She turned at the last moment and her sword punched through the dog's sternum.

The bone made an awful crack, and the creature fell limply next to its companion.

Arianne turned to the fire-lit clearing. Jack was still shooting as attacker after attacker charged into the circle of flames. The growing threat didn't intimidate Jack as he tracked each target with professional serenity and hit each mark with near-perfect accuracy.

Jack wasn't just a bounty hunter—he was a weapon.

The trees around them cast long shadows in the firelight, adding a bone-chilling atmosphere to the already terrifying attack. Arianne crouched in the shadows outside the fires, watching as the last of the attackers tracked toward the sound of Jack's gun, ignoring her completely.

Arianne's sides heaved, still recovering from the run and her fight with the dogs. She winced as her side began to ache, and she receded into the forest beyond the flames. Five attackers remained, an easy number for Jack to handle himself. Arianne had done her part—there was no need for her to brave the flames or kill anyone.

Until Jack's rifle misfired.

"Shit," they both cursed in unison.

The tribespeople took advantage of Jack's hesitation. The hunting party turned on the tree with a crashing wave of weapons and limbs. Injured *Feras* advanced on the tree as well, and Arianne's jaw hung open as she witnessed firsthand why firearms were not the preferred weapons against them. Any *Fera* who hadn't received a killing blow to the head or heart was rising and moving toward Jack like an undead army.

Jack lightened the herd with his attack, but ten were still advancing slowly on the tree. Including the five uninjured Feras.

Arianne bit her lip. She needed to buy Jack the precious time he needed to fix his rifle. She knew what she needed to do. She just needed the courage to do it. *This is just like training with Kalfas*, she reminded herself. *Attack, duck, and keep moving.*

The fire became the least of her worries as she lunged at the ten adult *Feras* out for blood. She didn't have to win—she just had to stay alive long enough to give Jack the time he needed. Arianne attacked the closest *Fera*, a female with cloven hooves like a deer. Ducking low, she swept her sword across her calves, slicing her Achilles tendon. The female yelped as her legs buckled.

Nine.

Arianne's legs almost gave out as the other attackers whirled around on her. Nine sets of hungry, savage eyes bored into her very soul. Some bared their teeth, displaying horrible, sharpened fangs. Others' tails swished in anticipation. All looked otherworldly and haunting—painted faces and bone masks shadowed by the fires and night.

"Now, I know we got off on a rough start—" Arianne began.

Four attacked at once. She yelped, rolling out of the way as a spear was thrust at her. In the tangle of limbs and sharpened weapons, Arianne hunted for previous bullet wounds. She spotted the first on a male's shoulder. She locked onto that target. As Arianne lunged at another female, she threw the hilt of her second sword backward into the male's injury. Though the female dodged Arianne's attack, she heard the male bellow in pain. Arianne took advantage of his distraction and sliced her sword across his stomach.

A killing blow.

Arianne's world slowed as the male fell to the ground at her side. It had been easy—too easy, like breathing. The heat of the fire singed her skin, blood roared in her ears, and yet all she could focus on was the sickly thud the male's body made when it hit the ground.

It felt wrong. It felt awfully familiar.

She'd killed before.

Murderer, a ravenous voice in the back of her mind whispered. She'd always been a murderer. She thought the realization would make her catatonic, but something else took over. Something deep and instinctual. Arianne needed to live, and nothing else mattered.

The worst thing was that she knew how to do it.

"*You'll be the most powerful weapon in the world*," Leon whispered to her from a long-forgotten memory. "*The world will tremble beneath us.*"

Eight enemies remained.

Arianne's involuntary hiss of pleasure sent shivers down her spine, everything inside of her preparing for what was to come. Her sight narrowed until all she could see was her next target: a huntress, knocking an arrow at close range. Arianne chucked, something dark and dangerous seeping like smoke from her pores as she met the huntress, sliding beneath her bow and slicing through her thighs. Arianne barely registered the *Fera's* scream as she fell. Nor did she blink when she thrust her sword through the female's neck.

Seven.

Arianne's hearing became near supernatural. As she crouched over the dead huntress, she could hear two more *Feras* approaching behind her. Her smile was bloodthirsty as her lips curled over her bared teeth. Angling her swords backward, she jabbed them behind her, feeling the satisfying glide of her swords meeting flesh. Two cries followed. Two bodies fell at her side.

Six and five.

Arianne stood, breathing deeply. She didn't want to think about how natural it felt to let go or how much her body rejoiced in the violence. *Survive, and then you can think about what this means.* Arianne's eyes narrowed as she whirled on three more attackers. That one word repeated inside her head: *survive, survive, survive.*

She might've despised her biological father, but her years spent in Pacific had made her forget one of the most essential parts of her being—a piece her father had ingrained into her very soul. Arianne was a survivor, and she was ashamed she'd forgotten.

"Come on!" She challenged her next victims as her grip tightened on her swords that dripped with the crimson blood of their friends.

Two more tribespeople attacked together while a third hung back. Arianne utilized both of her blades to keep the two males at bay. Where one male's spear met her right sword, the other's blade met her left. Something awful inside of her bloomed with excitement when she realized both of her attackers had been injured by Jack.

They were too slow to survive her.

The male with the spear was favoring his right leg thanks to a bullet through his left thigh. Arianne focused her attention on him. The male managed an arcing blow that caught her in the arm—but she didn't feel a thing. She wrinkled her nose in annoyance. She needed to single out one opponent at a time. Throwing the second attacker off balance, Arianne was afforded a few rare seconds to target the male with the spear. He sparred with her for a few blows, but he didn't last long under the weight of her full attention. With the first of the males discarded, she turned and attacked the second before he could recover his balance.

Four and three.

Arianne whirled on the last of the three males. She could feel the blood from the spear attack trickling down her arm, but she was too focused to feel pain. The blood from her wound became a distant reminder of her mortality. Some part of her still understood she could bleed, but she'd lost the part of her that *cared.* Sides heaving with effort, she locked eyes with her next target and bared her teeth.

Satisfaction filled her veins like a roaring tide when the male took a startled step backward.

"Feral," he whispered.

"You wish," Arianne replied.

The male was gushing blood from a bullet wound in his side. She was surprised he hadn't died yet. She was happy to finish the job. The male ambitiously took the offensive, and Arianne humored him with a smile as she dodged his sloppy attacks. She knew the male was fighting on limited time so she didn't need to attack him to win—even a *Fera* couldn't operate forever with so much blood loss. She continued to parry and step away from the male's advances like she was dancing to her own silent rhythm. It wasn't long until the male slowed, and his blood loss finally caught up to him. As the male attempted to deliver a sloppy downward strike, she finally decided to end his suffering. With a haunting grin, she stepped to the side of the attack and jabbed her sword into his exposed side.

Two.

"Arianne!" Jack screamed, the sound penetrating her battle haze.

Arianne turned, and her breath caught in her throat. Jack was captured. One of the remaining attackers had managed to pull him out of the tree. Jack was pressed against the male behind him, a sharp blade held to his neck. The attacker holding Jack grinned at Arianne—he knew he had her cornered.

"Drop the swords," the last attacker muttered from behind her.

The command only made her tighten her grip.

Half of Jack's face was visible in the glow of the fire burning to his right. "Forget about me," he gritted against the sharp blade. "The entrance is a two-day hike from here, where the Artery crosses over a river. Tell the guards inside that Blackjack sent you a message!"

Arianne shook her head. "Not without you."

Something like sadness filled Jack's eyes. "Did I grow on you, Princess?"

"Bow, and maybe we let you live." The attacker behind Arianne pressed a blade to her back. She tensed as she felt the sharp metal press against her side, warning of a deadly blow to her kidney. The hunter snarled, "You'll be a great addition to our tribe."

Her eyes widened. They didn't want to kill her. They wanted to trap her and force her to be a tool for them. Arianne's breathing slowed, and the primal fog she'd found herself in lifted for a few short moments. They were going to treat her like a weapon—a caged animal—just like her father had.

She began to shake with rage. She refused to be controlled by anyone ever again.

They were going to kill Jack and then imprison her. The combination of two awful possibilities channeled her focus. When did it start to matter so much to her if Jack lived or died? Arianne turned her attention to Jack who tried his best to look calm, but she could feel it: he was terrified.

One look at him and her mind was made up.

She was an idiot—Jack'd already given her Leonueva's location. Why would she risk her own life now? The answer was simple: because Jack did something *good*. If Jack could do something good, could she really leave him behind? Even with his life on the line, the first thing he thought to do was give her the information she needed to get to Caesar and Jaya back.

Jack was mere inches away from her, yet he felt so impossibly out of reach. Slowly, the bounty hunter shook his head. He knew her well enough to know she might try to risk it all for someone she'd only met weeks ago.

"I find it funny—" Arianne whispered as her body began to shake in anticipation.

The attacker behind her stepped close enough that she could feel his breath on her neck. Jack shook his head again. She only smiled back.

Without warning, Arianne jabbed her right sword backward into the male holding a blade to her back. At the same time, she jabbed her left sword forward, past Jack's side, and into the stomach of the last attacker. Jack expertly pushed the forearm that was holding the blade to his neck away and ducked out of the way as the male behind him fell.

Arianne kicked backward, knocking the dying male behind her away. A deadly smile came to her lips as she turned to watch the male crumple. "—that you didn't see that coming," she finished.

Zero.

But even the pain of her injuries was not enough to shield her from the awful realization of what she'd just done. A new clarity came to her eyes as she observed the burning clearing before her.

"What did I do," her words were hardly more than a whisper.

Jack wrapped his arms around her, "You saved my life," he responded in a quivering voice, "holy shit, you saved my life."

Arianne couldn't take her eyes off of the clearing, she barely registered Jack's hands holding her up. All those people... dead because of her. The bodies surrounding her, the bodies she'd felled, were gruesome and haunting and damning.

All of that pain and death was from her, and it was almost enough to make her throw up as the iron-rich smell of the blood she'd spilled filled her nose. concentrated on the crackling flames inching ever closer to her, too horrified to move. For once, she didn't care if the fire burned her. After what she'd done, she deserved it. Her jaw went slack as she remembered the blood on her hands—blood that had been hidden for years.

"I killed them," she whimpered.

Murderer. The singular word echoed inside of her head as the memories came flooding back. She began to sway as she teetered on the verge of passing out. How could she forget? How did she never remember what she was?

The ghost of Leon's hand rested on Arianne's shoulder. *"Well done,"* he purred.

And suddenly, she was a little girl again. Leon's words lightened her heart. *Praise,* Leon was giving her praise. Glee lightened her emotions at the chance to make her father proud. She didn't realize she was trapped in a memory until she saw the bodies. Arianne was powerless as more victims materialized before her. She watched as she killed each of them and then turned to Leon—hungry for praise—after each death. Even as a child, Arianne had been Leon's executioner—and she'd looked forward to it.

"How could I have forgotten," she moaned as she watched the lives she'd claimed in the past play like a movie in front of her.

Somehow, killing again triggered the repressed memories from before.

"Hey," she was distantly aware of Jack trying to soothe her, "we need to get away from the fire. Can you move?"

Arianne was too lost to respond. The ghosts of her past surrounded her, the emotion of their loss suffocating her. Slowly, she counted. Seventeen. She'd killed seventeen people while living under Leon. *Seventeen.* She wished it was just her mind playing tricks on her, but she knew it was *real.* It was all so terribly real.

She could remember each and every one of their names.

"Why didn't I remember?" Arianne begged, hands clawing down her face.

"Remember what?" Jack asked, shaking her lightly. "Come on, you've got to let me help you!"

She was a coward, a coward who couldn't even live with what her father had turned her into. She was a coward who chose to forget instead of endure the pain of her terrible sins. Leon hadn't just damaged her body all of those years, he'd effectively damaged her soul. How could she still be the hero with so much bad?

"Oh god," Jack muttered, and Arianne felt his hand pressed to her side. "Okay, we need to stop the bleeding. Just stay with me, come on."

Arianne didn't know how to respond. Tears streamed down her cheeks. She was lost in some terrible in-between. Was Jack someone from her past or present? Were those wounds she felt ripping into her body given to her by their attackers or Leon?

She was falling, her shock and horror forcing her deeper and deeper into herself. The surface felt like miles away, and she was certain she didn't ever want to come back up. She hit terminal velocity as past and present blurred together—her suffering the only thing holding their concussive forces together.

And then her falling stopped, the spiral downwards halted by the soft melody of a violin. The strings brought a strange harmony to her, filling the darkness with its calming sound. Then, the guitar and piano joined forces with the violin and the three instruments wove together to create a rope back to the surface.

As if from miles away, Arianne heard Jack's voice. "Focus on the music." His words were like soft pillows cushioning her fall. "Whenever I get overwhelmed, I listen to music. Focus on it."

So she grabbed hold of that rope of melody and let it guide her to the surface. Soon, she was back to the present, anchored by Jack's music device. Jack smiled down at her as he carried her, a spark of relief filling his eyes, "You're going to be alright," he promised.

And to her surprise, she believed him.

Chapter 31

Blackjack

Jack knew that Arianne was a *Fera*.

He'd suspected it for a while, but now he was certain. No human could flip such an otherworldly switch. One moment, she'd been a cowering amateur, ready to be skewered. The next, something primal took over. She became life and death and the very energy that ran between it. Each kill she took looked as fluid as breathing, and her injuries seemed little more than pesky bug bites.

Jack had almost forgotten about his misfired gun when he watched her kill that first tribesman, her eyes pooling pure black. He'd never seen anything like it. It was like she'd been possessed by some ancient deity of war. It was both beautiful and terrifying. That tribesman had been right when he'd called her feral. It was the only thing Jack could equate the phenomena to. But when a *Fera* turned feral, the change was permanent.

"I killed them," Arianne moaned from his arms.

Jack looked down at the woman—no *female*—and his heart broke. No, the female in his arms was far from feral: she felt pain and remorse. So then, what happened? He shook his head, focusing on his balance as he carried Arianne further away from the flames. They needed to get as far away from the sight as possible: it was a beacon, and Jack wasn't sure how much forest the flames would consume before they stopped.

The world around him smelt like ashes and death, gunpowder and iron. Jack did his best to fight the thick, smoke-filled air as he ran, but the more he inhaled, the more his lungs burned. They needed to keep moving before the very fire they'd lit to save their lives killed them.

"Hey," Jack tried to soothe his travel companion as he fought to carry her. "Just focus on the music," he reminded her, "focus on the lyrics."

He softly sang along to the song in an effort to calm himself. His reassurances to Arianne aside, there was no denying they were in deep shit. He needed to try his best to keep calm for both of them if they wanted a chance at survival.

Arianne's gray eyes stared up at the canopy above, "You have an amazing voice," she whispered.

"You should've heard my mother," Jack replied.

"What was she like?"

He almost stumbled. He hadn't spoken about her much. The memories always hurt, and they allowed for a level of weakness he wasn't able to afford. But if Jack could keep Arianne focused on the present and away from a panic attack that would only make her injuries worse, he would do it.

"She was beautiful," Jack began wistfully, "eyes the color of honey. I guess that's where I got mine from—she would always call me *Miel* when I was a kid. And we would go to the living room every night after dinner and practice whatever new song she found in her books."

"How did she die?" Arianne trailed off.

They approached a stream, and Jack waded across, thankful for an excuse to remain quiet as he concentrated on not slipping into the darkness. Further from the fire now, it was growing harder for him to see in front of him. They only needed to travel a little further until he could find a clearing away from the danger. He hoped the stream would help keep any ambitious flames from following them for the time being.

"How did she die?" Arianne asked again once they crossed the stream.

A clearing came into sight, and Jack let out a sigh of relief as he set Arianne down on the grass, "We need to close up that wound," he said softly, ignoring the painful subject.

Arianne's eyes cleared as she looked at the sky above her. "I've never seen stars like that before." Her words came out in a long breath of amazement.

Jack paused his efforts in tearing off a part of his sleeve for a bandage and looked up. The endless deep indigo stared down at him as millions of glittering stars speckled across it like freckles. So far away from the lights of civilization, the celestial bodies from millions of miles away were allowed to shine their brightest. Some bright specks stood alone surrounded by night while others clustered together in deep clouds of glowing light.

It reminded him of home.

"I've only ever lived in cities," Arianne winced, adjusting ever so slightly to increase her view of the sky.

Jack placed his hands on her shoulders and held her down, "Don't move," he instructed as he pulled up her blood-stained shirt, revealing the reopened wound. He winced at the angry gash, gushing liquid as thick and black as oil in the darkness. "We're going to have to stitch that back up," he warned, retrieving his bag full of the few goods he'd managed to salvage before they ran.

Face paling, Arianne sat back and nodded tightly, "Just get it over with," she winced. Her eyes went back up to the sky, "At least I'll have a nice view to distract me."

Jack couldn't stop his hands from shaking as he pulled the first thread through Arianne's torn skin. He risked a glance down at the female. She looked sickly, but she didn't let out more than a whimper as Jack continued. Brave, she was so brave, he realized. Why hadn't he ever seen it before? The Pacifican below him was tougher than he had ever been willing to give her credit for.

"You're looking at me like I have a second head," Arianne tensed.

"Some Jokers in Cartel can't handle pain like this," Jack responded, not looking up from his work, "Y-you're treating it like it's nothing more than a bad hang-over."

Arianne gagged as Jack pulled the deepest part of her wound closed and he feared that she might pass out. Instead, after a pause to push away the nausea, the female actually laughed. "I've had a lot of practice," she admitted.

Jack slowed. "Practice?" He looked down, the pieces connecting, "because you're a *Fera*," he breathed.

Everything made sense now: why she hated Cartel so much, why she cared about the tribes, and why she'd run away from Pangaea. Arianne was a mutant, and mutants were treated like animals by Pangaea... and by people like him.

Arianne stiffened beneath him. "I guess it was only a matter of time before you found out."

Jack had to focus on applying a new bandage to Arianne's side so he didn't devolve into shakes. "And you were afraid of me knowing," he breathed, "because you were afraid I would see you as less than human?"

Was that what he'd become? No better than a slaver? Was he really so lost that people looked at him and saw him as someone who contributed to that awful cycle of oppression? He slumped backward with a long sigh: that's *exactly* who he'd become. The realization made him nauseous as though he was the one with the gaping hole in his side.

Arianne paused for a long time, the sound of her ragged breathing the only thing filling their charged space. "Yes," she admitted quietly.

Jack's head whipped up to look at her, fire burning in his eyes. "I have *never* dealt in slaves," his voice was desperate and searching as if he needed Arianne to understand. "Slaves were the one part of Ace's business I refused to participate in."

Until that final night in France.

Jack shook at the memory. He really had lost himself to Cartel. He looked down at his right wrist, the ace of spades tattoo mocking him. Who was he kidding? Why was he surprised Arianne saw him as nothing more than another grunt from Cartel? He was *branded.* Cartel owned him.

And suddenly, he couldn't lie to Arianne anymore. He didn't know when it all changed, but it had became apparent to him that he couldn't just treat her like a means to an end anymore—no matter how detrimental that would prove to be. Arianne saved his life, she'd been given the option to run with all the information that she needed and had chosen to protect him all the same.

Arianne had chosen to save *him*, not his information. She deserved more than his lies. She deserved his trust more than anyone he'd met in over a decade.

"I was planning to sell you to Ace when we reached Leonueva," Jack admitted quickly before his common sense stopped him, "but I *never* considered selling you because you were a *Fera*."

As soon as Jack said it, he winced. Every ounce of his career professionalism was cursing at him for betraying his plans.

Arianne was quiet for a moment, then, "How chivalrous of you. So, you're just a backstabber, not a prejudiced asshole."

Jack blinked. Where he'd expected fury, he only heard slight levity in her tone. "Excuse me?" He asked in confusion.

Arianne managed a half chuckle before wincing in pain. "I wasn't born yesterday, Pangaea Boy, I knew you would try to double-cross me eventually. At least," she locked eyes with him, her large gray irises enchanting in the moonlight, "that's what you originally planned to do."

Jack read the unspoken question resting between them. Was that still his plan?

"I can't," his confession came out in a painful breath. "Y-you're," he searched for words, "good, Arianne. You're the first good I've had in a while."

If Jack betrayed her after the loyalty she'd shown him, he would prove to be the worst kind of human being. For the first time in a while, he didn't *want* to be seen that way. Arianne had saved his life and that had flipped an integral switch. Something inside of him was yelling at him now: that female resting below him was his last chance.

If he wanted to turn things around, it was now or never.

Arianne's eyes darkened, "I'm far from good," she admitted, "Those tribes-people I killed today?" She winced, "They brought back memories. They weren't the first people I killed. The people I was forced to be around as a child made me their executioner."

Arianne's confession chilled Jack to the bone. But, to his surprise, it didn't deter him, "You're good for *me*," he abridged with a small smile, "I don't think anyone in this war has a clean conscience."

Good for *him*. Yes, Arianne was good for him. She'd done something no one had been able to do and shown him there was more than just sinking deeper and deeper under Ace. Jack looked down at Arianne, really *looked* at her. He didn't know what it was about her, but she made him want to at least try to be some semblance of good. She made him want to dream of something better, to fight for what he once had. In such an unsuspecting—sometimes annoying—person, Jack could see himself wanting to be better in her presence.

He *trusted* her, and that was the most damning thing of all.

"I guess I would be a pretty big disappointment to you if I died tonight," Arianne said wryly.

A genuine laugh escaped Jack's chest and he was amazed at how good it felt to let humor back into his life. "I might just miss you, Princess," he managed, his lips tipping upward in entertainment.

"Do you mean it?" Arianne's voice was growing weaker as her eyes started to flutter closed.

Jack took the female's hand and squeezed it softly, "Would I have wasted my breath if I hadn't?"

A small smile fought its way to Arianne's mouth as she was pulled into uncon-sciousness, "Just checking," she whispered before breathing a strained laugh.

And then Arianne's head fell to the side, her body finally claiming the rest it so desperately needed. But even asleep, her blood-caked hand didn't leave his. Despite the pain and exhaustion, she looked at peace in her sleep. She looked like hell, but she was beautiful with her sandy blonde hair framing her bloodied and bruised face like a halo. He paused, the realization striking him. He thought that small firecracker below him was beautiful.

"You might not be Pacific's hero yet," Jack whispered, "but you're mine."

Jack's lips parted in surprise as if he'd just been hit with a blow. He looked down at Arianne once again and he was terrified and excited all at once as his heart fluttered at the sight of her.

I'm in so much fucking trouble.

Chapter 32

Arianne

Waking up was next to impossible.

Rain greeted Arianne as she stirred awake, pain lacing up and down her spine. She didn't dare to stir from her spot on the ground. God, everything hurt. She looked up, noticing their gray tarp had been hung above her head to protect their hastily constructed camp from the rainstorm. Jack must have erected the roof while she was asleep.

Jack. She turned her head. The bounty hunter was seated with his back to her as he stared out across the meadow beyond their camp. With so much mid-summer humidity, the rain had become a constant that watered the forest and turned it a vibrant green.

Arianne wished she could appreciate the beauty, but all she felt was hopeless.

Jack turned when he heard her stir. "How are you feeling?"

She winced, but she didn't attempt to move. "Like hell," she muttered.

The bounty hunter clenched his teeth and offered her some jerky. "I know, but we need to keep moving."

The thought of continuing on made her shake her head. "What's the point?"

She could hardly survive in a forest, what would she do when the real test came? Arianne winced at the memories from the night before that still haunted her. For all she knew, there were more awful memories to come when she returned to the city. She felt helpless with the fear that she couldn't even trust herself. What made it worse was she'd just started to believe she could handle herself on her suicide mission.

"We took a hard hit last night." Jack nodded in agreement. "But we can't give up now. We're so close."

Arianne gritted her teeth as she forced herself to sit up. "About last night," she murmured.

Jack turned to her, and for the first time, she felt like he was actually *looking* at her instead of simply tolerating her presence. Her stomach flopped. "We don't need to talk about anything if you don't want to," he replied slowly.

Arianne nodded curtly. "Thanks."

Where would she even begin? With the fact that Jack knew she was a *Fera*? Or maybe how he acknowledged he was going to double-cross her? She was still trying to figure out why she wasn't pissed at him for that little confession.

She sighed. When did it all become so complicated? When she left Pacific, things were black and white. There were her allies, and there were her enemies. And now, as she analyzed the bounty hunter she'd been strapped to for the past few weeks, she realized a gray space existed that she didn't like to think about.

"It's okay to feel overwhelmed," Jack continued, "I know how I felt those first few months in Joker training. I was lost and terrified. Alone." His shoulders slumped. "What I'm trying to say is: you're *not* alone. You don't need to fight this on your own."

The breath caught in her throat, and Arianne felt tears begin to sting her eyes. She'd been fighting alone her entire life: the memories of her childhood, the secrets from her friends, and the isolation of being locked on the island. As she analyzed Jack, her defenses weakened, and she wondered what it would feel like to have someone else to lean on.

"Thanks," she replied, too overwhelmed to say more.

Jack hesitantly rested his hand on her knee. "We'll figure it out. But first, we make it to the city and find your friends."

"What?"

Jack waved off her surprise. "It's fine. I don't need your city's coordinates. I'll give you my help pro bono." He winked. "You can't afford my professional services anyway."

Arianne shoved him, pretending to be offended, but in reality, she was relieved. A part of her was still wary of Jack's true allegiances, but it was a good feeling to know she wasn't entering Leonueva alone.

"My offer still stands," Arianne said, "if you help fix all of this, I can fight to get you citizenship."

Jack's levity faded. "I wish it was that easy," he admitted, "but I owe Ace a debt. She won't stop hunting me until I pay it back—or die trying."

Without another word, Jack stood and began packing up their meager camp. Arianne winced, terrified she'd ruined one of his rare good moods. At the core of it all, she felt terrible. How could she live with herself if she saved the Pacifican squad but left Jack behind? She realized then that if she left him in that city, she would feel like she hadn't saved everyone.

The hike that day was slow. Her injuries forced them to take more breaks than she was proud of, and the rain made the rocky ground of the sloping mountains slick. Somehow, they made decent progress, and by the end of the gloomy day, they could see the Artery in the distance.

Jack pointed to the large scar the Artery cut through the dense forest, "Leonueva is just beyond that." His finger traced the river running through the mountainside below them. "The Artery makes a bridge over the river. There's a sewer entrance into the city in there."

Arianne's shoulders slumped, the exhaustion from the past few weeks finally hitting her with the finish line in sight. "That was easy," she breathed.

"Easy as rocket science." Jack rolled his eyes.

"Oh, Haris wouldn't have a problem with that..." Arianne's voice trailed off as she realized Jack had no idea who her friend was.

Homesickness panged deep in her chest. She hoped Haris was okay. She hoped that everyone waiting back on the island was okay. With a deep breath, Arianne took in the last stretch of her hike ahead. She would be back at home on the island soon, and everything would be right with the world again.

While Jack disappeared to set up camp, Arianne remained behind and looked out over the vast expanse of the forest. Awe finally pushing its way past her sorrow. She'd never seen so much green in her entire life. The smooth peaked rolling hills of a dying mountain range grew out of the forest and made her wings itch to fly. She lost herself, simply imagining herself falling from the rocky outcroppings scattered about the mountains just to catch herself and sail over the rustling trees. The idea was just beautiful enough to make her forget about her dizzying nightmares—if only for a moment.

Arianne missed the feel of the wind rushing through her hair and the drop in her stomach when she went into a free fall. She risked a glance behind her at her traveling companion and frowned. Even if she could fly low enough to avoid Pangaea's radars— and that was a big *if*—she still had Jack to worry about. Sure, he knew she was a *Fera,* but she still wasn't sure if she trusted him with all her secrets yet.

"Arianne! Get in here! You're going to get soaked!"

He was right. The rain was coming down in a fury now, angry droplets splashing with each impact against her face. Arianne made sure that her emotions were in check before rushing underneath the cover of the tarp Jack erected.

"Here," he extended a bowl filled with another one of his salves. "This should help with the pain in your side."

Arianne took the bowl with a grin. "The only pain in my side here is you."

"Good one," Jack smiled in a way that threatened to melt her traumatized, frozen heart.

A silence fell over them as Arianne began to overthink the days to come. She knew everything was filled with uncertainty, and honestly, it was easier not to talk about it. Could she simply leave Jack behind once she freed the Pacifican squad from Ace? Was she sure she trusted him?

Arianne's troubled thoughts followed her even as she tried to sleep. Between the stress of the upcoming day and the lingering pain of her injuries, she couldn't relax and it wasn't long before she gave up on sleep entirely. Forcing herself to stand, Arianne ducked out from under the tent and began to pace the rain-soaked clearing beyond. The storm had passed sometime after dinner, and now only a few dark clouds lingered to rival the light of the moon.

The night was peaceful. If only she could pause long enough to take a deep breath. She paced through the grass, the blades sparkling silver from the remaining dew reflecting the moonlight. For a few fleeting moments, Arianne was almost crazy enough to run away and disappear into the wild beyond civilization forever. It would be so easy to just leave everything behind and become one with nature like some mythical forest wraith.

"Can't sleep?"

Arianne was startled. It always amazed her how the bounty hunter seemed to sneak up on her so easily. Jack was like a ghost, existing on the fringes of humanity, only appearing when he wanted to be seen. But that past week had shown her Jack was far more human than he wanted people to believe.

"I'm just a little stressed out," she admitted wryly.

Jack stepped out of the shadows of the tree he was leaning on. The moon cast dramatic shades across his face that defined his nose and cheekbones. Her breath caught: he looked stunning. Wordlessly, Jack walked up to Arianne and extended one of his earbuds, signaling her to put the device in her ear. With a raised eyebrow, she obliged, anticipating the music to start playing, just as Jack had done for her during the day. However, no sound emerged.

Suddenly, the world around her brightened. Night transformed into day, and the tree-covered mountainside morphed into rolling green hills dotted with white and yellow flowers. Arianne spun around in awe, and in the distance, beyond one of the hills, lay a quaint town nestled on the edge of a forest. She almost believed she was in heaven.

"I used to come here when I got stressed out," Jack began, his hands going to his pockets as he looked around. "Recently, though, I didn't think I deserved to be here. I haven't let myself come in a while."

"This is your home back in France," Arianne realized in amazement. "You're simulating the memory with the earbuds."

Jack nodded, his eyes filled with conflict. "Ace's only gift to me. It's a smaller version of a technology she calls a Simulator."

"It's beautiful," Arianne gasped.

Jack's face twisted with pain. "Mende, France," he admitted, "it was all destroyed just over ten years ago."

Arianne stilled. Mende was the name of the Pacifican outpost where Jaleel Leroy had once lived before its coordinates were betrayed. Pangaea had reduced that peaceful mountainside village to ash. There were no recorded survivors, or at least, none that were known.

Arianne turned to Jack. Slowly, the bounty hunter lowered his head in sorrow.

"Your mother died in the bombing," she realized in horror.

"And my father," Jack spat bitterly. "My mother died protecting my sister," he continued, shaking his head. "My sister never walked again. Our house fell on our mother and crushed my sister's spine in the process. My Pèpè and I were the only ones in my family who made it out unscathed."

Arianne fumbled for words. "But you're a Pacifican! Why didn't you ever go back?"

Jack looked down, his voice laced with anger. "They never came."

A chill ran down Arianne's spine. She now understood why Jack despised Pacific. He'd lost his home and family because someone in Pacific had failed to protect them, and then they were forgotten.

The town in the distance changed, and soon, the only thing that remained was a distant cloud of smoke. The valley around them filled with ash so thick it looked like a snow squall. Jack fell to his knees and grey clouds of debris puffed around him.

"My Pèpè found a cabin on the outskirts of town and took care of my sister and me. We didn't know what else to do. We didn't know who to trust anymore. Then, one day, Pangaea came looking. I don't remember much—just my sister's scream."

Jack's hands went to his ears as he stared at a point far beyond the meadow. Arianne landed on the wet ground next to him, reminded that they were only in a simulation. Despite the ash coating the ground, rain-soaked grass was what truly sat below. She held Jack's shoulders, trying to ground him, understanding how painful those memories were for him.

"A Pangaean soldier found our cabin while on patrol," Jack went on, his voice filled with despair. "I was returning from a hunt, and I was so scared. The next thing I knew, the soldier was on the ground, and my rifle was smoking in my hands. And Genevieve," Jack's hands raked down his face, "I never saw her look at me like that—like I was a murderer."

The simulation darkened as if Jack's very memory was shrouded in shadow. The ash faded, replaced by small flecks of red blood staining the green grass at their knees.

"I knew more of them would come for me, and I knew I couldn't bear to see my sister look at me like that again," Jack continued, his voice heavy with the memory. "So I ran."

Arianne's lips parted. "Your first kill," she said slowly.

Jack buried his face in his hands. "When I tell you I understand how you felt yesterday—I understand," he admitted, his voice wavering. Taking a deep breath, he collected himself and rose to his feet. He extended a hand to help Arianne up. "I ran to Paris, where Ace found me half-starved in an alleyway and offered me food and protection. I didn't look back."

Silence enveloped them. Arianne focused on his tight grip on her hand, knowing she was the only thing keeping him grounded. She squeezed his hand back and looked up at him reassuringly. She was surprised to see relief lingering there beside the pain.

"What was it like for you?" Jack asked, his voice soft. "To run away from everything you knew?"

"I don't remember much," Arianne began. Her mind went back to the fragmented memories she had of that day. "I remember fear, desperation, and pain. And then I woke up in Citadel."

Arianne suddenly went numb, her mind fighting to keep the worst of the memories at bay. She closed her eyes and tried to piece together the fragmented events of that day, or any day from Pangaea. But the more she tried to connect the pieces, the more they resisted coming together.

"I..." Jack trailed off, his face filled with remorse. "It's easier to shut it out."

"Then to remember," she finished knowingly.

Arianne nodded. She couldn't stop herself from running her hands down his muscled arms. The conversation they were having was stripping her raw and she wanted—no needed—the physical contact of someone else who understood.

A half-crazed laugh escaped her chest. "I feel *guilt* for leaving," she admitted. "I can't describe it, but I feel like a failure for running away. To this day, it's so much easier to push it all down than to..." She looked up at Jack, and her heart nearly stopped as their eyes met. "T-to talk about it," she stammered.

The simulation brightened around them. At first, Arianne thought the sun had returned. Then she looked around and realized they were surrounded by thousands of glittering fireflies. Gaping, she watched the small balls of fire swirl in the air around her as they left charming trails of yellow light in their wake.

"Beautiful," Arianne gasped, her face bathed in the ethereal glow of the fireflies.

Jack smiled down at her, his lips curving in a way that made her toes curl. "You get it, Princess, you actually get it," he said in amazement.

Arianne was keenly aware of how close they stood. Warmth grew between them as she moved her arms to brace herself against his chest. She almost gasped as Jack's hands rose to her lower back and pulled her closer. Her heart began thundering so loudly in her chest that she was terrified that Jack would hear her.

"We're fuck ups together, right?" she asked.

Jack reached across the space between them that simultaneously felt dangerously close and millions of miles apart. Softly, he put his hand under her chin and lifted her face towards him. In the soft glow of the fireflies, his stunning bronze skin and chestnut hair became devastating.

"Together," Jack whispered, agreeing.

Arianne froze as she realized she was wading into dangerous waters, and then admitted she didn't care one bit. A chill sent goosebumps across her body, "What about after?"

She was starting to hope Jack wasn't just going to be a passing character in her life. For a moment, she let herself wonder what it would be like to go beyond that war and their rivaling allegiances. What would they become? She wanted the chance to find out.

"After?" Jack asked, his tone becoming enticingly flirtatious.

Her mouth dried out as anticipation made her fingertips tingle. She knew she should stop and walk away. What was going on between them shouldn't happen. Jack had to return to Ace, and Arianne had an island to protect. But, what was so wrong about pretending?

Arianne rose to her tip toes, her mouth hovering just above his. Her eyes fluttered closed as she ran her hands down Jack's chest and across his hips, "You have a choice," she leaned to whisper in his ear, "We could forget about all of this, or—"

Her hand slowly snaked up Jack's body until she was cupping his face. After weeks of hiking, scruff covered Jack's lower chin, and it itched the inside of her palm. A low grumble escaped Jack, and she smiled, realizing he was struggling to hold back just as much as she was.

She was deeply aware they stood on the precipice. One shift in either direction would lead to two very different outcomes. One direction was the smart choice: keep allegiances clear and keep her distance. Unfortunately, the other direction was becoming impossible to ignore.

"Or," Arianne repeated slowly, her voice becoming low and taunting, "we can explore whatever 'together' means for us."

"Together?" Jack asked, his chin tilting so his lips hovered just before hers.

"Together."

Jack's voice was low, "I like the sound of that, Princess."

"Don't call me Princess," Arianne protested with a grin.

She didn't know who moved first. But as soon as Jack's lips were on her own, strong and searching, she knew she made a mistake. She wanted more, more, more. And that was dangerous.

She fell into him and happily let him deepen the kiss. Jack cupped her face, and butterflies filled her stomach as she ran her fingers through his tangled curls. She had never known kissing someone else could feel so good. She wanted more. She wanted everything. She didn't care that they had been strangers, enemies, a week ago. All she cared about was that it felt right. Somehow, she'd found someone who genuinely understood her, and it didn't matter that they existed on opposite sides of that war.

At that moment, she was crazy enough to think it could work.

And then the spell was broken. Arianne moved too far to the side and stretched her stitches. A wave of pain shot from her bullet wound and rippled throughout her body. She buckled, the lightheadedness making her want to vomit. Jack caught her before she collapsed.

"Ow," Arianne managed, looking up at him with a pinched smile.

Jack grinned, helping her to her feet. "Leave it to you to try and start something less than a day after almost dying," he quipped.

Arianne ran a hand over his face once more, the nausea making her want to curl up and sleep for the next two days. "Can you blame me?" She bit her lip, "Stick around, and maybe we can finish what we started."

"I'd like that," his gaze was softer than she had ever seen. The difference between the Jack she'd met on Citadel Island and the Jack looking down at her was like night and day. "Let's survive the city first," his eyes were light as if the weight of the world had been momentarily lifted from his shoulders.

Arianne knew they were mostly pretending. She knew surviving the next few days would be a stretch. But for a few fleeting moments, forgetting about it all felt nice.

Chapter 33

Jaya

Jaya leaned against the prison bars that separated her from her sister's cell. Kalinda's gentle hands reached through the barrier, braiding her bright purple hair. As Kalinda worked, her fingers scraped Jaya's scalp soothingly, and Jaya closed her eyes, allowing herself a rare moment of relaxation as her sister styled her hair like she'd done hundreds of times before.

Even when they were kids, Kalinda had always braided her sister's hair whenever she felt stressed. Growing up, Jaya had despised her hair for the attention it brought her, but Kalinda's braiding made her feel beautiful. Thanks to her hair, she could share those precious moments with her sister daily.

"Stay still, won't you?" Kalinda chided as she completed the braid. "You're no better at this than when you were a child."

Jaya grinned.

"Hey, Kal," Rhino called out, twirling the longer section of his silver hair. "Can you do me next?"

Kalinda snickered. "Mate, break us out of here, and I'll braid whatever you want."

A mischievous glint sparkled in Rhino's eyes. "You might regret that offer."

Jaya blushed. "Rhino!" she exclaimed. "Your president is right there!"

Rhino jolted, turning his head to Caesar, who was seated on his cot. "Caesar—I mean, Mr. President!" he stammered. "I'm sorry! I was just trying to lighten the mood! That's all!"

Caesar grinned, waving off Rhino's concerns. "It's quite alright, Lieutenant Adams." To Jaya's surprise, the President winked. "I've already seen the hair you're talking about."

All color drained from Rhino's face. "If I had known you were at the house that night, I would have never even considered the streaking dare."

Caesar chuckled, and laughter rippled through the room. Jaya even managed a smile. While morale wasn't perfect, Caesar's presence had significantly improved it. With Caesar back, the team had identified every Pacifican in the building and was slowly forming an escape plan.

It wouldn't be easy, but at least they had a chance.

The prison block doors opened, and to Jaya's dismay, it wasn't a Ward delivering their food. Pandora marched in, her face as unyielding as stone, bleach-blonde hair flowing straight behind her. Blue Krait followed closely after, like a shadow.

Another woman followed them. She had the same ghostly features as Pandora and glacial blue eyes so pale Jaya feared they could see through her. Unlike Pandora's fine-pressed black suit, this woman wore a floor-length white lab coat that had a white hood she kept over her head. With her features shadowed by the hood, the woman looked more like a wraith than Pandora.

Jaya's mouth went dry as the woman's eyes locked on her. "Is this the specimen?" The woman asked in a heavy London accent so unconcerned she might've been ordering a coffee, not inspecting prisoners of war.

Pandora moved to the woman's side. "Yes, Mother," she nodded, folding her hands behind her back. "That's the *Fera* who can change colors at will."

Jaya's heart threatened to stop. Hera Richards, the Matriarch of the Richards family and the world's most infamous *Fera* researcher stood before her. The European Scientist General approached Jaya's cell, studying her like an animal in a zoo, her gaze filled with cold calculation and morbid curiosity.

Kalinda reached through the bars to grab her younger sister's hand, and she grasped it tightly. Her heart was racing a million miles a minute under Hera's awful stare. What was Hera going to do to her?

In desperation, Jaya tried to catch Blue's eye. The Snake had warned her about Hera's lab but had never shared more details. What secrets were Blue hiding? As if sensing Jaya's questions, the Snake lowered her yellow eyes in shame.

Bile rose in her throat. She was doomed.

"Ah yes," Hera said mildly, "it will make an interesting addition to my lab."

No, no, no, no, Jaya's eyes widened as she squeezed her sister's hands tighter. To make matters worse, her stress was slowly turning her hands a shade of deep green and the color was rising up her forearms. There was no hiding her abilities now.

Hera watched Jaya's reaction with growing interest, "Pet, see to it she's brought to my lab immediately."

With a swish of her lab coat, Hera turned and left the prison block, followed quickly by her daughter. Blue remained behind; her snake eyes shadowed. Jaya shrunk closer to her sister as Blue approached her cell.

"Wait," Jaya began to hyperventilate, "Wait, no," she could hardly breathe, "Blue, where am I going? What's going to happen to me?"

"This is cruel and unusual punishment," Caesar protested, his voice filled with barely controlled rage. "As prisoners of war, we have the right to see a commanding officer and a fair trial!"

Blue frowned, "She's not a prisoner. She's a *Fera*," she sighed, lowering her head. "*Feras* have no rights, not in the Murray Monument."

Jaya shook her head, her voice trembling. "No, no," she cried, "they can't take me!"

Kalinda did her best to comfort Jaya, rubbing her thumbs over the back of her sister's hands. "Look at me," she demanded quietly. "Calm your heart. You're brave—braver than I'll ever be. I'm so proud of you."

Jaya slowed her breathing, focusing on her sister's face, memorizing every detail. She remembered the burnt honey-colored skin, the rounded nose, and her bright hazel eyes. Jaya memorized her sister's jet-black hair as it cascaded down her shoulders. In those moments, she fought to remember every last feature that she could. She knew she might never see her again.

"I love you, *Didi*," Jaya whispered.

Kalinda leaned forward and kissed Jaya's forehead. "I love you too."

"Oh," came a new, deeper voice, "did I miss something interesting?"

Caesar sat up straighter. "Prince Andre—Your Highness," he corrected himself. "I'm asking to keep my people together. Subjecting one of my Lieutenants to experimentation is cruel and unusual punishment and is certainly not legal under the Pangaean Constitution—"

Andre raised a black-gloved hand, silencing the President. The prince regarded Kalinda, who clung to Jaya, without any visible emotion. Jaya wiped away a stray tear, feeling a surge of anger. Not only did Andre appear unmoved, but he also seemed amused.

"Do you think I care about a tiny little *Fera*?" he cooed, glancing at Jaya. "She actually looks cute, all bright green like that."

Jaya shrank next to her sister, mortified and blushing orange.

"Oi!" Kalinda barked at the prince. "What's your problem?"

Andre turned his head to Kalinda, a smile cracking on his humorless lips, "Why, isn't it the nurse?" He asked, leaning towards Kalinda's cell. "Oh! Is she your sister?" Andre's jaw ticked. "Too bad."

"And I would've thought you'd have more consideration for little sisters," Caesar challenged.

Jaya glanced at Caesar in confusion. Andre was known to be an only child. What was Caesar referring to? Judging by Andre's seething scowl, there was something more to his words.

Andre turned on Caesar, his eyes blazing with newfound fury. "What did you just say to me?"

Caesar held his ground. "How about we ask your mother?" He retorted.

Andre took a step back, a dark shadow crossing his face. The prince looked furious, and his chilling glare sent shivers down Jaya's spine. Baring his teeth, he asked, "My mother?"

"Josephina Valentino Murray," Caesar replied. "*Lo entiendes?*"

A low growl escaped Andre's throat. "*Tu conoces a Josephina?*"

With the tension between Andre and Caesar growing, Jaya nearly missed the sound of the prison block doors opening once more. A man entered, the dim light of the prison shading all but the grin on his face.

"Well, of course, he knows Josephina," the man's deep, smooth voice resonated like the finest red wine. "She was raised with him."

For the first time since Caesar's arrival, Jaya saw the President's slowly growing rage finally break through his calm demeanor. Caesar held his head high, wearing a deep frown. "Griffin," he scowled.

The man walked under the dim lights, chuckling lightly. "Come now," he said, "we all know I haven't been called that name since my Ascension."

A chill swept over Jaya as she finally took in the man who'd joined them in their cell. He was strikingly handsome with golden blonde hair and eyes so blue they seemed capable of piercing steel. Everything about him was immaculate, from his well-groomed hair and clean-shaven face to his perfectly fitted suit and muscular frame. The only imperfection was the right side of his face where three claw-like scars left angry dark pink gashes in his skin.

The energy coming off of that man told Jaya he owned every room he stepped into and would dominate anyone who dared to try and take it away from him. The power that man's presence held was heavy, thick, oppressive.

He was an academic, a warrior, a Commander.

Leon Murray.

Jaya's heart stopped as she realized the enormity of the power standing before her. Leon was everywhere, everything, and she was nothing more than an ant to him. It shook her to her core.

Leon's eyes returned to Caesar, a mild amusement flickering across his face. "I never thought you'd be leading these idealistic rebels," he remarked. He waved his son aside and approached Caesar's cell. Jaya despised how effortlessly beautiful the Commander appeared as he smiled down at Caesar. "Look at how far you've fallen. I can't wait to watch you hit rock bottom. We have a lot of catching up to do, old friend."

Part III

Into the Lion's Den

Chapter 34
Blackjack

Leonueva.

Jack stared up at the towering skyscrapers in awe as he took a deep breath of air that smelled of electricity and oil. He realized he already missed the leafy freshness of the forest. The sewer systems had smelt far from great, and upon resurfacing inside Leonueva, he learned the city didn't smell much better. With a high population density and millions of machines whirring on oil and electricity, the air smelled like any urban center: full of waste.

He leaned down and helped pull Arianne out of the sewer tunnel, careful not to pull too hard and aggravate her stitches. The female climbed out from the manhole and stood to her full height to stare at the city with awe. Jack watched her curiously. His wonder about the city had faded years ago, so it was interesting to see someone stare at the buildings with newborn interest. Amazement made the Pacifican glow as she gaped at the shining lights of the modern buildings and the technological marvels that came from novelty and money.

Lots and lots of money.

Jack was certain he'd looked the same way when Ace brought him back to Leonueva. The new capital of Europe had the advantage that no other city in the world had: youth and a population built strictly of the wealthiest citizens and military.

An electric train built on a magnetic levitation system shot past, hardly making any noise. Jack brushed Arianne behind him as the tailwinds of the train rustled his hair. In a city born of modern technology, Leonueva had no need for cars. Leon might be terrifying, but he wasn't an idiot. When the great Commander designed his city, he built it with everything carefully considered. Leon's city seemed to live and breathe on its own.

Much like most of Pangaea, Leonueva was a masterpiece built on the bones of millions—but a masterpiece all the same.

"Damn, they've got a nice little utopia here, don't they?" Arianne breathed, looking up at the street littered with passersby. "Could almost make someone forget they're owned by an oligarchy that leaves half of the population in poverty." The Pacifican shrugged. "Oh, I almost forgot about the slavery thing too. But, what do I know?"

Jack managed a small chuckle as he scanned the street. "Okay, we need cover until nightfall. We got to regroup and figure out a plan."

"I thought we had a plan," Arianne eyed Jack.

He shrugged. "Wasn't sure we'd make it this far."

"Don't blame you there."

Jack led Arianne down the busy sidewalk. Their outfits got a couple of glares from some Elite shoppers, but as long as they stayed with the thick crowds, he was confident they wouldn't attract much attention. He watched as a Ward—dressed in their classic black and red uniform—patrolled the sidewalk across from them. Wards were not above random identification checks, so he needed to ensure they kept a low profile.

Luckily, he'd been avoiding Wards for his entire adult life.

Jack reached behind him and grabbed Arianne's hand. He paused when he felt how clammy her palms were. He turned to look at the Pacifican. "You good?" He asked with a raised eyebrow.

Arianne's gray eyes darted around the crowds. "Fun fact about me: if I start making jokes, it's because I'm stressed the fuck out."

Arianne bit her lip, which made Jack want to push her up against the store window to his side and kiss her right there. He pushed down on the thought, hating that he had a whole new slew of urges he needed to learn to control. The memory of her lips brushing against his left his head spinning.

Hey, idiot, you're in a city full of people who want you dead.

Arianne looked down. "I shouldn't have come here," she whispered. "What was I thinking?"

Her voice was terribly small, and Jack could practically feel her fear coming to the surface like a rising tide. He turned to the female and wasn't surprised to see the stricken look in her eyes. Before Ace had numbed him to the horrors of Pangaea, he'd made that same expression more often than he would have liked.

"Do you want to talk about it?" Jack asked, a hand rising to the small of her back.

Arianne's jaw clenched as she studied a small patrol of Wards marching down the street. "Not here," she whispered. "Let's just find somewhere to rest before I have a mental breakdown."

From the strain in her voice, he could tell she wasn't kidding.

"I get this is a lot," he began.

Arianne paled as they walked. He looked up, noticing what she was staring at. At the center of the city rose a towering black skyscraper. The windows were built of the darkest glass that had the entire building standing like a shadow above the city even in broad daylight. Jack's blood chilled. The Murray Monument.

In all his years in that city, he'd never stepped foot into that building, and he certainly wasn't planning on it anytime soon. Ace might be intimidating, but at least she wasn't the Lion that sat atop the obsidian throne.

Arianne's eyes didn't leave the tower. "It's a lot coming home," her voice lacked its characteristic fire.

He blinked, turning his head to her. She'd never denied that her father was a Pangaean Elite. It made sense that her family most likely came from the city. But still, the realization was shocking. Arianne, a Pacifican soldier, and mutant, was the daughter of some obnoxious Elite who called that city their home.

Her terror of Leonueva took on an entirely new meaning.

"Your father won't find you," he leaned forward to whisper in her ear.

"That's the plan," she replied tersely. As if a switch had been flicked, her daze faded as her classic bravado took over. "All right, let's go mess with your boss."

"I like that idea," Jack grinned.

For the Capital of Europe, Leonueva was a small city. It made sense. The wards that kept the city glamoured against onlookers could only cover so much space, and Leonueva only had two purposes: housing the upper class willing to live there and maintaining the stationed military base. With such a small city, the pair made it to his impromptu hideout just as night fell.

Streetlights flickered on as Jack led Arianne down an abandoned block. That area of the city was barren and forgotten. All the buildings were unfinished and the road was yet to be paved. Vines snaked up the skeletal structures, warning that they hadn't been touched in years. Jack gazed at the eerie construction sites as they stood like barren trees in the night. Most people were deterred from that part of town, but over the years, he'd gained a strange level of comfort around the abandoned lots. He liked the idea that even in Leon's perfect city, there were still imperfections where money or interest had run out before construction was finished.

The existence of those barren streets reminded him he wasn't the only thing in the perfect city that had been left behind to rot.

Lonely figures walked down the dusty streets. Arianne stepped behind Jack as she watched them warily. He gritted his teeth and turned to the Pacifican. "They won't bother us," he promised. "We hardly look like we have anything worth stealing."

Arianne looked down at her dirt-covered and torn Pacifican briefs with a nod. "We look pretty terrible," she admitted.

"Most of them came here through the military," Jack explained, "Unfortunately, once they're stationed here, they can't leave—even if they get discharged. Ace owns most of them now. They're probably addicted to whatever new drug she's peddling."

Arianne's gray eyes were cloaked in shadow, "There's so many of them."

"Ace has been leaking her people into this city for years now," Jack frowned, "Leon might turn a blind eye to her, but she's slowly rotting this place from the inside out. Ace has it made in Leonueva: gambling, drugs, and slave trade directly in the heart of the most concentrated population of Elites in Europe." He shook his head, "She has a monopoly and no shortage of money from her clients."

"And she has my friends," Arianne's eyebrows furrowed together, "and my dad."

A man walked suspiciously close to the pair, and Jack wrapped his arm around Arianne. He knew she could handle herself, but he also knew her bullet wound could make her vulnerable for the next few days. The darkness was almost complete, and Jack could feel his instincts warning him to get inside soon. With daylight on their side, the homeless around them might be more timid, but in the dark, there was no telling what they would do.

"Let's get inside for the night," Jack instructed, guiding Arianne toward a building. "We'll regroup tomorrow and figure out how we're going to get past my boss."

The building was far from up to code, but Jack had relied on it since the day he found it during Joker training. They picked their way to a false wall he'd erected near the back of the first floor. Moving a floorboard, he could wedge his fingers underneath and pull the panel he had cut backward. Beyond the rough carving of drywall was a steel door with a lock. Jack pulled up another floorboard and produced the key.

The door creaked open, revealing a staircase to the basement. Feeling around, Jack found the construction light he'd erected above the stairs, and he flicked the switch. With a *clink* and a soft hum, the old yellow lights revealed a dusty concrete staircase leading downwards into a shadowed basement.

Arianne raised an eyebrow, "If we hadn't just spent weeks together in the Darwin Zone, I'd be convinced you were taking me down there to kill me."

They carefully picked down the stairs until they reached the concrete-walled basement. Jack let out a sigh of relief at the sight of his mattress and spare couch. Exhaustion pulled at his limbs as he dropped his bag and collapsed face-first on his meager bed. It wasn't much, but after weeks of sleeping on the forest floor, that musky mattress felt like a five-star resort.

Jack turned when he realized Arianne hadn't moved from the entrance to the stairs, her face washed in the work lamp's yellow light. It was hard to miss her surprise at Jack's small base, and embarrassment pulled at him. He just brought this female—who he sorely wanted to impress—to a construction site.

He winced, "I know it's not a lot, but it's home," he managed.

Arianne frowned, electing to sit on Jack's couch, "I'm happy we have a place to rest," she breathed. "But, is this all Ace has given you?"

She looked troubled.

Jack pursed his lips. "Ace gives me enough. I only come here so I can have a break from her nonsense." He looked down, his eyes softening as his calloused hands ran over the sheets of his mattress, "This place reminds me that she doesn't completely own me. I don't know, this might be a dingy basement, but it reminds me that—to some extent—I'm still free to come and go as I please."

It was the only distinction he had from her *Fera* slaves.

Arianne's breath came out slowly. "And that's why you were desperate to pay off that debt."

His head shot up to look at her, and guilt made his stomach clench. "I'm sorry," was all he managed to say.

The Pacifican nodded, suddenly unable to look him in the eyes. Her hands fidgeted above her thighs as her jaw worked in thought. "I was so ready to see you as the bad guy," she began. "I was ready to hate you for taking Jaya, Caesar, and Rhino from me."

Jack's shoulders slumped. "I'm a bad person, Arianne," he admitted slowly, "you didn't get that wrong."

Jack had sold his life—his entire identity—away to Ace. He had killed, stolen from, and broken people and their families. He was ready to admit he was an enabler of the trading of human beings. Sure, he didn't actively trade sentient lives, but he did stand by and let it happen. No, he wasn't good. Far from it.

But maybe helping fix what he'd wronged with Arianne could be a first step in the right direction for once.

"Everyone does bad things, including me," Arianne's knuckles cracked under the pressure of her fidgeting, "it's the choices you make after that define if you're good or bad."

"A choice," Jack looked down, "I don't think I've had one of those in a while."

Arianne shook her head, "Of course you have. You chose to help me."

Jack nodded, "That's a nice sentiment, but I meant a choice in how my life will turn out." He held up his right wrist and displayed the ace of spades tattoo to her, "As soon as this was put on me, I didn't have any choices."

"Why did you come back to the city then?" she asked.

Disappointment settled like a rock in his stomach, "because I don't know anything else. And even if I ran, Ace is more powerful than a Pangaean Elite. She would find me." Jack paused, wondering if he dared to say the last part. Then he looked into Arianne's eyes. Though their color was as cold as steel, her gaze was welcoming and warm. He slumped, "And my sister Genevieve," he explained, "she's still alive somewhere."

"Genevieve," Arianne repeated, "you've been muttering her name in your sleep."

He hugged himself as a pang of sadness that physically ached washed over him, "She's everything to me. I couldn't live with myself if running meant Ace took her as collateral for my debt."

Arianne rose and moved to sit at his side. Slowly, she put her hand on his thigh, the warmness of her touch spreading through him like wildfire. Arianne leaned into Jack, and rested her head on his shoulder, "I had a brother," she offered as tears misted her eyes. "He meant the world to me too. I understand how much it must tear you up inside being apart from your sister."

Jack was surprised at the sting of tears at the back of his eyes. Without a word, he leaned into Arianne, his face falling into her hair. The female's dirty blonde waves were frizzy and tangled, but they smelled of morning dew and pine. It reminded him of home and their long hike through the forest he was slowly starting to miss. He inhaled deeply and felt the overpowering feeling of anxiety, worry, and loss slowly weaken.

With Arianne at his side, he felt less alone. Suddenly, he wasn't sure what to do if he was ultimately forced to remain behind in Leonueva. Sadly, he didn't know if he would ever meet someone like her again. Arianne was impulsive, wild, and aggressive, but she was also empathetic, vulnerable, and fiercely loyal. Most of all, she understood him more than anyone he'd ever met.

"A choice," Jack said.

"What?" Arianne asked, leaning away from his side to look up at him.

He frowned, "You mentioned figuring out what comes after all of this," he began, lacing his hand in hers, "One day, I want to be able to wake up in the morning and know that the life that I'm living was my decision."

He wanted to be the person his mother always dreamt he could be. He wanted to be worthy of the name his mother had given him—the name passed down through his family for generations. He wanted to live up to his father's legacy of kindness and brilliance. He wanted to protect his sister and be worthy of her love once more. Most of all—he looked at Arianne as his hand softly cupped her face—he wanted to find out what he could become with someone like her at his side.

Jack was willing to bet that together, they could change the world or reduce it to rubble. And even though he'd just realized all of this, he knew he would fight to the end for a chance at that future.

"I like the sound of that," Arianne's eyes fluttered shut as she leaned forward.

Her lips were soft as she kissed him. She was slow and careful as she moved into his lap and ran her hands through his hair. He sighed at her closeness and then reached a hand to the small of her back to pull her even tighter to his chest. Arianne's back had always felt strange when he held it, as if there was something more than just her uniform resting there, but he didn't mention it. The first rule of *Fera* courtesy was to never ask what their mutation entailed unless they offered it. If Arianne never asked why his wrist had healed so quickly, he wouldn't ask any questions about her. Besides, he wouldn't ruin that moment for the world.

Hands sliding down to her hips, Jack held Arianne softly as he fell into his bed. She fell with him as her arms braced above his head. He grinned, marveling at her corded muscles from years of training. Arianne was as beautiful as she was terrifying, and he was crazy enough to want more. He lunged upwards, claiming her lips once more, and she melted into his chest.

Then she began to kiss down his jawline. His eyes rolled backward as she kissed his neck. Breathing heavily, Jack ran his hands down her generous backside as a sigh escaped him.

He was so lost in Arianne that he made a major mistake: he stopped paying attention to his surroundings.

"Well, ain't this sweet? I would apologize for interrupting the moment, but I just don't care."

Jack's eyes widened. Instinct took over as he grabbed Arianne's shoulders and pulled them off the bed and behind the cover of his couch. There Jack knelt, producing a gun from his hip and cocking it.

"Fucking awful timing," he muttered.

Arianne grinned at Jack's side, a hunting knife appearing in her hands, "Let's try to focus," she winked.

Arianne stood up, quickly throwing the knife at one of the newcomers with an evil grin. Someone beyond the couch shouted in annoyance, followed by a heavy thud on the floor.

"Come on, Blackjack," drawled a man, "that ain't no way to greet your friend!"

Jack's eyes widened, "Jamie?" He stood up from the couch, hands raised above his head. Sure enough, Jamie—in a cowboy hat—was standing in front of two more Jokers. A third Joker lay on the floor with a knife in his shoulder from Arianne's throw. Jack stared at the group, "What's going on?"

Jamie pouted, "I thought you were never gon' come back!" The American sighed in his thick accent, "I thought you done abandoned me!"

Jack's jaw fell open as his blood went cold, "Did Ace send you?"

"Of course she did!" Jamie exclaimed, "You don't think you could just mosey into *la ciudad* without good 'ol Boss knowing, did you?" The younger man put his hands on his hips, "She's mighty disappointed that you didn't stop in, Blackjack."

Every nerve in Jack's body tingled, and he exchanged a look with Arianne below him. Something wasn't right. Jack eyed the men behind Jamie again, "She made you a Joker," he realized.

Jamie pointed a double-barreled shotgun in Jack's direction, "Oh, she did better than that, seeing as your position was vacant."

Jack bared his teeth, "Well, I'm back now. You can tell her that I'm not some toy to be fetched by her dogs. I'll stop by when I feel like it."

"We heard the news that you brought a Pacifican friend," Jamie's grin was predatory as his eyes raked over Arianne's body like she was nothing more than one of Ace's dancers. "Well, she seems like more than a friend." Jamie nodded at Arianne. "Don't get your feelings in a twist, sister. Blackjack loves his lady friends."

Arianne gritted her teeth in rage at Jack's side, "Last I checked, who I fuck is none of your business. Now who are you, and why should I care?" She muttered a few words in Spanish that Jack could only assume were some well-placed insults.

Jamie blinked, "A Spaniard," he whistled low, impressed, "Be careful, friend, they're spicy."

"Well aware," Jack seethed.

Another knife appeared in Arianne's hands, "I'll ask again, *quién eres*?"

Jamie swung his pistol around on his pointer finger. "You're looking at Ace's new top dog," he boasted, "They call me Texas Hold'Em now, but I'll let you use Tex to save your breath." Slowly, Tex raised his right wrist and proudly displayed a freshly inked ace of spades tattoo.

"Tex?" Jack pressed, "You're an idiot. You're letting Ace own you. She only did this to piss me off!"

Tex's eyes widened, and rage glittered underneath his dark brown eyes, "It was always about you! Maybe I was talented enough to make Ace appreciate me for my skills."

"Come on," Jack waved the younger Joker off. "I kept you alive in there!"

Memories from the grueling Joker training flashed through his mind. When he was numb, it had been so easy to brush off all the terrible things they'd been forced to do. Long nights fighting until they were bruised and bloodied, hospitalizing the weakest links, and killing relentlessly. Some part of him that was still good had fought to keep Jamie alive amongst all of those brutal assaults. And now—after only a few days—Jamie had been manipulated into becoming Blackjack mark two: Texas Hold'Em.

Time away had shown Jack just how easily Ace could manipulate a lost *child* into being her angel of death. Jack realized then that he had never been a professional; he'd been an idiotic boy manipulated by a criminal genius. Watching it happen to someone else in real-time rocked him to his core.

"And I wanted a friend!" Tex demanded, waving his gun, "and I thought you were too good for that." His eyes flickered back to Arianne, and hurt flashed across his face, "When I heard reports of you gallivanting through the Darwin Zone with *her*, I realized you were just too good to be friends with me."

"Come on, Jamie," Jack pleaded, "look what she's doing to you!"

"Fuck this, I'm bored," Tex waved to a Joker behind him.

Tex raised a hand to cover his face with a mask Jack had assumed was a fashionable addition to his techwear outfit. Jack realized too late that Tex was putting on a gas mask.

"Get down!" Jack shouted.

But it was too late. The masked Jokers behind Tex raised canisters as they began to diffuse yellow noxious smoke. Jack attempted to cover his face to fight the aerosol, but he knew it wouldn't help. The small, ventless basement filled with the gas faster than he could hope to escape.

Arianne and Jack exchanged one more glance at each other before they hit the ground with a simultaneous thud.

Chapter 35

Arianne

As soon as her eyes opened, Arianne almost rocketed towards the ceiling like a startled cat. She didn't recognize the white marble floors and the dark wood paneling on the whitewashed walls. When she managed to raise herself from the ground, she felt her stomach drop.

A stunningly beautiful woman watched her with catlike interest from her seat at the edge of her glass desk. She wore baggy, militaristic black joggers with straps that hooked around her sculpted shoulders. A white tank top started as a turtleneck and hugged her torso until it stopped just above her belly button. On her crossed feet, the woman wore shining black military boots, and her long black hair was tied in boxer braids as they fell down her back.

Power and confidence radiated from the woman. It was a different kind of power than Leon's: feminine, entertained, and happy to remain in the shadows. Yes, catlike was the perfect definition.

Arianne's eyes tracked to the stunning ace of spades tattoo drawn in swirling patterns across the left side of the woman's face. The winged female didn't need an introduction to know who was lounging in front of her. The kingpin of Europe, the Boss of Cartel, the Queen of the Underground. Ace.

Arianne almost spat the name. Ace smiled down at her, her teeth as white as the tank top she wore. "You must be Blackjack's friend. I've been anxious to meet you," Ace purred, her voice rich and deep with a fading African accent.

Arianne wiped the dirt off her pants as she stood up. "I wish I could say the same to you," she grumbled, refusing to break eye contact.

Before Ace could respond, Jack hopped up and quickly took his place in front of Arianne. "Really?" He growled at his boss, "Was that really necessary?"

A lazy smile grew on Ace's face as she jumped down from her desk. Even without her boots, the kingpin was strikingly tall. With her broad frame and long legs, she could have been a descendant of the ancient giants of Grecian myth. The woman smiled down at Jack as she approached him and pulled him into a hug, "My Blackjack," she said, "I'm so glad you've made it back alive. I was so worried."

Jack sat stiffly in Ace's arms, but the Cartel leader didn't release the embrace. Arianne wanted to spit at the woman for such an affected form of compassion. She'd heard of the many ways in which Ace had tormented Jack over the years and knew that Ace saw Jack as nothing more than an object.

And now they were at the mercy of such a woman. It made Arianne sick.

"I'm sorry I took so long," Jack's head dipped in subjugation as Ace stepped away.

Arianne frowned. That was how the game would be played then: they needed to stroke Ace's ego if they wanted to get out alive. So much for the element of surprise.

"I will find a way to forgive you," Ace waved Jack off as she walked back behind her desk.

Arianne's stomach dropped as Ace's gaze turned hungrily to her, "Who's your friend?"

Ace's dark eyes looked over Arianne with an unrestricted curiosity that made her fingers curl. Ace assessed her like she was a product to be sold instead of a human being to be negotiated with. Arianne gritted her teeth as she committed that look to memory: she would make Ace pay for treating her like that.

Right after she saved her people.

Jack recovered quickly, "She bargained to be brought to you," he began with a side glance at Arianne, "After we recovered the Pacifican squad, she convinced me that she could give you a better deal for her people."

Arianne cleared her throat as her mind whirled. *Come on, you thrived on spewing bullshit back on the island, this is no different.* She offered her best smile to the Underground Queen, "I know selling my squad for information could be valuable to you, but an alliance with Pacific could be just as lucrative."

Sure, the last thing Arianne wanted to do was make a deal with a monster like Ace, but she didn't have a choice anymore, seeing as she got captured before she could make a plan. She either found a way to entice Ace into making a deal with her, or she became Ace's new bargaining chip. From the interested gleam in the kingpin's eyes, Arianne knew she was thinking the same thing.

Ace's long and sharp acrylic nails methodically tapped on her desk as she thought, "Interesting," she said slowly, eyelashes fluttering as she looked back at Arianne.

The Pacifican clenched her jaw so tightly it hurt, "Will you quit staring at me like I'm some prized sheep?"

Jack winced, but Ace blinked in amusement, "Well, that's because you are," she sang. "I hate Pangaean politics as much as the next woman, but there's no denying this war is in a deadlock." The Cartel Boss rolled her eyes, "Two countries unable to attack the other because they can't find them—whatever, I don't care." She pointed a finger at Arianne, "But the Units I could earn from breaking that deadlock? Now, that's something I care about.

Arianne tensed, "Give me a chance to convince you otherwise."

Ace hummed, dark eyes looking upwards in consideration. "All right," she said, "what's a few more days? Give me some time to do my research, Pacifican, and we'll reconvene then. And since I'm so nice, I'll give you the business partner treatment: private rooms in my casino, a personal servant, and a playing card of 5,000 Units!"

Jack stilled at Arianne's side. "That's a generous offer," he replied politely, "but we prefer to wait until our meeting."

Ace winked at her prized investment, "Come on, you're a talented gambler. Business deals should be made in good faith. I give you both my best accommodations, and you give my clients and guests something to watch."

Arianne watched a silent interaction pass between Jack and Ace. Jack's jaw worked before he looked down and nodded. Arianne scowled at Ace's sickly sweet words. She hated how easily the Boss pretended she and Jack were her valued guests. Arianne knew the truth underneath: they were her prisoners.

A *Fera* female with pointed ears and neatly straightened brown hair appeared in the office and nodded at the pair. Arianne's mouth dried out. She'd never seen a *Fera* slave before. She began to sway, and Jack knowingly placed a hand on her shoulder to steady her. Arianne felt Ace's eyes watching her as the *Fera* servant guided them from the office.

"This was never the plan," Jack whispered to Arianne as they walked behind the *Fera* female.

"Kind of noticed that when we woke up on the floor of your boss's office," Arianne hissed back.

"I just want you to know that I'm not trying to fuck you over," Jack reassured her, "I'm as in the dark as you are."

Arianne nodded, letting out a long breath. The thought had crossed her mind that this was all some kind of elaborate ploy on Jack's behalf. She eyed the bounty hunter at her side, knowing there was still a chance that he could be double-crossing her, but some part of her told her to trust him. Besides, trusting Jack made her feel slightly less hopeless about her current predicament.

They walked a few more paces in silence before Jack turned to face Arianne again. "Whatever you do, don't draw attention to yourself. The casino is a kill box. If you don't conduct yourself right, we could get in a lot of trouble."

"More than we already are? I mean, seriously, how did you not consider Ace was watching you?"

"Arianne, please," Jack hissed back as he pinched his nose.

The Pacifican rolled her eyes. "Fine, I promise to lay low. Happy?"

The traveling pair walked in heated silence the rest of the way. Arianne regretted snapping at him, but she also couldn't hide a small prick of annoyance. They were both caught terribly off guard by something as predictable as Cartel keeping tabs on them. Exhaustion pulled at her, and she knew their tiredness from the hike had made them sloppy, but that didn't make the mistake any less painful.

A vibrant cherry oak door approached on her left, and the *Fera* female stopped and sketched a polite bow. "This is the women's room. I hope you find everything to suit your needs," her voice was soft and quiet.

Arianne couldn't help but stare at the slave. She was a beautiful *Fera*. A second take revealed tail billowing behind her dress and slightly pointed teeth. The female saw Arianne looking at her and looked down in shame. Guilt hit Arianne with a powerful blow, she should've known not to stare. She knew how staring made her feel. Arianne wanted so badly to reach out to the female and tell her everything was okay, but she wasn't in a safe space, and no words dared to reach her lips. Arianne looked away, ashamed she was hiding her own abilities out of fear of ending up like the servant.

The servant avoided eye contact with Jack, "Come with me. I'll help you get comfortable in your quarters, Master Blackjack."

Jack cringed at the female's address. Arianne nodded at him, telling him she understood completely. What Ace was doing to *Feras* in Europe was despicable, but if they wanted to survive those next few days, they needed to play by Ace's rules.

Arianne's hands didn't inch toward the door until she saw Jack stop at a room a few doorways down. The *Fera* female bowed to Jack and then walked away. Arianne and Jack looked at each other, and Jack held up eight fingers. *Meet me at eight o'clock.* Nodding, Arianne entered her room cautiously, scared of the possibility of what was waiting behind it.

She opened the door fully and sighed as she scanned the space. No unwanted surprises. Just another beautiful room built from Ace's terrible blood money. There were no ceiling lights in the room, but everything seemed aglow with blue. The bed, a soft white cloud, had a similar fluorescent glow flowing out from the bottom. Those same lights came out of every crease in the walls. Arianne felt like she was underwater. Despite being trapped in Leonueva, the room made her feel at ease for a moment.

Setting her bag down on the bed, she investigated the bathroom. She almost dropped to the floor in relief when she saw the shower. After a quick check for cameras, her clothes were on the floor, and she sighed in relief as hot water cascaded down her back.

A shower had never felt so good.

Finding a washcloth, Arianne scrubbed off all the dirt that had formed a barrier over her skin from the last few weeks. Next, she massaged her hair and scalp with shampoo and conditioner until her hands cramped. Finally clean, Arianne allowed herself to close her eyes and enjoy the marvelous heat, a small groan of delight escaping her.

Eventually, she forced herself out of the shower and into the steamy bathroom. Arianne dried herself off, feeling like a whole new person without all the dirt, grime, and blood. She was specifically happy about the lack of blood flaking her fingertips—no longer carrying a physical reminder of the deaths she'd sowed in the Darwin Zone. For a second, she could forget the awful hunters and the tribespeople. Her vision blurred as she gripped the edge of the sink.

Arianne's breathing slowed, and she concentrated on the white marble of the sink to block out the images of the dead around her. The tribespeople and the seventeen people she'd killed under her father's command. Twenty-seven in total. Her hands gripped the sink so hard the stone cracked. Her hair, soaked and dripping, fell at her sides, cooling her and making her shake with cold and terror.

What scared her most was that she'd forgotten what Leon had made her do. She hated to think about an underlying sinister side of her that had been capable of such carnage. What if she'd forced herself to forget so she wouldn't lose control one day? Her teeth began to chatter. What if she did lose control?

What if she couldn't stop herself?

When she arrived at the island, she'd convinced herself so thoroughly that she could be that innocent little girl that she'd forgotten almost everything. She'd been so hell-bent on being normal that her mind had blocked thousands of sins she'd committed as a Murray. For so long, she'd tried to be a perfect angel for Citadel. For so long, she'd wondered why she didn't fit the mold.

Now she knew why. The second she'd gotten blood on her hands, she was faced with the fact that she'd been lying to herself for years. She wasn't a hero. She wasn't an angel sent down to protect her people. She was born and raised to be a weapon: Leon's weapon. And the worst part was that, in the rush of it all, she'd enjoyed it. During that fight against the tribespeople, something had taken over her that reveled in the chaos and bloodshed—and a part of her craved to feel that way again.

What she had done that night thoroughly disturbed her. It wasn't because she'd killed, but because she'd caught a glimpse of what could happen to her. She knew the consequences of letting her soul fester and rot because she'd watched it happen to Leon and her brother. She knew that if she didn't stop herself soon, there would be no stopping her. Bloodlust ran in her family like a genetic disease. Unfortunately, there was no cure—not one that she knew about. Soon, killing would become like breathing, and she couldn't let that happen.

Against her will, her eyes drifted up to the bathroom mirror. Arianne expected to see her father there staring back at her, but to her great relief, steam had clouded the mirror enough that she couldn't see the reflection. Arianne wasn't sure she could bear the sight of her father just then. She did not want to look into that mirror and see the look of approval reflected on his face.

Approval she'd used to crave. That had been a shock as well. The memories brought back the emotions she'd felt when she killed: fear had been there, but there had also been desire. A desire to please her father.

Did she still crave his approval?

Arianne left the bathroom, she was distantly aware of her feet padding across the cold ground but she was still too lost in thought to care. Slowly, she removed her towel, preparing to look down at the ugly wound on her side. She analyzed the stitches, relieved that the threat of reopening it had mostly passed—even if the wound still hurt like hell. Taking her towel, she began to work it over her wings to dry them off as much as possible. She knew it would take hours for them to dry completely, but she much preferred the feeling of damp wings to soaking wet ones.

With a frown, Arianne moved to put her muddied jumpsuit back on. She was halfway through stepping into her khakis when she heard someone tsk, "Oh my. My master will not be pleased with your outfit."

My wings, they saw my wings.

Reflexively, Arianne lashed out. She whirled on the newcomer as her protective instincts took over. Arianne had her forearm lodged into the female's throat before she realized the person below her was the servant from before. The female gave a frightened gasp, and Arianne quickly stepped away from the pointed-eared *Fera*.

Arianne was breathing hard from the sudden burst of adrenaline when she allowed her clenched hands to relax, "What?"

She lowered her defenses—another *Fera* was less of a threat than one of Ace's goons.

The female still looked at Arianne warily, "Y-you um—won't be allowed in the lounge with clothes like that."

Arianne played with her wet hair and tied it into a bun. "Do you have an extra T-shirt and shorts? Clean ones would be wonderful."

The female put her slender hands on Arianne's shoulders and guided her to sit on the bed. "I have an outfit for you. Now let me help you with your hair," she said delicately. She took out Arianne's tie and let her long hair fall down past her shoulders.

"What's your name?" Arianne watched as the female carried over a short blue dress and placed it on the bed. Arianne looked at the female and then at the dress, "It's okay, you can talk to me."

The slave's large eyes investigated her assigned charge warily, "I don't have a name," she whispered, "we all lose our names when we're bought."

Arianne eyed the female. That wasn't the truth. The truth was the female didn't trust her. A wise choice considering the place that they were in. "Are there more of you?"

The slave's grip seemed to stiffen, "Yes," she said distantly, "Ace picks the 'prettiest' of the males and females to work for her. She sells the rest."

"That's despicable," Arianne hissed.

The female let out a soft breath as Arianne expanded her wings wide enough to fold them tightly into her back. She felt the female's breathing slow behind her as she helped guide the back of the dress over her wings. The fit was tight, but if Arianne kept her hair down, she could hide the slight bulge of her wings enough to pass as normal. She shivered as the female ran a clawed finger curiously down one of her golden feathers before zipping up the dress.

"My name was Carol before my parents sold me," she whispered slowly as if in a trance. When she spoke again, Carol's voice ached with longing. "Your parents didn't sell you?"

Arianne looked down, "I ran away."

She could feel Carol's eyes on the scars lining her upper back above the zipped dress, but she didn't dare comment. "It's common for *Feras* in Europe to be sold into slavery now," Carol muttered in disgust, "They can make their parents a lot of money."

Something squeezed in Arianne's chest. Of course, she'd heard of the slavery epidemic in Pangaea, but she hadn't known it had become so terrible. Asia was where the slave trade began, and they'd been the first to legalize it. In Europe, the trade was still illegal, but there were whispers that Leon was in the process of changing that. And Arianne's wonderful host was most likely the ringleader of it all.

"This isn't right," Arianne hissed, "you're just as much a person as everyone else."

"My master said I shouldn't discuss this subject," Carol said in a voice that was no louder than a whisper.

"Well, your master can fuck right off. I don't care what she thinks. This isn't right, and you shouldn't be treated like this." Carol was silent as she walked into the bathroom to grab things for Arianne's hair. Arianne stood up, took the supplies from Carol's hands, and placed them on the vanity. Then, she took Carol's clawed hands in her own, "Look at me: we're both different, and us different people need to stick together. You can trust me with anything you say."

Carol's large eyes looked down, "I never thought I was going to be a slave—my parents loved me." Quietly, she guided the Pacifican to sit again and combed her hair, "But then my parents got into debt. You can't get money anywhere anymore—not unless you're born with it. My dad was going to get killed for it. The debt collector took me from my family instead. He claimed I would be worth my parent's debt and then some at auction. My dad still begged for them to take his life instead." The servant let out a long sigh, "It's been almost ten years."

A silence fell over them as Carol started blow-drying Arianne's hair. She could feel Carol's eyes sweeping over her back. The servant pulled out peach cover-up makeup and quickly painted over the scars that were not successfully hidden by her hair and dress. Arianne looked down at her hands, unable to describe how those scars had gotten there or even why she deserved them.

"You look exhausted. How long has it been since you've properly slept?" Arianne asked, hoping to fill the tense silence.

"Only a couple of days. It's nothing I'm not used to, I promise," Carol sighed.

"Please, rest in my room, shower, and sleep for as long as you would like."

For a moment, Carol allowed herself to look excited before clouding her emotions and looking back down. She slowly shook her head, "I can't. It's my job tonight to make sure you and Jack are perfectly comfortable."

Arianne put her hand on Carol's shoulder, "Nothing would make me happier than to let you relax tonight. Please make yourself comfortable." Carol opened her mouth to protest, but Arianne only tilted her head up to silence her, "And if your master has a problem with it, you can tell her to bring it up with me."

Chapter 36

Blackjack

Jack collapsed onto his bed, groaning in relief. Sometimes, when he rested on the plush mattress, he wondered why he ever left Ace's quarters. Then his eyes drifted to the sole decoration on his room's walls: a picture of a Crowned Eagle in flight. As he analyzed the majestic bird, he was promptly reminded why he preferred sleeping in a half-finished building.

He was the opposite of that bird—free in flight. He was caged, trapped. If he were anything like that eagle, his wings were clipped long ago.

A knock came at the door, and Jack rolled his eyes as he forced himself out of bed. He opened it to find one of Ace's bodyguards waiting outside. "Ace wants to talk to you," the grunt growled.

Jack curled his upper lip. "Let me take a shower, and I'll be down." The man seemed to object, but Jack spoke up before he could. "I'll be there in no more than ten minutes."

If he was about to get his ass handed to him again, he at least wanted to look good while it happened.

Showered, shaved, and in a suit and tie that had been placed outside his bathroom, Jack rushed to Ace's office. The route was painfully familiar—he was used to running through the halls from his room to Ace's quarters after years of last-minute summons. Typically, the walk was met with the usual sense of obligation and duty, but now all he felt was mild annoyance and caution.

The boss was sitting at her desk, her various braids tied back with glittering golden ringlets. "It's so great to have you back," she beamed.

Jack analyzed the woman warily. "You called?"

"Ah, yes," Ace set down the glass tablet she was playing with. "We have a lot to discuss." Any warmth in her eyes faded as she glared blankly at him, "Tell me what happened in Brest, Blackjack."

Jack's throat tightened. He was well aware of the direction the conversation was headed. He considered himself fortunate that Ace hadn't already severed ties due to that botched mission.

Shaking his head, he mumbled, "I don't know. One moment, everything was proceeding smoothly, and then suddenly, there was this *Fera* like none I'd ever encountered. He freed all the slaves." Jack shook his head, the memory foggy from the concussion he'd sustained from the attack, "I tried to stop him, but he was too fast. Even for me. I don't remember anything after I attacked him. The next thing I knew, I was waking up in a Pacific hospital."

Ace ground her gold-plated teeth in frustration. "That deal cost me a lot of money, Jack. I would've killed the other guys, but you're the only one that survived."

Jack muttered, "You won't kill me."

"Excuse me?" Ace leaned forward, her tone sharp.

Jack shot her a glare. "I said, you won't kill me."

Ace twisted a thin braid around her finger. "Don't think I haven't considered it, boy."

He winced. "You wouldn't kill me—it would be a waste of your investment."

That was all Jack was to that woman: an investment. He was a weapon created by his boss, honed over years of training, and certainly more valuable alive. Jack had the best aim in Europe and could track anyone down like a bloodhound. Ace wouldn't risk the commodity he'd become.

"Do I detect defiance?" Ace raised a perfectly sculpted eyebrow. "Allow me to remind you who provided you with a home when you were nothing more than a street urchin. Who fed you and kept you out of the military," she smiled, "or worse."

Jack's gaze involuntarily shifted to the attractive male slave standing behind Ace, offering a decanter of wine. A shiver ran down his spine.

Straightening his posture, Jack retorted, "You won't kill me, and you won't touch Arianne. She's not property to be sold." He added firmly, "If you need to generate income, deduct it from my casino winnings—I don't care."

Ace smirked. "It seems someone has developed feelings for the Pacifican. Besides, I've already confiscated your winnings as losses for what happened in Brest."

Rage boiled up inside of Jack, its energy scalding his tongue. So many things came to mind for what he wanted to call the woman smirking in front of him. Each name was worse than the last. But for Arianne's sake, he bit down on his tongue as hard as he could.

"No," Jack spat back, "it's just... I owe her."

Ace laced her hands under her square chin and analyzed Jack just long enough to make him uncomfortable. After a painful pause, she smiled. "There go your eyes again—so bright." She mused, "You always were the most beautiful of my pets."

Jack clenched his hands. He wished he could rip Ace's eyes out of her head so she would stop staring at them.

Ace clocked Jack's growing annoyance, "I have a question for you, Blackjack: Do you want to kill me? Is that it? Do you want to kill the woman who gave you everything you could have ever wanted? I have always treated you like a son, and you insist on spitting in my face every time."

He scowled. Unless being treated like a son meant being treated like a glorified slave, he wasn't buying her bullshit anymore. Jack could barely control his anger anymore. "You've taken everything away from me, and then you have the gall to call the scraps you drop at your feet kindness."

His freedom, childhood, family, and earnings were gone. Jack had finally awakened to the realization that he was nothing without Ace. He despised it all—the transformation Ace had wrought upon him and the absence of any choice in the matter.

Jack's voice trembled. "I won't let you do the same to her." As he observed Ace more closely, he realized she looked satisfied. Jack's jaw slackened as he uttered, "You've already sold her."

Ace waved her hand dismissively. "I'm disappointed it took you so long to figure it out," she chuckled. "Of course I have. Do you think I didn't have a buyer lined up by the time you entered my city?"

My city. Ace saw Leonueva as her city. While Leon owned the upper class, the less fortunate reported to Ace. Jack was willing to bet that when it came to sheer numbers, Ace had more of Leonueva's citizens following her.

The Cartel boss reclined in her chair, a grin adorning her face. "It's out of my hands now. Some of my representatives reported you were accompanying an unidentified woman. A contact within the Pangaean military has promised me a reward of fifty million Units if I deliver the Pacifican asset into their custody."

A chill washed over Jack. It didn't matter that he'd chosen to protect Arianne—the outcome remained the same. Ace intended to auction her off to the highest bidder, and somehow, it was all his fault.

"Wait," Jack interjected as he contemplated his options.

Ace chuckled with a note of skepticism. "Even you can't make fifty million Units within a week, Blackjack."

"I can't, but ticket sales can," Jack declared.

For better or for worse, he 'd gotten to know Ace well during his years in her shadow. He intended to use his knowledge of her to his advantage. Ace had ascended from the lowest rungs of society through her expertise in gambling. She relished challenges and games, almost too much to resist. Now, the only question was if he was confident enough in his own gambling skills to go toe-to-toe with her.

"Let's play a game," Jack offered, "you versus me. The winner determines what happens to the Pacificans."

"I'm listening," Ace smiled, her obsidian eyes widening with interest. "But I must warn you: I can only offer up Arianne's future as fair trade."

Jack slowed. He knew Arianne wouldn't leave that casino without the other Pacificans. Unfortunately, he only cared if Arianne made it out alive. Arianne might hate him forever, but he could live with that.

"That's fine," Jack breathed slowly.

"Next," Ace continued, "fifty million Units is not something I'm willing to gamble away, my Blackjack. You must know that."

"No gambling," Jack continued, "think about this as a win-win situation for you." Ace nodded for him to continue. interest making her black eyes sparkle like obsidian. Jack had to keep his tone steady as his insane plan fell into place. "You host a little tournament of sorts. Have Arianne and I go through games or trials of your choosing for all of your clients to watch. You can sell tickets for people to buy. If the games make you more than your asking price, then you let Arianne go. If they don't, you keep the money. Best of all, you have new customers you can auction her off to and drive up her value."

Jack winced. He hated talking about Arianne like she was a product, but he didn't have much choice. Showing Ace a more lucrative route was the only way to get his friend out of that casino with her own free will intact. Ace wasn't a woman who could be swayed by morality.

Ace considered for a long moment. Her eyes, lined with glitter, looked back and forth as if weighing every factor in the deal. Slowly, the Cartel boss began to nod, "This certainly sounds like more fun than working with those Pangaean snobs," she continued to assess. "The novelty will give my clients something to look forward to. Yes, I like this. Here's the plan: we'll have a collection of three trials. You must make fifty million over the three trials and not a Unit less."

Jack's brain quickly did the math. They needed to make seventeen million Units per trial. Ace's casino hardly made that in a night. He knew the odds were not promising, and if he knew Ace, the challenges would be far from easy, but it was better than giving up Arianne without a fight.

He swallowed hard as Ace extended a hand glistening with golden rings. Slowly, Jack offered his hand in return. Bile rose in his throat when he saw Ace's brand on the inside of his wrist, and he was terribly reminded how idiotic he looked making a deal with the person who owned him.

Ace's grip was powerful as she shook his hand once. "We have a deal, Blackjack." She snapped her fingers at the beautiful male *Fera* behind her. "This calls for celebration. Wine!"

The slave stumbled forward, quickly replenishing the Underground Queen's wine goblet with dark crimson liquor. Jack frowned, unable to look the slave in the eyes as he poured a second glass for him.

Ace raised her glass in cheers, "Keep up these bright ideas, Blackjack, and once you're debt-free, we'll have a wonderful partnership together," she beamed.

Jack raised the glass to his lips, "I can't wait."

Then his eyes settled on the clock above Ace's desk: eight. He stood up abruptly, "I should get going," he managed.

Ace gave Jack a knowing look. "Go enjoy your time with the Pacifican. You don't have much of it left."

Jack's heart fell into his stomach as he turned to leave Ace's office. Though he didn't want to think about it, his boss was right. Whatever the outcome of those next three days, Arianne would leave, and Jack would be forced to stay behind. He buttoned up his suit coat to distract himself. He didn't want to think about how empty that reality made him feel.

"Arianne?" Jack asked as he sped into their shared corridor.

The door to Arianne's room opened, and she poked her head outside. "Jack," she breathed. "I was worried something had happened."

Jack stilled as she stepped out of her room. She looked far from the female he'd come to know in the Darwin Zone. Her mane of hair had been straightened, and it shone without weeks of forest grime built up around it. Her face was lightly dusted with makeup, giving her a softly striking look in the dim hallway lights. And her dress, Jack couldn't help but smile. The light blue fabric—sparkled with delicate rhinestones—made her gray eyes pop with color.

"Wow," was all he could manage.

"It's crazy how great dressing up makes you feel." She looked down, "Even when your life is falling apart."

The sadness in Arianne's voice struck him. He could only imagine what she was feeling. He lunged forward, offering her his arm, "Come on, we both look too good to waste it moping around. Let's try just to enjoy ourselves for a little bit. It might just make you feel better."

Arianne lifted her chin, and the haunted look in her eyes faded slightly, "That sounds really good," she breathed.

Jack guided her to the main casino floor, his conversation with Ace still hanging over him like a dark cloud. Still, he did his best to shake away his more negative thoughts for Arianne's sake. She needed a little time to exist without worrying about what came next, even if that was only for a few hours.

They explored the casino, stopping to try their luck at some slot games on the periphery of the space before diving deeper. Arianne eyes glittered in interest as she observed the flashing roulette tables and a bar illuminated in neon lights. Ace's casinos had two segregated levels: a main floor for general admission and a second, more exclusive level for Ace's high-rolling customers.

Pangaean Elites were pricks so self-absorbed they couldn't even stand to gamble next to commoners.

Arianne looked about ready to burst with excitement. "Come on," she tugged on Jack's arm. "Let's see why you earned the name Blackjack."

The suggestion certainly enticed him. It had been weeks since he'd indulged in his favorite pastime: screwing Ace's casino out of every Unit he could manage. But he wasn't quite ready to mingle with the crowd yet.

"First, the bar," Jack said.

Arianne raised an eyebrow, "You know that *Feras* can't get drunk," she whispered.

Jack nodded as he pushed through the crowd to reach the bar, "so does every other person in this room. Do you really want them questioning why you're not drinking?"

Arianne looked down, considering, before shaking her head. *Feras* had much quicker metabolisms than their non-mutant counterparts, which meant their bodies processed alcohol too quickly to feel the effects of intoxication. This was a well-known fact and a common tactic people used to single out their mutant peers who were attempting to hide in plain sight. If Arianne and Jack wanted to avoid extra attention, a logical first step would be to ensure they had a drink in their hands.

The casino floor was broken up into two segments: the gambling area and a club-like dance floor that wrapped around the bar like a river. Jack took Arianne's hand and led her towards the growing line of guests waiting to order a drink.

Ace didn't miss a single detail in the design of her casino, and her bar was no exception. The construction of the bar was a work of art in itself, with liquor shelves rising six levels at the back wall. Bottles lining the shelves were filled with clear and amber liquid and glittered in neon blue light, making them shine like a beacon in the casino's low light. Considering everyone in that building was looking to live out their most delinquent desires, a watering hole for alcoholics was certainly meant to be a beacon to guide their nightly endeavors.

Jack tapped his hand on the clear glass countertop and laid his palm flat on the surface. A laser rose from underneath the glass to scan his handprint: Ace's way of tracking people's accounts while on the casino floor. Jack's identity popped up alongside his shining allowance for the night: five thousand Units. A woman approached from behind the bar, well, the bartender looked like a woman at first glance. Like most of Ace's Dealers at the various tables, the bartender was a Puppet.

Puppets were a rare—and new—commodity found in the upper levels of Pangaea. They were robots created to complete repetitive tasks for their owners like pouring a pre-programmed list of cocktails or shuffling decks of cards. *Fera* slaves were still favored over Puppets due to their ability to do far more complex tasks, but Puppets were growing in popularity.

"Two rum and colas, please," Jack told the Puppet.

The Puppet attempted a nod, its depthless black eyes looking down to obtain two chilled glasses. Many saw Puppets as beautiful with their flawless faces paired with bright-colored wigs. The symmetry and sleek design made them look striking like a well-rendered animation brought to life. Jack didn't get the appeal, there was something about their expressionless faces that put them firmly in the uncanny valley in his opinion.

Some even used Puppets for more intimate desires. Jack was revolted at the thought. He preferred his partners *human.*

Or mutant.

Jack turned to Arianne as his breath caught. Her eyes glittered as they reflected the neon of the bar, a strange wonder striking her as she analyzed the Puppets and sparkling drinks. Then she tilted her head to look at the towering liquor shelves, and her sharp jawline popped in the flashing dace floor lights. There was something breathtaking about someone so deadly looking so beautiful and in awe of the world around her.

"My friends and I would go to this bar called Shipwreck," Arianne said, pulling Jack from his thoughts. "It was always a fun place to dance at the end of a long week."

Jack took his drinks from the green-haired Puppet and guided Arianne away from the bar, "You dance?"

Arianne perked up. "Do you?"

"Not in a long time."

A devious smile came to Arianne's face as she set her drink down on a high-top table behind her, "Well, Pangaea Boy." She began as she offered a hand, "Try not to step on my toes."

Jack considered, his eyes going to Arianne's outstretched hand. The logical side of him was screaming to keep a low profile. No good would come from him displaying any form of affection, especially not in a room full of potential enemies. Still, there was a part of him—which was becoming impossible to ignore—that got excited at the prospect of dancing. A small smile came to his face. He could just imagine placing his hand on the small of Arianne's back and twirling her just fast enough to rustle her sparkling skirts.

Unfortunately, Jack had developed a pattern of listening to the emotional side of him over logic in recent days. His desire to dance with Arianne overpowered his Blackjack-esque logic almost immediately.

Jack smirked, "I guess I could bear one dance," he quipped, taking her hand.

Arianne pulled Jack onto the dance floor, which was crowded with more of Ace's guests. Wordlessly, she guided his left hand to her side, and she held his right hand out next to them. Arianne moved first, her body gliding fluidly through the rhythmic steps of three. Jack breathed, allowing his defenses to lower for a few moments.

Arianne was dancing an informal brand of salsa to the pounding electric music. Jack tracked her steps once more. *One, two, three. One, two, three.* The stiffness in his limbs faded as he fell into step with her, his hips swaying. Arianne paused and twirled. Instinctively, he raised his arm to guide her, just like he'd done countless times with his sister as a child. His parents hadn't discriminated: if there was a musical art form, they had it within their house. He couldn't stop a smile from coming to his face.

"Not too shabby," Arianne complimented, waltzing around Jack.

"You aren't so bad yourself," Jack grinned, pulling Arianne tightly to his chest. "Where did you learn to dance like this?"

She collided with Jack. "Caesar," she breathed. "He's from Spain, like my mom." Arianne's face softened. "He didn't want me to lose sight of her culture."

Jack pivoted on his foot and dipped Arianne. She gasped as he leaned down, stopping mere inches from her face. "Maybe I'll have to teach you how the French do it," he whispered.

Arianne's hands clawed into Jack's shoulder, and she bit her lip. "Do tell me more."

Jack pulled Arianne back upright with a devilish grin. "We like to keep our partners *very* close," his voice dropped tauntingly low as he pulled Arianne tightly to him. Arianne giggled and allowed Jack to take the lead as they danced.

"Aye!" Someone yelled, "Save a dance for me!"

Jack slowed, quickly brushing Arianne behind him at the sound of the voice. His eyes narrowed when he saw Jamie—no, *Tex*—leaning on a high table with a smoking cigar hanging from the corner of his mouth.

"What do you want, Jamie?" Jack grumbled.

Texas hold'Em pushed himself away from the table and sauntered up to Jack, "I'm wondering what your play is, asshole."

Jack took a step closer to Tex and absently flicked the cowboy hat off of the younger man's head. "How about you take a nice walk and reconsider if you want to talk to me like that," he growled.

To Tex's credit, he didn't flinch. "How about you tell your little girlfriend about your deal with the boss."

"Little?" Arianne squeaked, "I'm pretty sure I'm taller than you!" She paused, her attention returning to Jack. "Wait, what does he mean?"

Jack dragged his hand through his hair, seriously contemplating how much it would cost him to teach the little shit in front of him a lesson. He leaned forward toward Tex, his upper lip curling in a scowl. "How about you mind your own fucking business?"

Tex smiled and the sweet-smelling smoke of his cigar wafted into Jack's nose. "Haven't ya' heard? You're old news. *Replaced.* Any of Ace's business is my business."

Jack scoffed. There was no way he was being replaced by a cheaper copy that easily. He clenched his fists. "And who told you that?"

Tex glanced back over at Arianne and infuriatingly blew her a kiss. "You're soft now," he sang, "and everyone can see it. It won't be long before Ace sees it, too, I reckon."

Jack's glance towards Arianne betrayed him. Was he weak now? Was waking up and realizing just how thoroughly Ace had brainwashed him make him weak? Jack clenched his teeth, fighting hard to keep up the Blackjack continence that had kept people terrified of him for years. Maybe Tex was right: giving a shit about someone else was making him weak. It was breaking down his walls that he erected to keep himself alive and to keep his emotions from crippling him.

Walls that kept the real him—the version of him still worthy of his family's name—hidden away.

Arianne's hand snaked into his. To his surprise, she stepped protectively in front of him and pointed a threatening finger at Tex. "You keep talking, and I'm going to find out just how far down your throat I can shove that cigar," she warned.

In response, Tex unleashed a cloud of smoke into Arianne's face. He managed a sneer for a fraction of a second before Arianne moved. Jack barely clocked the blow. One moment, Arianne's hand was at her side, and the next, she was delivering an expert chop to Tex's throat. Tex gagged, hands going to his neck in surprise before falling to his knees.

Arianne frowned down at the Joker. "Have fun choking on that Adam's apple."

Jack's mouth slacked open in amazement. "Am I allowed to ask if we can go back to your room?"

Arianne turned to Jack, and he was surprised to notice her cool frown, "I think I want to go back to my room alone, actually," she replied.

Jack couldn't help but look disappointed. "What do you mean? At least enjoy the casino with me for a little longer."

Arianne turned with a flick of her golden brown hair, "I'm going back to my room."

"Arianne, wait," Jack lunged to catch up to her, "what's wrong?"

She whirled at him, "You made a deal about *my* people's future with Ace without telling me?"

Jack wilted, "I was going to tell you. I just wanted you to have a few hours to relax before that."

Arianne crossed her arms, "You do realize that I'm behind enemy lines and trapped by a criminal kingpin who wants to sell me. There is no way in hell that I'm *relaxing*. What was the real reason for hiding this from me?"

With a crushing bite of disappointment, he realized that Arianne's own walls—steel and impenetrable—were back up as high as they could go. Jack looked away from her. "I was honestly hoping to give you a little bit of a break," he began, looking down. "Before Ace tries to auction you off," he admitted quietly.

"Excuse me, what?"

"Ace has a bidder within the Pangaean military offering fifty million Units," Jack said. "She was probably going to sell you off tonight—I made her consider a different option."

Arianne's eyes narrowed into deadly slits, "what makes you think you had any right to *offer* me off like that?" She shook her head, voice rising.

Jack raked a hand stressfully through his hair, "I don't!" He shot back, "but Ace was ready to cash in. I was the only person out of the two of us who she might listen to. I hate her, but I *know* her. I know what propositions she might jump on."

Arianne physically shivered as she hugged herself, "What did you propose," she asked so quietly that he could barely hear her over the music.

Jack paused, looking at the female in front of him. Arianne had lived her entire life controlled by what other people planned for her. First, with her father: trapped to be his weapon and seen as less than human despite her Elite blood. And then, with Pacific: resigned to the island to protect her from her bloodline's wrath. And now there he was—no better than any of them as he made decisions without her consent.

Jack took a step back, a chill running through him at the distance he felt growing between them. "A tournament of sorts. Ace will put us through three trials, and she'll sell tickets for an audience to watch."

"And there was no other option?" Arianne asked, still suspicious.

Jack held out his hands, surrendering, "Look, I hated doing it, but in my professional experience, we were treading on thin ice. I saw an out, so I took it. If we can earn more than fifty million Units in the three sessions, you're free to go."
"

Arianne considered, and Jack could see the anger inside her cooling as she assessed her options, "And you?"

Jack shook his head, "I can help, but Ace wasn't willing to negotiate for me."

"So you bargained yourself to give me a chance to get out." Arianne's eyes lowered. "That's a shit deal," she said, annoyance finally subsiding.

"You're not responsible for my debt," Jack sighed, "let's just worry about winning this thing." He didn't have the heart to mention how slim their chances were of beating Ace at her own game.

Jack accompanied Arianne on her walk back to her room. He wished he could find words to spark a conversation, but he couldn't think of a subject that wouldn't light like tinder in a campfire. From Arianne's reaction, he knew he made a mistake—it wasn't like his moral compass was well calibrated after years of misuse. Still, he needed to add that mistake to his ever-growing list of fuck ups.

First, he betrayed *good* people and got himself, Arianne, and the Pacifican squadron in that mess. Next, his original intentions to sell Arianne made him sloppy, so he didn't hide his cargo from Ace. That miscalculation gave Ace ample time to make a plan to turn a profit with Arianne long before they arrived in Leonueva. And most recently on his terrible list, he did the one thing he abhorred and dealt in lives without consulting the very people he was dealing with.

No matter how much Jack wanted to help Arianne now, it seemed like it wouldn't be enough. Best intentions didn't matter if they came about too late.

Arianne raised her hand to open the door, but she paused to turn to Jack. "Thanks for walking me back," she said lamely.

She sounded tired. Jack couldn't blame her.

Jack reached for Arianne's hand, and she subtly moved just out of his reach. Jack tried his best to hide the sting of disappointment. "Do you want any company?" he asked awkwardly. "I know how it feels to be alone in a place like this."

Arianne's walls were almost as high as they'd been when he first met her. Her arms were crossed, her eyes as hard as steel. She didn't look angry, just protective. Jack was surprised at how much it hurt to know he'd been pushed out. And for a short while there, he'd been allowed inside those defenses—and all he did was wreak destruction once inside.

"I'm just going to get some rest," Arianne replied quietly. "Alone."

Jack pursed his lips, managing a nod. *Right. Boundaries.*

After going through so much together, it was easy for him to forget they'd only known each other for a handful of weeks. And in that time, they'd only been friendly for a handful of days. Maybe he, the emotionless Blackjack, had become too clingy because he hadn't had a connection like that in years.

And that made Arianne's wariness even more jarring.

"Of course," Jack fumbled, "goodnight, Princess."

"Goodnight, Jack."

He couldn't help but smile sadly as the door was slammed shut. Letting out a long sigh, he slid down the wall. After growing so used to their friendly taunting, the absence of it left him feeling cold and lonely.

After a few moments of wallowing in his own self-pity, Jack realized that looking like a rejected puppy in a hallway was not his best look. Standing up, he set off back toward his room to continue his moping in private. He felt more like a ghost haunting the corridor than actual flesh and blood. The change he'd undergone in the Darwin Zone was easy to ignore when surrounded by the unknown. Now that he was home—not that Ace's Casino deserved to be called a home—the difference in how he saw the world was jarring. He had a constant point of reference between his two viewpoints, and the comparison wasn't pretty.

Taking his hand and guiding it along the wooden wall, he lost himself listening to the soft thumping his fingers made as they flicked over the panels. Just a month ago, that walk had meant nothing to him—he'd moved with confidence of his place in the world. Now, the hallway seemed to go on forever without meaning, much like his life. Guilt, annoyance, and sadness built up inside of him until it hit an overwhelming crescendo. Stumbling into this bedroom, he locked the door before someone heard his shockingly loud sigh.

Jack didn't know what he was going to do anymore. He knew he needed to help Arianne and her people, and he knew he was already on the path to failure. And what if he did succeed? Could he really just go back to his empty life as Ace's right-hand man? Could he bear it?

Jack knew the answer. It kept him awake well into the night.

Chapter 37

Jaya

Jaya was drowning under the sterile white lights. The cold metal examination table stung against her backside. She felt exposed in her paper-thin hospital gown, but even a winter jacket wouldn't shield her from the scientists' stares. The purple-haired Pacifican squinted as she stared into the blinding light above her and knew she couldn't stand another *day* of it.

And she'd only been in there for three.

A scientist looked down at Jaya from his spot next to her bed, his gloved hands typing notes of his observations onto a thin glass tablet. Another scientist sat at her side in a rolling chair, scraping some of Jaya's dead skin into a vial with a scalpel. All of the scientists wore uniform outfits, but they were not the typical coats she was used to seeing on the Helvig twins. The scientists in that lab wore white coats that looked closer to robes than jackets with flowing sides that fell below their ankles. The uniforms also had hoods that covered their jawlines, chins, and hairlines in a polymer-like fabric. The way the scientists acted was vastly different from what she was used to in Citadel—these researchers bordered on robotic. Their uniforms covered so much that little individuality emerged through the cracks. If Jaya hadn't known better, she would've suspected they were part of a religious sect instead of a research team.

"Subject has a transparent top layer of skin," the scientist with the tablet reported. "Further analysis is needed to determine if it carries specialized chromatophore cells similar to those found in chameleons."

Jaya's lips wobbled, her skin betraying her as it began to turn blue. She winced and closed her eyes, sensing the scientists' growing interest.

The scientist scraping her skin noted, "The Subject experiences skin color changes from variations in emotion. Further testing tomorrow will be on temperature adaptations."

Jaya was shaking now. She felt horribly claustrophobic under the undivided attention of those researchers. She was nothing but a freak to them—a sideshow attraction. She was far less than a slave in that basement. At least a slave was recognized to have emotions and a mind. Jaya was nothing more than a lab rat to those monsters. They even kept her in a cage—when they didn't leave her out on the freezing observation table.

"Doctor Richards," the masculine scientist reported as the sound of heels clicked across the lab. "I'm requesting a skin biopsy tomorrow morning."

Jaya's face was shadowed as a third presence appeared above her. She did her best to bite her tongue as Hera Richards leaned over her, piercing blue eyes glittering with interest. Jaya averted her gaze, scared her skin would change colors again if she witnessed Hera. She hated how the General Scientist acted like she was just another species to be studied, not a human being with a soul.

What was she kidding? Research was *all* Hera cared about.

Jaya had been thrown through test after test thanks to Hera's orders. Oxygen efficiency tests, blood draws, strength trials, and endless probing from Hera's underlings. Never once had the General addressed her directly. She wasn't even called by her name until she was returned to her cell at the end of the day.

If she was returned. The night before, she'd remained on that uncompromising metal table, hooked up to wires and breathing apparatuses throughout the night. Naturally, she'd hardly gotten any sleep.

Hera pursed her lips. "Do the biopsy now," she announced, "I want to look over the results tomorrow morning."

"We don't have a sterile room ready," the scientist with the scalpel announced. "And we won't be able to administer anesthesia." The scientist paused, considering, "I guess we could do a local anesthetic?"

Hera looked at her new research subject, her pale eyebrows furrowing in calculation. "Monitor her brain waves. I want to compare her pain sensors to those of other subjects for my increased senses hypothesis. I want to understand how much stronger *Fera's* senses are—including pain."

Jaya didn't process what was happening until she saw the research assistants leave to collect supplies. She watched, her heart rate rising as she saw the female assistant pick up a scalpel and a sample collection jar. Jaya's purple-green eyes widened in fright as she focused on the length of the scalpel and its needle-sharp edge. Anxiety peaked as she realized the blade was meant for her—she couldn't do anything but sit there and watch it come closer.

A whimper escaped her lips, "Wait, no," she pleaded.

Her panged painfully in her chest as she felt the cold brush of an alcohol wipe glide across her shoulder. Jaya wanted to crawl out of her skin and *run,* and she fought against her restraints to no avail. Her heart thundered louder, louder, louder as she started at the scalpel meant for her shoulder once more.

Her entire body tensed as one of the scientist's rubber-slick hands pulled at the skin of her shoulder, and she barked in pain as the scalpel dug into her skin. The sharp cutting motion of the blade burned as the still-drying alcohol came in contact with her wounded flesh. Breathing rapidly, Jaya closed her eyes tightly and tried to forget about the uncomfortable pain of someone digging into her shoulder. Even with her eyes closed, she could feel the hotness of her blood as it dribbled down her arm. She almost threw up.

Hera didn't express an ounce of care over Jaya's discomfort as she monitored the brain waves coming through on her tablet, "Interesting," she muttered. "Still a juvenile."

"Excuse me?" Jaya squeaked through painfully clenched teeth.

Hera blinked as if noticing her for the first time. "Your readings are relatively comparable to a human's," she explained, interest in a new subject to observe making her more talkative. "You haven't gone through second phase maturation."

"What?" Jaya asked breathlessly.

"Second puberty," the scientist with the tablet muttered as he recorded more information.

Jaya sucked in a breath to counteract her discomfort. She didn't know what was worse: being ignored or the fact that those scientists knew she could communicate and still treated her like a lab rat.

The procedure hadn't lasted longer than a few minutes, but Jaya had exhausted her jaw from clenching it against the pain all the same. The stitches were nothing compared to the sickly feeling of a chunk being removed from her shoulder, but they still weren't pleasant. Jaya sat back, staring up at the blinding examination lights in the hopes that it would send her into some sort of trance and take her away from that place.

"Stain the cells so we can observe them tomorrow morning," Hera ordered, the clicking of her heels signifying her departure.

Jaya closed her eyes against the throbbing pain of her shoulder, hoping to will herself to sleep. A trail of tears streamed down her cheek as the feeling of utter hopelessness settled in her gut. She missed her sister, she missed Caesar, and most of all, she missed home. She imagined she was relaxing on the shoreline, the metal slab she was resting on replaced by a beach towel laid across the sand. The calming memory of salty breezes and sun-warmed skin eventually lulled her into an exhausted sleep.

"Wake up, let's get you back to that nice homey cell."

Jaya blinked awake. The scientists were gone, and the lab was dark. She'd been left like a piece of lab equipment to be used the following day. She was starving, desperately needed to use the bathroom, and had a dehydration headache.

She turned to the sound of the voice that had woken her, "Blue?"

Blue's yellow eyes glinted in the darkness. "Who else would it be?" she muttered, unlocking her restraints with a swipe of a card. The Snake was oddly careful as she guided Jaya to a seated position.

"What are you doing here, Blue?"

Blue stepped away from the table and began expertly swiping through Jaya's laboratory files, projected on a small screen. The short-haired *Fera's* eyes narrowed as she read. "Okay, no dieting or sleep tests are being run," she mumbled to herself, "we're good to go."

"What's going on?"

"They left you to sleep here," she explained, "but seeing as it won't ruin any of their tests, I'm taking you back to the Pacificans for the night."

Jaya almost slumped with relief, but then she remembered she was talking to her enemy, "Why?" She asked cautiously.

Blue looked to the side before sighing, "Because I know how much it sucks to be left on that table." The Snake's sarcasm quickly returned as she put a hand on her lithe hip, "But if you would prefer to remain in the comforts of hotel medieval torture, be my guest."

"I need to pee," Jaya breathed as if in answer.

After stopping at a bathroom to let Jaya relieve herself, Blue led her towards the elevator that would take them up to the Murray Monument prison block. Typically, she tried her best to observe the demarcations on the different floors, but she was too tired to try and see much.

Blue, on the other hand, lingered on the touch screen in front of the elevator. "Maybe we can stop at the third floor for food," she whispered, her black-painted nails pointing to the screen.

Jaya blinked, realizing what else was listed on the third floor: the communications center. She didn't respond, seeing as there were cameras in the elevator, but she managed a slight nod in thanks to the Snake. Maybe Blue couldn't help them escape, but there was something reassuring knowing the female was rooting for them in her own small way.

Blue selected the first basement level for the prison block, and the pair stepped onto the elevator. Jaya scanned the space for cameras before turning to the other *Fera*. "Why are you so nice to us?" she whispered. "You're the only one who hasn't been actively awful to us since we got here."

Blue looked forward, her expression unchanging. "Pangaea's not my home."

"The tribes?"

The eastern female bit her lip. "I shouldn't be talking about this."

"The slave traders kidnapped me too," Jaya admitted quietly. "My sister saved me."

Blue was quiet for a moment. "I've said too much," her forked tongue stuck out in a hiss.

Jaya examined the Snake "Help us get out," she pressed, "and we can get you back to your people. Why wouldn't you help us?"

"It's complicated," Blue mumbled, her typical response.

Jaya's eyes went to the Snake's control collar, standing out like a black band of obsidian against her porcelain neck. "We can get that off of you."

"It's more than just that." She straightened as the elevator doors opened. "Let's go."

The pair fell into a tense silence as they left the elevator, the only sound coming from Blue's black boots as they squeaked across the tiles. Jaya considered the female in front of her curiously. There was so much hidden underneath her intimidating stature and piercing yellow eyes. Where had she come from? Why was she being kind to the Pacificans when there was a good chance it could get her killed?

Blue flashed a badge from her hip to a Ward standing guard outside the prison block, and the man nodded, swiping his access card to let the female in through the steel doors. Blue waited until the doors were closed behind them before saying, "Leon's angry about something," she warned in a whisper. "I'm not sure what, but Pandora says that it's something to do with your President and the prince."

Jaya frowned, "What should we do?"

"Be careful," Blue finished, opening the final door to the Pacifican prison block, "Leon's volatile when he's angry."

Kalinda cried out in relief when her sister was led inside. Jaya's heart lightened at the sight of her teammates: Rhino, Lyn, Carter, Gunner, Kalinda, and Caesar. Everyone was still alive, which was no longer guaranteed with Leon back in Europe.

Blue didn't acknowledge Jaya as she closed the cell behind her, keeping up her façade of bored indifference for the cameras. But Jaya saw deeper than that. Blue was a *Fera* trapped in a concrete city enslaved to a terrible woman—far away from the freedom of the Tribes where she belonged. Maybe Blue couldn't free herself, but she'd risked herself to provide the Pacificans with as much comfort as she could reasonably offer. Even if Blue wasn't a perfect ally, her warning words still had merit. Her last statement to Jaya flickered in her mind and chilled her bones.

What could she mean by Leon being *volatile*?

"Jay!" Kalinda cried, lunging to hug her sister through the prison bars. "I was so worried when you didn't come back yesterday!"

Jaya closed her eyes and allowed herself a few blissful moments her sister's arms. "*Didi*," she sighed.

Rhino thundered up behind Jaya and joined in on the hug. "Glad you made it back, little dude!" He boomed.

"Rhino, I'm not little, you're just huge."

Jokes aside, she was relieved to be embraced by the warmth of friends and family. The threat of returning to the laboratory and the uncertainty of their futures faded for a few moments, and she took a deep breath. They were alive right now, and that was all that mattered.

"Jaya, I'm glad you're back," Caesar said from his seat on the cot behind Kalinda.

Jaya separated from her sister and Rhino. Her stomach dropped as she beheld the Pacific President. Caesar's face was bloodied, one of his eyes blackened and close to swollen shut. Her mouth dried out. She didn't need to question what'd happened: Pangaea was attempting to get information out of him.

"Caesar," she breathed, slipping down the bar in despair at the sight of her beloved President, "what did they do to you?"

"What did they do to *you*?" Kalinda barked in concern, her hand running a soft trail next to the fresh stitches in her shoulder.

Caesar folded his hands together. "Negotiations," he managed.

Kalinda gripped Jaya's hand. "And you?"

Jaya shook her head. "More of the same. Hera's people, poking and prodding me." She shivered, "I can't think about how many more *Feras* have gone through that."

"Hera." Caesar's eyes were troubled. "Be careful about what you say around her. She's in Leon's Inner Circle. It's safe to say that anything that she knows, he knows. But Hera doesn't like losing her subjects—you should be safe for the time being." The President rubbed his temples, "I know that's only a small silver lining for what she's putting you through."

Jaya nodded, her eyes beginning to sting at the reminder that she would be taken back to that horrible, white-washed lab the following morning.

Then, the room was filled with the mouthwatering smell of tomato bisque, coffee with a hint of hazelnut, and herbal tea. For a moment, Jaya wondered if her starved body was producing hallucinations in the form of tantalizing smells. Then she heard the familiar clang as the prison block doors were slammed shut, followed by the squeaking of a wheeled cart.

Caesar's eyes widened, and Jaya whipped her head around to see a beautiful middle-aged woman walking into the room. The woman was pushing a cart decorated with bowls filled with deep orange soup, plates of scones, and steaming water for tea or coffee. Jaya almost lunged for the cart out of pure desperation.

"I know this isn't a silver lining," the stranger said, "but it's the best I could do."

The woman was small, a few inches shorter than Jaya, but unlike Jaya, she had generous curves. She had kind hazel-green eyes and a full head of dark brown, wavy hair. She didn't look like most of the people who delivered their food. Instead of the typical Ward uniform, the woman wore a gorgeous deep maroon jumpsuit with a matching belt tied around her midsection. Unlike the Wards, the woman carried an affectionate yet powerful air. Something told Jaya that the woman in red wasn't supposed to be there. In the same breath, she had a feeling that the woman went wherever she wanted.

"Team," Caesar said breathlessly. "Meet Josephina Valentino Murray: the Mother of Europe—my oldest friend."

Chapter 38

Arianne

The night of Ace's first trial arrived sooner than she'd expected. She had spent the previous day resting and preparing herself for whatever strange games the Cartel boss would devise. Ace had never specified the nature of the trials—whether they'd be mental, physical, or a combination of both. Knowing her luck, it would likely be a mix.

Carol silently secured Arianne's hair in a long braid and assisted her in donning a pantsuit that Ace had deemed appropriate for the occasion. Shortly after, there was a knock on the door, and Jack entered, holding a note.

Arianne turned her attention to him, her heart skipping a beat. She and Jack hadn't left things on the best terms the night before. She could sense the caution in his handsome amber eyes. He was treading lightly. For a moment, she avoided the intensity of his gaze, mindful of his attempts to protect her but unable to shake off the sting. Everyone in her life eventually tried to determine what she did, and she was tired of it.

She didn't even want to attempt to bring up the other elephant in the room: Jack had initially planned to sell her. Did he ever change his mind? Was this all just an act to make her cooperate? She knew the likelihood of her suspicion coming true was a small one, but it still bothered her that her mind went there. Could she really trust someone who'd been so adamant about betraying her people *days* ago?

Jack looked troubled as he sat down in a chair across from Arianne. "This is from Ace," he said, handing the note to her.

"You spoke to her?" The Pacifican asked warily.

Jack nodded, "I didn't want to go into this trial blind. She didn't give me much but this note." He moved to say more but paused as he beheld Carol behind Arianne.

"Jack, this is Carol. She's with us."

Jack narrowed his eyes at the *Fera* behind her, "Arianne, she could easily be a spy Ace planted in here. She needs to go."

Carol stiffened and Arianne's braid dropped out of her clawed hand. The Pacifican turned and placed a reassuring hand on the female's thigh. Carol's large cat eyes widened as she shook her head and stood to leave.

"No," Arianne said. "She's a friend. Us different people stick together."

Carol smiled wide enough to show her elongated canines.

Jack looked over at the servant apologetically. "Right," he corrected, "we could use any friend we can get. Just, um, don't call me master."

Carol bowed her head respectfully, "Us different people stick together."

Arianne opened the note and read the message out loud:

"Hello, *Feras*, Traitors, and Pacificans. I have come up with three games for you to play. The theme is simple: lessons in gambling. Each game embodies a specific lesson. Figure it out, and you will have the tools to beat the game. I'll add another wager to keep things interesting: beat me in all three games, and I will give the surplus of over fifty million Units to Jack's debt." Arianne and Jack exchanged a quick look before she kept reading. "I have sold fifteen million in ticket sales—a little low if we're trying to make fifty—but either way, I'm making money. For your sake, you better hope enthusiasm will build with each night. Your first clue is as follows:"

> *"Card games are meant for luck,*
> *Counting cards could win you a buck.*
> *Could you beat the dealer at their table?*
> *Come forward only if you are able.*
> *Compete and hope you don't bail—*
> *—Ace"*

Arianne glanced down at the riddle, eyebrows furrowing in frustration. "What the hell does that mean?"

Jack ran a hand through his hair. "How are we supposed to solve a riddle when the last line is incomplete?"

Arianne crossed her arms in annoyance. "What am I supposed to do? If this is the clue to winning the challenge, then we're toast. I have less than an hour to determine what it could mean." She frowned at Jack. "And now she's added your freedom as an extra wager to torment us."

"Don't let the riddle bother you," Jack took the paper and stuffed it into his jacket pocket. "Ace could've easily sent that to us to throw us off our game and stress us out."

Arianne rubbed her temples. "Well, it's working."

"The last line of the clue has to rhyme with bail," Carol said slowly. "I don't know what, but it has to rhyme."

Jack grinned at the *Fera* servant. "That's a good point, thank you."

The female smiled. "Anything to help." She tied the end of Arianne's braid and carefully wrapped it over her shoulder. "Good luck."

Arianne tried her best to give her new friend a reassuring smile, but the queasiness in her gut made her smile seem more like a wince.

Carol and Jack left Arianne to get dressed. Ace had selected a fashionable blue jumpsuit for Arianne, complete with a matching white jacket with—to Arianne's delight—extra stretchy shoulders. Once dressed and confident her wings were convincingly hidden inside her outfit, she busied herself by thinking over Ace's riddle. She knew Jack would scold her for overthinking, but how couldn't she?

Everything relied on those trials. If she couldn't win and make the games interesting, she wouldn't get enough money to free herself or Jack. And there was no way she could save the people she loved if she was the one being sold.

Luckily, Jack arrived back at her room before she could think herself into an anxiety attack. The bounty hunter had donned a tech wear outfit similar to Ace's preferred style, and Arianne had to admit that the fashion was striking. Jack wore baggy black joggers tucked into leather boots, a long black jacket with a collar that rose to his nose, and a hood covering his classically wavy hair. Arianne gave the bounty hunter a once-over, jarred at the new person she saw in front of her. This wasn't the Jack she'd gotten to know in the Darwin Zone. This was Blackjack: the right-hand man of Cartel.

If Jack was going to be in front of thousands of eyes, he couldn't afford to drop his infamous façade.

"What?" Jack asked, a concerned eyebrow raising.

Arianne shook her head, "Nothing, just—different."

He shrugged. "Appearances." Then he gave Arianne a once-over with those bright honey-colored eyes. "You look good," he said, voice muffled by the collar of his jacket.

Arianne fought the butterflies that fluttered in her stomach at the compliment. Fortunately, the Jokers meant to guide them to the game arrived, and she was spared from making a fumbling mess of herself.

The first Joker was a severe-looking man with tattoos on every inch of visible skin and piercings through his ear lobes, nose, and lips. The man frowned at the pair of challengers. "We're going to be taking the train out of the city," he instructed with a jab backward at the small team he'd brought along. "Any funny business and the games are canceled: Boss's orders."

The small team of Jokers led Jack and Arianne down a series of stairs into a cavernous underground space. Ace's Casino had been erected on top of Cartel's many tunnel systems leading into and out of the city. Arianne noticed the tunnel underneath the Casino was equipped with its own train station leading to the main underground network. The station wasn't much: a singular magnetic levitation track with a three-car train waiting in the gloom. Granted, anything constructed with the specific purpose of undermining Leon Murray was impressive, in her opinion.

The magnetic levitation system was virtually silent as the train pushed off from the station and down the tunnel. Arianne did her best to observe the track in case any information could help with her people's escape, but the tunnels swept past too quickly for her to get a good look.

The train ride didn't take long, though, given the various forks and turns in the tracks, she knew it would be next to impossible to duplicate the route on her own. Jack, on the other hand, seemed familiar with the path. "Just as I thought. She's taking us to the stadium," he concluded slowly as the train slowed to a stop. "She hosts larger events there from time to time."

"Good or bad?" Arianne asked as the Jokers guided the pair off the train and up another flight of stairs.

Jack looked behind him at the tattooed Joker, pointing a semi-automatic in their direction with little more ceremony than someone would a television remote. "It's Ace," he said flatly. "It's never going to be good."

Their conversation was halted when the group exited the tunnels, and Arianne spied the monstrous structure awaiting them just a block away. Naturally, she'd seen sporting stadiums before from old copies of movies made before the Great

Disaster, but she had never imagined what seeing one in real life would be like. Even in its misused and decaying state, the sporting stadium was unlike any structure she'd seen in her short life: towering but ovular and carrying a grandiose sense of excitement.

In the days before the Great Disaster, thousands used to assemble there to witness sporting events, but now, most of those sports had faded into history. Pangaea had little interest in investing in culture, finding it more convenient to maintain control over the masses by keeping them occupied with ceaseless work and minimal television programming. But she wondered what that stadium must have been like in its prime: hosting the world's most talented athletes and performers and filled to the brim with people bursting with life and entertainment.

The pair barely reached the stadium before being ushered onto the field. Arianne had to squint against the bright lights, revealing thousands of masked spectators crowding the seats, all with their eyes fixed on her. The heat of their silent stares sent shivers down her spine, and she couldn't help but feel the painful irony from her curiosity just minutes before. Had the performers of the past felt objectified and frightened like her? Or was this just the nature of Pangaea: stripping everything that once had warmth and life down to its base and lifeless form?

Arianne did her best to stand strong against the crowd. Each observer remained as silent as a vulture, patiently awaiting their next prey. Even Jack, who'd become desensitized to the horrors inflicted by Cartel, grew pale under the scrutiny of the thousands of beady eyes. Arianne felt bile rising in her throat as she and Jack crossed the worn plastic grass toward the center of the field. There, Ace awaited them, holding a microphone, her hands adorned with acrylic red claws and glistening golden rings. The Cartel Boss extended her arms, displaying her ornate tiger pelt coat as the challengers approached.

"Welcome to night one!" Ace's voice resonated throughout the stadium. "Welcome to the game show, *Win Your Freedom!*"

The stadium lights pivoted to illuminate the challenge Ace had arranged behind her. It resembled a board game, with thirteen rows of cards, each large enough for Arianne to lie on. There were fifty two cards in total, forming a complete deck. The first row consisted of aces and their respective suits: spades, hearts, clubs, and diamonds. Subsequent rows followed the same pattern, increasing in number until the thirteenth row of four kings.

Ace gestured toward the grid of cards behind her. "The rules are simple: only one card is safe enough to step on for each number. You may place one foot on any card without consequence, but your punishment—or reward—will be dealt out as soon as you place both feet on your chosen card. But I warn you: with each mistake, the punishments become deadlier."

The crowd erupted in cheers, and Ace's tattooed face lit up with excitement as she reveled in the applause. In that one moment, Arianne saw Ace and everything she stood for perfectly. Ace loved entertainment almost as much as she loved being at the center of it and she would go to whatever extent needed to feed such a desire.

Jack shook his head beside Arianne as he observed the deck. "The odds of us selecting the correct card each time are smaller than even I can calculate. Less than a fraction of one percent. I don't like it."

Arianne let out a dry laugh. "Counting cards won't work here, will it? But that's the essence of it, isn't it? In any gambling situation, the greater the risk, the greater the reward."

Ace leaned forward and attached a microphone to each of the challengers' collars, her obnoxiously long red nails making the task more complicated than it should have been. After a few moments of fiddling, Ace stepped back and smiled as a giant stop clock appeared on the old jumbotron above. "Now that everyone can hear you, you have half an hour, challengers!"

At Ace's final word, the clock began to count down. Arianne and Jack ran up to the first group of cards, the pair's heads swiveling as they investigated the playing field in front of them. Jack jumped on his toes and shook out his hands, "Okay, with thirty minutes, that means we have two and a half minutes to figure out each round," he calculated.

"Don't forget to add in time lost every time we get a punishment," Arianne mumbled, scanning the cards. "The first card is the ace of spades," she said quickly, "it has to be."

Jack looked down at his right wrist, where his brand stared up at him. "It would make sense. Ace never misses out on an opportunity to use her favorite card."

The challengers nodded to each other, and in unison, they stepped onto the ace of spades. A sound chimed, like a key on a piano. Arianne looked at Jack. "That's good, right?"

She didn't have a moment to breathe before an electrical current coursed through her body. Jack and Arianne screamed as they threw themselves off of the card and landed in the dirt behind them.

Ace, who was now lounging in her personal viewing box, grinned down at them. "Good idea," her voice boomed as the crowd laughed, "but incorrect."

Arianne's arms shook as she tried to make herself stand. Her entire body had begun to cramp up from the surge of electricity. From a quick look at Jack, she could tell he was struggling too. "That was only our first mistake," he wheezed.

Arianne got his point: they didn't have much room for error—especially if they wanted to put on a good show and bring people back. Or lessen Jack's debt. The twelve levels stretching out before them appeared even more formidable than before. How could they possibly manage to select the correct card thirteen times in a row without making enough mistakes to kill them?

Their second choice had to be approached with more calculation.

Arianne frowned. "Ace clearly anticipated we would opt for the ace of spades first. She doesn't seem inclined to let us win. So, what if she chose the complete opposite card instead? The one farthest away from the ace of spades?"

Arianne hated how her voice could be heard booming throughout the stadium. Even their panicked thoughts were laid out for thousands to hear. People were laughing at her pain, sipping cocktails while she fought for her freedom. It was dehumanizing.

Jack's face turned to the card furthest to the right. "The ace of diamonds," he breathed.

She shrugged. "It's worth a shot."

The pair stepped on the card. Another note pinged, similar to the one that sounded after they stepped on the ace of spades—Arianne could tell the notes were different, but she didn't know what they indicated. Unsure of the outcome, she held her breath as they waited. Her heart threatened to stop with the anticipation of punishment.

When no painful repercussions materialized, Ace applauded, "Good job using psychology, Ari. Very clever of you. But that won't work every time, I'm afraid."

"Ace won't kill us," Arianne reasoned, "we're both an investment she can't afford to lose."

Jack shook his head, "No, she knows we won't *kill ourselves*. She wants us to quit before we encounter a level we can't handle."

"But we can't do that," Arianne countered. "If we don't make this exciting, people won't come back tomorrow, and we won't make enough to get out." A silence fell between them, and they both knew that losing also meant that Jack wouldn't make any progress in reducing his debt.

The bounty hunter frowned as he looked at the foursome of twos in front of him. "Well, let's give this one our best guess then." Stressfully, he pulled his collar away from his face, and she caught sight of his grimace.

Arianne nodded for him to proceed, watching as he cautiously stepped forward onto the two of clubs. The piano key played, and then a spike shot up from under the card. Jack barely cleared the space before it made him a human kebab. The crowd cheered.

Jack fell backward and landed beside Arianne, his eyes wide with terror. "Scratch that. We have fewer mistakes than I thought," his lips quivered as he stared at the spike that had nearly taken his life.

Her breath caught at the sight. She turned her head towards the clock—they'd already lost eight minutes. They were falling behind in time. "Give me the letter," Arianne ordered as she helped Jack up.

Jack quickly pulled the note from his jacket and passed it to his partner, still breathing heavily from the adrenaline rush of almost losing his life. Frantically, she scanned over the clue Ace had given her:

> *"Card games are meant for luck,*
> *Counting cards could win you a buck.*
> *Could you beat the dealer at their table?*
> *Come forward only if you are able.*
> *Compete and hope you don't bail—"*

"Well, the last line makes sense now," Arianne began, "we can only move forward if we're sure. But we can't count cards in this game."

Jack leaned in next to her. His lips moved as he read the other lines. "The dealer is Ace, and this is a card game," his voice trailed off.

"Card games are meant for luck," Arianne repeated.

He shook his head. "If you're relying on luck, you're not playing the game right."

Arianne scanned over the cards in front of her. "Say that again."

"If you're relying on luck, you're not playing the game right," Jack repeated as a smile began to come to his face. "Ace's riddle says the games are *meant* for luck, but that doesn't mean you should use it!"

"That's it!" She shouted in joy as she turned to Ace. "That's the lesson: it's never about luck."

Ace gave the pair a half nod from her luxurious viewing box. "Took you long enough."

Arianne turned back to Jack, who was now squatting and staring at the cards in deep concentration. "That's all well and good, but I can't find a pattern," he frowned.

"And we'll be dead before we can make it far enough along the grid to see one."

Jack's haunted amber eyes looked back at the spike. "Well, the pattern isn't diagonal," he swallowed hard.

As if to test, Arianne placed one foot on the two of spades. Another key played. She then set her foot on the two of hearts, and she heard a different note sound.

Jack stiffened next to Arianne, "That cord was D major."

"You can recognize pitch," she said in amazement, "do you know how rare that is?"

The bounty hunter shook his head, "I've always been able to do it. I never thought much of it."

Arianne played the key to the ace of diamonds—the card they'd successfully cleared—behind them, "Okay, what was that?"

"C major," Jack responded without hesitation. "So let's find another card in C major." Arianne played the keys of each suit of the two cards in front of them until Jack heard C major play again. It was the two of spades that time. Without another word, the two jumped forward.

From behind them, two masked assailants surged forward. Arianne screamed in surprise as one attacker clamped her in a headlock and forced her to the ground. The impact was jarring, and she clenched her teeth in an effort to steady herself. She managed to shift her weight and roll away from the cards and onto the plastic grass. The black turf from the artificial field coated her face and filled her mouth, and she was forced to spit out the pesky plastic debris in annoyance. When she regained her footing, the attacker drew a knife.

Arianne pouted, "That's not fair."

Jack positioned himself with his back to her, raising his hands defensively. He cursed, "I thought we were done with this nonsense after we escaped the woods."

"Do you recognize them?" Arianne inquired, scrutinizing the masked attackers.

Jack nodded. "They're Jokers," he confirmed, "some of them were part of my training."

"Any weaknesses?" Arianne squeaked.

"Do you want the good news first or the bad?" Jack quipped.

Arianne evaded an attack from one of the men and delivered a solid blow to the man's collarbone. "Give me the bad news," she managed.

Jack grabbed the arm of one of the Jokers and twisted it until there was a sickening pop, "I may have lied about there being any good news." He winced as he kicked the Joker away.

The Pacifican Major had to stifle a yelp as one of the Jokers' blades grazed her thigh. "Well, at least you find this funny!" She retorted, sweeping her leg low to throw the Joker off balance, her hands burning from a rash from the turf.

Jack slid on his knees to dodge an attack and knocked another Joker to the ground. "You're the one—" he paused to jump and grab the attacker's hands "—who told me to laugh more!"

Arianne chuckled as she punched her assailant in the groin and pinned him down as he doubled over. With a swift movement, she unmasked her Joker. He was a boy, no older than seventeen.

Jack frowned as he threw off the mask of his own youthful Joker. "They're trainees," he sighed. "We got lucky."

Arianne tossed the boy aside in annoyance. "I guess the real deal comes next."

Jack was still staring down at the boy below him, expression conflicted as his hair fell over his face and covered his eyes in shadow. Did he know them? Was he remembering his own time as one of them? Arianne reached out to his shoulder to comfort him, but he shrugged her off.

"Let's focus on the challenge," he mumbled.

Arianne tried her hardest not to get offended. She knew how jarring it was to relive horrible memories. Instead, she focused her attention on the last two spots they hadn't attempted. "It's either the two of hearts or the two of diamonds." To test, she put a foot on the two of diamonds and looked at Jack. "What was that key?"

Jack, still distant, took a moment to respond. "That was A major." Arianne then played the two of hearts, "and that was D major."

The winged female thought for a moment and tried to recall her days of playing guitar. "If we are following a musical pattern, D comes after C."

Jack looked at the riddle once more, "'*Compete and hope you don't bail.*' Carol said the riddle was incomplete and that the last line would rhyme. What rhymes with bail?"

The clock ticked down, constantly reminding them how close they were to failing. Arianne began to sweat. "We have less than ten minutes," she hissed. "Okay, bail—we got hail, sail, male, pale, whale, quail." She shook her head, "Not helping."

"Scale," Jack whispered, "scale rhymes with bail!" He pulled out the riddle one last time:

> *"Card games are meant for luck,*
> *Counting cards could win you a buck.*
> *Could you beat the dealer at their table?*
> *Come forward only if you are able.*
> *Compete and hope you don't bail—"*

"All the letters of the clue start with C, and the first correct card we landed on was played in C major. C major is the most popular musical scale on a piano," Arianne pointed out with glee.

"Okay, the next key on a piano after C major is D major, then E, F, G, A, and B." Jack listed quickly, "Let's go for the two of hearts: that was in D Major."

They stepped forward onto the two of hearts and winced as the D major key echoed out across the silent stadium. When no punishment materialized. The crowd erupted into applause.

The pair looked at each other in amazement. "I think we're onto something." Arianne smiled.

"I hope so," Jack breathed, the bruise blossoming on his forehead warning they couldn't afford another mistake.

The next group of cards came up, and Arianne played each with one of her feet until Jack pointed out E major. "Three of diamonds," Arianne whispered as they stepped forward. The key played, and surprisingly, they were still alive.

With the pattern figured out, the pair rushed through the next levels of cards. "F major, four of spades," Jack commanded. "G major, five of clubs." The clock ticked down to under five minutes, and the crowd—once silent—had begun to stir in anticipation.

"A major," Arianne tried, testing out her rusty music skills. "Six of hearts?" Jack nodded, and they stepped forward. The energy in the crowd grew to electric levels. She could feel the reverberations of their shouts through her bones.

"B major, seven of diamonds," Jack said as they jumped forward. They moved, and the key played. The bounty hunter looked up at the clock: three minutes left. "We have five more rows."

"But a musical scale only has seven keys," Arianne continued.

She played the next four cards, and Jack listened quietly. "They're all in minor key now!" he exclaimed. "It's like a piano: C major and C minor are separated by seven keys. We need to find C minor."

Arianne looked hesitantly at the eight of clubs, which they'd quickly identified as C minor. "I hope you're right," she sighed as she stepped forward.

As the clock wound down to three minutes, the two were still alive. They ran through the next rows: nine of spades, ten of spades, jack of clubs, queen of hearts, and finally king of diamonds.

The stadium was ready to burst with excitement as the clock wound down and the challengers approached the last row of kings cards. The pair landed on the king of diamonds in unison. Jack and Arianne grasped their hands together tightly as they waited for the resounding piano chime. The key sounded like the final note in a symphony, and the crowd erupted. Even Ace burst from her seat in celebration.

Arianne's breath caught. They'd done it. She spun and jumped into Jack's arms, her heart lighter than it had been in days. For the first time since she'd arrived in that city, she felt like there was a chance—however small—that she could find a way to succeed. Jack's hands were warm as he held her, his breath shaking from the intoxicating combination of relief, disbelief, and joy. The crowd drowned out in her ears, and for a moment, it was only her and Jack, embracing and sharing breath as the world slowed. She leaned back to look at him and smiled as they once again proved they were a formidable pair when working together.

Jack leaned his forehead against hers, and she felt tears sting in her eyes. She was one step closer to saving him, too.

Ace made her way down into the center field, her tiger pelt coat trailing majestically behind her. Her face was bright with excitement as she reached the challengers and held their hands up to the sky to announce their victory. Arianne's breath came out in long, heaving gasps as she took in the crowd. Just minutes ago, the audience had been waiting for her death. Now, they were cheering for her victory.

She decided Pangaea was indeed a strange place.

"Cutting it a little close there, didn't you think?" Ace muttered to them, covering the microphone.

"Gotta keep it interesting," Arianne shot back a little breathlessly.

Ace chuckled, and Arianne glared at the kingpin. She was happy her voice sounded comical because every bone in her body wanted to grind the Cartel boss to a pulp right then and there. She just might have done it too if the edges of the stadium had not been lined with armed guards. Even if she had been physically well enough to fly—which she knew that she wasn't—Ace's men would have her gunned down in seconds.

"Arianne and Jack, everyone! Since I love rhyming so much, I thought I would share with all of you the last part of the riddle you received on your tickets: *Can you win using this scale?*" Ace cried out. "Bring your friends tomorrow night for the next game!"

Chapter 39

Blackjack

Jack peered down at the unopened letter Ace had handed him after the first challenge. Hair still damp from the shower, droplets trickled down his forehead and onto his lap. Lost in thought, he paid little attention to it. The earlier challenge continued to haunt him. The boys they'd faced in the stadium, Jack had recognized them. Months ago, he'd been involved in their training. They were newcomers to Ace's organization, homeless kids plucked from the streets of Leonueva. Jack knew that, much like him, they'd seen no other way out. He couldn't help but wish he'd urged them to flee when he had the chance.

At that point, they were beyond saving.

A knock on his door roused him from his reverie, and Jack sighed as he rose from his seat. He'd had enough of Ace for a lifetime, and he certainly didn't have any more patience for her that night. However, as long as Arianne was engaged in Ace's games, he would be at the kingpin's beck and call.

He opened the door with a frown, only to find Arianne standing there, her smile faint but present. Jack hesitated, uncertain of how to react. Going into the first challenge, he'd resigned himself to giving her space. But after how well they'd worked together in the challenge, he was reminded of how close of a team they'd become in such a short time.

That had to mean something, didn't it? Maybe Arianne saw it too.

"Hey," Arianne began timidly. "I couldn't sleep—I just kept thinking about everything."

Jack stepped aside to invite her in, "I get it."

Arianne had changed from her challenge pantsuit into a tee shirt and shorts. No longer needing to look like the unwavering Blackjack, Jack had opted for more comfortable clothes as well. He now wore a pair of his old training shorts and a tank top. It felt strange wearing the outfit. With his missions for Ace or nights spent avoiding the Casino, he wasn't around enough to wear his clothes from his training days.

Jack pulled awkwardly on the neck of his tank top, suddenly aware he might be revealing more than he was comfortable showing—even to Arianne. Scars from Joker training sessions, botched missions, and Ace's old-fashioned lessons marked up his arms, and he felt his hands cross over his chest to guard against the more prominent lines. And the scars were the least of his worries.

Maybe those old clothes were a little too small for him now. Jack frowned, quickly pulling on a sweatshirt. "Talk about what?"

"I saw you freeze up during the challenge today. When you looked at the boys."

"Oh, that." He sighed. "They just... Reminded me of another time."

She sat down on Jack's bed. "Go ahead and vent, I don't mind."

"They reminded me of *me*," he finally forced out.

"Right," Arianne nodded, "you trained to be a Joker."

Jack flopped onto the bed beside her, his hands resting on his stomach. "Those days weren't fun. Jokers are brutal, and their training borders on torture. I was barely a kid, just thirteen when I started." He glanced at his calloused hands as if their scars and calluses held the memories of all he'd endured. "They strip away who you are, make you forget yourself."

He couldn't even pinpoint when the brainwashing began to take hold. For the longest time, he'd been content, even grateful, that they had removed his humanity. The Jokers had erased the pain he once carried and replaced it with purpose and a means to survive. But now, as he looked at Arianne, he realized something: emotions could hurt, but they made life worth living.

Jack was gradually relearning how to enjoy being himself again, even though he still struggled to define who that truly was.

The weight of his parents' deaths, the disappointment of his grandfather, and abandoning his sister—maybe he'd been a coward, but it had been too easy to hide behind a mask. It had been simple to lose himself in a life he believed was necessary for survival. Removing that mask was difficult, but it was better than living in denial.

"I climbed the ranks quickly," Jack continued, "Ace always had her eye on me, grooming me to be her right hand for years. Once I outgrew the Jokers, I started handling more covert missions on my own." He shook his head, tears starting to burn behind his eyes, "And the things she had me do, the people she had me work with—it made it so much easier to keep losing myself."

Arianne rested a hand on his thigh and nodded for him to continue.

"Ace invested her best trainers in me, and by seventeen, I was arguably one of the most dangerous people in her organization. By then, I was too far gone to care much about leaving."

Jack played with his hands, eyes scanning the ceiling as he fought to find words to explain a subject he'd kept secret for years.

"I never thought of leaving—I had respect there, and as long as I did what Ace told me, she let me have free reign of when I came and went. I didn't care about what people thought because they were terrified of me anyway. Deep down, I knew Ace didn't care about me. Deep down, I knew I shouldn't stay, but Ace kept track of how much money I owed, and with each mission, I got closer to making it rich. If I could just pay off my debt, then I could be someone."

Those past weeks had shown him how foolish that sentiment was.

Arianne squeezed his thigh reassuringly, "you were a kid," her eyes darkened, "they manipulated a kid."

"Even as a kid, I knew I was wrong," he admitted quietly.

But he wasn't a kid anymore, he was an adult who'd made the terrible decision to deal in human lives. He was so focused on freeing himself that he didn't think twice about dooming someone else to the same fate in exchange. Looking back, it sickened him. No wonder he'd struggled to tell Arianne the truth, he could barely admit it to himself. And now, despite his honesty, it still might be too late.

Arianne smiled softly as she rested her head on his shoulder. "Tell me about them. Tell me about your home."

Jack was going to be sick. He didn't deserve her kindness. He didn't deserve a friend—especially a friend like her. That was why he needed to beat Ace. If he could help get Arianne out of her debt with his boss, then his conscience might start to feel better—even if he was left behind.

"Well," Jack began, "I would've lived my entire life and died in that town if I could."

He closed his eyes, remembering his small hometown sandwiched between mountains and forest. What he remembered most was the *green*—the meadows, the trees, and the mountains all seemed to soak up the sunlight and glow. Sometimes, he struggled to believe his hometown was real. It felt more like a dream than a memory now.

He recalled one beautiful night in particular—a memory he used to play so often that the recording in his mind felt worn like an old vinyl record. It had been his sister's first true Mardis Gras out on the town. Trumpets played happily in the air, along with steady bases and guitars. The night was warm—spring had finally come—and the festival was loud and filled with smells of foods cooking out of every door. Lanterns hung on trees, and the sides of houses lit up the evening. Fireworks popped loudly in the air. Jack had painted his face purple and green.

He still vividly remembered the purple-feathered mask his sister had worn. She looked so enchanting as she watched the festival with wonder. "*Couleurs dans le ciel!*" she'd cried repeatedly, "Colors in the sky! Colors in the sky!"

Fireworks were always reserved for rare occasions—that was the second time he'd ever seen them. His eyes drank up the sparks, and his mouth widened into a smile of amazement. People danced on the streets, young couples kissed under trees, and others enjoyed food from vendors up and down the road. Jack had sat with his sister on the bench, just watching the sky.

Tears stung his eyes when he remembered Genevieve walking—not stuck in that wheelchair thanks to the Pangaean attack that had taken everything from countless families in that town.

Jack felt a hand on his shoulder, and the memory of his sister's feathered mask faded into a familiar set of gray eyes, "Everything's all right," she whispered soothingly.

Jack shook his head. Nothing was all right. He was stuck in a city made of concrete, not surrounded by forests and green. Genevieve and his grandfather were thousands of miles away. And without his family, there was no home for him. But Arianne couldn't know that—no one could. He didn't know if he was brave enough to admit that to anyone—let alone himself.

Standing up before it was too late to stop the tears, he rushed to the bathroom and shut the door. Gripping the sink hard, Jack looked in the mirror and saw his horribly bloodshot eyes. Then, one glinting tear fell down the side of his cheek, and he aggressively wiped it away.

What was happening to him?

Arianne knocked slowly on his bathroom door. "Jack? Are you okay?"

Jack. The name sounded foul to his ears. Jack wasn't his real name. Who was he trying to fool? He'd convinced the entire world—including himself for a while—that Blackjack was who he was. But he wasn't so sure anymore.

I don't want to be Blackjack anymore.

The jarring thought struck him like a freight train. This was why not feeling anything was more comfortable. This was why being a shell of his old self was more bearable. Because when he began to feel again, that was when the emotions were too much to handle. He could feel himself slowly going insane with the pain.

"I need a minute," he choked out.

"I can help. I know what this is like," she responded quietly on the other side.

Jack gripped the sides of the sink so hard that they threatened to break, "I need to be alone right now," he snapped in a tone far harsher than what Arianne deserved.

As soon as he said it, the anger faded, and shame replaced it. Why did he have to push away the one person in his life who was actually trying to help? The tears stung to hold back, and he blinked in surprise—he never cried, he hadn't cried in years. He'd forgotten the weakness he felt in his legs because of it. Jack's knuckles went white as he gripped the sink even harder.

Why did it matter? The past was in the past. Jack would never celebrate another Mardis Gras in his hometown or see his sister again. He made sure of it the day he killed that soldier—the day he ran away. The moment of weakness struck him, and his old self started to sound enticing. Maybe Tex was right. Maybe he was getting too soft. Maybe it was better if he forgot all of it, and lost himself to the mantle of Blackjack.

When he finally opened the bathroom door, the room outside was empty, and he couldn't help but feel disappointed. But what had he expected? Arianne wouldn't have stayed, not after what he'd said to her. Jack looked towards the bed, where Ace's letter remained unopened. He considered lighting the paper on fire as kindling to burn his entire room down, but he thought better of it.

The person he was a month ago would have strongly considered arson without an ounce of remorse. Granted, the person he was a month ago hadn't given enough of a shit to get worked up to the point of wanting to burn a building down. Now, Jack was stuck in an awful purgatory: too many emotions but also a new level of self-awareness that held him back from acting on any destructive urges. It was honestly the worst of both worlds.

Disappointed, annoyed, angry, and sad, Jack grabbed the letter, crumpled it, and threw it in the trash. Then, before his impulses worsened the shitstorm he was already in, he forced himself underneath the covers of his bed. Closing his eyes, he turned off the lights in his room to convince his body to shut down despite his anxiety. Screw Ace. Screw it all. He was going to sleep it all off and hope he had more emotional intelligence to handle it all in the morning.

Holy fuck, he was going to need a ton of coffee.

Chapter 40

Blackjack

Sleep did not subdue his desire to light Ace's Casino on fire, but it certainly gave him enough patience to keep the urges away. The bounty hunter finished his second cup of coffee as he attempted to compartmentalize the clusterfuck that had become his life.

Ace, the woman he'd been hopelessly devoted to for all of his adult life, was now at the top of his shitlist. Any rose-tinted glasses he'd once used to make his boss more palatable were gone, and he was faced with the utter monster that he'd become chained to. Anger, check.

He'd successfully managed to piss Arianne off in the time they needed to be a united front. He hated that he pushed her away when she had specifically come to him for comfort and company. Stressfully raking a hand through his hair, Jack had to clench his teeth to prevent a bothered hiss. Just when he realized how much he enjoyed her company, he had to screw things up. Disappointed, check.

Lastly, waking up with the residual sadness of lamenting over his family felt like the worst kind of hangover. At least, it felt how he assumed a hangover would feel. Though he never had one, he could picture the symptoms: a nasty headache, no desire to get out of bed, and an overwhelming cloud of misery. Yup, that certainly matched everything he was feeling. He missed piano lessons with his father, listening to his mother's beautiful voice, his Pèpè's herbology lessons, and most of all, he missed simply basking in the company of Genevieve. Sadness, check.

Fuck everything. He decided to attempt to drown his exhausting depression with more caffeine.

"Good, you're here," Arianne muttered from behind him, and Jack was forced to face the reality that he was so used to her company that he could recognize her voice—and got excited to hear it.

Jack turned, watching Arianne stroll into the Casino's dining area with Carol walking reverently behind her. Though Carol and Arianne had grown close over the past couple days, Carol still kept up her loyal servant façade by remaining a few paces behind her charge with a lowered head. Jack gave his travel partner a wary once over, aware he'd done an impeccable job at pissing her off the night before. As he expected, Arianne wore her annoyance as plainly as she did her baggy black sweatshirt and simple jeans.

"Can I grab another cup of coffee before you yell at me?" He yawned.

Arianne produced a letter eerily similar to the one Ace had given him the night before and slammed it on the table. "When were you going to tell me that we got another clue?"

Jack's eyes widened, "did you break into my room?"

Sure, he and Arianne had operated with very little privacy for the past few weeks, but that didn't completely remove the years he'd spent being in control of what the world knew about him—and the corresponding security of privacy it gave. Did she find anything else in his room? He paled. This was *not* the morning he wanted to deal with that.

The Pacifican rolled her eyes and flipped the letter to show where the envelope was folded and closed with a seal. She pointed a finger to the seal, "Ace has a sensor built in to notify her when the seal's broken. She sent this second copy to my room and made sure to inform me that the first one got lost in transit."

Jack sank into his seat, his headache worsening. Of course, Ace, in her endless desire to pry into his life, had used one of her signal seals to make sure he'd looked at her obnoxious clue. And when his boss realized he hadn't touched the letter, she decided to send a second one to Arianne to stir the pot.

"I was going to tell you," Jack rubbed his temples, "last night got out of hand."

Arianne and Carol exchanged a knowing look, and the feline female raised her eyebrows towards the Pacifican knowingly. Jack was painfully reminded of the unwavering power of the alliance of women against men, and he was glad he hadn't had much experience dealing with it until that point. It sucked: he was willing to admit he'd been a dick to Arianne, but now he was under harsh examination from two. The argument hadn't even started, and he was outnumbered.

Arianne crossed her arms, "last night got out of hand? Do you have anything you want to say?"

Now was his chance to apologize, the part of him who'd retained his social decency from his time before Cartel noted. But he hesitated. He wasn't too happy about the fact that very personal matters were being discussed in the middle of a relatively public dining area. Most of all, he wasn't fond of the fact that Carol—a female they'd met days ago—was privy to their personal drama.

Jack looked around, "can we talk about this in private—another time?" He hissed.

To his surprise, Arianne sat down with a long and annoyed sigh, "You're lucky we have a challenge to win, or I would not be talking to you right now." Using her finger, she pushed the note closer to Jack with more attitude than he thought was possible. "The competition today is at twelve in the afternoon. We don't have long to figure out a strategy, and the riddle is not helpful."

Carol, keeping her vow of silence, shook her head in disapproval as the soft tufts of her brown hair swept past her pointed ears. Curiosity slowly outweighed his dark storm of personal dread, and Jack reached forward and opened the note. His eyes quickly brushed over Ace's words, and he read them back out loud:

"'Seeing as the note I gave Blackjack has not been opened, I took the liberty to send you a second copy directly. Numbers from the first night are: seventeen million Units. Since I modeled the last challenge after Blackjack, this one will be for you, Arianne. I'll admit, I don't know much about you, but I will try to do you justice today.'"

Jack continued with the riddle written below:

"' In games like these,
Some say winning comes in threes.
Money goes to me, the head,
While the gamblers rush penniless to bed.
You may win one,
But I'll win two.
If you choose to compete, prepare to lose,
Figure out this clue, and winning will be a cruise.
-Ace'"

Arianne shook her head. "And that's my sticking point: did she just tell us that we're going to lose the next two challenges?"

Jack read over the clue again. "No, I think she's talking about the casino. Basically, she's saying that as long as the casino wins more than half of the time, then they're making money overall."

The Pacifican raked her fingers through her mane of hair, still tangled from sleep, "Ugh, enough with the riddles. This is bullshit."

Jack played aimlessly with his wooden coffee stirrer. "She does love her riddles."

Arianne cursed, "And we only have a few more hours to try and figure this out."

"If it's like last time, we won't be able to solve the riddle until we see the game. We'll just confuse ourselves more than anything else. That's what Ace wants," Jack warned.

Arianne stood up with a loud screech of her chair. With a grin, she swiped the yogurt and apple Jack had grabbed for himself, "Well, if we can't figure anything out, I'm going back to my room. I'll see you when we get picked up for the challenge," she announced with a scowl.

Jack bit back an objection at Arianne for stealing his food and let himself deflate with a long sigh. Before Arianne turned to leave, he brushed his ego aside long enough to mutter, "Arianne, I'm sorry."

"Like you said," Arianne grumbled, turning her back to him. "There's no need to talk about it now."

Now, more than ever, Jack wished he would have success in spiking his coffee with some syrupy liquor. Unfortunately, he knew he wouldn't feel a thing. Even now, his damn metabolism was processing his coffee too quickly for it to have an effect longer than a few minutes.

"God damn it," Jack spat, giving up and walking back to his room to take a depression nap.

He barely woke up in time to get dressed in another all-black techwear outfit before one of Ace's Jokers rapped on his door. He did his best to put on the perfect image of mild disinterest as he answered their incessant knocking.

"What," Jack said blankly, hoping none of the Jokers could sense he still hadn't recovered from crying his eyes out the night before.

Arianne was waiting with the squadron. Like yesterday, Ace had dressed the female in a business casual outfit. This time, Arianne wore a one-piece jumpsuit with black and white trim and a matching black leather jacket. Though she looked well put together, Jack had been around her enough to notice the ever-so-slight paling of her skin and clenched jaw.

"We're here to escort you to the train," the tattooed Joker from the day before grumbled.

The pair rode to the stadium in silence. Jack did his best to block out his nerves by inserting his headphones into his ears. The Simulator's music helped him pass the time as they traveled out of Leonueva and into the abandoned stadium. The constant beat of his music aided his focus as he repeatedly read Ace's clue in his hands. *If you choose to compete, prepare to lose, figure out this clue, and winning will be a cruise.* His eyebrows furrowed together. The only part of the clue he could decipher was that Ace was expecting them to lose. And that wasn't an option. Arianne needed to get out, and he needed to be debt-free as soon as possible.

Jack stole a glance at Arianne at his side. He wasn't certain what he would do once he was free, but he knew the first thing he would do was find her again—wherever she was.

Like the day before, the pair were ushered onto the field where Ace awaited them. During their hurried walk to the center, Jack leaned toward Arianne to attempt one last conversation. "Listen, I know I messed up," he began, "let me make it up to you."

The Pacifican kept her attention facing forward, her mouth a hard line. "We win the challenge, and we can talk after."

Arianne and Jack arrived next to Ace, and the Cartel leader flashed her teeth at the pair. "Thirty-seven million in total ticket sales as of five minutes ago," she whispered, "You might be onto something," she said with a wink toward Arianne.

"Cut the shit and just tell us what we have to do," Arianne muttered in response.

Ace wore a bright yellow puffy jacket that extended to her sides, emphasizing the warm undertones of her skin. Her long braids were tied up into twin buns atop her head, and her ears were adorned with large golden hoop earrings that reflected the midday sunlight. Ace was not only an Underground Queen but also a fashion icon. To Ace, beauty equated to power, which was why she always looked impeccable and surrounded herself with the most handsome of servants.

"I think I like you more and more by the day," Ace sang as she waved at the crowd. "Too bad we will most likely be parting ways tomorrow." She turned her attention towards the stadium, now packed to the brim. "Welcome to the second challenge! The rules of the game today are simple: if the contestants can solve the riddle, they win!"

Ace pulled a sheet of paper from her large yellow jacket and held it out in front of herself to read:

> *"In games like these,*
> *Some say winning comes in threes.*
> *Money goes to me, the head,*
> *While the gamblers rush penniless to bed.*
> *You may win one,*
> *But I'll win two.*
> *If you choose to compete, prepare to lose.*
> *Figure this clue out, and winning will be a cruise."*

Ace bowed mockingly to her challengers. "Good luck," she said, smiling, "you have all the time you need." She then pulled two Simulator headbands from her jacket. "Put these on and step forward if you wish to compete."

Jack cursed as he expertly fashioned the Simulator headband to his forehead. He then turned and helped Arianne do the same. The female curiously tapped the headband wrapping across her temples and behind her ears. "This is just like your Simulator, right?" She asked.

The former Joker pursed his lips. "Significantly more powerful," he warned.

The pair nodded to each other, and together, they stepped forward across the line Ace had demarcated in the plastic grass. The illusion sprung to life as though they'd stepped through a portal into another world. They were on a beach with sand to their left and lapping waves to their right.

From Jack's memory, it looked like the island of Citadel.

"Bitch," Arianne spat, confirming Jack's theory. She knelt, letting grains of sand trail through her fingers. "This all feels real."

Jack looked around, his suspicions rising. "What's her play?" He asked slowly. "No way she just sent us on a tropical vacation for a few hours."

"Help! Help!" A female *Fera* cried out from the opposite side of the beach.

The mutant was running towards them, hands frantically waving as she continued to shout. A Ward dressed in their classic red and black uniform materialized in front of her. Jack didn't have time to shout at the female to duck before the Ward raised his blaster rifle. Face as still as stone, his gloved hand crept towards the trigger.

Arianne took a lurching step forward. "Come on! We have to help her!" She exclaimed.

Jack looked around him at how convincing the scene was. "You have to remember this isn't real."

His words didn't reach his partner as she lunged towards the Ward. Arianne's twin short swords materialized in each hand as she ran, summoned out of thin air. Her feet kicked up sand as she sprinted, yelling at the female to run. Just as she closed the space within a few strides, the Ward shot the defenseless female down with uncompromising relentlessness. Arianne cried out in rage, the last few steps of her sprint quickening as she closed in for the kill. Her arms swept upwards. As she reached the Ward, she cut both of her swords downward in a sweeping motion through his shoulders. No blood spilled. Instead, the Ward hit the ground in a heap and then dissipated. The *Fera* disappeared as well.

Arianne landed in the sand alone, sides heaving as the sand absorbed her fall. "What? Where did they go?" She looked around in confusion.

Jack ran up to her. "It's not real, remember?"

The Pacifican shook her head. "No, no, it can't be. He felt real," she trailed off, eyes going to the swords in her hands. "These feel real."

Jack steadied her with a grip on her shoulder. "I know. Ace is trying to get in our heads. She's trying to throw you off your game. Look, Ace put you in your home, she's using Pangaeans—who she knows you hate—and she's using *Feras* as your motivation." He pointed to Arianne's headband glistening on her forehead, "she's built the perfect situation using what's in your head."

Arianne shook her head. "But why?"

"So that we can't think!" he explained. "Ace wants us to be so focused on what's going on around us that we don't have the headspace to solve the riddle.

"*'If you choose to compete, prepare to lose,'*" she recited the riddle with a shake of her head, "but I just won! I just beat that Ward."

"Help!" The same female from before appeared in front of them.

This time, she was running from three Wards.

"I'm going to need backup," Arianne lowered into a defensive crouch.

With half a thought, Jack willed a gun to appear in his hands, the very feel of the metal resting in his palms too familiar. *Not real, not real,* he repeated to himself. But what was this challenge? How did they win it? Did they win once they beat every challenger, like levels in a game? He raised the gun and fired three shots. All three Wards collapsed onto the ground and disappeared.

"That was easy." Arianne perked up.

"Too easy," Jack droned, looking up at the seemingly blue sky towards where Ace would be sitting outside of the simulation.

"Help me! Help me!" Two captured *Feras* appeared on either side of the pair. Three Wards surrounded each captive.

Jack narrowed his eyes. It would make sense if they were playing through predetermined stages because the levels were certainly getting harder.

"You take the ones in front of you. I got behind you," Arianne said, turning her attention towards the first set of Wards.

Jack couldn't help but smile. It felt like they were back in the woods. Bickering aside, they made a good team. As Jack fired off three more shots, he could hear the sounds of Arianne's enjoyment as she cut down the Wards behind him. He turned around just in time to see Arianne duck under a Ward's swing and jab upwards into his jaw. In that upward motion, all he could see was the broad smile on the female's face. Arianne was a warrior—and a good one at that.

The Ward dissipated, and she jumped up in excitement, "I could get used to this type of fighting," she breathed. "No blood. No death."

Jack huffed in response as they turned around to see that ten Wards had replaced the three Jack had shot down. "You detect a pattern?" He asked warily.

"Not one that can help me solve that riddle," she responded as she jumped forward.

Jack shrugged and joined Arianne in the assault. That time, as he swung and shot at the oncoming Wards, he noticed some resistance from the attackers. The battle was not as quick as it had been before.

Even Arianne was breathing heavily once the last of the Wards had disappeared.

"*Aidez-moi!*" Jack's head whipped around toward the girl who'd just called out for help in French. His heart slowed to a stop. He recognized that voice.

"Genevieve," he whispered in horror. And there, behind him, stood his sister—older than he remembered—but no doubt his sister.

Genevieve's bright red hair fell in long curls over her shoulders, her freckled face painted in fear. Jack furiously turned to where he knew Ace was sitting in her viewers box, laughing at him with that catlike entertainment. Jack pointed a finger toward his boss, "I'll kill you for that!" He bellowed.

Arianne turned to face the twelve Wards that stood between Jack and his sister. "Who's that," she asked in concern.

"My sister," he responded darkly.

"It's not real," Arianne repeated calmly.

He couldn't take his eyes off Genevieve. "Then how did Ace get an older image of her?" He growled, "Because I certainly don't remember her like that."

Ace had seen Genevieve. She knew where Jack's sister was. The implications of such a terrible woman knowing where to find his beloved sister turned his veins to ice.

Arianne's upper lip curled as she put the pieces together. "So not cool."

Once again, the pair became a whirlwind of limbs and weapons as they fought through the ever-growing mass of Wards. Jack shot three Wards down before he was pulled to the ground by a fourth. He dropped an elbow into the man's side and then punched him firmly in the nose. He wished he would have gotten the satisfaction of gushing blood—all he could see at the moment was red. Who the hell did Ace think she was, threatening him with his fucking sister?

Jack screamed with rage as he landed a kick to another Ward's gut. Screw guns—he wanted to feel every inch of that fight. As if in response, two sets of brass knuckles materialized on his fists. He smiled, whirling around to land a satisfying punch to the Ward's jaw.

From behind them, Jack could still hear his sister calling out for help. Her cries were slowly driving him insane. Arianne took down the last Ward while Jack raced to the man holding his sister. A swift sweep kick had the Ward landing hard on the ground.

Jack caught his sister, his entire body screaming at him to wrap around her and protect her from any further harm. His arms were shaking as he held her tightly to his chest, "It's okay, Gen," he muttered to her in French, words uncertain at first after years of mostly speaking English, "Everything is okay."

Genevieve's green eyes looked up into his, "Kes—" her words were cut short as the simulation washed her away in fragments of pixelated light.

Jack watched in agony as his sister faded from his arms. "No, no—Gen, come on!"

He folded without the weight of his sister. And then he was crying all over again, his breathing coming out in choked sobs. The life inside of him faded as he sunk into the sand at his knees. To have his sister in his arms and have her disappear moments later was excruciating.

He was faintly aware of Arianne kneeling at his side. Carefully, she wrapped herself around him. "I'm sorry," she whispered.

His lips wobbled. "It's not real," he repeated.

He desperately needed to believe it now.

Arianne reached for his hands, her eyes searching his. "This simulator might not be real, but the pain is."

He leaned into Arianne, trusting in her strength as he fortified himself. "Let's finish this fucking challenge already," he sniffled.

"I'll be honest," said a rich, masculine voice. "I didn't expect either of you to make it this far."

Jack's thought process slowed at the sound of that chilling voice. Next to him, Arianne's entire body took on an inhuman stillness. He hesitantly turned to see Leon Murray standing with all his intimidating might just a few yards down the beach. Even in the simulation, Leon's presence was oppressive.

Leon was calm and collected as a young *Fera* with blonde hair and the wings of an angel hung from his arm. A terrible smile came to his face as he pointed a pistol at the young *Fera's* head. Twenty Wards materialized before the Commander, their formation almost as daunting as the man they stood to protect.

Leon tilted his head—the three ragged and claw-like scars cutting through his eye caught the sunlight and made him look impossibly more sinister. "Kill any of my Wards, and the Little Beast dies."

"Arianne, what are we going to—"

Arianne's bellow of rage cut of the tail-end of his sentence. He turned in surprise, freezing when he realized Arianne's eyes had gone completely black—just like during the fight in the forest. He didn't have time to think about it further as a blaster materialized in Arianne's hand, and she sprinted towards the Commander. She fired shot after shot, each laser blast tearing a hole through the Commander's body. As Leon fell, the Wards disappeared around him.

But Arianne didn't stop.

The female was still screaming as she jumped on top of Leon, her knees digging into the dying Commander's chest. Arianne took her time lining up the killing blow, savoring every moment as she raised the blaster to Leon's head. The Commander *smiled* as Arianne delivered two more shots through his forehead.

Leon faded away, leaving Arianne panting in the sand.

"There should have been blood," she snarled as she stared at the dirt where Leon had once lay. "There should have been *lots of blood*."

Jack had seen Arianne fight for survival in the woods—but he'd never seen her like that. It was chilling to realize that the closest explanation he had was that she'd been possessed by something that survived off of adrenaline, rage, and fear.

"You could have killed the *Fera,*" Jack said warily, terrified of how he could see the reflection of himself in her black eyes.

Was this part of Arianne's mutation? Jack's eyes narrowed as he thought. It was unlike any mutation he'd ever seen. No, the only thing that came close in his knowledge was a *Fera* going feral.

Arianne's head whipped around so fast that the movement almost seemed animalistic. "Do you think I care?" Her black eyes went back to the sand. "He can't hurt me, that's all that matters."

"You thought killing me would be that easy?"

Leon reappeared above Arianne like an avenging ghost. His smile was dark and entertained as he raised his front leg and planted it firmly on her chest. Leon pushed Arianne into the sand with little more effort than stepping on a fly.

And to Jack's horror, she let him.

Arianne's black eyes faded to gray, terror dripping from every fiber within them. She wasn't breathing, she wasn't speaking, she wasn't *moving*. Arianne could have rolled away from Leon's hold or taken out his legs, but she did nothing but stare up at the cloudless sky above her.

Jack's lips parted. Arianne had gone catatonic.

"Look at you," Leon taunted, "you think you're so tough? All these years later, and you're nothing but a scared Little *Beast*."

"Arianne, it's not real!" Jack cried out, "None of this is real!"

"I can never tell when he's real anymore," she whispered. It was as if her soul had been torn into two dimensions. One part existed in that stadium, and the other was trapped in a long-lost memory.

Jack frantically looked around him for anything that could pull her from her trance. "Arianne! What did you tell me in the forest? Together! We do things together! So I'm going to need you to snap out of it so we can finish this thing: together."

Arianne's distant eyes blinked, and for a moment, her clarity returned. "Jack? Jack? Where are you?"

Jack shrunk. Arianne couldn't see him. Ace must've trapped her in a second simulation to feed the crowd's curiosity. She could hear Jack, but she was still lost. Jack stared at his partner and gaped at the pure fear plastered on her face.

Men about to die at his hands hardly ever looked as horror-stricken as she did in those moments. There was something different about her fear— subconscious and primal. He struggled to comprehend what Ace could have possibly shown her.

"Arianne! I'm right here!" Jack reached out to her, but she didn't register his touch. "I'm right here. Can you see me?"

"Not so tough when you're all alone? Are you?" Leon laughed as he leaned down and picked Arianne up by her shirt. "Oh, poor thing, you're shaking."

Arianne mustered enough strength to make eye contact with the Commander, but even that tiny ember of bravery was quickly engulfed by horror. She opened her mouth to speak, but no words came. Tears quietly started to stream down her cheeks. Suddenly, Jack couldn't take any more of it. He sprinted towards Leon and knocked the Commander to the ground. Arianne may have forgotten the world they were in was fake, but he hadn't.

The Pacifican was unresponsive as Jack hooked his arms under her shoulder blades and dragged her backward. If he went far enough, they would pass the edges of the simulation. He pulled as hard as he could, the sand making his calves scream in effort. Soon, the beautiful beach around them faded as they cleared the walls of the Simulator.

The noise of the crowd, once muffled from the simulation, surrounded Jack again as he laid Arianne down and knelt beside her. He did his best to block out the commotion as he prodded her lightly in an attempt to wake her from her trance.

"Come on," he muttered, "snap out of it. It wasn't real. It wasn't real."

Arianne's eyes were fixed on a point beyond the stadium, and her lips moved in inaudible words. What had Ace triggered in her mind that could cause that level of meltdown? Jack cupped her clammy face in concern. What had she *lived* through that would elicit that level of horror?

"Give up yet?" Ace's voice echoed from her observation box.

Jack didn't look up as he gripped Arianne's cold hand tightly. "No! Give us a minute!" He bellowed. Jack smoothed her sweat-soaked hair with his other hand. "Come on, Arianne. You're out. It's not real. Leon can't hurt you here."

Arianne screamed from some invisible horror, her hand squeezing his tightly. He bit back a groan of pain. Arianne didn't just come from a bad past. She was sick. Why had no one ever noticed? Why had no one ever helped her? Looking down and witnessing that much terror was almost too much for him to stomach. But he would, for Arianne's sake. He would stay there with her and ride it out.

"Quit, and she can go back to her room and rest," Ace offered snidely.

Jack ignored his boss. He refused to let her win after the awful tricks she'd played on them. "I'm here," Jack repeated, trying to reassure Arianne.

Slowly, Arianne's glassed-over eyes gained some clarity. "Jack?" She asked quietly.

He let out a sigh of relief, and he helped his female sit up slowly. "I'm here," he repeated.

Arianne took a deep and shaking breath, "It's over."

"What, the challenge?" He asked slowly.

She shook her head. "No, the worst part is over," she swallowed, looking up at Ace. "She's trying to break me. Too bad for her that I'm used to it." Her face hardened. "Let's finish this." Her feet were unsteady at first, but she slowly regained her confidence as she led Jack back into the simulation.

That time, forty Wards greeted them as the beach appeared once more.

"This is impossible," Jack sighed.

"Exactly," Arianne mumbled. "Ace was going to make it harder until we were forced to quit. But that's the point. Re-read the riddle."

Jack pulled the letter from his pocket.

"In games like these,
Some say winning comes in threes.
Money goes to me, the head,
While the gamblers rush penniless to bed.
You may win one,
But I'll win two.
If you choose to compete, prepare to lose.
Figure this clue out, and winning will be a cruise."

"What did you say about casinos this morning?" she questioned Jack, her face sickly pale.

"They need to win more overall if they want to make money."

Arianne nodded, her body still wilting with exhaustion. "Exactly," she breathed. "They'll give you a couple of wins to rope you in and think you're making money. But overall?"

"The house always wins," he said in realization.

Arianne scanned the battalion of Wards in front of them, the group so large that some were forced to stand in the lapping waves of the seawater, "This was never about beating the simulation. *'If you choose to compete, prepare to lose.'* It gets harder every time we win until we can't possibly succeed."

Jack scanned the beach. "The only rule of this game was to solve the riddle. It never said anything about fighting."

"The house always wins," Arianne breathed, "the only way to not lose is to not play."

In unison, the pair stepped back out of the simulation. Arianne looked up at Ace's observation box. A sickly sheen still haunted the female, but she looked confident as she prepared her final answer. The crowd silenced in wait.

"That's the answer," Arianne called up to Ace. "The theme of this game is that the house will always win. The point wasn't for us to win—it was for us to not lose."

Ace was silent for a moment as she stared down at her challengers. Jack rolled his eyes, knowing she was only delaying her response to increase the crowd's anticipation. Then, a small smile cracked onto her face as she began to clap. The crowd joined in, and the entire stadium became a cacophony of cheers.

"Well done," Ace said above the crowd, "I almost thought you wouldn't figure it out."

Arianne extended a vulgar gesture towards the Cartel kingpin before turning to march out of the stadium. Jack sent a glare of disgust toward his boss before he followed Arianne down into the train station that would take them back to Leonueva. Arianne was silent as she collapsed into her seat and stared out the window into the underground cavern beyond. A deep sigh escaped her as she wrapped her arms around herself.

Jack leaned forward in his seat and extended a hand. "Do you want to talk about it?"

The female shook her head. "I can't do this. I can't play another game."

"You have to. One more challenge, and you get out free."

But the fight in Arianne was gone. "I'm done," she announced flatly. "Fuck this stupid city—I just want to go home."

Jack recalled what the past month had put them through. The amount of shit they'd seen would've been enough to send most people running for the hills in a few hours. They'd put up with it all for *weeks*. He was exhausted, but he was used to it. He couldn't imagine what Arianne was feeling—her first time seeing the world, and this was the hand she'd been dealt.

"One more challenge and I'll get you home," Jack promised.

"And my family," Arianne pressed.

He looked down. He didn't know if he had the courage to correct her. Ace had never guaranteed the other Pacificans' freedom. But he didn't care about them. He cared about Arianne, and he needed to get her out alive.

Jack squeezed her hands, "One more challenge," he repeated, "and then I promise I will get you home safely."

When Jack reached his room, he almost folded in exhaustion at the sight of one of Ace's goons waiting outside. The woman was leaning on Jack's door, arms crossed. "Ace wants to see you," she reported flatly.

Jack shoved past her. "I have nothing to say to her."

"That mark on your wrist says differently," the guard taunted.

Jack curled his upper lip, feeling his Blackjack persona rise to the surface, "One more word, and I'll show up at Ace's office carrying your head."

He pushed the woman away from his door and slammed it shut behind him. Collapsing on his bed, he gave a few deep breaths to collect himself. Once he was certain he wouldn't take a bat to everything in Ace's office, he fixed his techwear jacket, ran a quick brush through his hair, and stalked to his boss's quarters.

When Jack reached Ace's doors, he threw them open in a fury, "Okay, I came like the fucking dog I am. What the hell do you want?" He spat. "And how the *hell* did you get a picture of my sister for that simulation?"

Ace's dark eyes shot up at Jack's tone, "I wanted to congratulate you on your most recent win," she said softly, her long nails delicately holding a glass of wine at her side.

"Don't avoid the question," Jack growled.

Ace shrugged. "It's just collateral—in case you don't do exactly what I say."

Jack froze. "You didn't find her. There's no possible way you found her. That's just an image of a girl that looks like her."

Genevieve was gone—hidden in the mountains of France with his Pépé as they had been for years. At least, that's what Jack had convinced himself of.

The Cartel kingpin raised an eyebrow. "Is that a gamble you're willing to make?"

Jack clenched his teeth as he took several calming breaths. "Why?"

"Because you did it, Jack. You and Arianne made over fifty million Units during these games. Fifty-three million, to be exact—those numbers came in minutes ago." She waved a tattooed hand. "Arianne will leave the Casino tomorrow after the final challenge.

"When is the challenge?"

A smile played across Ace's face as she sat back in her seat. "Can't tell you this time. It's all part of the game."

"And why Genevieve." Not a question, a demand.

Ace paused her drink as a drop of deep red wine slid down her cheek. It looked like a trail of blood. "Because I need you to make sure that Arianne cooperates. You see, I never had her little rebel friends. I suspect they're being held by the same buyer who was interested in your *Princess*."

Jack clenched his teeth so hard his jaw groaned with the pressure. "You're despicable. You're—" Rage made him clench his fists. "You're—"

"I'm what, Jack?" Ace asked, "Please, do tell me."

He raised his chin, staring down at the woman who so terribly held him by a leash, "You're a liar."

"Blackjack," the Underground Queen cooed. "Never once did I say Arianne was competing for her friends' freedom—did I? Now, she's proven that she has quite the talent for causing problems, so you're going to see to it that she stays put until the last challenge. If that doesn't happen, you'll find out whether or not I was bluffing about knowing your sister's location. What do you think?"

What were the odds that Ace truly knew where Genevieve was? Too high for him to be willing to gamble. His eyes narrowed in rage. "You don't want to know what I'm thinking."

But what about Arianne? How could he lie to her? She was going into that final challenge believing that her fellow Pacificans were trapped somewhere in the Casino. But Ace was right. Neither of them knew what Arianne would do if she knew the truth. Jack was stuck: lie and protect Genevieve or tell the truth and protect Arianne.

He wouldn't be able to live with himself if either of them got hurt.

"Oh, Jack," Ace sang as she leaned forward and held a white envelope between her fingers, "your final clue."

He furiously swiped the paper from Ace's hands and stormed out of her office.

In anger, Jack tore open the letter and unfolded the parchment. He'd expected a poem, but the only thing that stared up at him was a giant number two written in Ace's beautiful swirling handwriting.

"What the hell?" He burst out in anger as he crumpled up the paper and threw it at the wall.

Two. What could the number two mean? Was it the time of the challenge? No, Ace already said that the time of the challenge was part of the game. Then what? He paused, and his head whipped around to glare at the crumpled-up clue he'd left behind him.

The last challenge came back to Jack. *"You may win one. But I'll win two,"* he whispered.

His veins turned to ice as the realization struck him—it was a trap all along. There was no winning. Not in Ace's book. The casino always won, and Ace never said that Arianne would be leaving that casino free. She just said that Arianne would be leaving.

Jack and Arianne had beaten Ace once. But now Ace would claim two more wins: one against Arianne and one against him. Check and mate. Jack winced. *No, not Arianne.* He couldn't be responsible for losing her freedom—even if that meant risking his sister's safety. What would that make him if he stood by and let his friend get captured right after the last challenge? What did that make him if it was his fault?

It was time for Jack to decide what side he was on. He winced. He couldn't help but feel like making a choice was like fixing a broken arm: painful but necessary and ultimately brought on by a stupid mistake. A couple of weeks ago, the decision would have been easy, but then again, the decision was easy that time as well. Even though the verdict had changed, Jack was certain of his choice. The entire mess they were in was his fault, and he was determined to fix everything he had ruined.

One way or another.

Considering his sister's safety or not, his stupid life choices had put a good person in danger, and he *needed* to reverse it—which started with finding Arianne and coming clean about everything happening.

Even if that meant owning up to his lies and losing the first friend he'd made in years.

Screw their friendship. Arianne needed to get out safely.

Chapter 41

Jaya

Josephina Valentino Murray. The Mother of Europe, a *Queen* in her own right, was standing in their prison block, offering a band of rebels homemade soup.

Jaya watched Josephina in shock as she extended steaming bowls and poured hot coffee or tea for each of her teammates. Caesar's words in greeting struck her: *my oldest friend*. The Pacifican President smiled softly as he watched Josephina fix a cup of coffee for Major Cadmilus. Next, Josephina approached Caesar's cell.

Kalinda helped the president up, wrapping an arm under his shoulder to assist him in walking to the edge of his cell. The old friends locked eyes, and Jaya could feel the love of that stare all the way from her cold spot on the cement floor. The hard part was she couldn't detect if the stare was platonic or romantic. In her very limited experience, it seemed like both.

What was the story behind the unlikely pair?

Jaya's heart tore as she watched Josephina reach her lithe hands through the prison bars and caress Caesar's face. "Oh, what did they do to you?" She whispered quietly.

Caesar leaned into the touch. "It's been a while," he said.

Josephina cracked a small smile that was mixed with longing and pain, "I'm sorry I didn't come sooner. I was in Asia with Leon." The woman shook her head. "I wish there was more I could do."

"Excuse me?" Kalinda asked from underneath Caesar, "Um—Your Highness, ma'am, could you give my sister some food?" Jaya's cheeks flushed as the *Mother of Europe* looked her way. "She hasn't eaten in two days."

Josephina patted Caesar's unshaven cheek before turning towards Jaya's cell. The Mother smiled as she extended a large helping of soup through the bars. "I made it myself," she beamed, "let me know if you want seconds."

The bowl warmed Jaya's hands. The smell of cream, tomatoes, and garlic wafted up through the steam, filling her mouth with saliva. She barely managed a nod of gratitude before downing the soup whole.

"All right," Rhino muttered. "How did *you* end up with the king of darkness upstairs?" He pointed an accusatory finger at Josephina.

Jaya almost passed out from embarrassment.

To her surprise, Josephina didn't reprimand the larger *Fera*. Instead, she exchanged a look with Caesar. "I fell in love with the man, not the Commander."

Captain Lyn analyzed Josephina. "Is there any way you can appeal to his *gentler* nature?"

"Unfortunately not." She looked at Caesar again, "I can only offer more subtle assistance."

Captain Lyn crossed her arms after exchanging a look with Major Cadmilus. "Yeah, I was mostly kidding," she said flatly. The Captain turned to Caesar, "Sir, I understand she was your friend, but we're behind enemy lines. This is *hardly* the place—"

"Are the cameras off here?" Caesar interrupted, smiling at his old friend.

Josephina filled up Jaya's bowl once more before leaning next to Caesar. "Of course." Her grin was mischievous and slightly devilish. Jaya blinked, realizing that she *liked* the Commander's wife.

Caesar nodded to Captain Lyn. "Then I would like to reintroduce my friend, Jo," he reached through the bars, grabbed Josephina's hand, and squeezed it tightly. "Jo has been running interference for Pacific ever since I lost contact with her twenty-five years ago."

"Holy cannoli," Rhino gasped.

Jaya almost spit out her soup.

Josephina looked down shyly. "It's not much. I simply *modify* patrol routes before they get too close to your island. I do my best to eliminate any evidence I can when I come across it—mapping done by Air Forces or blocked signal waves, for example. I'm only good with information—but anything for an old friend."

Captain Lyn didn't uncross her arms. "I'll believe it when I see it," she muttered.

Josephina pursed her lips. "I understand if you don't trust me. I did come bearing some information. Leon has announced an execution that will happen in ten days. I don't know for whom, but he's already announced the event to the city's reporters."

A hush fell over the room, and Jaya's stomach bottomed out. All eyes landed on Caesar. Jaya swallowed hard, the very thought of the president's execution making her eyes sting. They couldn't lose Caesar, *anyone* but Caesar.

The Pacifican President looked down in consideration, his face classically cast in the image of a level-headed ruler instead of a man with ten days to live, "If my execution means the rest of your lives will be spared, that is a trade I'm willing to make."

Josephina squeezed her friend's hand ever tighter.

Ten days. They had ten days. Jaya looked down at her half-empty bowl of soup—her appetite gone. She didn't know what to feel. On one hand, the uncertainty of waiting was over. On the other, a timer was counting down.

"What's with all the sad faces? It's almost like you don't want to be here," Andre taunted, strolling into the prison block as his Ward's mask fell away to reveal his handsome, square face.

"Just an attempt at peaceful relations for once," Josephina chided, stepping away from Caesar. "Andre, *mira,* help me clean up this mess."

Jaya half expected the prince to laugh in his mother's face. She was shocked when, instead, he sauntered across the space and kneeled to pick up a few discarded coffee cups and bowls. Jaya and Kalinda exchanged a look. The prince—the ring leader of their misery—was leaning down to pick up his *prisoner's* dishes simply at the request of his mother. Josephina might have been small, but she wielded her own brand of power within the walls of a family who thrived on physical strength.

Andre grumbled, his eyes narrowing at Kalinda. "Don't get any ideas," he warned her. Andre approached Josephina and bent down from his impressive height to kiss her forehead. "Even an Heir bows to his mother."

Kalinda placed a hand on her hip with a smirk. "It's cute, that's all."

"Oh *hijo,* you used to help me make these scones," Josephina cooed, reaching up to pinch Andre's cheek. Andre tolerated his mother's touch, but Jaya could see his blood boiling from embarrassment below the surface.

"Like I said," Kalinda cooed. "Cute."

Andre ignored Kalinda, his attention turning to Caesar. "I've come to collect you. The Commander wants to have another discussion."

Caesar visibly slacked in Kalinda's hold. "If he's going to ask me about the location of the Serum again, I'll save you some time: I don't know where it is."

The Serum: a vaccine that carried all the uploaded knowledge of Pangaea within its creepily blue liquid. Every Commander received the vaccine on their Ascension day. With it, they gained knowledge of their regions' languages, the complex history of their empire, geography, and more. The uploading of knowledge directly into a Commander's brain made them effective rulers of such large areas but also formidable threats. How could anyone compete with someone who had extensive knowledge of battle strategies, martial arts skills, leadership methods, and history all at their fingertips?

Strangely, the procedure for making the Serum—typically protected by the newly minted Commander until a new one on a different continent needed to Ascend—had gone missing after Leon's Ascension. Despite Leon's competence, the rest of the world saw that slip-up as one of his greatest failures. For that reason, despite his growing age, the North American Commander still hadn't retired. Without the Serum, no Heir could truly ascend their throne.

Andre assessed Caesar coolly. "We know you don't know where it is," he replied, "or you would have traded it for your team's freedom days ago. Isn't that right?"

Caesar glared at the prince. "An astute observation."

Josephina paled as she watched the interaction between her eldest friend and son. Jaya realized what position the Mother of Europe must have been in: torn between loving her family and her friend as they devolved into war.

"Actually, the Commander wanted to get some blood samples from you," Andre corrected.

Josephina perked up, looking between Caesar and Andre. "Why is that necessary?"

Andre frowned at his mother. "Be careful. You don't want to look like you care about these people, do you?"

Josephina met her son's stare but didn't respond.

"I can assure you," Caesar sighed, "I'm the last member of the Ortiz Elite family. If you're looking for another distant member for inheritance purposes—you won't find them."

"Seeing as your parents signed off the rights of their estate to my grandparents, I'm the next inheritor of the Ortiz line." Andre grinned. "Beautiful palace you have in Spain, by the way. I wonder why you ever left it."

Caesar glared at Andre as the prince strapped him to the wheelchair waiting outside the cell. Jaya watched, distraught, as he wheeled Caesar out of the prison block, a rock of disappointment settling in her stomach. After days of being stuck in that lab, she'd only afforded herself a few short minutes surrounded by her loved ones before they were separated again.

She reached through the prison bars to grip Kalinda's hand. At least her sister was still with her.

The next morning, Blue arrived early to retrieve her for another day of tests. Kalinda had woken up with her sister to braid her hair before the Snake came to retrieve her. When Blue opened Jaya's cell, she paused for a moment to watch Kalinda finish off the last few strands of Jaya's purple braid. For a moment, Jaya could have sworn she saw Blue's yellow eyes lower.

"Showing affection will only give them more ammunition they can use to hurt you," she warned, pulling Jaya from her cell and handcuffing her.

The Chameleon looked back at her sister. "The minute you give up love is the minute you give up entirely."

"Whatever you say," Blue sighed, turning to walk out of the prison block.

As the pair of *Feras* walked, Jaya addressed the Snake curiously. "Did you know that Caesar Ortiz was a Pangaean Elite?"

The doors to the elevator closed before Blue responded. "Yes, it's important to understand the Elite inheritances, especially when involved with other upper-class families. I'm surprised the education in your tiny country neglected it."

"Pacific doesn't recognize the command of the Elites."

"Caesar Ortiz was the only descendent within the Ortiz Elite family—which controlled the southern half of Spain. Obviously, his parents knew they were being targeted and legally gave the rights to their inheritance to their trusted valet: Enrique Valentino." Blue rolled her eyes. "When they were killed, the Valentino family became the new reigning Elites of southern Spain, and Enrique legally adopted Caesar as his son."

Jaya's eyebrows furrowed. "How does that work?"

Blue hissed like the knowledge she was discussing was as basic as addition and subtraction. "A lesser Elite family in the area would have risen to power against a child manning his family's properties. With Enrique's experience, Caesar Ortiz would keep his inheritance and be protected. Unfortunately, when Caesar disappeared thirty years ago, the Valentinos remained in charge by default."

"Who killed Caesar's family?"

"Probably some rival family. It's not as uncommon as you would think. The deadliest thing to an Elite and another Elite. That's why so many lesser Elites flocked to this city—it's owned by Leon, so there's no territory to fight over, and they get the bonus of exclusivity."

Jaya nodded tersely, "You know a lot for being just another slave."

The Snake's eyes flickered for a moment. "I was something before I had this collar around my neck," was all she provided.

Blue Krait remained in the lab while Jaya went through her tests, hovering far enough away to remain removed while still being close enough to watch. By midday, Jaya was strapped to another metal table as the scientists ran tests on her vitals and brain waves. To her surprise, Blue moved closer with each test. By the afternoon, the Snake was resting on a wheeled chair a few yards away.

"Hanging out for the day?" Jaya asked.

Blue hardly paid her much attention. "It's nice to see I'm not the only one they're subjecting to this shit."

"How many *Feras* have they tested?" Jaya asked.

Blue shrugged, leaning back as she kicked her lean legs onto an empty metal bench. "Probably hundreds. Who knows when Hera started?"

The lab doors opened as Blue was preparing to bring Jaya back to her prison block at the end of the long day of testing. To her dismay, Pandora strolled in, her inhumanly blue eyes glowing softly in the abandoned lab's gloom. "I thought I heard you were spending a lot of time with the lizard *Fera*." Pandora chuckled, walking up to the lab bench Jaya was still strapped to.

Blue stepped away from the bench, crossing her toned arms as she raised a dark eyebrow at the Elite heir. "I was curious," she said with a fanged smile. "I don't see many other Asian *Feras* around here."

"Um, I'm from England," Jaya objected from her table.

"Whatever." Pandora waved both *Feras* off.

Blue's eyes shimmered with entertainment. The lengthy *Fera* strutted over to Pandora and hissed with her forked tongue. "What's wrong? Jealous?"

Pandora grinned up at Blue and grabbed the Snake's chin. "Possibly," she whispered.

Jaya's eyes almost popped out of her head as Pandora pulled Blue's face towards her and kissed her. Jaya craned her neck, shocked at what she was seeing. Not only was Blue enslaved to the Richards family, but she was also in a *relationship* with Pandora.

How could someone see Pandora—that maniacal monster of a woman—as someone worth loving?

Pandora finally let Blue go, stepping back with a lazy grin on her face. "Don't forget that you're mine," she said softly.

"Never," Blue replied as if in a trance.

And as quickly as Pandora had come, she turned on her heel and left.

Blue's expression was unreadable as she returned to unlocking Jaya's restraints. "I told you," she said quietly, avoiding eye contact. "It's complicated."

Chapter 42

Arianne

Caesar had been right. Arianne wasn't ready for any of this. She couldn't even handle a *projection* of her father. If she'd truly been in danger—instead of simply being inside a simulation—her mission would have ended then and there. And she would have gotten Jack killed along with her.

Her entire plan to return to Leonueva—it was too much for her.

But she was so close. One more challenge, and she could find a way to free her family.

A knock sounded against her door and Arianne sprung from her bed, wariness creeping up her spine. The clock resting on the armoire read quarter to twelve. What could someone possibly want at midnight?

Cautiously, she opened the door. Behind her, Carol stirred awake from her resting place on the couch. Outside, Jack was waiting, his eyes frantic. Arianne's stomach flopped. She didn't know if she had the energy to talk to him.

Still, she managed a sarcastic raise of her eyebrow, "What is it?"

"Can I come in?" Jack asked.

Something insistent in his expression made her agree, and she stepped aside to allow him in. Carefully, Arianne checked the hallway beyond before closing the door behind them. Then she eyed the bounty hunter warily, "What's going on?"

Jack took a deep breath, his gaze going between her and Carol. "I don't have much time to explain. You need to promise me that no matter what I'm about to tell you, you will trust me."

Arianne narrowed her eyes. "Well, that's promising," she said slowly.

He shook his head. "We need to leave now."

Arianne and Carol exchanged a look. "Leave? Why?"

Jack reached into his pocket and handed her a crumpled sheet of paper. "Ace wasn't lying. There's no *winning*." Arianne paled as she spied the singular two drawn onto the page. "Every win we get, Ace will win twice."

The Pacifican handed the note back to Jack. "No," she shook her head. "I can't just run away. My people are *here*. I need to get my freedom so I can help them."

Jack looked down, a shadow crossing his face. "Ace never explicitly said she had them."

Arianne's heart slowed to a near stop. "*What*?" Her hands began to tremble. "What do you mean my people aren't here, Jack?" She paced at the awful truth, "Don't you get it? I risked *everything* to come here!" By the end of her speech, her voice had risen to a furious shout.

All of it was for nothing. She'd successfully managed to trap herself in Leonueva for nothing.

"I'm sorry." Jack held out his hands in surrender. "Ari, if I had an *inkling* that your people weren't here, I would have told you. Ace fooled me, too."

She clenched her jaw, unable to look at Jack. "And how did she know to sell me?"

The bounty hunter's voice died in his throat as his shoulders slumped. "I didn't lie to you. My original plan was to sell you." He focused on the far wall of the room, "Even if that intent changed, my original plans made me sloppy, and I didn't think to shield your existence from Ace. She saw you coming for weeks."

For what might be the first time in her life, Arianne didn't know what to say.

"I'm sorry," Jack repeated, his voice sounding like sandpaper. "Arianne, this tears me apart inside."

Tears stung in her eyes as she brushed past the person she believed for a fleeting moment had been her friend. And maybe, someday, he could have been more. She didn't speak as she began packing her bags. As she shoved clothes, weapons, and rations into her tattered travel bag, a new plan began forming in her head. Hide in the city, regroup, and find her people. It wasn't the best plan, but it was better than sticking around for Ace to cash in on the small fortune Arianne promised.

"Arianne, can you say something, please?" Jack pressed, walking up to her side. "If you want to live, you need to trust me."

Arianne whirled on Jack, her crying eyes staring daggers into him. "The only thing I *trust* is that you'll screw me over." She shoved past him to finish her packing. "Whether you choose to or not. Come on, Carol. We're getting the fuck out of here."

Screw Jack. Screw completing that challenge to help cancel out his debt. Arianne had lost days in the casino, and her people were somewhere in the city, waiting for her. Her stomach dropped like she had let herself go into a free fall in the skies outside Citadel. What if her people weren't even in Leonueva? She shook her head. That was a bridge she would burn once she escaped Cartel.

Jack sighed. "At least let me help you escape. Ace can punish me all she wants after."

"Your misery isn't my problem anymore," she growled.

Jack shrunk under her glare but didn't respond.

Arianne should have felt bad, but adrenaline was slowly drowning out everything in her head. She'd let herself get distracted by a handsome Pangaean who managed to say the right things at the right times. It didn't matter if his intentions were good in the end. It only mattered that his actions ultimately screwed her over. Caesar, Rhino, and Jaya were in trouble, and she had made the rookie mistake of letting a stranger in.

The only thing that mattered now was the mission.

"Carol, now," Arianne barked, slinging her travel bag over her shoulder and opening the door to the hallway beyond her room.

Carol frowned, brushing past Jack to kiss him on the cheek. "Thank you," she whispered. If Jack heard Carol, he was too frozen to acknowledge her.

"We'll head to the servant quarters," Carol said, ushering Arianne out of the room. "There's a garage where goods get delivered to the casino. We can sneak onto a truck waiting there."

Arianne snuck down the hallway behind the female as Jack took up the rear of their group. She frowned towards Carol, "Why don't more of you escape that way?"

"We have nowhere else to go," Carol responded quietly. "Plus, none of us know how to escape the city."

"That's where I come in," Jack said darkly.

"No," Arianne countered. "I'm not leaving this city until I know where Caesar is."

Her will burnt as brightly as a dying star. She'd already run away from a family once. She wouldn't be doing it again. Caesar *raised* her. She'd been alone and afraid, and Caesar had made her better than she ever had a right to be as Leon's daughter. Leaving him behind wasn't an option.

And Jaya and Rhino were trapped too. She blinked away more tears as she started to run behind Carol. She would die before she left her friends behind. As for Haris, Arianne refused to return to the island without his father.

"We got friends!" Jack warned, his wavy hair shielding his eyes as he whipped his head around to spy into the hallway they'd just left. "They just broke into your room—we're out of time!"

"Faster!" Carol called, "We can get to the servant tunnels and lock them out. It should buy us time." She sped off down the corridor, her *Fera* speed carrying her towards a small door at the end of the hall.

"Come on, Jack!" Came Tex's mocking drawl, "Ace gave ya' one job! Keep her in place!"

Jack turned, running backward as he fired a few shots behind him. "Oh, was that what I was supposed to do?" He questioned once the ringing of his gunshots faded. "Guess I fucked up!"

Jack's gunfire provided the group enough cover to dive through the metal door leading to the servants' tunnels. Carol shouted, closing the doors behind them and locking out their pursuers. The female sighed as she slid down the closed door, large eyes closing in relief.

Jack reloaded his dual pistols, amber eyes flickering in the gloom of the tunnel. "We can't stop here. We need to move."

Arianne observed the group around her, "First, we need a plan."

Jack, who'd put one ear to the metal door, jumped, "Get down!" He shouted, leaping at her and dragging her to the ground.

Not two seconds later, Arianne's ears were pierced by the terrible barrage of gunfire as bullets pounded into the door. The first few bullets only punctured the metal, but the next round found their way through the dented door as they ricocheted into the tunnel beyond. The steel door was still standing, but it looked more reminiscent of Swiss cheese than a barrier. Jack's weight fell on top of her, and she had a moment to turn and face him after the recoil. She blinked at his grit jaw and intense gaze, and she hated how her stomach flopped at the idea of him above her.

You're supposed to be pissed at him, dumbass.

"Crawl!" Jack demanded as he pointed at a turn in the hallway.

Arianne snapped out of her daze and followed behind Carol, crawling on their elbows and knees. Bullets shot above her head and splintered the wall in front of her. Those bullets would've torn her apart if Jack hadn't been paying attention.

Once again, he'd shown her how terribly inexperienced she was in the field. Years of training could never replace the real thing. Two weeks ago, she'd been stupid enough to think she could take on the world because she knew a few fancy tricks. That overconfident female would've been torn apart by those bullets—if she'd even made it this far.

Rounding the corner, Arianne jumped up and risked a glance around the edge of the wall. The gunfire had created enough openings in the door that she could see what was waiting for them beyond. And it wasn't good. She searched her mental archive of weapons from school with a huff, "the bastard brought a fucking Gatling gun."

"Gatling gun?" Carol asked, eyes wide.

Jack stood up slowly. "Big gun with big rounds," he spat. "Also known as a big fucking problem."

Arianne looked up and down the hallway they'd found themselves in. "Carol, how much further?"

"Not far," the female responded.

"Jack," Arianne turned to the bounty hunter. "Any plans?"

Jack leaned against the wall, his face darkening as he raised his gun. "I wouldn't call this an idea, but it's better than nothing."

Jack closed his eyes, listening for the pause in the Gatling gun fire. When their followers began to reload, he moved. Turning out from the safety of the corner, he ran towards the Swiss cheese door and placed his guns into two of the bullet-pierced holes.

Biting his lip, Jack placed his pointer fingers on the triggers. "Here goes nothing," he muttered.

Jack fired twice, his deadly precision confirmed as two bodies hit the floor. Momentary distraction clinched, Jack sprinted back to the safety of the turn in the hallway just as more gunfire began to chip away at the steel barrier. From the dismal look of the door, it wouldn't be long before Texas Hold Em' and his team broke through. As soon as Jack reached Arianne and Carol, the three scrambled away down the hall.

"Not bad," Arianne managed as she ran next to Jack.

Jack clenched his jaw. "I couldn't get myself to kill Jamie," he whispered.

Arianne glanced sideward, frowning. "No one's blaming you for being human."

Blaming him for being a dumbass who kept secrets from her was a different story.

Before she could remind Jack of how much of an idiot he was, a low growl sounded, cutting through the hallway like a rumble of thunder. The sound triggered something primal inside her that had every nerve in her body alert in warning. Concerned, Arianne risked a glance towards Jack running at her side and realized that he was equally unnerved. When the inhuman growl sounded again, she felt goosebumps crawl up and down her body, and she was made terribly aware she had never heard anything quite like it.

Her entire body was telling her one thing: *run*.

"Oh no," Carol whispered as her eyes widened in terror.

Jack slowed to a stop, the hair on the back of his head raising like the hackles of a cat. "Leave it to her to throw it back in my face," he muttered through clenched teeth.

Arianne heard footsteps pounding and sickly claws gliding down metal. Her muscles tensed in warning. Whatever was coming for them didn't sound good. Jack reloaded his pistols as he frowned at his fellow conspirators. Even Carol, far from a warrior, bravely unsheathed her claws. A cold sweat broke out on Arianne's forehead and she drew her twin short swords.

"You know what's going on?" Arianne squeaked.

Jack rocked back and forth on his feet as a bead of sweat broke out on his forehead. "Ever fought a feral *Fera* before?"

Her eyes widened in terror. "No!"

When the creature rounded the corner, Arianne quickly realized how much she wanted to go home. Her mouth dried out in utter horror as a seven-foot female made of pure muscle, oily green scales, and deadly sharpened claws barreled towards her. For a moment, Arianne was frozen as she stared into the depthless black pits of the creature's eyes.

Fuck. Me.

Jack reacted faster than Arianne, lunging to fire a few quick shots at the *Fera* before jumping out of her warpath. "Time for a hands-on lesson!" He shouted.

To Arianne's dismay, Jack's bullets bounced off of the female with little more than a scratch. She quickly realized the *Fera's* skin was as thick as an alligator's. It would take a point-blank, high-caliber shot to the head to knock that creature down. Her stomach bottomed out. Jack, their team's best chance at killing the beast, couldn't even draw blood.

With a cry of annoyance, the creature fell onto all fours and dashed forward. Its muscled shoulders rippled as its claws sunk into the tiled floor below it. Using its momentum and strength, the feral beast made a beeline toward Arianne.

Arianne yelped at the sight. She desperately wanted to close her eyes and open them to find that the past three weeks had just been a *terrible* dream. But she knew the feral female running at her was *real,* and denying it would only put her six feet under. So, the only choice she had in those moments was to push forward and pray it was enough to let her see another day. As the Darwin Zone had taught her, fear needed to become a distant memory. The only thing that mattered was that the next death wasn't her own.

First survive, Arianne. First, survive.

Arianne let out a screaming battle cry as she ran to intercept the feral *Fera.* She registered the echo of her feet as they hit the tile, and the world slowed down around her. A calm fell over her as her breathing increased and the *Fera* neared her. Arianne was ready. One moment, the *Fera* was running at her, and the next, its massive tail filled her vision. The tail's power knocked the breath out of her and sent her crashing into the wall to her side.

Arianne wheezed, drywall crumbling around her.

The *Fera* let out a victory cry that displayed her dripping, sharpened teeth. Arianne scrambled to catch her breath as her pounding heart became a painful thumping beat in her chest. But she couldn't move—she couldn't escape with her lungs starved of oxygen. The *Fera* stalked closer, its haunting black eyes reflecting Arianne's horrified face. Despite all of her body's desperate pleas, she was frozen and cursed to watch the creature of her nightmares close in for the killing blow.

It suddenly dawned on her that she was going to fucking die.

Carol sprung from behind the feral *Fera,* wrapped her arms around its head, and twisted. Her attack knocked the creature off balance enough for Jack to land a perfect shot to its left eye. His bullet hit its mark, sending blood splattering from the soft tissue of the *Fera's* eye socket. The female roared, stumbling as it clawed at its face in pain. Their combined attack made the creature retreat just far enough to give Arianne a window to move.

Carol, as graceful as a cat, rolled out of the way and sprung towards Arianne. The servant was kind as she sheathed her claws and offered a hand. "Are you okay?" She asked.

Arianne nodded, hot with embarrassment. "Thank you," she breathed, still fighting for air.

The feral *Fera* recovered faster than Arianne hoped, and the female turned its attention to Jack. The bounty hunter fired a few more shots, but each one only succeeded in annoying the *Fera*. Scaled lips curling back in a growl, the Alligator swept her clawed hand in a deadly blow to Jack's abdomen. Arianne cried out in terror, but Jack managed to duck under the attack, his black joggers letting him slide effortlessly across the waxed marble floor.

With the feral alligator still distracted, Arianne had time to recover. Taking a deep and wheezing breath, oxygen finally returned to her bloodstream. Making sure she wasn't dizzy, she double-checked the grip on her blades and tested her footing. As she prepared for her next assault, Arianne scanned the space around her. Where were their other followers? She decided to make an announcement to the group.

"Where's Tex?" Arianne called.

"Feral *Feras* are unpredictable! Ace won't risk losing her people!" Jack answered, shoving Carol out of the way from a sweep from the *Fera's* tail.

Jack's shout got the female's attention. The Alligator whirled on the bounty hunter as her arms recoiled backward and prepared for a strike. Arianne saw her opening as she beheld the *Fera's* exposed backside. She took it without hesitation. Teeth grit with effort, she jumped and angled both blades downward into the thick muscles surrounding the creature's spiked spine.

As her sharp blades cut into the soft flesh below the scales, the creature screamed in pain. Arianne blinked. The scream sounded alarmingly *human*. She paused for a critical second, reminded that they were indeed fighting a poor female who'd been tortured to that terrible point. Disarmed, she was thrown off of the *Fera's* back. Her body hit the marble ground hard—the impact making her neck ache. She corrected herself quickly but realized with dismay that her blades were still lodged in the creature's backside.

"Shit," Arianne spat.

Without her swords, she didn't have a defensive countermeasure planned when the Alligator directed its attention toward her. Even Arianne wasn't fast enough to escape as the *Fera* closed the space between them with a roar of rage. She was forced back against the wall and flinched against the *Fera's* hot breath and dripping fangs.

Arianne's chest heaved as those feral black eyes of death looked hungrily down at her. She saw her life flash before her in those dark depths, and—if she was honest with herself—the life she saw wasn't one she was proud of. The Alligator reared back, its right claws preparing for the final strike. But as the creature ripped her hand through the air, her claws never struck Arianne.

A figure lunged and intercepted the Alligator's attack. Arianne recoiled in shock as the Alligator's claws sunk deep into her savior's gut. The momentum of the attack drove the Alligator and her new prey into the wall beyond. The entire room shook with the impact, and the wall splintered, sending dust and drywall crumbling down. Arianne scrambled to her feet, rushing to save whoever had just saved her. Then she heard a sickly *crack* as the *Fera* recovered and forced all its weight down on the crumpled form underneath it.

There was nothing left to save. Arianne slowed in awful realization. Her eyes locked on the swaying tail of the Alligator as its jaw unhinged and its teeth neared the limp body underneath her.

"Carol!" Jack shouted, "God damn it!"

"Carol!" Arianne screamed as guilt quickly replaced her horror.

Her nose detected the familiar metallic smell of blood as the Alligator dug into Carol's flesh. Red was everywhere: splattered across the wall, coated underneath the *Fera's* claws, and speckled across her arms. The *Fera* went into a frenzy as it ripped into Carol and tasted more of her blood with an eerie grumble of hunger and satisfaction. The creature dug deeper, and all Arianne could do was watch, her mind unable to process the thousands of emotions rushing through her head at concussive speeds.

"It's my fault," she whispered in a trance, unable to look away as Carol was dismembered beyond recognition.

The Alligator was bleeding out from the blades in its back, yet it didn't cease from its awful digging. Arianne gagged, and her knees wobbled as the creature continued to claw into Carol. Viscera dripped from the *Fera's* claws, shining a sickly pinkish white in the hallway lights, and the sight of that stringlike sinew hanging from its mouth and fingers was what finally made her vomit.

"We have to go!"Jack wrapped his arms around her waist and pulled. "We're out of time!"

"Carol!" Arianne cried out, "N-no! We can't leave her! I promised I would get her out!" She fought against his pulling. "I promised!"

Jack shook Arianne, gripping her face, steadying her, "*We keep moving,*" he screamed.

Arianne stumbled behind Jack. She struggled to focus on running as her mind replayed the critical seconds between her mistake and Carol's sacrifice. It was all her fault. Why did she deserve to live if Carol's death was all her fault? If she hadn't felt mercy for that creature, if she'd just been a god-damned professional—

"Rule one of Pangaea," Jack huffed, running at Arianne's side. "Live first and deal with the mistakes you've made later."

Arianne nodded, but her heart ached. She'd just met Carol, yet the female had been willing to give everything for her simply because she'd been the first person to treat her like a human being in years. Life wasn't fair. It took more than it gave. Even a bright spark in a place of darkness like Carol could be snuffed out in the blink of an eye.

"I'm the one who advocated for Ace to save that *Fera*," Jack admitted, lowering his head. "This isn't your fault, Arianne."

The words settled on her numbed senses. All she managed to do was nod as they continued running. The delivery garage appeared—the warehouse's large rolling doors were open wide, displaying the loading bays and the cool darkness of the night beyond. For the first time in days, Arianne could see her freedom within reach. She willed herself to keep it together for just a few more minutes.

"And the grand finale has arrived!" A feminine voice boomed throughout the tunnels and garage.

All fight inside her dissipated as a firing squad of twenty Jokers filed into formation from behind the bay doors. The masked mercenaries produced their firearms and lined each at Jack and Arianne. The pair slowed to a stop, raising their hands above their heads.

Ace waltzed out from behind her Jokers, clad in a glistening black latex one-piece, her glitter-lined eyes glowing with entertainment. "You two certainly put on a show!"

Jack shook next to Arianne. "You tricked me," he growled.

Ace pouted at her bounty hunter. "I'm disappointed you fell for it so easily, my Blackjack."

Arianne started to tremble with rage. "This was all a sick fucking game?"

Ace waved her off, dozens of golden bracelets clinking with the movement. "Even I can't plan how that beast will react." The Cartel boss grinned. "But I will say, that outcome was certainly a crowd favorite." She pointed to a camera on the wall to Arianne's left.

Ace had been broadcasting their chase the entire time.

"We collected the fifty million Units," Jack growled. "Let Arianne go."

Three SUVs with black tinted windows slowly rolled into the cargo bay. Ace's braids whipped around as she turned to watch the cars arrive, and a smile grew on her tattooed face. "Half right," she sighed. "I'll let Arianne go, but some new information has come to light. Fifty million Units is far too little a value for a—" Ace paused, considering. "What did you call her Blackjack? *Princess?* Hmm, oddly fitting."

Arianne's jaw dropped. "What."

Ace tapped her temple with a sharp pink nail. "Come now, sweetheart, the Simulator goes two ways. Just like you can see what memories the simulation pulls up—so can I."

The blood drained from Arianne's face. "I don't know what you're talking about."

Ace was giddy as two Wards emerged from the first SUV, lining up behind the last vehicle in their small caravan. "What I'm talking about is that you're worth far more than a small fortune," Ace explained. "You just financed my newest Casino in England, *Princess.*"

"Don't call me that," Arianne growled lowly.

"Don't call her that," Jack replied in unison.

Ace turned her attention to Jack. "Did you figure out the final lesson? Lesson one: you can't win with luck. Lesson two: The house always wins. But what's the third?"

Jack's amber eyes heated until they looked like molten rock. "I don't give a fuck about your games anymore."

His annoyance didn't phase the Boss. "Blackjack, to my side, please," she commanded boredly. Then she waved at Arianne. "I'll give you two more clues, and maybe you can guess the lesson of this third challenge."

Jack's jaw tightened as he took a protective step in front of Arianne. "No."

"Don't forget who you work for, Blackjack," Ace sang.

Jack didn't move from his stance. "I haven't," he said sadly with a glance behind him. "But I also didn't forget our deal. Let Arianne go free, and you have me, Ace. You have me forever."

Arianne stilled. "Jack," she said slowly, reaching toward him. Sure, she was pissed at him, but he didn't deserve a life chained to Ace.

Jack turned to her, his hands warm as they gripped her shoulders. "Ari, you get free, and you *run*," he pleaded. "Don't look for me, don't turn back, just *run*."

She shook her head. "Together, Jack," she whispered, gripping his hands. "You promised."

Jack couldn't give up. He *couldn't*. He'd changed. He'd learned how to live and *feel* again. Arianne couldn't leave him behind. She looked into the eyes of someone who'd effectively become her partner in crime. They'd been through more hell in a month than most friends would go through in a lifetime. This couldn't be the end.

Just as she couldn't leave Jaya and Rhino, she wouldn't leave Jack either.

Ace cleared her throat. "To my side, my Blackjack."

"You get a chance, and you *run*," Jack begged. "It's too late for me."

Arianne looked down at their conjoined hands. She wasn't leaving, not without him. Because no matter what type of front Jack tried to put up, she saw past it. Jack was a dreamer, an artist, and someone who cared so much that it hurt him.

Jack attempted to smile, but it faltered, and Arianne could have sworn she saw silver tears brimming at the edge of his eyes. He squeezed her hand one last time before taking a regretful step towards Ace.

Arianne glared at kingpin, suddenly feeling cold without Jack at her side. "All right, bitch, what the hell is going on?"

Ace smiled, walking up to run a tipped nail down Arianne's cheek. Her insides recoiled at the touch, but with so many guns pointed in her direction, she didn't dare to move. "Sweet thing, did you think he was your friend?" Ace turned to wave at Jack. "Did you really think a few measly weeks could change the weapon I've so carefully honed over a decade?" She leaned forward to whisper in Arianne's ear. "And did you think you could run from your past?"

Arianne's eyes widened, the bittersweet sting of Ace's words sending fear to the tips of her wings. "If you know so much, then you know running isn't my specialty," she hissed.

A deep, husky laugh came from Ace's chest. "Oh no, dear, I know you prefer the *flight* option when faced with that age-old fight-or-flight question. Isn't that right?"

Arianne's toes curled in an effort to keep herself from attacking the Cartel Boss. She wished she could watch that horrible woman bleed, but one look at the Joker firing squad warned her such an action would be far from worth it.

Ace scanned Arianne's rigid body with interest. "You want to kill me, don't you?" She poked Arianne's chest. "And you haven't even heard the whole story."

"Ace! Let her go, and I'll take on the debt difference," Jack barked. "You'll have me forever—for free."

"As interesting as that sounds, I think you'll want to hear my alternative bid, my Blackjack. It might be too good to pass up." Arianne and Jack turned their heads towards the sound of the closing SUV door. Ace fixed her long black braids. "Arianne, I would like to introduce you to my newest guest."

All she needed to see was that awful strawberry-blonde hair for her knees to buckle underneath her.

No, no. Anyone but her. Anyone *but her.*

Hera Richards strolled from the small caravan of SUVs surrounded by a small squad of masked Wards. The Scientist General wore the rare alternative to her typical white hooded lab coat: her black and red military uniform. The many badges from her years of service glittered across her chest as her light hair flowed in straight, silky strands around her face.

The queen of Arianne's nightmares looked no different than she had a decade ago.

"So, you two have met before," Ace's dark eyes sparkled in interest.

Hera's expression didn't change as she walked up to Arianne. Arianne's blood went cold as she glared up at the scientist who'd subjected her to days, weeks, months, *years* of experimentation as a child. Any hope she had left faded as her bleak reality washed over her.

"I've never seen this woman before in my life," Arianne breathed, but she couldn't even find the energy to make those words believable.

Hera's ice-blue eyes were freezing as she raked her gaze across Arianne. The woman looked down at her with disdain as she extended a finger. With a small flick, the scientist General pulled Arianne's golden angel necklace away from her chest and raised an assessing eyebrow. Arianne dropped her head in defeat.

"We can play hide and seek as long as you'd like," Hera whispered, "but you and I both know where that necklace comes from. I don't think you want me to embarrass you in front of your new friends and show everyone the other ways I can identify you."

"No, ma'am," Arianne whispered and then blinked in shock at how easily those words left her mouth. Despite what she'd thought, years of habits built underneath Hera came back without an ounce of struggle.

"Good girl," Hera straightened and turned to Ace and Jack. The woman snapped her fingers, and a Ward delivered a briefcase to Ace. "I hope that is enough compensation," she said with disinterest.

"And may I introduce Blackjack," Ace gestured to her side. "My prized *partner*."

"What," Arianne and Jack said in unison.

Hera reached out and shook the hand of a stunned Jack. "Honor to meet the architect behind the greatest hostage capture in this war."

Arianne narrowed her eyes, a deep ache settling in her chest.

"The second half of the deal would be a new brokered alliance with the Pangaean government," Ace said proudly, turning to Jack. "As a reward for your role in making this happen, you'll receive ten percent of the profits from this sale and a very lucrative position as liaison between Pangaea and Cartel."

Arianne's heart slowed to a stop. "What?" She whispered again.

Jack stumbled backward. "Wait," he breathed. "No—Ari, I didn't plan this!"

Arianne glanced down at the frigid concrete below her as two Wards cuffed her arms behind her back. Defeat made her numb. Hera *owned* her once again, and despite all of her efforts, Ace still sold her like any other *Fera* slave.

And Jack...

"Have you figured out the lesson yet, Arianne?" Ace asked, lifting her face with a single pointer finger.

Arianne ripped her head away from the Boss. "I'll kill you for this," she whispered in a low rage, "Don't think that I won't."

The kingpin turned to Hera and laughed. "Do you know how many times someone has told me that?" She shook her head. "Looks like I'm still alive. Still don't want to guess the lesson of this game?"

All the rage inside of Arianne finally boiled over, and she lunged at Ace. "Don't make deals with assholes," she barked.

Ace jumped out of Arianne's reach with a giggle as two Wards lunged to hold the winged *Fera* back. The Underground Queen backed away, hardly phased. "Close. Never trust anyone when it comes to money."

Arianne curled her upper lip at Ace in disgust. "I never should have trusted you."

Ace put a hand to her face sarcastically. "Oh, that's not what I meant," she said as her eyes drifted suggestively towards Jack.

Arianne watched in dismay as Ace turned back to Jack and Hera. Jack looked between the two women in alarm as Hera extended her ghostly hand one last time. Arianne's jaw dropped as she realized the deal presented to Jack: he was being *rewarded* for betraying Pacific. And on a more personal—and painful—note, he was being rewarded for betraying her.

Caesar, Jaya, Rhino, and the entire Pacifican squad weren't held by Cartel. They were held by her Father inside the Murray Monument. The colossal mountain—one Arianne thought she'd almost climbed—just turned out to be a false peak. The true peak was still thousands of feet above her.

And she was out of energy.

"What will it be, Jack?" Ace hummed, "You can have everything you've ever wanted: freedom, money, and power. Or," Ace turned to Arianne, "you can end up like her. What will it be?"

Jack looked over at the female who'd become a friend, his eyes pleading. Arianne ripped her gaze away. It was suddenly too painful to even look at him. She knew what he would choose. Deep down, she'd known what he would choose all along.

Together... that was just some bullshit they made up in the woods. Ace was right. A few weeks of fantasizing didn't change years of reality.

The bounty hunter shuffled nervously. "Please don't," he begged Ace, "please."

"'*No, please*,'" Ace mocked. "Hush, you've made enough bargains. You only have a choice left."

Despite knowing the pain she would feel watching, Arianne raised her head. A small part of her *hoped* she hadn't been an idiot—she hoped she'd been right about Jack.

Jack didn't look at Arianne as he turned and shook Hera's hand one final time.

Hera's smile was serpentine. "Pleasure doing business with you, Blackjack."

Jack had done all of this. He wasn't sorry. He was *capitalizing* on her pain. Arianne saw red.

"I trusted you!" She bellowed, and she lunged against the Wards' hold as a terrible mix of horror and pain rose inside of her. "You have no fucking idea what you just did to me!"

"Arianne," Jack whispered, unable to look up.

Her name on his lips burned. It felt like a mockery—a blatant example of the trust she'd given him thrown back into her face. Now, he couldn't even look her in the eye as he sided with her enemy and profited from her misery. Because of someone who had claimed to be her friend, she was at the mercy of Hera. Arianne gazed blankly forward in a daze, a wave of nausea making her dizzy. She couldn't believe how quickly her entire world had gone to shit.

It was all Jack's fault. And with that truth now painfully clear to her, she felt every emotion she once had for the bounty hunter fade until only hatred remained. After everything they'd been through, Jack was now worth nothing to her.

"Arianne," Jack pleaded again.

"You don't get to say my fucking name," Arianne responded in a low and haunting whisper.

Live first and deal with the mistakes you've made later—Jack's words from minutes before came back to her. Arianne looked at him in disbelief. He'd never lied to her. He'd been honest about his goals all along, but that didn't make the pain of his decision hurt any less.

She felt the anger she'd stolen from her Father slowly start to take over her fear like a reflexive form of defense. If it had to be her against the world, *so be it.* That strange calm she felt before battle washed over her and she welcomed the primal feeling of rage as it wrapped around her like a protective blanket.

"I'm going to kill all of you," a voice that wasn't hers escaped her mouth. She got sick pleasure from the shock and fear that washed over Jack and Ace's faces.

Hera frowned as she pulled a dart gun from her hip. "All right," she sighed. "That's enough. I'm not dealing with that the entire ride back."

Ace turned to Hera. "She looks feral. You've seen this before?"

Arianne's legs coiled beneath her, but just as she moved to lunge, Hera shot three darts into her chest. She stumbled back, her vision going blurry as her breath caught. The calming presence that took over her fought the drugs rushing through her in a dizzying battle between sleep and destruction. Eventually, even her *Fera* metabolism failed against enough medication to keep three grown men down.

Hera watched her new purchase collapse to the ground with mild interest. "Confidential," she muttered. "But she's not feral. Not yet, at least."

As the drugs pulled her under, she saw Jack stand and return to Ace's side. Her last few moments of consciousness were spent watching the bounty hunter cordially apologize to his boss with a face built of perfect disinterest. Arianne realized with dismay that he looked every inch like the Blackjack she'd met in that interrogation room back on Citadel Island. She was forced to wonder if any part of their journey had been real or if she'd simply been fooled by one fantastical ploy.

A single tear ran down her cheek as she closed her eyes and became the property of the Murray Monument once more.

Chapter 43

Jaya

Five days until the execution.

Jaya fought back a shout of discomfort as an ice-cold needle was inserted into her forearm. Squinting her eyes closed, she couldn't decide what was worse: the thought of Caesar's impending doom or the experimentations to come. She was tired, so very tired.

"You never mentioned," Blue muttered as she inspected a black-painted nail. "How did *you* get yourself stuck in this situation?"

Jaya eyed the Snake at her side. "Really not an appropriate question," she hissed.

Blue's yellow eyes bored into hers. "Oh, I'm sorry to offend you," she responded sarcastically. "Slavery, human experimentation, and torture are on the table here—I almost forgot that hurting people's feelings is strictly off limits here at our lovely war-crime central."

The Chameleon sighed and banged her head lightly on the table underneath her. "You should have all the answers. You were following us for weeks."

"Following Bradley Shaw," Blue corrected.

Jaya frowned. "For what reason?"

Blue shrugged. "I should say that's classified, but I don't really give a shit about that. You're not leaving here anyway, so what the hell. Our intel says Shaw is highly *suggestible*."

"Suggestible?"

Blue leaned back with a grin. "He's easy to manipulate."

Jaya's stomach lurched as she considered the ramifications of Bradley Shaw—their vice president—in Pangaea's pocket. "And did you succeed in manipulating him?"

Blue shrugged, obviously enjoying prolonging Jaya's apprehension. "I'm sorry, that's above my pay grade. Not that I'm getting paid."

The purple-haired female raised an eyebrow, "How did *you* get yourself stuck in this situation?"

The Snake's jaw tightened. "Fair question. A series of stupid decisions that took me from my home in Japan and sent me halfway across the world."

"That's not the full answer."

Blue's eyes narrowed. "There are details about my past that I haven't even shared with Pandora," she said. "And I would like to keep it that way."

"Like your name? No one names their kid after a poisonous snake."

"Especially my name." Blue's forked tongue curled with a hiss.

"How about friends?" Jaya closed her eyes, thinking of Arianne and Haris waiting for her back on the island. "Did you leave any friends behind?"

Blue's face softened in a rare moment of admiration. "One, back in Japan. We used to dance together. From what little I've heard, she's world-renowned now."

"Was she from your tribe?"

Blue's head shot up. "She was from... before my time in the tribes."

So Blue wasn't born in a tribe. She'd been given to one.

"Tribespeople are not your friends. The tribes say *amica,* which can be roughly translated to 'friend,' but it means much more. An amica is your family, your protector, and your friend all in one." Blue leaned forward, holding her hands together in consideration, "You die for your amicas: you live and breathe through them."

Jaya's breathing slowed. *Amica...* the waves of the sea surrounding her island home washed across her memory. She could almost taste the salty air and feel the spray of the cool water as she rode her surfboard to shore. And there, right next to her, was Arianne. Joy shining on her face as they raced.

Arianne was her amica.

"Some advice," Blue started, "don't think about your life before this place." The Snake gestured to the white-washed lab. "This is your life now. You'll only make yourself miserable imagining what you had before."

Jaya nodded, fixing her gaze on the blinding laboratory lights above her. "No way out?"

Blue was quiet for a moment as if considering her next words carefully. When she spoke, her voice was soft. "That's why my hair is so short." She let out a long sigh, "I grew it out long enough to give myself another way out, but they caught me before I could jump off the chair. They cut my hair every month now just to be safe."

Jaya's breath caught in her throat.

"I should get going," Blue whispered, standing up to leave.

Jaya's eyes burned as she stared at the lights above her, but that time, the burning wasn't from the brightness.

The lab was haunting at night. The typical quiet Jaya had grown accustomed to in her cell with the other Pacificans didn't exist down there so deep below the ground. Even when the day was over and the lights were turned off, there was a constant low humming from the equipment throughout the lab. The first few nights she'd spent in that terrible place, it had been difficult to sleep due to the insanity-inducing buzzing tickling her ears. Now, the noise was as familiar as the sandy beaches of Citadel.

Jaya rubbed her eyes, remembering her conversation with Blue earlier that day. She needed to *stop* thinking about home. Her memories would drive her insane long before that humming did.

She was about to fall asleep, curled into the corner of her new holding cell, when she heard footsteps thundering down the hallway to the lab. Her eyes burst open, and she watched as a squadron of Wards approached the windowed doors to the lab from the elevator beyond. The purple-haired *Fera* frowned in confusion, it had been hours since the lab had gone dark and the scientists went home. Despite Hera pulling a few late nights, not much happened after hours—especially not a patrol of Wards stomping around.

Hera took up the rear of the patrol, her black military uniform almost absorbing the shadows of the hallway. The scientist General moved to the front of the group and swiped her badge to open the doors to the lab, and the fluorescent lights burst to life in response. The Wards followed their General, a new prisoner held limply in the center of their patrol.

Jaya would have recognized that wavy, honey-brown hair anywhere. "Ari," she whispered in horror.

Hera's head whipped around, her icy eyes focused on Jaya. "You know the Little Beast," she smiled. The scientist General turned to Arianne's limp body with interest. "Pacific," she said slowly. "That's where you've been hiding all of these years."

"Ari!" Jaya cried as her hands shook the bars around her cage. "Ari, wake up!"

Jaya shook her head in denial. What she was watching couldn't be real. Arianne couldn't be in the capital. Her mind spun with possibilities. Was their island attacked? Did Bradley Shaw betray them?

Her heart thundered in her chest in panic. "Arianne! Please wake up!"

Hera ignored her lab subject as she pointed to the Wards. "I want a constant perimeter around this lab. No one except personnel that I authorize will be allowed in." Hera pointed to Jaya. "No subjects inside the lab will be let out. We cannot let word get to Commander Murray about Subject One—not until I get enough data to prove we need to keep her alive."

"Ma'am," one of the Wards questioned. "Is Commander Murray allowed inside?"

Hera sighed. "Obviously, but he rarely comes down here. I'll try my best to keep him away for now." She looked at Arianne, who'd been strapped to an observation bench. "I can't lose this specimen just yet."

"Ari," Jaya breathed.

Hera marched for the exit to the lab, the lights shutting off in her wake. "Report back at first light tomorrow," she commanded. "We're operating on limited time, so I suggest we all get some shut-eye."

The doors to the lab closed behind Hera and her squadron of Wards. Jaya was left in darkness again, the space only slightly illuminated by the the soft light emanating off some of the machines. She fought the darkness to look at her friend. Arianne was unconscious, her eyes squeezed tight.

Dread pulled at Jaya at the endless possibilities of how Arianne, who should have been safe back home, was now in that lab. What was going on outside of those walls? She ground her teeth in frustration. She'd only been separated from her squadron for a short while, but a lot could happen in a few days.

Then Jaya heard a slight groan of pain escape Arianne's lips, and she turned to see her friend move ever so slightly against her restraints. Arianne's eyes opened slowly, but to Jaya's surprise, she didn't look around. The winged female's face was blank as she stared upwards at the ceiling.

Defeated.

"Arianne!" Jaya cried once more.

Slowly, Arianne rolled her head towards the sound of Jaya's voice. She expected some surprise or terror to come to Arianne's face at the sight of the haunting lab, but to her dismay, her friend's expression was blank. Defeat washed off her in waves. The sight made her stomach flop.

"Ari? What are you doing here?"

Arianne turned her face to stare emotionlessly at the ceiling above. "Isn't it obvious?" she muttered tonelessly. "Your rescue has arrived: ta-da." Her head then made a loud *thunk* as she let it fall back onto the examination table.

Jaya's jaw dropped open. "What?" she hissed, "Ari, you were supposed to stay on the *island.*" Annoyance bubbled up inside her, "Y-you didn't listen! Now there's one more person we'll have to save!"

Jaya's fright at seeing her friend in the Murray Monument quickly turned to anger. When would Arianne ever listen? Back on the island, Arianne's undying ambition and will to fight and forge her own path had been motivational—it had been a driving force for Jaya at the academy. But now, removed from academia and thrown into the real world, she quickly realized those traits were the *opposite* of what was needed to be a good soldier. Instead of adapting to adulthood, Arianne remained that same headstrong girl who flippantly ignored orders and selfishly desired to prove the people around her wrong.

Now look where that landed her: trapped next to Jaya and ready to suffer the same fate as a lab rat. Most of all, Jaya was furious that the relief she once had knowing her friends were still safe on the island had just been crushed.

"You couldn't even see us off!" Jaya's frustration boiled over. "Caesar and I were leaving, and you couldn't even get past your stupid jealousy and see that we needed your support! And now look at you, you *had* to be the hero! You *had* to do whatever Arianne wanted to do! As always!"

A long hiss escaped Arianne's lips as she slammed her gray eyes shut. "Can this wait, Jay?" She said quietly, "I really need you to shut up right now, please."

"Shut up?" Jaya squeaked, "Did you just tell me to shut up?"

"I'm dealing with a lot right now," she replied flatly.

Jaya shook the bars of her cage. "*You're* dealing with a lot? I'm in a cage! Underneath the capital of Europe! You don't get to say that!"

Arianne let out another painful hiss. "And here comes the headache. Those damn tranquilizers always gave me headaches."

She paused her rant, her lips parting in confusion. "Wait, Ari," she said quietly. "What do you mean?"

"Home sweet home," Arianne grumbled, and her finger pointed to a water tank behind her.

Jaya went still at the disdain in her friend's voice. Breath hitching in fear of what Arianne might reveal, she followed her finger to the tank: a large cylindrical container built of glass and steel now filled with hundreds of gallons of dark water. Her eyes widened. She always forgot that Arianne had a *water* adaptation as well—something that would make containment in such a barbaric prison less horrifying. Instead, such an adaptation made a water tank a novel environment for tests and a next-to-impenetrable enclosure.

Then, the final incriminating piece fell into place and connected all the terrible dots. There, next to the tank, was a child's drawing of a stick figure warrior with white speckled wings and long white hair. Strix: The Champion Arianne claimed had been her hero since she was a child. Bile rose in her throat once she realized that Arianne—a much younger Arianne—had drawn that picture to look up to while she was put through hell.

And those sick Pangaeans stuck it up next to her watery prison—like a child's finger painting proudly hung on the family fridge.

"Why didn't you tell me," Jaya whispered.

Arianne shook her head, her voice taking on that distant sound that Jaya knew all too well. "Talking made it real," she replied.

A deep chill rocked her to her core, making an involuntary shiver escape her. "How did you escape?"

"I don't remember."

"Why did you come back?"

Arianne finally turned her head to look at Jaya, her heart breaking when she saw her friend's tear-stained eyes. "Because they took you."

Jaya's lips trembled. "We're going to get us out of here, Ari."

But it was too late. She could already see Arianne drifting toward that far-off place deep inside her mind. Arianne shook her head, tears glistening as they fell down her cheeks. "They have me now." Her voice cracked. "They won't let me go again."

"No, Ari, you can't focus on the bad right now!" Jaya shouted, "Come on, we're going to get out! We're in this together! Focus on me!"

"Together," Arianne trailed off as if those words hurt like a spear to her chest.

"Yes, Ari, come on, focus on me," Jaya pleaded. "We will get out of here if we keep our hope!"

But her words were useless. Arianne was gone, lost to her terror. For the first time, Jaya understood just how awful the visions that haunted her were. And for the first time, she couldn't comfort her friend, her sister—her amica—when those episodes came.

Watching Arianne disappear was her new form of torture.

Chapter 44

Arianne

Arianne was numb. The pain was a distant memory at that point. It had to be if she wanted to survive with a hint of sanity. She would rot in that lab, hooked up to countless machines and monitors.

Just being back inside those walls had decade-old memories rushing back to her at concussive speeds. Everything was so terribly familiar: the tests they ran on her, the scientist uniforms, and the nostril-burning scent of sterilizing alcohol. Other memories surfaced as well. She remembered the other subjects she'd been tested with, and she remembered each of their deaths from fatigue, extreme experiments, or the side effects of going feral.

Jack had betrayed her. Jaya, Caesar, and Rhino were trapped in the heart of Leonueva. And she was powerless to fix any of it.

"How curious it is to observe the decline of a rebellion," Hera sang as she walked into the private observation room.

Arianne looked away from the ghostly woman. She refused to show Hera a speck of the panic steadily rising in her chest. She took a couple of steadying breaths, reminding herself to be numb in the scientist General's presence. If her memory served her correctly—and she was well aware it usually didn't—Hera took any reaction and used it as a weapon. She couldn't afford to give her antagonizer more power.

Hera frowned, "I was hoping you would be willing to speak to me. I have many things that I could offer you."

"The only thing you can offer me is the Pacificans' freedom." Arianne knew she wasn't leaving that decrepit basement, but maybe Jaya and Caesar could.

Hera pouted mockingly. "You know I can't do that, love," she said in her obnoxious English accent.

Arianne turned her head away. She was done talking.

The ghostly woman straightened up, a cunning glint coming to her cold eyes, "You have the resolve of your father—who would have guessed?"

A fire burst to life inside her chest. "Mention him one more time, and I'll gut you."

The scientist General strolled to Arianne's observation table. "You have his anger as well. Interesting." Arianne bared her teeth and spat at the General. Hera wiped the saliva off her face with a chuckle. "And your mother's spirit."

"Shut. Up."

"Oh, I have so many questions for you, Arianne Murray. How did you find Pacific? Why did you leave Leonueva? You were an heir to one of the most powerful families in the world, and you gave it up."

"That's not my name," Arianne replied stiffly, her eyes returning to the ceiling above her. "And don't ask questions you already have the answers to."

Arianne had never been an heir. She'd been a monster, an experiment, a *weapon*. Leon never saw her as his daughter, only a tool he could use to rebuild the world.

Hera picked up a tablet from the table next to her and began to scan the projected contents of a document. "Then let's find some answers, shall we?"

Arianne focused on the ceiling before a panic attack gripped her with its icy cold hands. "Why don't you go plant a tree to replace all the oxygen you're wasting? It'll be a better use of your time instead of trying to get answers out of me because let me clue you in on something: I fucking hate you."

"Is that so?" Hera replied, lightly entertained. The pale woman raised a pair of forceps. "How about we pry your eyelids open for a few hours, just like old times? I remember that was one of your favorite exercises." She lifted her tablet. "It would also be pretty informative in testing your nictitating membranes."

To her surprise, she didn't react to Hera's threat. A steady calm of familiarity took over her. Arianne let out a long breath. "Go ahead then."

And with those words, Arianne felt the precipice of the terrifying, slippery slope before her. She knew the numbness that protected her like a warm embrace would take over her again. The person she was, the daughter Caesar had raised, would wash away like footprints in the sand when the sea brushed across it. Pangaea did something to her when she was a child—something terrible. It had rotted her core, and it was only a matter of time before that rot returned to the surface.

Something warned Arianne that the parts of herself she'd forgotten were far worse than anything Leon had ever been.

"Don't worry," Hera muttered, writing something into her document. "Leon doesn't know you're here."

"And why would Leon's most trusted General lie to him?"

Hera looked up from her glass tablet. "Because you're special, Arianne. In all my years of research, I've only seen one other *Fera* like you."

Arianne rolled her eyes. "Yeah, yeah: a *Fera* with two mutations," she huffed, used to Hera's obsession over her abilities.

Arianne was the first *Fera* Hera had ever seen with two distinct mutations. Her novelty was what sparked the General's interest in mutants. Through Arianne, Hera saw breakthroughs in understanding the growing mutant race and a whole new era of insight into what their capabilities could bring. If *Feras* with multiple mutations existed, what did it mean for their range of abilities? As a child, Hera had promised to help unlock the potentials of Arianne's genetics and—by extension—help Leon forge Europe's newest weapon. To Hera, Arianne's multi-mutation potential was unlimited: once mature, she could be stronger, faster, and brighter than anything Pangaea had ever seen.

Leon couldn't wait until his newest weapon came of age and turned him the most powerful man in the world.

"Precisely," Hera replied, pulling latex gloves over her hands.

Arianne stilled, her body recoiling at the smell of latex and rubbing alcohol. "Hate to disappoint you, but compared to other *Fera's*, I'm normal," she muttered with a hint of disappointment. "All these abilities you claimed I would have—I don't. Maybe the two mutations counteract instead of compounding the effects of the gene."

Hera flipped Arianne's forearm and ran a chilling antiseptic wipe over the inside of her elbow. "Do you know why most slaves are traded after adolescence?"

Arianne averted her eyes as Hera produced a needle to draw a blood sample, and she had to press her eyes shut against the sting of its sharp tip, puncturing her skin. God, she hated needles. They reminded her too much of her childhood, and that made a phobia so great that she felt like she was about to crawl out of her skin.

"I don't know," Arianne ground out.

"For a *Fera,* you don't know anything about your people," Hera condescended.

How could she? *Feras* were scattered everywhere, and most were in hiding. Even in Pacific, there was only a small population of mutants, and most were too concerned about fitting in to test their abilities.

"What's your point?" Arianne barked as Hera slid the needle out of her arm.

Hera knocked on the observation room door, and a hooded scientist walked in to retrieve the blood sample. Two Wards filed inside after the scientist and began unstrapping Arianne from the observation table. "Follow me," Hera instructed the Wards. "I want her hooked up to the carbon dioxide exchange and heart monitor over there."

Arianne followed behind Hera, and the guards around her placed her in a chair on the main lab floor. The winged *Fera* looked around, finally able to observe the space in the light. The lab had changed a lot since she'd last seen it: new technology—along with updated floors, lights, and tables—told her Leon had given Hera a pretty penny for her studies. Even with the lab looking so different, she couldn't fight the sickly feeling of déjà vu.

Hera waited with crossed arms as the Wards strapped Arianne to an observation chair. A scientist quickly arrived to hook her up to the monitors. "*Feras* finish maturing later than humans." The scientist General explained while she waited. "While their adult features mature around the same time, their secondary characteristics can arise in their early to mid-twenties. We call this Second-Phase maturation."

"Can arise? Not *will* arise?" Arianne asked.

"Good ear," Hera remarked as she took a wet rag and wiped it over Arianne's neck until her gill slits appeared. "A total of five-gill slits," she mumbled to an assistant who was staring at Arianne like a carnival attraction. "I've learned a lot more about *Feras* since when you were my first subject," she waved her hand in a gesture that showed she was vastly proud of herself, "I have a better idea of what to look for now."

Arianne's eyes drifted to Jaya, who was on a sleep monitor across the lab. She frowned as she took in her friend's vibrant purple hair spilling over the lab table. "How many people have you tortured in this hell hole?"

Hera's attention went back to the monitor. "I've observed the characteristics of over one hundred and seventy-five different *Feras.* A few of those subjects had mutations that represented a fish—which gave me some insight into the nature of your aquatic adaptations. I learned your second *Fera* mutation is not based on just any fish—it's most similar to a shark. I'm curious to see what other traits that mutation will give you as you age."

"You didn't answer my first question," Arianne said through her oxygen mask.

"Ah, yes!" Hera snapped her fingers. "*Feras* can enter the second phase of maturation, but they don't have to. My geneticists have marked an epigenetic phenomenon that supports the hypothesis that *Feras* can suppress their abilities. In an effort to hide, they can passively delay or block their second-phase maturation."

Arianne looked down, considering. "Domesticated," she said with realization.

"Yes, it seems there's some scientific explanation behind that insult." Hera shrugged. "Domesticated *Feras*—or *Feras* trying to pass as human—unknowingly block their second-phase maturation and stunt the growth of their abilities. I could go into DNA methylation, but I wouldn't want to bore you."

"General!" A hooded scientist seated at a microscope called. "Come look at Subject One's red blood cell count. It's through the roof!" Hera rushed to her assistant's side and peered through the microscope. "This many erythrocytes would aid in faster healing and higher oxygen efficiency."

"They're higher than when she was a child, showing a positive relationship between age and increased phenotypic change." Hera looked back toward Arianne in amazement. "The only number this compares to is Subject Sixty-Seven."

"They're currently lower than Subject Sixty-Seven, General." The scientist seated at the microscope retorted.

"Who is this Subject Sixty Seven?" Arianne demanded, her confusion turning into increased frustration.

"The only other Level Two *Fera* that I've found," Hera responded, leaning down to observe the microscope. "And while you would like to think you have a chance at normalcy, I'll have to destroy your hopes. Subject Sixty-Seven gave me greater results than I could have ever dreamed. The Subject's strength, endurance, intelligence, and healing were statistically greater in every category compared to a normal *Fera*. Granted, Subject Sixty-Seven was a mature *Fera* while you're still a juvenile. We'll have to fix that."

"What?" Arianne asked.

"High stress can trigger inert abilities and begin the maturation process." Hera turned away from Arianne and pointed to her assistants. "Base numbers are taken: authorize the start of Subject One Maturation Study."

The General pointed to two more scientists waiting at Arianne's other side. Panic filled every inch of her body when she saw what one of them was holding—a *whip*. As the flashes of memories of Leon delivering painful lashes across her back came to the surface, they were met with greater clarity. The scars were not just from torture—they were part of an elaborate *experiment*. Arianne closed her eyes and recoiled at the resulting ache in her scars.

"General," a scientist reported. "The Subject has severe bradycardia—heart rate is below thirty BPM."

The blood inside her began to boil. Arianne started to struggle and kick against her restraints. Her senses suddenly sharpened into laser focus, and the rolling storm of fear and anger coiled until it was a living beast inside of her chest. Hera couldn't do this to her, not again, not again, *not again!* And as if in response, something deep inside prepared to rocket to the surface.

"Don't worry," Hera said with interest. "A *Fera's* BPM can healthily operate in the range of twenty to two hundred and fifty. Considering Subject One's oxygen efficiency, she'll be fine."

Arianne's chest ached, and her breathing increased until she was hyperventilating. She continued to fight to free herself from the chair as every bone in her body was yelling at her, *screaming* at her to move. That beast of emotion was now writhing inside of her, yelling at her to run as far away as possible. In those moments, it didn't matter if she gave up on saving her people. Nothing was worse to her than reliving those nightmares.

She didn't care if that made her a coward.

"General," the scientist warned. "The Subject's heartbeat is rising and fast."

Hera stiffened. "Instinct is taking over." She paled, turning to yell at the Wards. "Restrain her! Now!" Hera pulled a communications unit from her collar. "Backup, we need backup!"

But it was too late. In a savage yank, Arianne felt the restraints break beneath her feet. A Ward rushed at her, but he was little more than a fly as she released a swift kick that sent him into the wall. By the time the next Ward converged on her, Arianne's hands had broken free. With an ease she'd never known, she grabbed the second Ward's neck and threw him into the first.

Arianne jumped up, an excited smile coming to her face as she recognized that rush that had come to save her. After learning its strength in the forest, she'd learned to crave it. The primal side of her had taken over once again, and it wanted only one thing: *survive.* She was more than happy to give in to that desire as she whirled on Hera.

Hera watched in awe and fear. "A feral-like protective state ability that I've only recorded in Level Two Mutants," she said in amazement. "After all these years, the whip still worked to trigger it."

Arianne's guttural voice wasn't her own as she converged on her captor and torturer. "You *whipped* me as a science experiment?"

Arianne lunged, but a blinding blast shot her backward as blue light surrounded her vision. Suddenly, she was weightless, the energy from the impact shooting her through the air. Arianne hit the wall next to the downed Wards with a booming crash. The impact should have kept her down, but she didn't feel pain—not in that state.

Jumping up, Arianne ran at her new attacker: a blonde with glowing blue eyes. At first glance, the woman looked like she had a seemingly ordinary right arm, but as Arianne closed the space between her and her new target, she realized the woman's limb was far deadlier than flesh and blood. With a shout, a blaster erupted from the woman's arm and fired another shot of energy at Arianne's chest. The second attack was strong enough to stun her even in her Instinct state, and she shot backward as she collided with the wall for a second time. But that time, Arianne didn't rise.

The otherworldly and intoxicating presence faded as her injuries overpowered her, and Arianne was left exhausted and half-buried in the lab's drywall. The woman—no, cyborg—approached Arianne, blaster arm still raised with a scowl. With new clarity, she blinked at the cyborg, a faint recognition pulling at her broken memory.

"Nice to see things don't change," the cyborg muttered. "You're still wreaking havoc."

Arianne blinked, a name surfacing in her mind. "Pandora?" She asked, but as soon as the name reached her lips, memories of the blonde became infuriatingly intangible.

Pandora curled her upper lip at her, an emotion on her face resembling disgust. "Fuck you."

Arianne was still reeling when she felt a sharp pinch at the back of her neck.

Hera stepped away, holding a dripping needle in her gloved hand. "Keep her sedated," she instructed her daughter. "And put her in the tank. She's too volatile to test consciously." The General sighed. "Just as I feared, triggering her maturation with stress will be too dangerous if Instinct surfaces every time to protect her. We'll have to put her body through stressors while she's unconscious."

Arianne felt the burning sting of the sedatives as they poured through her bloodstream. She fought the dizzying effects, but even she couldn't stop the urge to sleep that pulled at her body like a riptide. The world started to slow. Still, she managed to look at the destruction that she'd caused. Velcro restraints were torn to shreds, and the concrete wall lurking behind the crushed drywall was all but crumbling on top of her. The chair she'd been sitting in was dented beyond repair.

Did I do that? Arianne wondered, her body beginning to sway.

Her nerves didn't register Pandora's touch; she only felt the pressure of the cyborg's hands as she grabbed underneath her shoulders and dragged her away from the wall. The world fazed in and out of focus and Arianne's limbs went numb until they were dragging limply at her side. The steel water tank drew closer, a floor-to-ceiling window at its front displaying the dark, watery depths that would soon become her new home. Even as her mind slowed to a halt, she could feel the venomous barbs of dread sink deep into her soul.

And there, next to the tank, was an old drawing of Strix. Mocking her—welcoming her.

Arianne felt her fate split like a fork in the road. There were two possibilities: either she would die in the tank or re-emerge, like a venomous wasp from a cocoon, as Hera's new weapon. She wasn't certain which was worse.

Hera knelt next to Arianne as Pandora dropped her at the base of the tank. "That was just a taste of your potential," the General whispered from what seemed like the end of a long, dark tunnel. "We've only just begun to unlock the secrets of your genetics. And at the end, I will gift Leon the weapon he's always dreamt of. I doubt his common whore of a wife could do that."

Chapter 45

Blackjack

"I thought I would find you pouting up here," Ace muttered, her heels clinking on the metal ladder as she climbed to the casino roof.

Jack looked out over the city below him, his legs swinging over the ledge as the wind buffeted his hair. He didn't acknowledge his former boss—now partner—as she sat down at his side. The pair stared out across Leonueva, lit up against the indigo night above them. Just below, Jack could hear the faint sounds of the slot machines and crowds of gamblers preparing for another night of debauchery.

He shook his head, his teeth grinding against the urge to push Ace off the roof. A quick glance behind him showed Tex, not-so-casually pointing a blaster in his direction. Frowning, Jack turned his attention back to the city skyline.

"I'm just relaxing before I have to report tomorrow," he replied evenly.

Jack should be happy. He should be *excited*. The following morning, he would head to the Murray Monument to celebrate the execution of a Pacifican rebel and the beginning of Cartel and Europe's new alliance. Tomorrow, everything would change. Jack was being promoted—he would start to make *real* money. Ace wouldn't just be his owner and boss anymore; she would be his partner. Wasn't that what he'd always wanted?

But he knew good things shouldn't feel that shitty. He lowered his head and let out a long sigh.

Ace patted him on the back. "That girl made you soft. You used to be perfect! You were a doer—an executor of my will without question. And now you can't even enjoy a good thing when it comes to slap you in the face."

Jack scowled. "We should have aligned on the plan instead of blindsiding me. I could have handled it better if I knew what was going on."

It was the abridged version of what he wished he could say. He wanted to scream at Ace, to call her every single insult that went through his head when he watched Arianne carted away, but he kept silent. Jack needed to hold his tongue, or else he'd end up just like his friend: trapped and sold as a slave.

He squeezed his eyes shut against the memory of Arianne's frightened face.

Ace picked at one of her nails, now painted a glittering green. "You never would have gone through with it if I didn't give you the shove," she taunted. "Would you?"

"No."

Ace leaned back. "That's the one lesson you still need to learn," she replied. "I just can't get it through your thick skull. You need to check your god-damn morality at the door, Blackjack. No one in this industry will give a fuck about hurting someone else's feelings. The moment you hesitate is the moment you'll drown." The Cartel boss cracked her knuckles. "I didn't get to where I am by being nice. Sometimes, you must become your worst nightmare to make it out here."

Once upon a time, Jack had been okay with that mantra. The allure of becoming someone with power and money had given him purpose. Now, all he could think of when he thought of his future was the person he'd stepped on to obtain it.

Ace reached out and grabbed his chin, turning his head to face her. "I know that look," her glittered eyes darkened. "Don't fuck this up for us. Do I need to remind you how much I've done for you? Despite all your failures this past month, I've given you everything you could have ever wanted."

Jack stared blankly forward, not focusing on Ace. He frowned in the kingpin's grip. What did he want? *One day, I want to be able to wake up in the morning and know that the life that I'm living is my decision.* It felt like a century ago that he'd said those words to Arianne. Ignoring the lives he'd ruined just so he could finally have power—unfortunately, that *was* his choice.

But it wouldn't be one he was proud of.

The short time he'd spent with Arianne had woken him up. He liked to pretend he could be just as ruthless as Ace, but that wasn't the reality. Feeling emotions *hurt*, but he would much prefer the pain to a life of numbness. The only catch: he had to stop making decisions that made feeling emotions hurt like a thousand arrows directly to his heart.

"Understood," Jack muttered. He understood Ace's warnings, but that didn't mean he was going to heed them.

Ace smiled, standing up. "Good," she said, as casually as though she'd already forgotten the weight of her threats. "I hope I don't have to remind you how much you're worth." Jack rolled his eyes. It was the same story Ace held over his head since he was a teenager. Ace's nostrils flared. "Do you think I'm bluffing?"

Jack glanced at his former boss out of the corner of his eye, a fraction of the disdain he held for her escaping him as his eyebrows furrowed. "You said it. Not me."

Ace stiffened. "Do you have *any* idea who your father was before he ran off with your savage of a mother and joined that lost cause of a rebellion? Do you have *any* idea what that blood running through your veins is worth?"

Jack jumped to his feet. "Don't talk about my parents that way!" He shouted, a painful image of his mother's body buried beneath the rubble of his home coming back to him. His mother had *died* protecting his sister, and he would be damned if he heard anyone speak poorly of her. "My mother was an amazing woman—not some savage. And my dad—"

"Your father was an idiot who was lucky enough to be too rich to lose all of his fortune to stupidity. If I didn't think you were more valuable as a tool than as a paycheck, I would have sold you for those fortunes years ago." Ace pointed threateningly at him. "You fuck this business deal up, and I'll come to collect."

Jack flinched, taking a step back. His mind went back to the simple ranch he'd grown up on, tucked into the mountains of France. It certainly hadn't been much, but it was home. Money, power, and influence were not words he considered when he thought of his humble family.

He shook his head. "You have the wrong guy. I have no idea what you're talking about."

Ace grinned, leaning close to Jack. "Hmm," she pondered. "It seems like Mommy and Daddy weren't honest with their children. Are you serious? Do you not even have an inkling of who you are?"

Jack straightened, staring down at Ace with a new form of confidence. "I'm just Blackjack, right?" He droned. "That's all I am, and that's all I ever will be."

"Sure," Ace scoffed. "And Arianne was just a Pacifican Major."

Jack blinked. "What do you mean?"

Ace stood up from the edge of the roof. She waved goodbye, moving to join Tex at the ladder. "Welcome to the high rollers table, Blackjack," she sang. "You've just been dealt into the most dangerous game in the world. I suggest you learn more about your fellow players—and your own hand—before you make any more bets."

Jack's lips parted in confusion as Ace descended into the chaos of her Casino below. Her words sounded like a warning, a way to scare him back into the safety of her games. And yet he knew she was telling some version of the truth. The moment he walked into the Murray Monument and threw himself into Pangaea's politics, he would have a target on his back for the rest of his life.

Playing it safe and following Ace's directions was the smart way to go. Ace knew that by keeping Jack in the dark, he would be forced to follow her plans if he wanted to survive. But he was tired of Ace, and he refused to continue living at the expense of others. He might be the greatest idiot in all of Pangaea, but he would rather be an idiot than live one more day as Ace's punching bag.

Jack was going to fix everything—even if it killed him in the process. Sure, even if he survived, he would have all of Pangaea and Cartel hunting him down for the rest of his life, but what was new?

His mind was made up, but that didn't mean he was excited. "*God fucking damn it,*" he cursed himself and his newfound morality.

He was going to die in the Murray Monument, and the greatest irony of it all was that it was his plan.

Chapter 46

Blackjack

The ominous spire of the Murray Monument bathed Jack in shadow as he cautiously stepped up the black marble staircase at the entrance of the building. He was winded, but not from the exercise. With his thundering heart, he just couldn't seem to catch his breath.

Glistening obsidian windows rose dozens of stories above him. He squinted his eyes to where he could just see the uppermost floor through a thin layer of clouds and imagined Leon, the Lion of Europe, sitting on his throne in wait.

If Commanders had thrones.

Jack bit his lip to fight the rising tide of nervousness as he walked up the final steps towards the entrance. *You're going to die today,* a voice at the back of his head muttered. No wonder his heart was ready to burst out of his chest.

A tall Ward dressed in an officer's black and red uniform waited stiffly at the center of the lobby. Jack stilled his approach, assessing the man as his instincts warned of a threat. The Ward focused his hazel eyes strictly on Jack, confirming he'd been waiting for the bounty hunter. From the severe look on the man's face paired with the perfectly trimmed curly brown hair and finely-pressed uniform, Jack could tell the Ward was all business. That put all of his plans at risk.

As Jack approached the Ward, he allowed himself a moment to take in the majesty of the lobby around him. The room had three-story walls, built with the same sleek marble that the stairs outside of the tower had been constructed with. And carved from the marble, welcoming any guest into Europe's capital, were two black statues of lions poised to strike. Even being made of stone, the beasts looked deadly enough to chill his bones. The warning the hulking statues represented was not welcoming either: inside those walls, everyone was prey.

And Leon, the patriarch of the Murray pride, was simply the current leader in a long line of hunters.

"Beautiful, aren't they?" The Ward asked, folding his arms behind his back.

Jack eyed the pointed fangs of the marble lions. "From my experience, the most beautiful things are often the most dangerous." Riches, luxurious Elites, poisonous animals, Arianne...

The Ward turned on a sleek black boot, and Jack caught the glint of a double-sided sword strapped to his back. The Ward continued through the lobby, expecting Jack to follow. "You'll find many beautiful things in the Murray Monument," he mused.

Jack joined the Ward in the elevator, and an awkward silence fell as the doors closed. As the elevator climbed, Jack risked a look up at the towering Ward at his side and analyzed his uniform. From the officer's decorated breast to the red sash across his chest, the man emanated importance.

"Would I be able to see the prisoners before the execution?" Jack asked as the elevator climbed higher.

He could devise a further plan if he could just find Arianne and her people. From Hera's correspondence with Ace, he knew the execution was planned for noon, meaning he only had an hour before the war with Pacific officially began.

For years, Pacific and Pangaea had been quietly fighting a cold war. Pangaea would attack a Pacifican outpost—like Jack's home—and Pacific would raid a Pangaean armory or naval vessel. Most people knew about the tensions rising between Europe and the rebel colony, but the battles and lives lost behind the scenes went mostly unnoticed.

But an open execution done by the Commander himself? Even Jack knew what that meant. Leon was declaring all-out war against Pacific. And Jack wouldn't forgive himself if he played an active role.

The Ward raised an eyebrow. "Having second thoughts?" He questioned with a taunting grin. "And here I thought the infamous Blackjack had no feelings."

That was before he had the pleasure of waking up.

Jack put on his Blackjack façade one last time, letting a dark smile spread across his face. "I just wanted to take a moment and admire my good work."

The Ward reached out a hand and clapped him on the back. "*That* I can understand."

He gave Jack a half smile and turned to the touchpad on the wall next to the door. With a simple wave, the building's floor plan appeared below his gloved hands, and he quickly typed in a code to unlock the screen. Jack smiled as he slyly watched him work, memorizing the passcode and navigation of the software for later. Sure, he wasn't certain how he would lose his tour guide, but gathering information for when the chance presented itself didn't hurt. The Ward selected a basement floor, and Jack stumbled as the elevator jolted to a halt and reversed directions to go downwards.

The doors to the elevator finally opened, and the hallway beyond branched off from different entrances carved into its metal walls. As Jack followed his guide, he did his best to keep track of the various doors, including one that led to a separate flight of stairs. A Ward seated at a desk at the center of the corridor fumbled and saluted the pair as they approached. The officer waved the Ward off, and it took no more than a flick of his head to instruct the Ward to open one of the doors lining the corridor. Jack watched the interaction with interest, further noting the importance of his escort.

What Jack hadn't expected beyond those closed doors was chaos.

He recognized Caesar Ortiz and the rest of the squad he'd arrived with in Romania. Behind their prison bars, the Pacificans were in a fury, pounding on the ground and walls and shaking the very bars that kept them confined.

The Ward at Jack's side unsheathed his double-edged sword from his back. "Get the *fuck* away from her!" He bellowed with rage.

Jack realized then that the Pacifican squadron was the least of their worries. The true chaos was coming from outside of the cells.

A woman with beautiful dark brown curls lay on the ground with her hands held above her head. Behind her stood a woman around Jack's age with sleek bleach-blonde hair and a blaster for a right arm pointed at the downed woman's head.

Behind the cyborg stood Hera—casually watching the scene unfold from her resting spot on the far wall. The scientist General uncrossed her arms as she took in the outraged Ward at Jack's side. Just like days before, Hera was the picture of cool confidence. Jack knew then that Hera's relaxed state was a warning more than anything. Hera planned for chaos; she was *comfortable* with it. Wariness crept in through his nerves, and he took a cautious step away from the Ward at his side. Years with Cartel had taught him to sense a coming fight like the smell of rain before a storm.

"Ah, the *Prince* has arrived," Hera taunted, her icy eyes going to the black-clad Ward.

Jack blinked at the man next to him. *Prince*. The Ward wasn't just an officer—he was Prince Andre Murray, Heir Apparent to the Commandership. And Jack had spoken to Andre like a commoner. He paled, taking another healthy step backward.

"*Hijo!*" The woman on the floor shouted. "Stop!"

Andre's eyes threatened death as he pointed one tip of his sword at the cyborg. "Back the fuck away from my *mother*," he spat. "That's an order, Richards."

Jack was seconds away from sprinting out of that room. Pacific's President, the European Prince, the General of Europe's armies, and now, the Mother of Europe. The powder keg of the war was about to go off, and he wanted to be as far as possible from the explosion.

But he wouldn't run until he knew what the hell he was running *from*.

"Attacking my daughter would be treason," Hera's voice boomed throughout the room. The scientist General stepped defiantly in front of the cyborg—her daughter—and somehow managed to glare down at the towering Prince of Europe. "Your blood may give you rank, but even you cannot overpower the law."

Andre was shaking with a cold fury. "Get my mother off of the ground," his voice was low and murderous.

Hera turned to smile at Josephina as the cyborg ripped the queen off the floor. "Josephina Valentino," the General purred. "You're under arrest for treason against the Empire."

Josephina blew a stray strand of curly brown hair from her face and then scowled up at Hera in defiance. "Josephina Valentino-*Murray*," the woman spat. "Don't you ever forget that he chose me over you."

The scientist General's cool façade cracked momentarily as her upper lip curled. "I'll never let him forget that you chose that man," she pointed at Caesar, "over your Continent!"

All eyes in the room turned to Caesar. Out of all the Pacificans, Caesar was the only one who'd remained silent throughout Josephina's arrest.

Finally, the Pacifican President spoke. "The only person who should be punished is me," he whispered, his coffee-warm eyes locking with Josephina's. An unspoken conversation passed between the two, and Caesar broke his gaze from the European Queen. "It's too late anyways," he finished.

Josephina's teeth were bloody as she smiled at Hera. "Pacific is coming," she warned with a slow shake of her head. "This elaborate trap that you've planned for me—you think I didn't see it coming? Do you think I didn't know you were looking for any reason to undermine me? You're out of time."

Hera roared with rage, "You're the one out of time!"

With that, the powder keg exploded. Andre lunged at the cyborg, reaching for his mother. Hera dove to the floor for cover. There was a blast of blue light, and Andre was launched backward into the wall behind him. The concrete behind the prince cracked.

Jack ran.

The Ward from the main hallway sprinted past him, hardly paying the bounty hunter any mind as he ran towards the chaos of the prison block. Turning his head to ensure he wasn't being followed, Jack dove into the elevator. Behind him, smoke was billowing from the doorway as Andre and the cyborg continued to fight.

He didn't have long until someone realized he was missing.

Frantically pressing the elevator *close* button, Jack didn't give himself a moment to breathe until he was secure behind the hulking doors. His frazzled mind fought to remember the elevator code as his fingers waved nervously over the projected touchpad. *What was going on back there?* He didn't have time to dwell over obviously complicated Pangaean politics. The only thing he was worried about was that Arianne hadn't been in that prison block.

He'd been granted a precious few moments. He couldn't waste them.

There was a soft *beep* as he correctly input the code, and then the floor plan he'd seen with Andre minutes before appeared. He scanned up and down the many levels of the Monument, looking for any indication of where Arianne could be kept. He looked for any floor marked *Richards* or other prison levels—but found nothing. His anxiety rose to the boiling point. Every second he wasted staring at the Murray Monument's dozens of floors was a second the cyborg or Andre could catch up to him.

"If I was a psychotic super scientist who spent millions of Units on a human being, where would I hide her?" He hissed, continuing to scan.

Then he found it: the unmarked level a floor below him. There could be dozens of other places on that map where Arianne might be hidden, but if he were trying to hide someone —or something—he would put them somewhere people would neglect to look. With a cold hiss of air through his teeth, he took his chances and clicked the button.

The elevator jerked downwards, and Jack gave himself those few short interim moments to prepare for the worst. As soon as the doors opened, he broke into a sprint, knowing he needed to search the floor quickly if he wanted to give himself enough time to check elsewhere in case his hunch was incorrect. When he realized what was beyond the elevator shaft—a giant lab shrouded in darkness outlined by shining floor-to-ceiling windows—he knew Arianne was there.

His heart slowed to a stop. They'd put Arianne in a lab. He'd sold her to be an experiment.

He didn't have long to act on his discovery when he heard the distinct clicking of heels coming from the darkness down the hall. His fingers curled in anticipation as a *Fera* sauntered from the shadows, her deadly yellow eyes glinting with a predatory light. Jack sized her up, realizing that she was tall even without the six-inch heels she was so expertly walking in. He analyzed her lengthy body and lean limbs—his training warned of frightening speed and incredible flexibility. He knew with one assessing glance that if the snakelike female attacked him, he would have his work cut out for him.

The female smiled with her blue-painted lips. "You're not supposed to be down here," she hissed.

Jack recognized the black control collar around the *Fera's* neck, and he realized—with a touch of sadness—the female was a slave. He didn't want to fight someone against their will, but he knew he couldn't save Arianne unless he got past her. He lowered into a defensive crouch. "Would you be down here if that collar wasn't on you?"

The female bared her teeth, displaying sharpened vampire-like fangs. "An oddly personal question for someone I've just met."

"Blackjack, nice to *beat* you."

The Snake blinked, "what?"

He attacked.

The female reacted faster than anticipated, expertly flipping backward to dodge his swing. As she slid across the ground—with extra dramatic effect—she drew a set of twin daggers from her thighs. Crouched low in the darkness, she bared her fangs like the animal she so eerily took after.

Jack felt naked in his simple sports coat and dress pants—and exactly *zero* weapons.

"Knock me out, and you can get inside," the Snake whispered.

"What?" Jack asked.

The Snake didn't bother to respond as she lunged, her limbs a fury of blades. Jack dodged and parried the blows, expertly stepping backward as he threw up fists and forearms to block the daggers before they could break his skin. The female didn't show fatigue or discouragement from his parries as she continued her assault with a low swipe to his calves. It was then that he realized she wasn't going for killing blows—only easy strikes meant to draw blood.

Jack had dealt with plenty of mutants in his years in Cartel—enough to have seen that behavior before. It only meant one thing. Following his hunch, he reached out, grabbed the Snake's right arm, and twisted hard. The female screamed, dropping her dagger with a loud clang in the empty hallway. She recovered fast, lunging with her left hand, but Jack was faster as he blocked upward with his forearm and suspended her arm in midair. The female cursed, her forked tongue escaping her lips with a hiss of frustration.

"Venom-dipped blades?" Jack asked tiredly, "Little cliché, don't you think?"

"You're fast for a human." The female's eyes narrowed.

Jack smiled at her. While she was distracted, he raised his foot and delivered a kick to her stomach. The female slid across the room from a blow more powerful than expected. With a moment to breathe, Jack managed to quip, "Who says I'm human?"

The female recovered quickly, dashing at Jack with another barrage of attacks. "Blue Krait," she greeted, switching her last blade between her hands with each swing. "But you can call me Blue."

Jack palmed Blue's first blade in his hand. Dropping below her swipe, he turned and delivered a cut across her side. He felt his blade dig into soft flesh with satisfaction. Before the Snake could retaliate, he rolled across the ground and out of the way.

Blue shouted in pain, "You think I'm susceptible to my own venom?" She taunted.

Jack shrugged, "It was worth a try."

"You're here to free the *Feras?*" Blue asked breathlessly.

"Who's asking?"

Blue straightened with a flip of her short black hair, "I'll repeat: this collar will force me to keep fighting you. The only chance you have to get inside without my interference is to knock me out. But fair warning: the collar tracks my heart rate. If it detects that I'm incapacitated, it will send an alert. I can't guarantee how much time you'll have after that."

Jack pointed at the female with the venom-tipped blade, "You're one strange *Fera*."

"Not strange—but I'll admit I'm confused," Blue quipped, attacking again.

Jack analyzed the Snake's movements for patterns and weaknesses as she converged on him again. Controlling his breathing, he could take himself back to the training floors in Cartel. Suddenly, everything felt like muscle memory from his years fighting on those mats. He fell into a familiar system: watch for an opponent's mistake, trust his body to react, and capitalize. The idea of Blue being just another opponent in Joker training cleared his head enough to concoct a solution.

Blue was hyper-flexible, which was a nightmare to defend against, but it also meant she was prone to hyper-extension. Hyper-extension left the body defenseless for a few vital moments—if someone knew where to look. Jack was patient as he dodged attack after attack, never striking, only watching. Then, as he predicted, Blue lunged too far as her legs spread wider than she could quickly retract from. There was his chance: she was off balance and wouldn't be able to dodge in time.

Jack moved.

In a very Arianne-like attack, Jack swiped his foot towards Blue's extended leg. The blow knocked Blue off her feet and her body went horizontal as gravity pulled her downwards. Jack winced as her head hit the concrete with a sickening thud and then bounced off the ground with the initial impact. Blue's body slackened as her head finally came to rest on the floor.

Even with her body in shock, Blue fought the concussive blow, her flickering eyes darting to his, "She's coming," she warned.

Jack stepped above Blue and felt an emotion he hadn't felt in years: pity. He pitied the mutant below him, and he wished he could do more. But he didn't have time. "Who's coming?" He asked through gasping breaths.

"Go," Blue hissed, "make... sure... I'm... down."

He nodded, delivering a swift kick to her temple and hoping it was as close to painless as possible. He winced as the Snake's otherworldly yellow eyes finally closed, and her head rolled to the side. Jack clenched his teeth, his training screaming at him to kill her.

He could practically hear Ace curse at him. *"Stop being so soft! If you don't kill her now, she'll come back for you later!"*

He shook his head against the hiss from his boss's ghost. He refused to be that person anymore.

Unfortunately, he didn't have time to dwell on his moral crises. Just as Blue warned, her collar began to beep like a ticking time bomb. Scrambling, he searched her body until he found the access card to the lab. The collar's beeping intensified—his time was running out.

Swiping the card across the lab's glass doors, they opened with a furious rush as cool air spilled from the lab. Jack shivered, but it wasn't just from the air conditioning. His eyes scanned the dark space, his assessing gaze going over the beeping contraptions and steel examination tables. Hera *experimented* with sentient people in that awful place. His hands clenched as he realized there could be people in the world worse than Ace.

That wasn't a world he wanted to be a part of.

Then he saw the cages. They were as unnerving as a graveyard, forbidding and barren. If Jack had forgotten where he was, he might have convinced himself they were dog crates. But the cages were too large for any canine. He was plagued with an awful inkling of what Hera was capable of. If Hera could experiment on humans like they were animals, then it wouldn't be a stretch to imagine she would store those humans like animals as well.

He ran towards the cages, lights in the lab flickering on and off as they followed his movements. He was uncertain what he would do if he saw Arianne trapped inside one of them, but to his surprise, all the cages were empty—spare one. Jack realized immediately that the occupant was not Arianne, thanks to her vibrant purple hair. The Desi female was crouched in the back corner of the cage, her brilliant fluorite eyes wide and assessing as she watched him approach.

Jack had heard enough stories about the female from Arianne to recognize her—even if he hadn't met her on that fateful mission to Romania. Jaya Bahri: the Pacifican Lieutenant. Arianne's best friend.

"Jaya?" Jack asked, his hands going to open the cage.

"You," she growled.

Guilt squeezed his heart. "I know, I know," he repeated. "You can yell at me once we get out of here."

He opened the cage door, but the Lieutenant didn't move. "Why should I trust you?"

"Seeing as I just let you out of a fucking cage, I think you're going to have to give me the benefit of the doubt."

The purple-haired *Fera* crawled out, eyes wary. "What's going on?"

Jack sighed. "We don't have much time. I was invited to watch an execution in under an hour. Pacific is en route, and someone is *definitely* on their way to ensure you don't get out."

Jaya considered his words. "It's today, then," she said in a chilling whisper. "They're going to kill Caesar."

"I'm here to make sure that doesn't happen," he reached down to help Jaya up.

Jaya hesitated, withdrawing her hand, "Why the change of heart, huh?"

Jack let out a long sigh, "that's an extremely long story. I guided Arianne to the city, and let's just say I owe her a big fucking debt. Do you know where she is?"

Sadness flickered in her eyes, but the Lieutenant quickly righted herself and pulled her body from the cage to point to a water tank constructed on the far wall. Jack's breath caught at the sight, and his feet absently carried him toward the metal monstrosity—half in awe and half in horror. As he neared the tank, his movement triggered the illuminating lights at its base, and the murky water burst to life, the white lights shining like an awful display.

And there, suspended in the water, was Arianne. With the white light around her, she looked ethereal. His knees weakened. She was asleep, her body adorned in a black wetsuit-like fabric bobbing peacefully inside the tank. Bubbles rose from her neck where five gill slits passively opened and closed, taking in water. Her honey-brown hair rose above her head, its strands glittering in the soft light as they floated in the still water. And most strikingly, two golden brown wings hovered limply behind her back.

His jaw slackened. Arianne had *wings*. How had he missed it? Maybe he'd been so focused on hiding his own secrets to notice she'd been keeping some of her own.

"Y-you care about her," Jaya said in surprise, her face confused as she turned to assess his expression.

Jack's mind slowed to a halt. All he could manage was a hand to the window of the tank—as if that could provide comfort to the female whom he'd condemned to such an awful fate. "I don't deserve to care about her."

Jaya rushed to the control systems to the right of Arianne's prison. "Help me get her out, then!"

The world sped up again, and Jack was reminded of what precious little time they had. "Tell her I'm sorry." He spent one final moment looking into the face of the female who'd become his greatest salvation—and greatest regret. "Get her out of here, please."

He brought Arianne into that hell. He couldn't live with himself if he was responsible for getting her caught in the crossfire in the war beginning just floors above. Worst of all, he wasn't brave enough to be there when she woke up. He didn't want to see the look of betrayal in her eyes again.

"Where are you going?" Jaya demanded, hands frantically selecting different controls to free her friend.

Jack quickened his pace towards the lab doors. He knew if he didn't leave before she woke up, he would never leave her side again. Unfortunately, he still had things he needed to do. "I'm needed upstairs. I'll try and buy your people as much time as I can!"

Jack ran through the lab, past Blue Krait—still unconscious on the ground—and towards the elevator. Just as the doors closed around him, the entire building rocked from a quaking blast. He gripped the elevator handles, knowing that a quake could only mean one thing: Pacific had arrived.

Jack was too late. The war had begun.

Chapter 47

Jaya

Jaya fought to make sense of her brief conversation with Blackjack. The man seemed different, haunted. When she'd seen him last, he'd been a force of uncompromising malice. Now, he was risking his life to help them. She worked her jaw but knew she couldn't afford to dwell on it. On the battlefield, no matter what form it took, a soldier couldn't question a change of fate. All a soldier could do was keep moving and hope she survived.

"Come on, Ari," Jaya gritted. "Help me out here."

Her hands fumbled across the tank's control panel. There were too many dials and buttons, and she was hopelessly lost. Palming the access card Blackjack had left behind, she swiped it across every panel, but nothing happened.

Arianne was trapped, and Jaya feared only Hera had access to let her out.

"You idiot! You just *had* to come to Leonueva. You couldn't stay safe at home!" Jaya jumped up onto the roof of the tank, and she began pulling on the tank's door handle with all of her *Fera* might. But even she wasn't strong enough to get the door to budge. "I love you," she strained as she tried to pull again, "but I really don't like you right now!"

An outside blast rocked the floors above and shook the lights in the fixtures just above her head. The Chameleon paused her struggles for a moment, listening in the eerie silence that followed in an effort to discern any information of use. So deep below the ground and surrounded by the basement's thick concrete walls, she couldn't hear much, but she did know one thing: skyscrapers didn't just shake like that out of nowhere.

Leonueva was under attack. Blackjack hadn't lied. But why did he decide to help them? Who called Pacific? All of those questions were things she didn't have time to answer.

That was when the lab alarms began to flash. The lab—once shrouded in darkness—became washed in deep red light. Jaya's lips parted. "That's not good."

Then she remembered Blackjack's warning: someone was coming for her.

Jumping from the top of the tank, Jaya searched the lab for anything she could use as a weapon. Panic made her fingertips tingle as the lab alarms grew louder. Something deep inside of her was warning her that she was out of time. And then, as if her anxiety summoned the entity, a figure appeared beyond the lab doors, its features covered by the gloom.

Jaya found a tranquilizer dart gun. She fumbled as she loaded the gun and took cover behind a flipped lab bench. Fear crept up her spine when she heard the airlocks on the lab doors open. The sirens stopped, bringing the lab back to its awful silence. Red continued to flash, and she willed her skin to match the blood-like colors of the lab to give herself a fraction of cover.

Boots squeaked on the clean white ground. Jaya calmed her breathing, fighting to locate her attacker as they stalked closer. Anticipation made bile rise in her throat as the adrenaline of the coming fight rose to a crescendo. The Pacifican Lieutenant risked a look around her cover, and with the flashing red alarm lights, she finally saw the hunter outlined against the darkness. Pandora.

Jaya stole a look behind her at Arianne, and she knew with a deep-seated sense of dread that she wasn't going to leave that lab without her friend. Which meant—somehow—she had to beat Pandora. Jaya waited, crouched behind her cover as the blonde Elite stalked through the lab, a sick entertainment bringing a smile to her face. As Pandora turned her back on Jaya to investigate the examination tables, the female knew it was now or never.

Willing her *Fera* stillness to take over, Jaya was as quiet as a shadow as she rose from behind the lab bench to sneak closer to Pandora. She knew she only had one shot—good thing she had been the best shot at her Academy. Baring her teeth, the Chameleon fired before any nerves could take over.

The tranquilizer hit home, embedding itself into Pandora's backside.

The woman turned too quickly to be human, her glowing blue eyes shining in the darkness as they locked on her. Jaya dove beneath the lab bench just in time to avoid a blast of hot blue energy, and she shouted as the heat of the blast singed the hairs on top of her head. Jaya shrunk further underneath her protective wall, the smell of burnt hair stinging her nose.

"Hello, purple one," Pandora taunted. "Did you really think that would work on me?" Jaya's blood chilled as the empty dart that had delivered the sedative to Pandora clinked on the ground past the bench. "I used to micro-dose that stuff whenever I got bored in here."

Jaya rolled her eyes in exasperation, "What's your problem?"

Pandora gave a low chuckle, "Honey, we'll be here all day with that explanation. Unfortunately, I have a schedule to keep, which includes making sure extenuating variables don't mess with my mother's plans."

Jaya didn't respond as she focused on the sound of the cyborg's footsteps. As Pandora neared her cover, Jaya moved behind a set of shelves on her silent bare feet. The Chameleon peered out from behind her new spot as Pandora converged on top of her old position. The cyborg barked in annoyance, blaster arm raised and ready to strike.

"Come now," Pandora purred, "I think we're both too old for hide and seek."

"Can you blame me?" Jaya replied, thinking back to their first altercation in Moscow—she'd crawled onto the ceiling and used her advantage of surprise to overpower Pandora. "It worked so well last time."

Pandora's footsteps moved away from her, and confused, Jaya peered out from behind the white shelves to determine where her pursuer had gone. The cyborg had her back to her once more, proving she didn't particularly care where Jaya was. To Pandora, Jaya was trapped in that lab with her and *not* the other way around. Pandora had walked to Arianne's tank, her pale face illuminated by the white lights underneath the water as she took in the submerged captive.

"Interesting," Pandora said, "you didn't run when you had the chance, purple one. Almost like... You care about her." Pandora ran a hand down the glass of Arianne's prison and laughed humorlessly, "That was your first mistake."

"Let's test that resistance," Jaya muttered, firing two more tranquilizers at Pandora.

The cyborg turned, her attention snapping to the sound of the dart gun. Her blue eyes blazed in annoyance as her arm separated to fire another blast at the Pacifican. Jaya was thankful for her lizard-like grace as she rolled behind the cover of another lab bench to protect herself from the attack. Breathing heavily, she listened carefully for another chance to move as she assessed her situation: no weapon, no way to beat Pandora alone, and she couldn't leave without Arianne.

She was stuck.

Pandora casually walked across the lab. "Here's how it's going to go," she explained. "She'll leave you, just like she left me, and you'll spend years wondering if she's dead or alive." Pandora roared in annoyance, and Jaya heard her fire another blast. "And then, you'll realize she's forgotten all about you."

Jaya's breath caught at Pandora's claims. Pandora had *known* Arianne as a child. Had they met in the lab? Was Pandora just another one of Hera's sick experiments? The Chameleon looked at her friend's sleeping form, her mind screaming at her for answers that would make everything make *sense*. As she stared at her best friend, an idea arose: she couldn't beat Pandora alone, but two might just do the trick.

Drawing a breath to steady herself, the Pacifican jumped out in front of Arianne's tank, a wry grin coming to her face at her plan. "You can't blame someone for escaping a prison," she countered. Just like she had never blamed her parents for failing to rescue her, Pandora couldn't hold that pain over Arianne's head either.

Pandora turned, jaw clenching as she lined up her shot. "I can blame them for leaving me behind!"

Jaya waited as the white-hot energy of the blast pooled in front of Pandora's arm. Her body screamed at her to run for cover, but she waited. *Come on,* she willed Pandora, *take the shot.* Pandora screamed with rage, and her blaster fired, sending a burst of hot blue plasma toward Jaya. Trusting her reaction time, she dodged the blow with a swift tuck and roll.

The blast hit home, colliding with Arianne's tank, and Jaya smiled as the glass cracked. She turned her attention toward Pandora, a small part of her feeling sorry for the innocent child that had been corrupted in that lab. But she couldn't do anything about the past, and there was certainly no part of her that felt bad for the monster Pandora had become.

Jaya frowned as she climbed to her feet. "The difference is, Arianne won't leave me behind." It didn't matter if they fought. It didn't matter if they didn't see eye to eye. She loved Arianne, and that was enough.

In one swift movement, Jaya grabbed an examination chair and swung it at the tank's cracking glass. Water erupted as the cylindrical wall shattered into millions of glistening fragments. She dove out of the way, covering her eyes as a torrent of water and glass exploded outwards. Pandora screamed as the wave converged on her, tiny shards of glass digging into her skin and speckling the water with red.

"Arianne!" Jaya cried out. "We need to fight!"

Arianne's gray eyes snapped open. She landed on the floor in a crouch, water cascading around her like an ancient goddess of the sea. Arianne's hair was dark as it stuck to her face, her wings falling at her sides like a heavy cape. The winged female collected her shaking limbs underneath her, muscles bunching up in preparation for an attack. Jaya felt chills as her friend took a deep and slow breath, her lungs expanding as her mouth breathed air for the first time in days.

Then Jaya watched as those gray eyes pooled to black.

With a roar that shook the laboratory, Arianne shot at Pandora with all the fury of an avenging angel.

Chapter 48

Arianne

Josephina had taught her to fly.

Those first moments in the air, the wind crashing against her face, the feeling of weightlessness—Arianne felt like she could do anything.

When she landed from her first flight, her life changed forever. She met her mother at the top of the Murray Monument, and as she fell into her, they both began to cry. After months of practice under the cover of darkness, their efforts had finally paid off. Arianne, born to touch the sky, had taken her first step toward her destiny. What she never knew until she'd woken up in the waters of the Aegean Sea was that destiny also included leaving her family.

Josephina had known that, and still, she gave her daughter the power to abandon her.

The nightmares never left her. As a child in Pacific, Arianne couldn't reconcile the beautiful peace of the island with the fractured memories of her home. She struggled to handle the guilt of leaving her mother and brother. Even so young, she knew she'd been given a chance she wasn't supposed to have.

Kalfas taught her discipline. The pain, the hurt, and the fear went into hours of training. Blood, sweat, and tears were the only things that kept her memories at bay.

Leon trained Arianne to be a weapon. Kalfas promised to make her a hero.

Her days became consumed with training and the endless endeavor to find a new lesson, a new technique, to force her body to master. Every martial art, outdoor sport, and endurance practice was on the table—all in an effort to hone her burning energy and mold her into something *worth* the life she'd stolen.

Because in her mind, every minute outside of the halls of the Murray Monument was not something to be taken for granted. To Arianne Murray, heiress to the Commandership, freedom wasn't in her birthright. So, she spent every free hour in that gym with Kalfas until the smell of salty sweat on leather followed her into her dreams.

Arianne would be a hero. She would become *more* than the life her father had forced on her.

Punching bag after punching bag fell to her ambition. Years went by. For a young female fated to die in Leonueva, she grew in spite of the hand the universe had dealt her. She would become like Strix: The Legend of the *Feras*. Whenever she grew tired, whenever her injuries stacked up, she would remember where she came from and keep building. Purpose made all the pain bearable. Purpose consumed her.

And then, one day, that purpose was taken away.

Kalfas lied to her. Caesar lied to her. Her *mother* lied to her. Despite everything Arianne had convinced herself of, her fate never changed. Leonueva was her birth, life, and death. Leonueva, Leon, Pangaea... they *defined* her. They owned her.

Arianne was only slightly aware of the prison she resided in. She could feel the weightlessness of her watery grave, and she was resigned to let herself fade away. Anything was better than failing again. Anything was better than being reminded that she was never meant to be the hero of her story.

As if summoned by her misery, a memory came to her, its foggy tendrils floating up to her in the bubbles of the gloom.

She was seated with her mother in front of their living room fireplace. She felt the warmth of the flames as her mother ran soft brush strokes through her shaggy hair. Josephina hummed softly, her hands careful as she worked out tangles in the golden strands. Even beneath the surface, Arianne started to cry as she held onto the memory and curled deeper into Josephina's arms. She decided that, if she could, she would stay there until her life was finally pulled away from her.

"You have the heart of a fighter," Josephina whispered, "that is a blessing and curse, *Chica Angel*." Arianne's eyes fluttered closed as the brush moved soothingly across her scalp. "Changing the world takes a lot of pain, and many quit before they even begin. But you, your fire will keep burning when most others' go out." Her mother let out a deep sigh, "I wish I could take that burden from you. The only thing I can do is beg you to keep going."

Though she tried to hold onto her mother's warmth, her mind had other things to tell her. Arianne tried to swim back towards her seat by the fireplace, but the safety of fire and her mother's voice sunk deeper and deeper into the recesses of her mind as she was washed into a different scene.

Arianne slammed onto the solid wood floor of the ground, her body recoiling at the painful landing. Kalfas stood above her—bow staff pointed at her head. She couldn't have been older than fifteen at that point. The young fighter stared up at her trainer with annoyance as she fought to catch the breath that had been knocked out of her. They'd been training all day. Her entire body shouted in exhaustion. Sweat dripped down her face in the relentless Mediterranean heat, and her limbs stung with countless scrapes and bruises. She had lost every match they fought, and her head was pounding. She wanted to go home.

Kalfas's face was furious as he glared down at his trainee, "Again!" He barked.

"I'm done. We've been at this for hours!"

The Pacifican General frowned as he stepped back and leaned on his bow staff. "The difference between winners and losers is simply that winners refuse to lose." Kalfas focused his olive green eyes down at Arianne intently, "So what will it be, child? Will you accept failure, or will you continue the game?"

Arianne smiled, jumping to her feet and raising a set of twin batons in her sweat-soaked hands, "I haven't lost yet," she responded with a wry grin.

"That's what I thought," Kalfas challenged.

Arianne lingered on those memories as her mind bounced back and forth between the warm comforts of her mother's company and the intoxicating thrill of training. Her entire life, she'd been taught to fight. The very will to keep going had been bred into her bones from both her parents. She might hate her father, but she certainly wouldn't squander that specific gift. Even when she fucked up time after time.

And for once, as she watched over her past like she was watching her favorite scenes in a movie, she realized that failure was okay. The odds had been stacked against her for her entire life, and she would fight those impossibilities until her last breath. And maybe, just maybe, she'd become something from that.

Winners refuse to lose, Kalfas's voice repeated in her head.

That didn't sound too bad. Arianne would win or die trying—whatever came first.

Then, she became vaguely aware that someone was calling for her.

Arianne...

Arianne...

Arianne!

The calls sounded like they were coming from a fading wraith clinging to its last moments of corporeal presence. Her ears focused on the ghostly sound, confused for a moment whether or not the voice was coming from the past or present. She let the calls become like a tether she could grab hold of and pull her to its location. As she grew closer, she recognized Jaya's voice like a lighthouse in a storm. Then, her best friend's calls were nearly on top of her—screaming and frantic.

Suddenly, water rushed past her head, and Arianne felt her stomach drop as her weight pulled downwards. She snapped back to consciousness as she scrambled for purchase in the waterfall she'd woken up in. As her eyes opened, she was aware of a flashing red lab, torrents of water, and bright purple hair.

Jaya's screams came into focus as one singular word registered in Arianne's hazy brain, "*Fight*!"

The world came back to Arianne as all the voices in her head joined together to scream that one word over and over again: *Fight! Fight! Fight!* She felt her body steady underneath her as the chanting rose to a crescendo and flooded her veins with adrenaline. *Fight!*

Maybe her density wasn't to simply die. Maybe it was to fight for every scrap of life she could get. And god damn it, she was going to do just that.

Chapter 49

Arianne

The inhuman calm took over.

Instinct, Hera had called it. Fear, rage, and power surged as Arianne sprung from her place on the ground. Crushed glass sunk into the bottom of her feet, but she didn't feel a thing. She locked eyes with Pandora and sprinted at her with unrelenting rage. The cyborg managed to dodge her first attack, but pure, unmistakable fear was painted across her ghostly face. Not that Arianne cared. She was told to fight, and fight was all she cared about.

The cyborg pointed at Jaya. "You idiot!" she screamed. "You don't know what you've done!"

Jaya ran to Arianne's side, joining her friend as the pair attacked in tandem. "I know we're winning!" The Chameleon countered with a high sweeping kick to Pandora's head.

Arianne blacked out, giving in to Instinct. The feeling was revitalizing, her body relishing in the extra burst of speed and strength. The world was a whirl of motion and energy as her arms, elbows, knees, and legs assaulted Pandora with a barrage of attacks.

As she moved, a voice thundered: *fight, fight, fight* in a steady rhythm at the back of her head. Each time she landed a hit, the pounding grew louder as if her violence was thriving on its own positive feedback loop—growing and growing and growing until either she or her opponent gave out.

Pandora fell onto the defensive, her arms raising as she attempted to block her attackers. Arianne locked onto a bloody cut on the cyborg's arm. Her primal fury went into a frenzy as her nose honed onto the *delicious* metallic smell of blood.

"Ari..." she distantly heard Jaya say in concern.

Arianne tackled Pandora as the pain and fear from her past few days in Pangaea fueled her. She wouldn't be trapped in that basement ever again, and everyone responsible would *pay*. Her focus turned to Pandora's cybernetic arm. Even in her frenzied state, she knew Pandora was little more than a human without her arm. And *weak* humans were far from her concern. With a growl, Arianne wrapped her arms around the cybernetic right arm, her plan in place. Then she was ripping and pulling, the robotic arm snapping and groaning underneath her vice grip. The cyborg flailed underneath Arianne, but there was no freeing herself from the female's rampage. Sparks flew, wires snapped, and metal groaned beneath her fingertips as she wrenched the arm from Pandora's body.

Pandora screamed, and it wasn't from pain.

Like a crack of lightning, Arianne went back to another time. A time when she'd heard the exact same scream escape the cyborg's throat. An image flashed across her mind—something from *before*. A younger Pandora lay on the ground before her, face crumpled in pain as blood gushed from the open wound in her right shoulder. Arianne looked down in her memory to see a bleeding *human* arm resting in her hands.

Oh my god.

Arianne blinked, and against her wishes, Instinct's possession faded as clarity returned to her. The realization was like a slap back to her senses, leaving her spinning, in pain, but on the path back to regaining her focus. As her concentration returned, she was awfully aware of the stunning silence of the lab. She stared lamely down at the bloody arm resting in her hands, bile creeping up her throat. It took another shake of her head to clear the fogginess completely. When she looked down again, the blood and gore of her hallucination had faded—leaving only the robotic arm behind.

Arianne's breathing was shaky as she looked up at her opponent. She wasn't sure what was real anymore. Was she still dreaming? Was her mind still stuck in some limbo between the eternity of the tank and real life? Or was she the very real reason as to why Pandora's right arm was replaced with a prosthetic?

Pandora pulled herself away from Arianne with her remaining left hand, her glowing blue eyes wide with fear. The cyborg's breathing was panicked as she fought to distance herself from the winged female. For a few short moments, the pair of experiments could only stare at each other.

"Ari..." Jaya trailed off.

Arianne couldn't look at her best friend. "Go," she muttered. "Find the others. I'll catch up."

"I'm not leaving you."

Arianne looked at Pandora again, and something told her there were still secrets in that lab that she needed to bring to light—secrets she'd forgotten.

She stood up, preparing for another attack from Pandora. Placing herself between the cyborg and the exit, Arianne shook her head. "Caesar will be on the top floor of the Murray Monument," she instructed. "I'm the only one out of the two of us who can make it in time. Go save the rest, and I'll meet you at the top floor."

"I'm supposed to get you out, too," Jaya protested one last time.

Pandora rose to her feet—whatever fear she once displayed had disappeared. Arianne raised her fists to guard her face. "Arguing isn't going to buy us time!"

Jaya nodded tersely, clearly looking unhappy with the plan. Still, the trained soldier didn't waste another moment as she turned on her heel and sprinted out of the lab doors. Arianne waited until she heard the doors close behind her friend before she initiated another attack. Pandora had recovered enough to be competent in the fight again, expertly dodging Arianne's flying kick with perfect balance despite her missing limb. Sparks flying from her shoulder, the cyborg matched the mutant blow for blow despite her disadvantage. Arianne cursed, annoyed at her loss of speed and tenacity without Instinct. The drastic difference in abilities between states left her feeling lethargic without the extra dose of power. But no matter how hard she tried, she couldn't bring that primal strength back to the surface.

Pandora laughed, drawing a blade from her thigh and forcing Arianne to the defensive. "She doesn't know who you are," the cyborg taunted.

The winged female raised her forearm to intercept Pandora's attack and winced as the blade cut through her wetsuit and tore flesh. "We're going to keep it that way!" She barked, grabbing onto Pandora's forearm and squeezing. "No one needs to die for knowing who I am."

Pandora cried out in pain, dropping the blade. "Is that what you're afraid of?" She taunted.

Arianne jumped out of the way, nearly missing a kick to her diaphragm. "Unless you're licensed, I don't need a therapy lesson from you."

Pandora dashed at her with a cry of rage. "Do you remember me, *friend*?" She spat, kicking again in the hopes of hitting her opponent while she was on the ground. "How much did you forget, huh?"

Arianne grabbed the cyborg's dropped blade and crouched low as she palmed it at a defensive angle across her chest. She refused to respond, choosing to focus on her next attack instead of giving in to her opponent's attempts to confuse her. The teal-eyed woman chuckled, her eyes' inhuman light glowing in delight as she dodged attack after attack.

"You don't even know *why* you can't remember," she smiled, ducking under Arianne's increasingly frantic blows. "It kills you inside, doesn't it?"

"Shut up!" The winged female cried out.

Arianne swung below her opponent's one-arm block and used the cyborg's forward momentum to land behind her. Pandora's back exposed, Arianne lowered herself and delivered a deep swipe through the cyborg's hamstrings. Pandora shouted in surprise and pain as her legs involuntarily buckled beneath her.

The cyborg fell, and Arianne landed on top of her. Arianne extended an arm to grasp Pandora's white uniform and pulled her close to her face, "What do you remember," she snarled.

Pandora's upper lip curled as she leaned closer, "like I would say *anything* to you."

A wave of rage crashed through her. Before she could stop herself, she delivered a punch directly to Pandora's nose. Crimson blood splattered in a satisfying crack as Pandora's face crumpled beneath her fist, "What do you remember," Arianne repeated in a furious whisper.

Still, the cyborg's smile didn't fade. Eyes already swelling from the broken nose, her teeth shone red as she looked up at Arianne. "I hope the memories haunt you," she snarled, "I hope you're given a taste of what you were until their shattered pieces slowly drive you insane. I'm glad you forgot me—if only so my ghost in your mind can torture you forever."

Arianne released her hold on the terrible woman's shirt in horror. She distantly sensed the reverberation of Pandora's body hitting the ground underneath her. Her hands dropped to her side, the blood on her fist blending with her memories of the past, "Because I stole your arm?" She asked in fright.

The Richards family heir laughed, bright turquoise eyes looking up towards the ceiling above her, "Because you left me," an awful chuckle croaked from the back of her throat.

Arianne pushed herself away from the woman, still laughing like she was half insane. Fear tightened her chest at the woman's insinuations, "What do you mean I left you?"

"Come on, I know you can do better than that," Pandora wheezed, the concussive blow to her face finally catching up to her. "Here, I'll help you: what does Leon hate as much as mutants?"

Arianne shook her head.

The fractured woman gave one last bloody smile as her eyes fluttered shut. "Impurities," she whispered. "Happy family reunion, sis."

Arianne felt detached from her body as she rose to her feet. The world swayed around her as she looked down at the cyborg below. *No, that can't be right*, she thought. That monstrous woman was trying to slow her mission down. She fought to push forward, to continue toward where Caesar was preparing to be executed, but she couldn't move.

Sister.

Pandora had to be lying, right? Still, Arianne couldn't move as she continued to stare at the woman lying bloodied on the ground. Though Pandora's face was swollen, she couldn't help but look for the similarities. Was it just a likely coincidence, or did their eyebrows have the same shape? They had the same muscled curve in their shoulders and strong chins—Leon's strong chin. Sisters. Though she didn't want to believe it, deep down inside, something told her it was the truth.

Pandora was cast away as a weapon and an experiment just like her. Her mouth parted in disgust, pity, and shock—they were both deemed unworthy as Murray heirs. Because of genetics, Pandora had been considered less than—just like Arianne. And that's when the ripping guilt hit her: not only had she left the one person who shared in her pain, she'd forgotten about her.

But why? How? How could she forget her own sister?

Half-sister. Pandora was the bastard child of Hera and Leon. Due to the power structure of the Elites and how wealth was passed on, marriage was essential to determine proper inheritance. Arianne hated that she knew how her father and other powerful Elites like him thought. Pandora might not be a *Fera* Elite, but Arianne was willing to bet she was the next undesirable thing. Even though it pained her to leave her sister again, she knew the little girl she'd once known in that lab was long gone. All that was left now was a concoction of hatred and mad science.

Arianne ran faster as the pieces started to come together.

Hera had always envied Josephina's position as Leon's wife and Mother of Europe. From a young age, Hera had been betrothed to Leon—something even Arianne remembered the scientist General bickering about. When Josephina gave Leon a *Fera* daughter, Hera sought to undermine her by giving him a human daughter. The only downside had been that Hera hadn't considered that Leon would view Pandora's bastard status as unworthy of the Commandership as a mutant.

Fast forward twenty years and Hera still hadn't given up her ceaseless quest to gain Leon's favor. Only that time around, she would use Pacific as the vessel for her rise to power.

Arianne had been the one variable Hera never considered—which was why the General paid top dollar to ensure her secret was hidden. Arianne was too valuable to science and as a trump card for Hera to kill, but that didn't mean she wasn't a threat. Because of that, only she could stop Hera's plans because she was the only person not factored into the master equation.

Knowing how deeply the Richard matriarch had sunk her claws into every factor of that day was frightening. It also brought on a new level of risk to everyone Arianne loved. If Hera proved to Leon once and for all that she was the woman he needed at his side by completing Caesar's execution, Josephina and Andre could be cast out. Obviously, Leon never *stopped* courting Hera completely if Pandora existed. That meant Hera already had one foot in the door.

Anger and frustration on her mother's behalf were like a boiler inside of her—bright and burning and energy-giving—as she found the staircase and took the stairs three steps at a time in bounding leaps. She couldn't risk taking the elevator anymore. It would be heavily monitored during the attack, not to mention a death trap with Pacific attacking the tower.

Her heart thundered in her chest, and she was uncertain whether it was from running, the possibility of seeing her father, or some dreadful—and much more likely—combination of both. The idea of coming face to face with her father rocked her to her core, but she couldn't stop and let herself think about it. If she didn't make it in time, everyone she loved would face Hera and Leon's combined wrath. And that eventuality was far worse than anything Leon could do to her.

"I haven't lost yet," Arianne repeated the words she'd muttered to Kalfas all those years ago. "I haven't lost yet!"

Screw her exhaustion. Screw her confusion. Screw her hopelessness and terror. She had one small chance to make everything right, and by Strix and every Legend she looked up to, she would find a way to do it.

Arianne burst through the doors of the lobby and into the chaos beyond. Even with her exposed wings and eye-catching wetsuit, no one paid her any mind as they scrambled through the cavernous space. Wards gathered in squadrons preparing to protect the tower, civilians swamped the stairs and elevators looking for a place to hide, and Pangaean soldiers crowded the entrance, creating a block-ade with guns and steel.

Outside, dust coated the atmosphere. The Murray Monument shuddered, and Arianne watched as a building outside exploded from a long-distance mortar launched into the city. It was only a matter of time before Pacific broke Leonueva's air defensive line and could stage a close-range attack. She smiled at the brilliance of such an assault. Pacific had found Leonueva's defensive weakness: air support. Why would a city waste time with a large Air Force division when it was invisible?

Maybe Pacific could win. Arianne held on tightly to that small kernel of hope as she prepared for what she was about to do. She needed to get outside, and there was only one way that granted her access to weapons before her suicide mission. Pouring on the speed, she ran at the line of soldiers standing guard at the lobby entrance. Luckily, the soldiers were so focused on the city beyond the doors to the building that they didn't notice her approach. She planned her next steps in the final seconds before she broke through the first row: grab a weapon, don't stop, get outside, and fly before they could shoot.

She ran faster to pick up enough momentum to carry her through the multiple rows of soldiers. She ran past the first line of men, extending her hands to steal two military issue short swords from sheaths from two men at her side. As soon as she felt a firm grip on the handles of the blades, she was sprinting through the last few rows before anyone could retaliate. She hated that those soldiers had been issued those blades to kill *Feras,* but right then, she needed weapons. And swords didn't run out of ammo.

Arianne broke through the outermost line of soldiers and sprinted into the chaos of the city beyond. Her bare feet screamed in discomfort as their already torn soles stepped across rocks and falling rubble. Once a safe distance away from the building, she looked at the sky above her. The air itself was clouded with smoke and building debris, making it hard to see past the buildings rising into the brown dust coating the atmosphere. Even though she couldn't see them, she could hear the sounds of screeching jets over the screaming of civilians.

Even with the polluted atmosphere, she didn't miss how the blue beyond the dust shuddered. Her mouth parted as a rippling wave of pixelated green, red, and blue swept across the sky. The wave erased the projection of a normal day and replaced it with a floating battlefield of smoking jets and fire. The fear of the people in the city around her increased as all of Leonueva realized their final level of protection—their invisibility—was destroyed.

For the first time in its history, Leonueva was exposed to the world.

She knelt, feeling her power coil throughout her limbs as her golden wings widened in anticipation. Taking one final deep breath, she jumped, her legs delivering enough downward force to crack the pavement beneath her. In one powerful flap, she rocketed upwards, the wind ripping at her soaking-wet hair in a satisfying gust.

Arianne focused her sights on the top of the Murray Monument, letting her wings carry her to the fight of her life.

Chapter 50

Blackjack

As the elevator slowly ticked upwards towards his meeting with death given human form, Jack looked beyond the windows to the sky beyond. His stomach dropped at the sight of the burning city below. Pacifican mortars materialized as they passed the city's invisibility shields and dropped on Leonueva.

The sight was terrifying: a seemingly peaceful sky one moment, and the next, bombs appeared out of nowhere to rain destruction and fear.

The building shook, and he gripped the railings in front of him once more, stomach dropping. There, at the edge of the glass building, he felt more exposed to the Pacifican assault than ever. But how did Pacific find them? He'd certainly been too vague to be helpful during his interrogations. No, someone else led the rebellious colony to Leonueva.

Jack thought back to the altercation in the prison block. The Pacific squadron, though imprisoned, had known that their people were coming. And the European Queen, Josephina, had been under arrest. He recalled Hera's seething remark to her: *You chose that man over your Empire.* That man was Caesar Ortiz, the Pacifican President slated to be executed.

An execution that would be made very difficult in the middle of a siege. Josephina must have been the one to contact the rebels in a desperate sacrifice: her city for Caesar Ortiz.

His ascension finally slowed as he reached the top floor of the Murray Monument. Jack's breathing stopped as his eyes observed the monstrous drop to the concrete city floor—more than one hundred stories below.

All things considered, it was ironic he was terrified of heights.

As the doors of the elevator opened, he realized the hundred-story drop was the least of his worries.

The penthouse beyond looked like a throne room from Ancient Europe. Instead of grand paintings and majestic red carpeting, the Murray family had redefined the titular grand hall of a tyrant with a modern twist. Majestic speckled white marble columns rose from the marble floor, their bases covered in lavish ferns. The entire floor was open concept, with every wall made up of the glinting black windows the Murray Monument was known for. A long dining table stretched between the elevator and the Commander's desk, and upon its granite surface sat a lavish spread of breakfast foods held on golden platters.

Three individuals sat at the table: Hera, Josephina, and a portly red-haired man dressed in classic Pangaean businessman fashion. Hera seemed pleased with herself as she drank a glass of sparkling wine and reached for a short stack of pancakes. Josephina, on the other hand, watched the scientist General with disdain as she sat unmoving in her chair. The final guest at the table eyed the two women with a concerned frown, sweat glistening across his forehead.

As Jack stepped out onto the floor, everything seemed... off. A war was beginning outside, and here, these people were eating *brunch*. Well, Hera was eating. Josephina and the other man seemed to hold the same disgusted surprise as Jack.

"See, Hera?" A voice boomed from the far window. "I told you our final guest would be punctual."

Jack felt goosebumps shiver up his spine at how easily confidence and power dripped off of each of those words.

He'd been so concerned with the table in front of him that he'd missed the dominating figure standing behind the marble desk beyond. Silhouetted by the light coming through the windows, the man was nothing more than a black shadow against the sunlight. He was tall and broad, with the glint of a broadsword just barely visible across his back. From the way Jack's instincts were telling him to run, he knew exactly who lingered there.

Hera sat back in her chair, her blonde hair hidden behind her signature white scientist coat and hood. "As usual, your foresight is unparalleled."

Leon Murray turned. He wore a handsome, blue-gray three-piece suit, so well fitted that even Ace would approve. The Commander's honey-blond hair was slicked back, the careful grooming matching his well-shaven face. Jack's eyes settled on the claw-like scars striking through Leon's right eye: his most infamous moniker. To everyone in Europe, the scars were a reminder that underneath the collected façade of their ruler existed a man to be feared.

Leon smiled. "Welcome, Blackjack."

Jack felt the blood drain from his face. From then on, his gift of autonomy—which most citizens enjoyed—was gone forever. Leon had seen his face and, with that familiarity, held power. Jack couldn't help but feel as if he was *owned* by the Commander now.

Jack bowed low, the power emanating from the Commander almost overwhelming him. "It's an honor," he breathed.

Leon strode from behind his desk, his long limbs steady and controlled, boasting decades of training to make his body almost as deadly as his mind. The Commander gestured to the table as he approached. "Well, have a seat. Despite what's going on outside, I would like to have a discussion like *civilized* people."

The bounty hunter's eyes darted to the crumbling city beyond. "What's going to happen?" He couldn't stop himself from asking.

The Commander raised his wrist and glanced down at a watch. "The city's lost. Thanks to an... *oversight.* Pacific was able to capitalize on a weakness I left exposed." Leon closed his eyes, practicing a powerful sense of calm. "No sense in losing our heads over the inevitable. I have an evacuation unit en route to take us to our old base of operations in Paris. My Advisor should be there to welcome us."

All attention at the table went to Josephina. Despite her involvement in the destruction, the Queen kept her hazel eyes high in defiance.

As the Commander sat down, everyone at the table sat up a little straighter, and their collective anxiety rose from uncomfortable to stifling. It seemed only Hera remained partially immune to the effects of orbiting so close to a dying star about to implode. Despite Leon's calm, Jack could sense the rage and anger coiling just beneath the surface. The bounty hunter felt his training rise up, preparing him to bolt at the nearest sign of trouble. Every ounce of his being wanted to be far away when Leon exploded, and seeing as someone could cut the tension in the room like a knife, he knew that it was only a matter of time.

Leon folded his hands. "I guess we can go forward with the execution."

Josephina's eyes widened, but she didn't speak a word.

Jack glanced around the room and realized Caesar was nowhere to be seen. His breath caught as he put the puzzle together: Leon intended to execute someone in that room. And Jack had just volunteered to take part in the lottery.

Hera was the picture of calm as she drenched her pancakes in syrup. "May I introduce our newest business partner," she gestured casually to the red-haired man at her side. "Bradley Shaw: Vice President of Pacific."

Bradley Shaw fumbled his fork in his hands. "Hello," he muttered, his nervous gaze flickering downward.

Jack barely registered the man as he scanned the room. Who was Leon going to kill? Was it Bradley Shaw, a rebel leader? Was it Josephina, the betrayer of Leonueva? Or Hera for undermining her Commander, working behind his back? Jack clenched his teeth. Was it him? Did he know too much? Was he going to get punished for Ace's crimes?

Leon had a right to kill every person in that room, and Jack was kicking himself for walking into it.

"Unfortunately, Shaw doesn't know the *location* of Pacific. Caesar was at least smart enough to not trust him with the coordinates of his little hideaway. *But* Shaw has agreed to be an informant for us. We'll lose this battle, but Pacific will take home the mole that will win us the war." Hera straightened, satisfied with herself.

Leon nodded, his clear blue eyes assessing the Pacifican vice president like a lion would its prey. "And how can we guarantee that he will cooperate?"

Hera's fingers tapped the marble table. "He and his family will be pardoned when we take the rebel capital."

"Perfect." Leon folded his hands. "We'll leave him behind to be scavenged by Pacific."

Bradley Shaw straightened, his beady eyes widening. "Wait! Y-you're just going to leave me here in—in a *warzone*?" He turned to Hera, a speck of authority entering his tone. "This was not the deal!"

Leon slammed his fist downwards, shaking the table with a startling boom. "You've committed *treason* against Pangaea," he thundered. "Every breath you breathe is because I allow it. There is no *deal,* only repayment for your crimes."

Jack began to sweat as he imagined that wrath targeted at him and he promptly froze like a rabbit hoping to hide from a hunter. He was suddenly reminded of the *Fera* slave he'd left unconscious down in the laboratory and the two females he'd aided in rescuing. He prayed Arianne was long gone. At least then, it would be all worth it when Leon killed him for treason. Honestly, he was just happy he'd made it that far in his plan.

"Next order of housekeeping before we leave," Leon continued, and Jack felt the heat of the Commander's gaze settle on him. "Blackjack," he practically purred. "I would like to cordially welcome you to this alliance. There could be a bright future between Ace's organization and my government. I have great plans in the works for the legalization of slavery, and I would like you to facilitate the bridge between government rule and private-sector commerce. Once the taxation code is finalized—of course. You'd be rich. I'll even make you an Elite for your service."

Jack's breath caught in his throat. The draw to such an offer was enticing. A month ago, he might have even taken it despite his distaste for slavery. Power, money, and status—plus a way out from underneath Ace. Sure, he would only be trading one evil for another, but with Leon, he could become so much more than a criminal Underground urchin.

Despite everything he'd learned, Jack still struggled to resist the urge to say yes. Sure, he would probably be arrested for treason once Blue Krait woke up, but he had always been one to make the choice that kept him alive for as long as possible. And if he denied Leon's alliance, he would be dead on the spot instead of in a few days.

Jack looked down—it wasn't like he had some other option waiting for him. If everything went to plan, Arianne would be taken home with Pacific, and there was no way he could follow her after everything he'd done. All things considered, his balance sheet was clean, and it was time to move on to a new chapter: he'd repaid Arianne for his crimes, and he'd closed out his debts with Ace. There was nothing *but* the next step forward with Leon. The bounty hunter shrugged. He was already going to hell; he might as well enjoy however much time that he had left on the earth.

Nodding, Jack summoned the courage to look the Commander in the eyes. "Sounds like we have a deal," he said in his best Blackjack voice.

"Wonderful," the Commander rumbled, "which brings us to the final item on the agenda."

Leon snapped his fingers at Hera. The scientist General produced a pistol from her hip. "I hear you prefer the old-fashioned bullet-in-chamber method over blasters," she said before expertly sliding it across the table.

Jack stopped the pistol with his hand, his eyebrow rising in confusion.

"I want you to kill my wife, Jack," Leon commanded.

"Take your soul and leave this building before you sell it to him," Josephina spat. "This is not your fight, and you do not want to put yourself in the middle of it."

Leon's calm façade cracked as he whirled on his wife. "Silence!"

Josephina angled her chin upward and looked down at her husband with unflinching calm. Jack was uncertain if any other person existed that was brave enough to glare at Leon like that. That tenacity…Maybe that was how Josephina, a commoner, had gotten the Commander to condescend and fall in love with her in the first place.

Jack watched in shock as Leon almost buckled under his wife's gaze. "I wish things could be different," he whispered.

And Josephina, the woman Jack had decided was the bravest person in the world, *smiled* at the Commander. "The irony of having all the power in the world and still being powerless when it matters."

Leon jumped out of his seat and turned to flip his chair across the room. He shouted in rage as he whirled back on the group, and Jack realized the Commander was dangerously close to snapping his thin veil of control. Silence fell after the clattering of the hurled chair ceased, and to Jack's amazement, Josephina was still unfazed. Perhaps after years with her husband, his intimidation had long since lost its potency.

The Commander focused his attention on Jack as he let out a long sigh to collect himself. A few strands of his slicked-back hair fell over his forehead, and Leon took a moment to comb the stands back with a shaking hand. "As you can see," he continued softly, "I have a well-founded issue with *trust.*" He turned to spit the final word at his wife.

Hera watched the scene with a delighted, cold gaze. "You seemed confused why none of the Pacifican captives were slated for execution," she said knowingly to Jack. "We never cared to execute an insignificant pest. A flea sitting on the flank of a dog is far less dangerous than a virus lurking within." She turned her attention to Josephina. "A beautiful virus, yes, but never very smart. It was easy: threaten to kill your little childhood crush and wait for you to play your hand."

Josephina scowled. Even in the face of death, she didn't wilt. "You think you've won? You traded an entire city to find me." She turned her head towards her husband. "I'll take that trade any day."

Hera's face reddened with rage, but she bit her tongue.

The Commander continued to pace, and with his movements, the powerful broadsword strapped to his back caught Jack's attention as the light from the windows bounced off it. The warning the weapon gave was chilling. If Leon decided to lash out in rage, no one in that room could stop him before he killed each and every one of them. Leon was large and trained, but he also had the Serum in his brain: beating someone who had the knowledge of every martial art would be a colossal feat—even if that person was human.

Above them, the ceiling started to open slowly. At first, the change went unnoticed, the faint humming of the panels above his head so fine-tuned that it could be easily ignored. As the ceiling opened wider, like a cover removed from a pool, the bright light from the sky above finally alerted Jack to the gaping hole a couple dozen feet above his head.

Just beyond the crest of the open roof, a Pangaean jet with its shining white hull circled lower and lower. Leon's evacuation team had arrived.

Jack had spent years learning how to identify Pangaean technology in order to scam Elites or weasel himself out of tight situations. Because of this, he could tell that the jet waiting above them was part of the newest class of aircraft. A perfect combination of jets and helicopters, the new models were capable of hovering in place, taking off anywhere, and reaching mach speeds. If his observations of Pacific's airships from his short time in their possession were correct, he knew Pacific pursuers could never keep up.

All of that considered, it meant that as soon as Leon reached that jet, he would be untouchable.

"Here's how this is going to work," Leon shouted over the chaos of the open sky above. "You have a ticket on that jet if you kill my wife. From my intel, you spent a lot of time with Pacifican affiliates. There's a chance you harbor feelings for their rebellion." He pointed to Josephina. "Like her. If I'm going to have you working with me, I need collateral."

Jack's arms were paralyzed. He couldn't reach for the pistol in front of him. Typically, holding the gun was the easy part. But now, for the first time, he hesitated.

Hera rolled her eyes as she pulled out a blaster and pointed it at Jack. "You shoot the whore, or I shoot you. Simple."

Josephina bared her teeth at Hera, a fighter until the end. The gesture reminded him of Arianne.

Leon extended a hand to Jack. "My wife is a close friend of Caesar Ortiz. Her death at your hands guarantees you can never go to Pacific. It's a win-win: I get insurance, and you get everything you could have ever wanted."

"Show us the 'best aim in Europe,'" Hera taunted lazily.

Jack shook, his eyes going to the ground. It was the opportunity of a lifetime—power, money, and influence. It was also life or death. Why the *hell* was he hesitating?

The conflicted bounty hunter looked up at Leon, Hera, Bradley Shaw, and, lastly, Josephina. Just as Ace warned, he'd stepped up to the most dangerous game in the world, stupidly thinking that *he* was the one with all of the cards. One last look at Leon reminded him that the Commander was the master of his domain—nothing happened in his city without his consent.

Jack had become painfully aware there was no way even he, the prince of trickery, could scam his way out of that situation. He snuck a look outside at the growing chaos for a quick reprieve from the decision laid out before him. The bounty hunter focused his hearing on the people screaming and the planes flying overhead because the sounds of war were more calming than that room's silence.

He sighed, closing his eyes. He knew he didn't have a choice.

If he held out, someone else would kill Josephina. Jack would have accomplished nothing but killing himself. He was wrong about becoming prey the moment he stepped into the Murray Monument: he'd been a hopeless rabbit stalked by the lion the second he'd chosen to return to Leonueva tainted by Pacific's influence.

Ace's words came back to him—as horrible as they were. *"The moment you hesitate is the moment you'll drown."*

To secure his future, he had to end someone else's. Doing that did not make him cruel. It made him a survivor. So he stood and took a calming breath as he raised the glinting pistol in front of him. The motion was as natural as walking, yet his heart threatened to beat out of his chest.

Despite himself, Jack risked a look at the rebellious hero he was about to kill. Josephina didn't beg or plead in her last moments. She simply closed her eyes and nodded. A moment of understanding passed between the Queen and her killer: Josephina didn't blame him, and she'd come to terms with her sentence long before that day.

Jack fired, the movement so familiar that such a monumental action almost felt inconsequential.

The bullet hit its mark, just like it always did. The slight kickback of the gun into his hand was the only thing that reminded him that what he'd just done was real. Josephina's head shot backward with the momentum of the bullet, and then her body went limp as it fell forward. It had been simple—easy. The simplicity of it all horrified him. He shook his head, suddenly queasy, and quickly threw the gun away from him in disgust. He couldn't watch as Josephina's breathing grew ever quieter.

She was dying. He'd executed a hero. He couldn't come to terms with the horrible thought.

Hera sat back in satisfaction. "Best aim in Europe indeed," she purred with delight.

Leon swayed, his eyes clouded as he gripped the table and lowered his head. Jack looked away as the Commander screamed. Maybe delegating the execution to Jack was more than just a good strategy. Maybe, deep down, even the terrifying tyrant of Europe couldn't kill his traitorous wife.

Jack barely had a moment to breathe in the aftermath of his actions when the windows behind Leon's desk shattered. His heart skipped a beat in shock, and he dove to cover his face from the glass raining down in glittering shards. When he recovered, he raised his head above the table just high enough to watch an avenging angel built of golden light and blood crash into the throne room.

The angel's eyes glanced at the dying Queen before settling on the tyrant. With a roar loud enough to rock the heavens, she bellowed, *"What did you do?"*

Chapter 51

Arianne

Arianne was out for blood.

Caesar, her dad, was nowhere to be seen. And her mother... if she weren't running on pure rage, she would have buckled to the ground right then and there. Josephina was dead, executed by Leon. They'd all been fooled into believing Caesar was the target.

And Arianne had been fooled into believing she still had time to make things right with her mother.

She was too late.

Then Leon turned—his face a mix of grief, confusion, and wonder. Arianne slackened as her gaze locked with his. Her heart threatened to stop beating. After eleven long years, Leon, *her father,* was standing in front of her. Fear, worship, hate, and *love* mixed together inside her to make a potent concoction that threatened to make her pass out.

The father and daughter stared at each other for what felt like an eternity. The world slowed to a stop. Arianne was lost in those blue eyes so similar to hers, and for a moment, every ounce of fight left her body. Her younger self seemed to shake her as an overwhelming desire to *please* her father took over her.

For a moment, her past desires made her pause. If he saw how powerful she'd become, he would realize how valuable she could be. Perhaps he could love her.

Then Arianne saw her mother face down: murdered by the tyrant she'd somehow found a way to love as a child. Clarity cracked the haze of emotion that once paralyzed her. She distantly registered the others in the room: Hera, Jack, and

Bradley Shaw. Even with a clear mind, she would have struggled to piece together what was happening.

"Back from the dead," her father mused distantly with a curious tilt of his head.

Arianne's eyes narrowed into furious slits as she pointed one of her blades in the direction of her father, "I didn't come back for you."

Leon composed himself with a quick hand through his frayed blond hair. "So that's where you've been hiding all of this time," he smiled.

"My name is Arianne Ortiz," she said slowly, "you took my dad. I'll kill you for that."

Leon lifted his chin in a sneer. "Your *dad?* Interesting," he murmured, eyes glittering with rage. The Commander risked a quick glance towards Hera and Jack. "So that's who you brought with you into the city," he realized slowly, sickly excitement growing.

"Arianne," Jack pleaded, "Caesar's not here. He never was. Go—please."

Her heart constricted as she looked at Jack. She forced down the tender softness she still felt when they locked gazes. She quickly ripped her eyes away from the man, reminding herself that he was in that room because he'd *profited* off of her pain and capture.

Even if, in the end, he hadn't wanted it.

Arianne didn't look at her former friend. "Stay out of this," she warned.

Leon reached behind him, pulling a painfully familiar broadsword from his back, *Lion's Fang.* Arianne's eyes widened—she remembered that sword. She gritted her teeth, pushing down the barrage of memories that fought to surface at the sight of her father approaching her. Leon used to train her with that very blade—he'd been the first to teach her the importance of melee weapons in the world of *Feras.*

And now, from the look of excitement on the Commander's face, he was ready to remind her why even *Feras* feared him. Leon walked slowly, savoring every moment, "And what will you do, Little Beast? Do you really think you have what it takes to kill me?"

Arianne's grip tightened on her dual swords as sweat pooled out of every pore in her body, "I didn't think I had what it took to look you in the eyes," she admitted. "We've already made it this far—let's find out how much further I can get."

"Arianne!" Jack cried out.

She ignored Jack's warning as she dashed at her father. Every minute used training in the gym, every hour wasted mourning the loss of her family, and every year spent avoiding her reflection out of the fear she would see *him* came forward in a blinding burst of energy. Arianne had a lifetime of seconds building toward the man standing before her, and she intended to use all of them to afford her one final shot.

For Pacific, for *Feras,* for Andre, for her mother, and mostly for *herself,* she charged forward. One more fight, one more victory, and it would all be over. The fear of living in Leon's shadow and the war between her new home and Europe would cease. Arianne would do it. She *had* to be the one to do it.

Leon shouted, holding his blade across his body to intercept her jumping attack. Arianne's dual blades swept down on top of the Commander's broadsword with a quaking crash. The reverberation of the deflection shook her very bones. She landed hard, barely managing a step to the right as her father swung downward with deadly might.

With a hiss, she fought to summon Instinct one more time. She continued to tense in an effort to stir the deadly force sleeping inside of her—but she got no response.

As if reading her thoughts, Leon heckled, "You can't control it anymore, can you?" Her eyes widened with shock, and Leon took advantage, lunging forward with incredible speed for his size. "It needs energy," he said knowingly, "and it looks like you've spent every last drop."

Arianne ducked under her father's swing, landing a forward jab across his left shoulder. Unlike other opponents, Leon didn't let pain slow him down, and she realized it would take far more than a scratch to phase him. The Commander continued his attacks as he delivered expert blow after expert blow. Arianne jumped back, barely escaping with her life from Leon's last assault. Sure, she was a *Fera,* but she *was* exhausted, and Leon had the advantage of reach and knowledge. With every attack she attempted, Leon knew every possible combination and counter. It was like battling one of Ace's Simulations: it learned and adapted, never losing, only adjusting.

"Did you really think you could beat me?" Leon hissed as her crossed swords blocked his heaving swing. With her knees lowered to brace for the block and Leon leaning forward into the blow, the Commander was close enough to her to whisper hauntingly, "I *created* you."

The winged female's pupils went to pinpoints, and she froze as those words circled around in her head and threatened to drive her mad. In her daze, she didn't see Leon's foot coming towards her stomach until it was too late. The impact forced the breath out of her body in one fell swoop, and she flew backward towards the windows she'd come in through. Her body hit the ground hard, the obsidian fragments of shattered glass digging into her skin as she rolled.

Arianne faintly registered Jack's screams.

She was powerless as she lay there, lungs spasming as she fought for air. Her ribs ached, and she knew at least a few of the bones were cracked. She was terribly aware that she was in trouble as her body—drained of energy—refused to pick itself up off of the ground.

Leon stalked forward, and his sword scraped across the marble ground at his side, making a toe-curling screech. He took his time—sensing that his opponent was all but defeated. Arianne squeezed her eyes shut in pain from her fall and the deafening sound assaulting her sensitive mutant ears. Her injuries were agonizing, her senses overwhelmed, and her heart shattered. The insurmountable tsunami of defeat combined to make it even harder for her to force her failing body to stand.

Then, she was weightless, held in the air by Leon's vice grip on her wetsuit. Her hands scrambled for purchase, finally grabbing a hold of her father's wrist and squeezing. The Commander didn't register the pain as he snarled at his daughter, a wicked smile twisting his face. Behind Arianne, the wind from the shattered windows buffeted against her exposed feathers.

Leon analyzed his daughter. "Have you ever heard of the story of Icarus?" he asked, bending his elbow to pull her closer to his chest.

Arianne didn't notice Leon reaching behind her to grab one of her wings until she felt the cold touch of his skin on her sensitive feathers. The idea of her father placing his hands on her coveted wings sent a ripple of fear and anger surging through her, strong enough to give her one last burst of struggle. She spit at Leon as she tried to wiggle away from his touch, but her father wasn't phased. The Commander ignored her outburst, a strange look of amazement coming to his face as he glided the back of his hand across the primary feathers by her shoulder. Then, he grabbed onto the cresting bone of her wing and began to squeeze. She struggled to move away—but to no use. Leon had her pinned, and any weapon she hoped to use was painfully out of sight.

Leon's hypnotizing gaze didn't break from hers, "Icarus: the mortal who attempted to imitate immortality until he flew too close to the sun." Leon leaned forward, his words tickling Arianne's ears, "he thought he could go toe to toe with a god—until his wings were clipped."

Leon squeezed until her wing snapped. Arianne bellowed in agony as white-hot pain shot straight up her back.

"I am your god, Arianne," Leon whispered as he gave his daughter one final shove.

Then she was falling, the ground rushing up towards her at terrifying speeds. She screamed, her body somersaulting through the air in a desperate attempt to level out. But the effort was hopeless as her left wing flapped uselessly at her side.

As she fell to her death, a memory came back: a fraction of the memory from the day she'd run away eleven years ago. The thought had a strange symmetry to her current fall, and she was crazy enough to find it beautiful. During her first escape, she had flown from that very window, crashing through the glass towards the freedom beyond. She looked up at the gaping hole in the side of that tower of obsidian in a combination of awe and disdain. It seemed she was only lucky enough to escape her fate with her life once.

She closed her eyes, the wind whipping past her ears. She'd failed. And her father had rewarded her with the cruelest death for a winged *Fera* that he could think of: the very free fall that had once exhilarated her. For a moment, she was brought back to the island, and the feeling of that fall was met with the scent of sea salt and fresh sunscreen. But this fall wouldn't end with her catching those warm Mediterranean updrafts and flying over the swaying palms. This time—falling from a monument that should have been hers by blood right—her wings would fail.

Just like everything else that she was a part of, she would fail. And with one final breath, Arianne accepted death.

As every ounce of hope left her chest, a shadow blocked out the sun above her. Her eyes burst open as she realized what was rocketing towards her: *Wings*. Large, light-absorbing, seventeen-foot *wings*.

"Arianne!" Blackjack screamed.

Her lips parted, but no words escaped her.

Jack collided with her, his powerful arms wrapping around her chest. With a jarring jolt, her fall was halted as his wings caught air from his free fall. The pair of winged *Feras* shot up momentarily before continuing their slower descent to the ground below. Jack barked in pain at the extra weight pulling downwards on his wings, but he never released his white-knuckled grip on her back.

Even with Jack's rudimentary gliding, their landing was far from cushioned. Arianne pushed herself away from her savior at the last moment to lessen the weight of his crash. She braced and rolled, her already scraped skin tearing on the sweltering concrete. When she finally stopped tumbling, she lay on the ground for a moment, her heart thundering in her chest and her broken wing throbbing from the impact.

But all the pain in the world couldn't shake her out of her daze. Alive, *holy fuck,* she was alive. She turned in amazement at the person who had, in a mind-bending twist of events, saved her life.

Jack, not practiced in a crash landing, took the fall much harder than her. The man—no *male*—cried out once more as he hit the ground at just shy of a deadly velocity. Arianne forced herself to stand as the winged male settled in an exhausted heap atop the Murray Monument steps: his dark wings splayed out across the expanse of the marble in unmoving mounds of feathers.

It was the most beautiful and heartbreaking thing Arianne had ever seen.

"Jack!" She cried out as she ran towards him.

The winged male rested, unmoving on the ground. His right arm was bent at an unnatural angle, and a large bruise was blossoming on his cheek from where his head had hit the pavement. Arianne began to cry as she slid to his side and started to shake him. He *couldn't* be dying. She wouldn't let him—not after everything they'd been through and sacrificed for each other. Not when she'd just been shown how much they were *meant* to be in each other's lives.

Arianne had never once met anyone like her. She couldn't lose them so quickly after realizing that she wasn't alone. Most of all, she couldn't lose *Jack*, the male who'd found a way into her vengeful heart and proven to her over and over again that he was so much more than the person Ace had forced him to become.

Arianne's bleeding fingers dug into his shoulders as she shook him harder, her breaths coming out in sobbing gasps. "Come on!" She barked, "Not you too! *Not you too*!"

She ignored the stomping of boots coming from outside of her vision. She ignored the implications of those boots: Pangaean soldiers were closing in around them. Whatever time Jack's sacrifice had bought her would be in vain if they didn't move. Arianne shook her friend harder, desperately trying to wake him and get them out of one last bind. She refused to believe that Jack could die for *nothing*.

"Come on, Pangaea Boy," she whispered in breathless gasps, "you promised we'd do this together. I can't do this without you."

The soldiers advanced, and she knew she never stood a chance against them alone. But with Jack, they might have enough luck for one last fight together.

Then, his eyes opened slowly, the amber surrounding the irises catching the sunlight and turning them to sweltering gold. "Keston," he sighed weakly.

"What?" Arianne asked in surprise.

Jack took a deep breath and pushed himself off of the ground gingerly. The male's dark wings draped behind him like a billowing cape as she helped him stand to his full height. He wavered, but a slight lean on her shoulder kept him standing. Arianne looked between the two of them with a sinking heart. They'd made it far those past few weeks, but their bodies had finally given out.

There wasn't much fight left shared between them.

Jack stood up straighter despite the advancing Pangaean soldiers. "My name is Keston," he repeated as tears came to his eyes. "Thought it would be nice to die as the male my parents wanted me to be." He closed his eyes as a distant smile brushed across his lips, "It feels better to die as myself than live one more minute as that lie."

She looked up at *Keston* standing above her, amazed at what she'd watched him become. "I'm glad I got to see the real you."

Keston looked down at her—the two finally seeing each other for who they truly were. "I'm sorry," he breathed, "for everything."

Arianne managed a small smile even as her heart swelled. She wasn't quite sure what they meant to each other anymore. She wasn't sure if she was ready to forgive him just yet. All she knew was that she wanted the time to find out.

She laced her fingers with his, "Let's survive one more time, and we can hash out who owes who later." She squeezed their intertwined hands, "I like Keston," she finished with a sigh, "It suits you."

"Hands up!" One of the soldiers shouted as the Pangaean squadron settled into position around the pair of winged *Feras*, "You're under arrest by the authority of the European military!"

But Keston wasn't looking at the soldiers—his gaze was fully focused on her. His eyes scanned her as if he was taking in her features one final time. "Promise me one thing," he pleaded.

Arianne was lost in his passionate stare. "Anything," she breathed.

Keston let out one more long breath as he looked up at the sky. "Take my body back home. Bury me next to my mother."

She didn't get a chance to respond before gunfire shattered her eardrums.

Chapter 52

Jaya

The world was crumbling around her. Jaya focused on her next steps as she ran to prevent herself from collapsing into an anxious heap. Her breaths came out in heaving gasps as she ran faster, the image of her sister waiting for her keeping her going. The hallways, usually teaming with Wards, were empty as the building's security prepared for the Pacifican attack. She was thankful for the open path as she turned into the prison block.

Jaya hated that she left her best friend behind, but she knew she needed to refocus her priorities. Arianne could *fly* to Caesar's rescue on the top floor of the Murray Monument. It made *tactical* sense to split up, but that didn't make leaving her best friend any less hurtful. She gritted her teeth, focusing on the faces of Rhino, Kalinda, Lyn, and the others waiting for her. It might hurt to run from Arianne, but it was the best chance they had at getting everyone out alive.

As she ran inside, she was surprised to see that the prison block was open. The floor was covered in blood, but no one was outside of their cells.

"Jay!" Kalinda cried out.

Rhino jumped up. "Jay!" He repeated.

A cry escaped Jaya's chest as she locked eyes with her sister, reaching out from her cell. "Kal!"

"What's going on up there?" Captain Lyn demanded. All business.

"Pacific has arrived. I don't know how much time we have but we must escape before the Wards resume their positions. Arianne is here." Jaya stopped to breathe, trying her best to report as quickly as possible. "She was trapped in the laboratory with me. She's gone ahead to stop Caesar's execution—"

She stopped when her eyes landed on Caesar, resting in the back of his cell. The President was covered in shadow, so still that she might have missed him if he hadn't shifted at his daughter's name. Jaya's lips parted in shock. If Caesar was still in the prison block—

"I wasn't the one they were after," Caesar's voice was dull, defeated.

Jaya blinked. "W-what do you mean?"

The President uncurled his hand, and inside it lay one of Haris's prototype wireless phones. "Jo. They were after Josephina. They waited until she incriminated herself in a desperate attempt to save me. Hera Richards apprehended her and her injured son just before you arrived." His head hung low. "Hera wanted to draw her out. Pangaea was never going to kill me. Not when I know where the island is, and they still suspect I know where the procedure to make the Commanders' Serum is."

Captain Lyn jumped up, pulling Major Cadmilus with her. "Enough chit-chat. We can catch up once we get our asses on a Pacific jet."

Jaya nodded. Running from the prison block, she found a key card left behind at the Ward's desk in the main hallway. The Chameleon quickly got to work unlocking the three cells that held her fellow Pacificans.

Rhino sprung from his enclosure, ducking down to scoop his friend up in a suffocating hug. "You crafty little shit!" He exclaimed. "How'd you get out?"

Jaya looked down, her mind still clouded from the fight with Pandora, as well as Arianne's escape. "Blackjack," she breathed. "Arianne must have followed our failed mission and forced Blackjack to lead her into the city." She still hadn't pieced all of the events together. "It was so strange. He *cared* about Ari."

Rhino placed Jaya down, and behind his large mass, Kalinda was waiting. Tears ran freely as Jaya ran into her sister's arms, savoring her familiar scent. If she'd learned anything from her time in this awful place, it was that her family was far more important than any mission she could ever be given.

"I thought they killed you," Kalinda whimpered.

"I'm okay," Jaya cried, curling in closer to her sister's chest

Captain Lyn and Major Cadmilus helped Caesar limp out of his cell. The President was wan, dark circles hanging under his eyes. "You said Arianne is here?" She nodded, watching Caesar's eyes darken even more with worry. "No," he gasped. "No, this can't happen."

Jaya frowned, sharing a gaze with the man who'd become like a father to her. She nodded subtly to inform him that she *knew*. She knew Arianne had grown up in that laboratory. She knew what kind of grief Arianne—and, by extension, Caesar—were experiencing because of that.

"I've summoned Kalfas," Caesar said, an ounce of his confidence returning. "We can't help Arianne from down here." The President held up the phone, the built-in GPS flashing red. "His jet should be waiting outside. We just need to find a way there."

The mission was set: the final run for their lives to the safety of the skies as Leonueva fell beneath them. At one point, Jaya would have been content with the success of the siege and the following collateral would have been inconsequential to her. Now, with her friends and family considered, her only motivation was getting everyone around her out alive.

Rhino took the lead, his naturally thicker skin providing a great shield in case their small squadron was surprised by a Pangaean attack. To her annoyance, the elevator was down when she attempted to summon it. She gritted her teeth, her stress levels rising: they would need to take the stairs. She turned, lips parting as she looked at Caesar, who was barely able to stand without the help of Lyn and Carter.

"The elevator's down." She winced.

Captain Lyn took over, snapping her fingers at Rhino. "Lieutenant Adams, carry President Ortiz. Major Cadmilus, you take the lead up the stairs. No time to lallygag!"

Caesar didn't object as Rhino scooped him up into his powerful arms. The group turned towards the stairs, falling into formation. Even though the former Captain was still grieving the loss of his squadron, he was newly motivated by the chance to see his wife and son again.

The Pacificans moved up the stairs. Kalinda, Rhino, and Caesar took up the rear while Carter, Lyn, Jaya, and Gunner shielded the front. Keeping Caesar alive was the main objective, and if Kalinda went down, there would be no chance of reviving any other injured people in their party. The formation made tactical sense, even if Jaya had personal reasons to support it. She was content with her expendability if Caesar and her sister made it home to Citadel.

"We've reached the first floor!" Carter exclaimed. "Do I advance?"

Lyn crouched behind her comrade. "Scope it out first," she instructed. "We don't have any weapons for cover."

Carter nodded, carefully opening the staircase door to the grand lobby beyond. "Front entrance is covered by a Pangaean squadron," he reported. "The emergency exit near the back is our best chance."

"I'll report to Kalfas," Caesar said from the cradle of Rhino's arms.

"Move on my mark," Captain Lyn instructed. "Let's keep the formation tight. Don't fuck this up. We've all got people waiting for us at home."

They moved, Carter taking the lead. Jaya remained low as she crept through the lobby, hating how exposed she felt. A hand came to her back, and she looked to her right, seeing Kalinda at her side. The field medic gave her a promising smile, and Jaya was reminded of the day her sister had saved her from the slavers. Kalinda's smile was warm, endearing, and promising. It seemed to say: *what's one more impossibility?*

Carter reached the back door, throwing the emergency exit open to the street beyond. There, standing watch outside the jet, was Kalfas—rifle in hand. At the opening of the emergency exit, alarms above the door began to sound, and Jaya's stomach flopped. Other sirens filled the air, but the specific blaring signal above the doors they were attempting to escape out of brought unwanted attention to their direct location. If the soldiers had ignored the emergency exit door because it was locked from the outside, they were aware of it now. At the sight of the escaping Pacificans, soldiers from the front of the lobby turned and shouted as they ran to intercept them.

Carter frantically waved his squad forward, keeping the door open with his foot. "Go!" He yelled.

Rhino and Caesar went first, followed by Jaya and Kalinda. Lyn pushed Gunner through the exit last. Jaya barely cleared the exit when she heard the cracking sound of gunfire over the sirens. Her training took over as she turned towards the deadly sound and stepped before her sister to shield her. But none of it mattered.

Major Carter Cadmilus gave one final salute. Then he closed the door, locking himself inside. Bullets ricocheted against the inside of the metal in terrible thuds.

"Major!" Captain Lyn screamed.

"Get on the damn jet!" Kalfas ordered. "He bought us *seconds*!"

Jaya fumbled her way onboard. She hardly noticed the takeoff as she stared at the door, slowly growing smaller and smaller below. Carter Cadmilus, her best friend's father, had given up the chance to see his son again just to buy all of them two critical seconds of time. She swayed, almost tumbling into the open air.

Another life lost for the mission. Her family might make it out okay, but there was another family at home who wouldn't be as lucky.

"Haris," Jaya whispered in horror.

Rhino's eyes were wide as he stared at the same door Jaya couldn't look away from. "Jesus fucking Christ," his lips trembled.

"Snap out of it. We're not done yet!" Kalfas demanded stiffly, walking around the cabin and shoving a rifle into the hands of each of the remaining soldiers on the jet. If the Pacifican General mourned Carter's death, he didn't show it. "You want to make it out alive? You want to make your teammate's sacrifice worth it? You load those guns and get ready to fight. We've got two more Pacificans to save."

Arianne and Josephina.

Jaya tensed, removing the safety from her rifle and taking up a position next to Rhino, leaning out of the opening of the jet. Black glass rushed past them as they scaled the daunting height of the Murray Monument. Her new priority was ensuring Arianne was *alive*—then, she would have all the time in the world to yell at her.

As they reached the top of the building, Jaya prepared to fire. What she wasn't expecting was the open roof... and the room beyond to be empty—save two people. She straightened as she recognized Bradly Shaw cowering behind the large marble table at the center of the room.

Kalfas pointed to two officers he'd brought along with him. "Get down there! Get them up!"

"Jo," Caesar whispered, his eyes going to the second figure visible from below.

The Pacifican officers rappelled down into the open penthouse. They retrieved Josephina first, placing her unmoving body on a plank before pulling her up into the jet. Everyone was silent as the Queen's body was brought aboard. Caesar lunged at her just as Kalinda launched into action. Jaya's breath caught when she saw the small trickle of blood on Josephina's forehead, recognizing the cauterized entry wound of a bullet.

They were too late. The execution was over, and Leon was long gone.

"Someone check for an emergency medical kit!" Caesar cried out.

Kalinda was careful not to move Josephina as she assessed the exit wound and worked to stop the bleeding. "She's low on blood," the medic warned.

Bradly Shaw was pulled into the jet, but no one paid him any mind.

The President held onto Josephina's pale hands. "Come on, *mi amor*," Caesar gasped. "Come on, stay with me."

The officers from below returned, one carrying an emergency medical kit in his hands. Kalinda quickly reached for it, her fingers fumbling to open the box and pull out the life-saving Second Blood. Her eyes narrowed as she injected the needle into Josephina's forearm.

"She's still breathing," Kalinda reported warily. "But the internal swelling could kill her. The exit wound is also keeping her alive as a place for swelling."

"Do what you can," Caesar blinked away tears.

"Even if I can stabilize her..." She trailed off, unable to continue.

Jaya frowned. Even if her amazing sister could pull Josephina back from the brink of death, there was no guarantee the Queen would wake up. Brain damage from swelling alone could make it impossible for her to regain consciousness. Breathing and basic functions were controlled in the brain stem, but waking up required far more.

"Alright!" Kalfas cried out. "We got action down on the street! Williams! Bahri! You might be interested in this. Let's go!"

Jaya tore herself from her sister's side. *Arianne.*

Hanging from the open door of the jet, Jaya and Rhino zeroed in on two winged figures surrendering to a horde of Pangaean soldiers below. Rhino shared a look with Jaya. She nodded, and the powerful *Fera* jumped from the jet with a yell.

Rhino dropped three stories, his battle cry shaking her eardrums. "It's game time!" He shouted, concrete cracking beneath his powerful feet as he landed in a crouch.

Jaya targeted the Pangaean squadron and opened fire. Rhino, a force of nature, barreled into the back of the unit, firing and taking down soldiers two or three at a time. Despite the chaos of the day, she felt a rush of calm as she discharged her weapon. There was something relaxing about following the well-practiced procedure of providing cover fire: breathe, aim, shoot.

And Arianne, swaying in exhaustion, gave her focus.

Kalfas stood at Jaya's side as they landed. "All right, rookie," Kalfas barked. "Let's finish this."

The world slowed as Jaya felt the battle fury take over. Gunfire drowned out her hearing. She vaguely registered Pangaean soldiers falling around her. Rhino raged on, his powerful shoulders rising above the chaos like a beacon in a storm. Jaya stood at his back, providing cover.

"I'm going to need a raise!" Rhino huffed as he trampled a soldier at his side. "And a vacation!"

"Can we get out of this first?" Jaya yelled above the noise, reloading.

"Gun! Gun! Gun!" Arianne cried out.

Jaya turned, realizing her friend and Blackjack had the advantage of the high ground on marble steps. She blinked, noticing the dark wings billowing from Blackjack's back. Quickly, she threw a downed soldier's blaster at her friend. Arianne caught the blaster, stepped in front of Blackjack, and opened fire. Her assistance was the final edge the Pacificans needed. Moments later, the last of the Pangaean squadron fell.

Then Jaya was running, sprinting up those steps toward Arianne. The winged female buckled, and she sank to the ground in exhaustion. Jaya bounded forward, reaching her friend just in time to catch her. Blackjack fell at Arianne's other side, and Jaya finally got a look at the feathered wings protruding from the bounty hunter's back.

Had Arianne known Blackjack was a *Fera?*

"Ari!" Jaya cried, brushing hair out of her friend's face. "What happened?"

Arianne's eyes cleared as she sat up, leaning heavily against the support of her two friends. "I fell," she said, turning to Blackjack. "He caught me."

Blackjack lowered his eyes. "You caught me first," he said softly.

Jaya looked at Arianne's wings. Her left one was fractured, the bone below her shoulder painfully bent. Then she turned her head up towards the Murray Monument looming above them, scanning the height of the paralyzing fall that should have claimed her friend's life. Then she turned to Blackjack. He'd exposed his identity to save her. *Twice.*

The bounty hunter's shoulders slumped. From the look of the deep purple bruise on his cheek, he was most likely fighting a nasty concussion. Jaya was surprised he was still awake.

Arianne's hand reached up to stroke Jaya's purple hair. "Hi," she whispered.

"Hi," Jaya smiled down.

All things considered, she could kill Arianne right then and there. But at the moment, she was just happy to see that her oldest friend was still breathing.

"How?" Arianne coughed. "How did Pacific find us?"

Jaya handed her the prototype phone. "Haris, that crazy genius. His phone has tracking capabilities. Caesar got the phone to Josephina Murray, and she summoned Pacific." She looked down, silently praying for the Queen whose life now rested in Kalinda's hands. "She was a rebel like us all along."

Arianne jumped up, a mix of emotions crossing her face. There was grief, fear, hatred, and love, but Jaya couldn't decipher why. "Y-you have her, right?"

The Chameleon tilted her head to the side, confused at her friend's sudden concern with the Pangaean queen. "Kal is taking care of her right now."

"I need to see," Arianne said, surging forward.

"Wait," Blackjack reached out and grabbed her arm.

Jaya read Blackjack's face. He was sad. As she exchanged a glance with the male, she quickly realized that he wanted a moment to say goodbye. She turned, noticing that Kalfas was making his way through the wreckage towards the three of them. All three knew what awaited Blackjack if he let Kalfas reach them: he would be arrested for conspiracy against Pacific. Even though every instinct was yelling at Jaya to restrain Blackjack then and there for what he'd done to her team, something also told her doing so was wrong.

At the end of the day, Blackjack was the only reason they were still breathing. Herself included.

Then she saw how Arianne was looking at the bounty hunter, and she knew there was something between them beyond travel partners. Going against every bit of training she'd received, Jaya nodded at the pair and stepped away. Even if the law dictated that Blackjack should go to prison for what he'd done, he'd also saved her life. Because of that, she decided she wouldn't be the one to put him away. If Blackjack wished to say goodbye, she could allow them a few minutes of privacy.

Jaya walked away from the winged pair, focusing on Kalfas advancing through the battlefield as he searched for the injured. The Chameleon approached her General, saluting. "What's our plan, sir?"

"Get the hell back behind the safety of our borders." Kalfas frowned down at a Pacifican soldier, his olive green eyes clouding as he knelt and retrieved his comrade's dog tags. "This feels far from a victory," he muttered.

A shiver ran through her as she took in the carnage. Pacific may have taken the city, but she had the awful feeling that they were somehow worse off than they were before. The growing storm between their two countries had finally broken. Like it or not, Pacific had started a full-out war with the attack.

"It feels like the floodgates have opened," she whispered in reluctant agreement.

Kalfas nodded. "Leon doesn't mind losing battles, but he is not a man that loses wars."

It was a painful reminder of the history lessons she'd received growing up in Pacific. Pangaea had lived under the guise of world peace by creating an empire that spanned all six inhabited continents. Wars were a thing of the past thanks to the unifying reign of Pangaea—the only exception being small rebellions that were quickly fettered out.

The only revolt that came close was the Selvian War, fought between the Selvian Tribe and a much younger Leon Murray. The Selvians had given Leon a run for his money—for a time. Then, Leon ruthlessly wiped that legendary tribe off the map, a flex of power that sent every other European tribe even further into hiding.

The war further isolated the already-reclusive tribespeople. For generations, the Selvians—with their powerful legion of Champions—had served as the respected voice of the tribes in Pangaean politics. When Selvia fell, any protection they afforded other tribes and the *Feras* within them dissolved, allowing the slave trade to leak its way into Europe.

"There's a very real chance Pacific will share Selvia's fate," Kalfas warned, confirming her fears.

The question was no longer *if* but *when*. Leon would return with a vengeance, and Pacific needed to weather the storm. Losing the Selvians had been the first blow to *Fera* rights across the globe, but any chance of saving *Feras* from enslavement would die if Pacific fell.

"We'll be ready," Jaya murmured.

Kalfas looked at her, a sigh escaping his lips. "You're still young," he began, turning to look up at the towering Murray Monument above him. "Being ready has nothing to do with it."

Chapter 53

Keston

Keston.

The name felt foreign in his mind. Just like the music in his head and the *Fera* genes running through his veins, Keston had fought to suppress his name and all that it had meant for years. Ace owned Blackjack through and through, so he'd shoved the last parts of his true self deep down, hoping that a part of him would always remain his own.

He was ashamed. After letting himself become the person that he was in Cartel, he didn't deserve to carry the name. Keston was someone's son. A musician, and a mutant boy from a small mountain village. Blackjack, on the other hand, was a killer, a *human*, a brainwashed drone with no sense of empathy or remorse. Blackjack was the antithesis of who Keston wanted to become, and so—with every passing day—that boy from the village was pushed further and further away.

Being Blackjack was certainly easier than addressing the millions of emotions that threatened to drown him, but he didn't want detached oblivion anymore. He wanted to *feel*. He wanted to be worthy of the name his family had given him for once in his life. And the way Arianne looked at him right then gave him an inkling of hope for a future where that was possible.

He gave Arianne a nervous smile. "Wait," he said, reaching out with his unbroken arm, his hand wrapping softly around her bicep. "We should talk."

She took a shaky breath. "Yeah, we should."

Keston stared down at Arianne, mind reeling as he thought of everything that needed to be said. There was so much wrong, so many secrets, and so many apologies—yet so little time. His lips parted, only one thought coming to the forefront of his mind. "I-I'm sorry I didn't tell you about..." He looked over his shoulder at his wings draped behind his back.

The subject felt foreign. For years, he had shoved the mutant side—the less desirable side—of himself down. Just the feel of open air against his wings was strange. He fumbled, realizing he still couldn't speak directly about the subject. After years of hiding as a human, mentioning his mutant gifts had become terrifying and forbidden.

He'd never even learned how to fly properly. When he'd lost his home, his mother had only just begun instructing him on how to glide. After that, displaying his *Fera* traits was too dangerous. Even though Ace knew about his true nature, he'd done his best to distance himself from that identity. He'd wanted Ace to see him as human, not as a slave. And the respect the human Blackjack received from other members of Cartel was far greater than what mutant Keston ever could garner. After years of hiding, his wings were too weak even to attempt true flight.

Arianne stepped forward, her hand reaching to touch his dark brown wings. She shook her head, a small smile coming to her face. "I'm sorry I didn't tell *you*. I guess we were so focused on hiding our own secrets that we didn't even think to see reflections of ourselves in each other," she responded quietly. "I understand why you did it, though. I think we both understand what would happen if the wrong people knew."

Ignoring the painful throbbing of his head and arm, he took in the beautiful female. "I think I finally found the right person to tell."

Arianne frowned, taking a step back. The distance between them was painfully cold when all he wanted to do was step forward and bury himself in her arms and beautiful golden brown feathers. But a lot had happened between them since such intimacy would've been an option.

"If you don't leave now, Kalfas will arrest you," she warned, her tone steeling.

He blinked at her sudden coldness. "I don't care about that right now," he said. "I care about making things right between us."

Arianne hugged herself, her head turning to look at the Pacifican jet. "We don't have that kind of time."

Keston frowned. *No,* he couldn't just leave the person in his life that he felt *connected* to behind. He couldn't describe it, but their connection went further than their shared mutant traits. Somehow, this random female had found a way to pull him from Ace's brainwashing and make him want to be more than Blackjack again. For the first time in years, he had hope, and it was because of her. His emotional compass had finally leveled out, its needle pointing to one thing and one thing only: her.

She was his true north. He couldn't throw that feeling away. But Arianne was right. His newfound freedom would disappear if he lingered long enough for General Kalfas and his men to arrest him.

Then, as his mind replayed their fraught time together in their final moments, he remembered an important promise he'd not collected on. A smile grew on his face. "Okay," he leveraged. "Remember back when you were interrogating me? You still owe me a question."

Arianne turned to him, and she seemed resigned and hesitant to play along like she once had. She shook her head, "I-I'm not in the mood right now, Keston. You need to go."

His heart lurched as he realized whatever small chance he had with her was slipping through his fingertips. His mouth dried out as he came to grips with the very real chance that, after everything they'd been through, he'd lost her forever.

"Together," his voice hitched, "if that word meant anything to you, could you please listen to me one last time?"

Arianne considered, a long sigh escaping her as she raised her head. " Okay," she looked up, her eyes misty.

Taking a step forward, Keston grabbed the small of her back and pulled her close to him, careful of her injuries and his own. He took in her scent, sea salt mixed with forest, and committed it to memory. For all he knew, this could be the last time he saw her. To his surprise, Arianne gasped and let him hold her close. With her body against his, he almost lost all track of rational thought.

But even Keston couldn't forget his one important question.

"Arianne," he breathed, butterflies filling his stomach. "Every part of me is screaming not to leave you. I know I fucked up, and I know there's no possible way we could ever explore whatever connection we found. You have your people in Pacific, and I know I can't come with you."

Josephina's body flashed before his eyes. No, he couldn't go to Pacific, nor could he ever tell anyone on that island what he did.

Arianne wrapped her right arm around Keston, her left arm still hanging limply at her side from her broken wing. Despite her injuries, she was soft as she ran her hand against his feathers, sending a chill of anticipation down his spine. "That's not a question," she leaned forward to whisper in his ear.

Keston searched those storm cloud eyes, every ounce of his being wishing things could have ended differently. "Do you feel the same?" He asked quietly. "Does some part of you want to figure out where this goes? Because if not, I'll leave you alone forever, but—"

"Yes," she breathed, the singular word like a soft breeze.

He paused, his mind unable to comprehend her answer. "What? You do?"

Arianne squeezed him tighter, her eyes blazing with that classic determination he'd come to admire so much. "Yes," she repeated. "It's complicated, but yes."

Hope flickered in his chest. Keston knew such a concept was dangerous to hold, but he fostered it and let it burn brighter and brighter inside him.

"When you saved me, and I thought you were dying," Arianne looked towards where they'd fallen from the height of Leon's tower. "I forgot about everything that happened between us. In those moments, I *mourned* the chance of finding out what it all means."

Keston smiled, his left hand sliding up to hold her face like he'd done a dozen times before. "This isn't goodbye then."

Ever so softly, he pressed his lips against hers. The kiss was too short, but he stopped himself nonetheless. The promise of claiming more than just her lips would keep him going until he found a way to see her again. The way Arianne leaned in for a deeper kiss told him she was anticipating their next meeting—however impossible—as well.

"This kind of feels like a goodbye." She frowned.

He fought every urge to beg her to run away with him right then and there. But Arianne had people waiting for her back on the island, and he had loose ends he needed to tie up before he could truly be free. Once all of that was said and done, once it was safe, there would be nothing stopping him from finding her again.

"How can it be a goodbye?" He chided, flicking her nose. "I saved your life *twice* today. You owe me a favor."

Arianne reached out, holding a block-like device in her hand that looked like a Pangaean Elite mobile phone. "I know this isn't much, but my friend made this phone. It can connect with the one I have back home—even through the Pacifican communication shields." She paused as if considering, and then, to his surprise, she removed her golden necklace from her neck. "Take this too."

Keston's eyes widened, recognizing the golden chain as the object that had comforted her many times during their journey. "No." He held his hands up. "I can't take this."

"Please," she insisted, "this necklace was given to me by my mother." Keston was shocked—he'd never heard her speak about her mother. "It protected me when I was a kid and I would like to think it protected me today as well. I want it to protect you."

Keston pocketed the phone and then hesitantly let her loop the necklace around his neck, "Thank you," he said once he stood back up.

He was terrified of the months ahead. For the first time since Ace found him in Paris, he was out on his own. That phone would become his lifeline: his only connection to someone else as he ventured out alone.

Alone... but free.

She nodded, taking a cordial step back. "Give me a call when you need that favor. I'll be there," she nodded to the golden angel with the sapphire eyes now glinting at his neck, "and you can give that back to me."

"Thank you," Keston whispered again, meaning every letter.

Arianne avoided his gaze. "Don't say that," she sighed.

"Why not?" He pressed, leaning in to get one last look at her stunning eyes. "I mean it. You saved me, Arianne. You're the one who showed me how to dream again."

When she looked up, he was surprised to see tears in her eyes. "Thank you always sounds like goodbye."

Keston stepped back, feeling the very physical thread that seemed to connect them grow tighter. He had to run now if he ever wanted a chance to explore the thing growing between them, but it felt impossible to leave.

"You're my compass," Keston promised, his heart stopping for a moment as he felt the truth of his words. "Everything I do guides me to you. This isn't goodbye, it's a 'see you later.'" He stared deeply into her eyes, knowing that final vision of her would be what kept him going until he saw her again and they got that second chance they'd promised each other.

"I'll see you later then." Arianne smiled, composing herself. "Don't get in too much trouble now, okay?"

"Where's the fun in that?" He asked.

And then, with one final laugh, he turned and escaped down the nearest alleyway. Keston could still hear his chuckle echoing off the walls as he faded into the chaos of the city beyond—the danger and madness comforting him like an old glove.

He would find his way back to Arianne, but he would make sure that he was a free male first.

Chapter 54

Arianne

By the time Arianne looked back, he was gone. She lowered her head as her heart sank. Some naive part of her wished that he would devise a brilliant way to fix everything and ride back to Pacific with her. Now, he was gone, and something inside her pulled as if he'd taken a part of her with him. She never would have believed that a stranger like him would grow to mean so much to her. Blackjack had been her enemy, but Keston had fought and sacrificed for her. The male she'd come to know had grown to mean so much more to her than just a mission.

Arianne hadn't lied when she said it was complicated. Keston's actions had hurt her and those around her—that couldn't be excused. But that didn't mean he was despicable, and it didn't mean those actions hadn't hurt him as well.

She'd run away from her family, was a child executioner, and even forgot her own sister. Those very thoughts made bile rise in her throat. She couldn't hate someone for the things they did to survive another day. Just like her, Keston was broken. They had both done things in the past they wanted to forget, but maybe they could help each other.

That's why it hurt to walk away. For the first time in her life, someone understood.

"Ortiz!" Kalfas's bark tore her attention from the street corner where Keston had disappeared.

The winged female turned to her old mentor, relief flooding her veins. "Kalfas," she breathed.

The tall General walked up to her, his stern face unreadable. "Where's Blackjack?"

Jaya appeared behind the General, her typical braid frazzled. The purple-haired *Fera* locked eyes with her and gave a subtle nod. Arianne nodded back to her friend, abruptly aware of the small token of gratitude Jaya had given to the mysterious male who had saved all of their lives. It seemed Jaya's time in Leonueva had changed her as well.

Arianne turned back to her former mentor, blinking in confusion. "He disappeared," she answered truthfully. "I couldn't stop him."

Kalfas considered for a moment, frustration clear on his face. "Not optimal, but we don't have time for more shit. Let's get to the plane before another problem presents itself—something you're unnaturally proficient in attracting." Kalfas's expression changed to one of annoyance as Arianne reached his side. "You," he gritted out with a frown. "You have no idea how much I want to kill you right now."

"Awe, Kalfas," she cooed. "You missed me."

The General frowned. "Do you have any idea how much trouble your shenanigans have caused? Disobeying a direct order is going to be a paperwork nightmare! And guess who has to deal with it?"

Arianne leaned over and hugged Kalfas, warmth filling her heart at the touch. "You can lecture me later. You missed me."

Jaya laughed as Kalfas stiffly accepted Arianne's hug, rolling his eyes all the while. "Don't make me say it, Ortiz."

"Am I under arrest?" Arianne asked.

"Most definitely," Kalfas shot back.

"Can I see Caesar first?"

"Whatever," Kalfas muttered, "since when do you listen to me anyways?"

Arianne separated from the General and ran toward the jet. The weight of emotion settled on her as soon as she walked onboard. Whatever relief she'd felt at the sight of Jaya and Kalfas dissipated when she saw her mother. Kalinda and Caesar rested on the ground, tending to the unconscious Queen. Arianne's knees weakened when she saw her mother's blood, but she forced herself to keep standing.

Every part of her wanted to rush to her mother's side, but she stopped herself. Josephina Murray was the First Mother of Europe, and by all accounts, Arianne shouldn't have any personal connection to the woman. Her focus shifted to the remaining Pacific soldiers waiting in the cabin. She needed to act like Josephina meant nothing to her.

Which was the worst punishment of all.

"Caesar," Arianne whispered, needing her father before the weight of the shitstorm circling around her crushed her.

Seeing Leon was enough to send her into a catatonic state, and that was without considering everything else that had piled up on top of it. Hera's new batch of experiments. Remembering that she had a sister—and had abandoned and mutilated said sister. Keston betraying her, then saving her, then leaving her. The fall of Leonueva. And her mother, dying on the floor in front of her.

The only thing keeping Arianne going was the fact that everyone she'd come to rescue was safe. Caesar was alive.

Her small whimper seemed to bring clarity to the President, and he blinked, turning to look up from Josephina towards his daughter. Kalinda, monitoring the Queen's injury at Caesar's side, turned and managed a welcoming smile towards her friend.

"Dad." Arianne's lips wobbled.

She was terrified Caesar would be furious. He had every right to be. She was almost too afraid to look him in the eye. She knew he'd almost lost her a dozen times over from her stupidity and ego.

But he wasn't angry—far from it.

Kalinda helped Caesar stand, and Arianne realized with a start that he was missing a leg. She mourned the injury for a moment, but the feeling was quickly eclipsed by relief. She would take losing a limb over losing the man who'd raised her any day.

"Arianne," Caesar breathed.

And suddenly, everything felt right again. As soon as her father's arms wrapped around her, she burst into sobs. Every ounce of fear about losing him evaporated. All of her ambitions, fears, hopes, and dreams faded into one aching relief: he was alive. Her dad—the man she loved more than anything in the world—was safe in her arms.

She wasn't a hero. She was just Arianne: a female who would tear the world down to protect the ones she loved.

"Dad," she cried again.

"*Tranquila*," Caesar stroked the wild mane of hair above his daughter's head. "Everything's going to be okay," he soothed.

She laughed weakly against his shoulder. "I came to rescue *you*. That's my line."

"We're going to have a long talk about that later." He let out a deep sigh, pulling his daughter in closer. Arianne was so relieved to be in Caesar's arms that the aching in her wing at the embrace was a distant sensation. "But not right now. I'm just happy to see you again, *hija*."

"I got some good news," she said, fighting back tears. "It's very unlikely I will ever do that again."

"*Aye dios mio*," Caesar muttered. "You give me more gray hairs than running a country."

The pair exchanged a chuckle filled with relief. Despite everything that had driven them apart, they were allowed a moment to simply enjoy the warmth of their embrace—such a simple act that had seemed impossible only hours ago.

The Pacifican jet took off moments later, and Caesar returned to Josephina's side while Arianne found a seat to take the strain off of her wounded back. She sat across the cabin from her mother—removed enough to look normal despite her constant monitoring. Rhino and Jaya remained at her side the entire flight. The three friends sat in stunned silence, relieved from the hell they'd just narrowly escaped. The feeling of Rhino's hand resting on her thigh and Jaya's fingers interlaced with hers kept her sane despite the pain and storm of emotions.

Once Josephina's condition stabilized, Kalinda approached the *Fera* trio, analyzing them with a deep frown. Without a word to the shell-shocked group, Kalinda replaced Jaya at Arianne's side and inspected her fractured wing. With expert hands, the field medic set the break and placed the wing in a splint before working on the rest of the trio's wounds.

As the pounding pain in her back subsided, exhaustion hit her like a wave. Eyes flickering closed, Arianne leaned against Rhino's meaty shoulder. After weeks of peril, she was safe. Her body finally claimed the rest it so desperately needed as she fell into the deepest sleep she'd had in weeks.

Chapter 55

Arianne

The following month passed in a whirlwind.

Hearings, meetings, and hospital visits—Arianne felt like she hadn't had a moment to sit down and breathe since her flight home. She certainly hadn't had enough time to process everything that had happened to her. She was in limbo: aware but unable to react just yet. After months of being in survival mode, all her body wanted was two weeks of sleep in a coma-like state.

But she wasn't done yet.

After the events of Leonueva, the individuals discovered at the Murray Monument were slated for cross-examination to ensure all their stories lined up. Jaya, Rhino, Kalinda, and Lyn had received a speedy trial in the days before. The captured squadron who had protected Caesar—and ultimately helped Josephina summon Pacific to Leonueva—were quickly regarded as heroes and given high honors.

Arianne's heart clenched. Her mother was now celebrated as the true hero of the skirmish—now named the Fall of Leonueva. Josephina's years of aiding in protecting Citadel's location had been publicly reported. Now, the entire island worshiped her as their unofficial queen. She'd been pardoned and offered Pacifican citizenship—if she ever woke up to reap the benefits.

Despite the work of Citadel's best doctors, there was a good chance that she never would.

Now, the only remaining trials were for Bradley Shaw and herself.

"Major Arianne Ortiz." The Head Chair tapped his gavel to get her attention. "Did you hear me?"

Arianne shook her head, pulling her mind from the movie of memories that hadn't stopped flickering since she'd returned home. The winged female blinked against the bright rays of island sunlight washing through the windows before her. "Yes?"

She was seated in a conference room at a long, broad table made up of the council of representatives who were charged with examining her role in the events. The council comprised of Kalfas, several other military leaders, and a select panel of Pacifican Senators. Caesar sat in the room as well, but he was removed from the table. As president, he had a right to listen to the meetings, but as Arianne's adopted guardian, he was too biased to judge.

The Head Chair, the leader of the Pacifican Senate, frowned at her from across the conference room table, his wrinkled face the permanent display of disapproval. "Do you have any changes you would like to make to your official written statement?"

Arianne eyed the document the Head Chair held in his wiry fingers. In those pages, her journey would be forever enshrined in the government record: her crimes, failures, and patriotism. She knew the review board's decision was out of her hands, and she was uncertain if her good deeds would ultimately outweigh her discretions. But she was okay with whatever outcome: her journey had taught her that actions—no matter how well-meaning—had consequences.

And for once in her life, she was *Fera* enough to own up to them.

But what was in the document didn't scare her. It was what she'd kept from it. Keston... she'd never once revealed his true identity, nor what their relationship had grown into. Once the statement was approved, the official record of the events leading up to the Fall of Leonueva would reflect a completely transactional relationship between a bounty hunter named Blackjack and the Pacifican Major, Arianne Ortiz.

The record would not reflect Arianne's potentially treasonous relationship with Keston nor his *Fera* nature. Jaya and Arianne risked purgery with their statements that Blackjack had evaded their attempts at his capture after the battle.

And the greatest lie of all was one Caesar and Kalfas had signed off on. In Arianne's statement, she admitted she had come in contact with Leon Murray. To avoid suspicion and full prosecution, she had to include one damning lie: *Major Arianne Ortiz had no previous relationship with any hostile encountered. Any actions taken by Major Arianne Ortiz were made in the best interest of the United Colonies of Pacific.*

The words were complete and utter bullshit.

Attacking Leon... even she couldn't rationalize it. Every ounce of her training should have told her to retreat and get behind the cover of her comrades. Every rational soldier could go on record and state how idiotic she'd been. And that was the kicker: she hadn't been thinking when she saw her mother and father—she'd just acted. Now, if she wanted to avoid a dishonorable discharge—and possible exile thanks to her personal relation to the Murrays—she needed to lie through her teeth and pray the Senate bought it.

She leaned forward towards her microphone that recorded every damning word, her tight uniform squeaking uncomfortably with the movement. "Yes, your Honor," she said. "All statements made in that document are accurate accounts of the incident to the extent of my knowledge."

And if word ever got out about how much bullshit she'd just spewed, she was intimately aware that she was taking Caesar, Kalfas, and Jaya down with her.

"Thank you, Miss Ortiz." The Head Chair smiled. "If there is nothing else to add, the review board has arrived at their verdict."

Her stomach twisted, and she turned to Caesar and Kalfas for any sign of encouragement. She didn't get it.

The Head Chair of the Senate cleared his throat. "Insubordination is grounds for a dishonorable discharge, Major Ortiz." Arianne wilted under his sunken eyes. "That being considered, your actions resulted in a historic win for our people. General Kalfas confirmed your instrumental role. The Council has also advised me on other important variables to consider in your case."

"Understood," She nodded curtly, her mouth drying.

The Head Chair sat back. "This war is far from over, Major Ortiz. That being considered, the United Colonies of Pacific need all the fighters they can get." Arianne perked up as he continued. "Due to your specific skillset and honorable actions during the Fall of Leonueva, your discharge sentence has been lessened to a military suspension."

She sagged in relief. "Thank you, your Honor."

"I'm not done," the Head Chair announced. "Your military suspension is contingent on your cooperation. You will be required to testify during Bradley Shaw's trial." His glasses glinted in the sunlight. "And that trial may bring about more information than this Council has assessed. Your sentence will be adjusted based on the results."

She gritted her teeth. So much had happened in those short few minutes at the top of the Murray Monument. And most of it was a blur. She was uncertain how much Bradley Shaw had discerned—which made her blood pressure skyrocket. What had Shaw seen her do?

Bradley Shaw was a traitor, and Arianne would do whatever she could to make him pay, no matter what pleas he sent her way. Her only fear was that Shaw would attempt to take her down with him.

"Next: counsel from your next of kin has given us other perspectives." The Head Chair continued, gesturing towards Caesar. "Your suspension will also be contingent on cooperation in psychotherapy." Arianne's lips parted. "We are well aware of your... impulses, Major Ortiz. We need your service, but we cannot condone sending one of our own on active duty until their mental state is stable."

Arianne lurched out of her chair, wings unfurling behind her. *No! You got it wrong!* She recoiled. She wasn't unstable, and she refused to be seen as a head case. She wanted to shout her objection but stopped when she witnessed the review board flinch back—fear in their eyes.

The winged female blinked, sensing an unease so thick she could cut it with a knife.

She wilted as the awful realization struck her that even in her home country, she was feared by the people she'd fought to protect. And the worst part about it was that they didn't even know the whole story.

"No," she said in a small voice, feeling herself shrink. "I-I'm sorry. I didn't mean to scare you." She held her hands up, looking pleadingly at the Head Chair. "I'm fine," she reassured him.

"Arianne," Caesar said calmly.

She turned to her father, betrayal making her shoulders slump. She heard every thought Caesar had in those three syllables. She looked deep into her father's warm, watchful eyes as the awful realization settled over her. *He thinks you're broken,* a savage, primal voice born of fear and hate whispered at the back of her mind. *He thinks you'll turn into* Him.

"I don't need help," Arianne pleaded. "I'm not a threat! I-I promise!"

Caesar stood slowly, raising his hand to silence the Head Chair as he attempted to soothe his daughter. "I know, *hija.* "Arianne blinked away terrified tears as her father laid a calming hand on her wings. "But you've been through a lot. They're just talks—okay? We just want you to feel better."

Arianne tore her gaze away from Caesar, his disclosure of her struggles without her permission making her feel backed into a corner. She knew she was getting worse: her blackouts were more frequent, now plaguing her with her childhood *and* the events of the month before. And her uncontrollable anger... she'd risked the entire battle because of it. Lastly, her dreams had devolved into nightmares of Hera's lab and forests filled with hunters following her scent. Deep down, she knew she needed help, but the idea of forcing it on her made her insides curl.

Maybe Caesar had a point. Maybe she *did* need help. But it still hurt like hell to know he was weaponizing her dreams of being a Pacifican officer to get her to comply with therapy.

She sat back down, calmly folding her wings behind her. Owning up to her actions felt a whole lot better before she realized that her actions scared people. Her *skill set,* as the Head Chair had called it, was a terrible weapon in Pacific's eyes: great, but only if it was pointed at the enemy.

"You just want to calibrate your weapon," she muttered delicately, uncertain whether or not she was saddened or enraged at the idea.

"Arianne, no," Caesar protested.

She avoided her father's burning gaze. They thought she was broken, but they also wanted to use her. What was it? Was she a threat, or was she their savior? Her nose scrunched up in annoyance. Who were they to say what level of broken she was allowed to be? Did they ever stop to think about how much sacrifice was needed for her kind of power?

Power was a gift and curse for a reason, and she was offended that they wanted to glorify her strengths while vilifying the pain she'd sustained because of it.

Thunder crashed in Arianne's storm cloud eyes as she looked up at the Head Chair. "You gained an inkling of what I could do from these reports, and you don't want to lose it. You want the weapon without the madness, but maybe you didn't stop to think if they're a package deal."

The fact that the people in that room were afraid of her wrecked her inside. She never wanted the people she saw as allies to cower before her. All she ever wanted was to *protect* them. But that sadness was slowly devolving into anger. The very people she wanted to protect were using their fear to justify reducing her to a weapon—just like Leon.

"Major Ortiz," Kalfas boomed, cracking Arianne's rage. "Sit down."

She blinked, clarity returning to her. As she took a deep breath to calm herself, she felt the entire room do the same. Filling her lungs in a rhythmic pattern of deep breaths, she managed to slow her thundering heart and sit back down. The room was deadly quiet now, and she was awfully aware of how every eye around her was fixated on her wings—exposed from her outburst. Those wings were a physical reminder that she was different, and different was dangerous.

Maybe Caesar and Kalfas had grounded her for reasons beyond protecting her from Leon. Once Pacific knew what she could do, they wouldn't see her as a citizen. They would see her as their sword. Arianne fought tears as she stared downwards at her painfully clenched fists. Pacific now understood what power they possessed from the mission reports of the inhuman-like feats she'd accomplished on her journey.

"I'm sorry," she breathed to the council and, to some extent, to her future self.

The Head Chair tapped his gavel on the table. "Then this investigation is concluded," he announced. "The files will be marked incomplete until the conclusion of the Shaw case. It is my honor to officially welcome you back to Citadel Island, Major Ortiz."

The Head Chair's congratulatory words washed over her like a tidal wave. Typically, Arianne loved waves, but this one threatened to pull her under. Numbly, she stood and saluted. It took all of her strength to keep her lips from wobbling and her eyes forward. Everyone in that room was scared of her, and whatever freedom she'd bought herself was built on a shaky mountain of fabrications. Arianne Ortiz was not real, but she would have to live behind that mask for the rest of her life if she ever wanted to keep her place on that island.

The Head Chair's eyes bored into her as if calculating when he could take a hammer to the thin ice she currently found herself on. She stared blankly forward at the wrinkled man, determined not to give him an ounce of satisfaction. She'd known from a young age that political power trumped even the strongest of *Feras*. She also knew that fear made people cling to whatever power they had. The Head Chair feared her, which made him dangerous.

"You are dismissed, Major Ortiz," Kalfas ordered, sensing the glares between Arianne and the Head Chair growing increasingly more predatory.

Arianne quickly turned and left the room before she broke down into tears.

Camera flashes blinded her as she left the Capitol building. Reporters from across the island and awestruck citizens were waiting eagerly on the building's steps to hear the results of the trial. She shielded her eyes and ducked her head against the barrage of questions and screams.

"Miss Ortiz!" A reporter called. "What was the verdict?"

"Welcome home! Anything you would like to tell the island?"

Arianne's breathing quickened. The flashes of the cameras started to feel like a barrage of blaster fire. The circling crowd suddenly felt like a patrol of tribesmen closing in on her. Her body went into a frenzied adrenaline state. She covered her ears, panic gripping her with its cold fingers as the shouting of the reporters merged together until they sounded like excited cheers in Ace's arena. Too much. It was all too much.

Spreading her wings, she crouched low and launched into the sky.

Months ago, she would have loved the swarming crowds and attention. Being on the cover of a Pacifican magazine and being called a hero would've been a dream. Now, all she wanted was to be left alone. She landed on the balcony of her home with a thud. The world spun around her as she stumbled up the stairs and into her bedroom. Crawling onto her bed, Arianne hugged her knees to her chest, wrapping her wings protectively around her. There, in her cocoon, she burst into tears.

"I take it back," she sobbed, rolling to her side. "I take it back!"

Sinking into that water tank, watching Carol torn to shreds by the feral Alligator, Josephina bleeding out in front of her, Leon kicking her from the tower, the fall that should've led to her death... she couldn't handle it. She wished it never happened.

But it did. Now, she was a "hero," just like she'd always wanted.

"I take it back," she whispered again, her throat raw from sobbing.

A hesitant knock came to her door sometime after the worst of her tears had dried. She softly mumbled for the guest to enter through her wall of feathers. Caesar walked in, his weight heavily supported by his cane and the new prosthetic he was slowly learning to use.

The President patiently moved a few feathers to see his daughter's face. Through the gloom provided by the shade of her wings, she saw him offer her a small smile. "Want to meet me downstairs?" He asked softly in Spanish.

Arianne sniffled. "I'm a little tired."

Caesar softly wiped a stray tear from her cheek. "Just trust me?"

"Okay, give me a minute."

Arianne changed out of her wrinkled military uniform and into a low-back floral dress. She enjoyed wearing things that didn't constrict her wings. She also appreciated the slight boost in confidence she got by looking halfway decent—even if her eyes were still hopelessly bloodshot and swollen.

With a long sigh, she stepped out of her dark bedroom, a slight headache coming on from the congestion in her sinuses. Slowly, she trudged down the stairs, her motivation drained. She stopped when she saw the balcony doors open, a fully furnished table beyond. Her lips parted as she approached, curiosity cautiously taking over her despair.

The setting sun turned the sky orange as palm trees decorating the shoreline beyond swayed in a calming breeze. For a moment, she was lost in the beauty of the scattered clouds, painted purple and pink in the dying daylight. With a sigh, she was reminded how easily she'd fallen in love with that view.

"I assumed you didn't get ice cream in Leonueva," Caesar said in greeting.

Arianne gazed at the decorated table in wonder. Caesar had set it with every requirement for the perfect ice cream sundae. Four flavors of ice cream, sprinkles, cherries, bananas, hot fudge and caramel, cookies, and whipped cream. Her mouth watered at the sight.

"There's a lot I need to apologize for," Caesar began. "I should've been honest with you from the start." The President casually began fixing his bowl of coffee ice cream. "Instead of grounding you, I should have taken the time to explain everything going against us. I just wanted to protect you, Arianne. My presidency should be my burden, not yours. The politics with the Head Chair and Pacific's desire for a weapon that could turn the tides of the war shouldn't be your problem." He let out a long sigh. "A long time ago, I promised to protect you. I guess that included my best efforts to give you something of a normal life."

Arianne took a spoon and began digging into the cookies and cream container, "Dad," she chuckled through a spoonful of ice cream. "I was born with giant-ass wings. I was never going to be normal."

Caesar let out a long breath. "You can't blame me for trying."

She grinned, deciding it would be easier to eat straight out of the carton. She'd been through hell—she deserved to gorge herself. She sat on the balcony railing, deciding to concentrate on piling as much whipped cream and sprinkles on the top of her container as possible.

"And I should have been honest about my relationship with your mother," Caesar continued.

Arianne perked up, dropping a cherry. "What?"

Caesar folded his fingers. "I've always been so proud of you. The odds you've had to overcome amaze me every day. And despite everything, you fight to be *good*, Arianne." He looked down. "That's also why I wanted you to stay on the island. I know all too well what the world does to good people—I wanted to protect you."

"My mom," she whispered, her mind going to the hospital bed where Josephina currently rested.

"The Ortiz's were a family of Pangaean Elites that reigned over the southern half of Spain," Caesar began. "My father grew close to his personal valet, Enrique Valentino. Your grandfather. My father's relationship with the Valentino family opened his eyes to the treatment of commoners, and he worked to change policies in his region." He took a bite of his ice cream. "Other Elites didn't like the threat those policies posed to their power and wealth, so they murdered my parents in an attempt to take their influence." He paused, shaking his head. "I was eleven years old."

"Dad..." Arianne trailed off. She couldn't imagine her father, the President of Citadel, a young orphan. In many ways, they were more similar than she'd thought.

"But my parents anticipated this," he continued. "My father gave all of his wealth and properties to his valet. Enrique and his family were to be the reagents of the Ortiz estate until I was old enough to assume the responsibilities as patriarch of the family. I grew up with your mother, Arianne, and I love her as deeply as I love you."

The winged female looked down, a mixture of emotions stirring within her. "Is that why you adopted me?"

Caesar shook his head as his hand reached out to hold hers. That small gesture reminded her of the first day they had met. "No, *hija*, "he breathed. "I chose to be in your life before I knew who you were." He gave her hand a soft squeeze. "I will choose to be in your life no matter what."

Arianne wiped away a new wave of tears. "I love you too, Dad."

"I'm sorry I never told you," he said again. "I was afraid of you growing up believing you were still in your family's shadow. I didn't want you to ever question what you meant to me. I promise you, Arianne, the greatest pride of my life will always be you." Caesar leaned forward, giving his daughter a long hug. "Do you have any more questions?"

Arianne pulled away from the President, a frown settling on her face. "If you knew my mom, how did she marry Leon? Why did you leave her for Pacific?"

The former Elite let out a soft laugh, one meant to shield pain hiding just underneath. "That's a long story for another time, *hija*." He pursed his lips as a haunted look fell over him, "that's the other thing I wanted to talk about."

"What is it?"

Caesar stood. Leaning on his cane, he moved beside her and rested his hands on the railing. The President looked towards the horizon, his eyes settling on the rippling line where the cotton candy sky met the darkening sea. Arianne jumped down from her spot and joined him, gently leaning into his side as he wrapped an arm around her.

"Being good isn't easy," Caesar breathed, dark eyes shimmering as they reflected the sun. "Everyone around me has suffered because of this thing called altruism. I wanted you to be the exception, but no one's immune. There's a lot of bad in this world, Arianne, and you only have two choices: fight it or succumb to it."

"I've realized," she said wryly.

"What you're going through..." He trailed off. "You're not alone. And I have to warn you, it won't get easier. That's the tradeoff. You can choose to be a hero, but you cannot choose the consequences." He shook his head. "Most of the time, you cannot even predict them."

"Caesar?" She asked, concerned with his wavering tone.

"We've all been through a lot." The President looked out over the domain he'd built as silver lined his eyes. "It's not going to get easier. I suggest you rest while you can." Caesar turned to move toward the balcony doors with a stiff nod. "Excuse me," he finished tersely before leaving.

The ice cream settled like a rock in her stomach. Suddenly, even her favorite treat didn't sound appealing. Straightening herself, Arianne hopped back onto the railing and sat, her legs swinging over the deadly drop down the cliff below as she tried to calm her anxiety.

Caesar was right. The Fall of Leonueva was just the beginning. There was no telling what would happen from there—what Leon would do, if Pacific could defend itself, and a million other variables. The only thing she could do was be happy she was still breathing and pray to whatever god that still existed that it remained that way. Arianne took a long breath, staring over the rocky island speckled with green below her. It seemed as if the only certainty was uncertainty.

Her prototype phone buzzed in her pocket as if answering her thoughts. Confused, Arianne reached into the spandex underneath her dress and pulled it out. On the screen was a notification labeled *Pangaea Boy.*

She grinned despite her better judgment. The trial over the past month should have been a warning that she needed to lie low, but she couldn't resist the pull of her excitement. She opened her phone and read the message as her fingers tingled with anticipation: *Ready for our next adventure, Princess?*

She scanned the darkening skies above her, thumbs circling over the keypad in her hands as she considered her response. She knew keeping in contact with him was foolish, but she was never one to follow the book.

Always, she replied to the winged male.

Closing the phone and placing it back in her pocket, she felt a stir she hadn't sensed in weeks. She wanted to move. She wanted to feel the wind rushing through her hair once more. Despite everything plaguing her on the ground, she yearned for the freedom the skies promised. Skies that, one day, she might not fly alone.

So Arianne Murray closed her eyes, leaned over the railing, and let gravity pull her down. Her powerful golden wings caught her, and she rocketed towards the moon rising above the sea. She shouted out into the night with excitement, and maybe, somewhere, another winged *Fera* cried back.

Epilogue
The Mourning Prince

Andre Murray stood over his mother's grave, a single tear betraying him as it fell down his cheek.

The prince stiffened as he raised his arm to wipe that shimmering sign of weakness from his face. Collected once more, he raised his chin, curled his upper lip, and waited for the last wave of sadness to pass. It didn't take much effort to replace his mourning with anger.

He glared down at Josephina Valentino-Murray's beautifully carved headstone in the heart of the Paris cemetery, hissing as his eyes started to sting again. For the fourth night that week, Andre fought to come to terms with his new reality. His mother—the only woman who'd ever loved him—was gone.

The leaves of the trees shading the graveyard rustled on a cold wind that warned of autumn. In response, he raised the collar of his uniform to protect against the chill as night fell. It seemed he'd inherited his intolerance to the cold from his Spaniard mother.

Everything reminded him of Josephina now.

"Out here sulking again, I see," came his father's voice.

The prince turned, watching Leon materialize from the trees. The Commander wasn't alone. He was followed by Hera and a new shadow that Andre didn't recognize. From what he could recall, Leon's newest lackey was a French Elite, but he'd never learned of a man who looked like that in his studies. How an unknown Elite could rise and become Leon's personal Advisor and overseer of the former capital in Paris was beyond him. The man stood at average height, but what struck Andre was that he looked far from French: he had dark curling hair and warm chestnut skin.

"I didn't know it was frowned upon to pay homage, father." Andre ducked his head into a respectful bow.

Leon regarded the headstone of his former wife coolly. "I would be wary of who you let see you paying respects to a traitor, son." Any ounce of grief Andre would have expected from his father had completely disappeared in the past week. What remained was a man who seemed utterly unfazed by the passing of his wife.

Andre glared at Hera, who now sat proudly at her betrothed's side. The scientist General raised her head and stared back. Now that she was unrivaled for Leon's affections, there was a new level of insufferable superiority in her air. He clenched his hands at the coup she'd performed against Josephina—the coup that had ultimately gotten his mother killed.

He scowled as a powerful surge of anger took over. In quick succession, Andre drew a blade from his belt, palmed it, and threw it at Hera's head. The dagger embedded itself deeply into a wrangled tree behind her. To the scientist General's credit, she didn't flinch.

"I understand emotions are high," Leon purred, casually stepping in the way of Hera and his Advisor.

Andre's eyebrows furrowed together. "You're not going to address that she *plotted* to frame my mother—your *wife*? Her daughter hospitalized me, and now you let her stand by your side?"

"Oh dear," Hera smirked.

"Things have been busy," Leon held his hands up, "I regret that I haven't been able to debrief you during the chaos and your recovery. Allow me to shed some light on the situation." The Commander turned on his watch, and a projection appeared above it. "Your mother was a traitor, son. That's something we all must accept. But, neither Hera nor I killed her."

The security footage of the front entrance to the Murray Monument flickered above Leon's wrist. At first, there was only debris and scattered crowds of panicked citizens running just beyond the marble staircase. Then, there was movement as someone ran from the lobby and onto the street. Andre felt himself still as a full-grown female in a black experimental wetsuit ran into the camera's frame.

And behind the female was a set of magnificent golden brown wings. Andre stopped breathing entirely.

The video continued to play as the female crouched down and rocketed into the sky. Leon paused the recording as the *Fera* turned mid-air to face the building. It was at that moment that her face came into view.

"Arianne," the prince's entire body threatened to shut down. "You lied! You told us she was dead! I mourned her for years," he seethed, turning on his father.

Leon studied the image of his daughter, fresh from the grave. "Yes, I'll admit I was quite surprised as well. Unfortunately, she didn't come back as the girl you loved. She's been brainwashed by that rebel island cause, and now she's a weapon programmed specifically for this family." The Commander closed the projection and lowered his head in a moment of silence. "A fact I experienced personally when she attempted to kill me." He paused, deep blue eyes locking with his son as he pulled a small glinting fragment from his pocket. "And put this bullet through your mother's head."

Leon tossed the metal ball toward Andre, and the prince caught it with a wince. Even though it had been weeks since the bullet was fired, the metal burned in his hands like it had only just left the barrel. His knees buckled as he held his hand to his chest to counteract the awful ache growing inside of him. In those moments, his world shattered and was rebuilt with a new purpose.

"The Arianne you knew died. This one just shares her face," Leon continued. "Do you know what I want you to do?"

The prince stood as his grief, agony, and anger melded together to create the passion that would carry him to his ultimate goal. "I'm going to kill her for taking my mother from me," he growled.

"Wonderful." Leon gestured to his Advisor. "Then let me introduce you to our newest resource: Monsieur Cassius Leroy. We had to keep him under close examination for a few years: dissociative identity disorder can be *tricky*. But we're quite certain Cassius has a hold over his alters now—isn't that right?"

Cassius nodded, reaching a hand out for the prince to shake. "I have control of the body now. Jaleel shouldn't be a problem anymore," he said in a rich Parisian accent. "The Leroy Estate is at your disposal, Your Highness."

"Now that we have everyone on board," Leon clapped his hands. "We have a rebel colony to destroy, the Serum to find, and a particular Little Beast to kill. Let's get to work, shall we?"

ENJOY THIS STORY?

PLEASE CONSIDER LEAVING A REVIEW!

TIME TO BOOK YOUR NEXT FLIGHT...

TURN THE PAGE FOR A SNEAK PEEK!

Eleven Years Ago

H is world both ended and began anew with that single explosion.

A bright flash followed by a quaking boom turned the peaceful home he once knew into a barren wasteland. The shockwave caused an immense and painful pressure in his chest, like someone had punched him with the full force of their power. The winged boy stumbled, tears pricking his eyes from the bright flash of light coming through the room's ruptured windows.

"Keston! Get down!" his grandfather cried, voice barely perceptible over the ringing in Keston's ears.

Pépé grabbed him and angled him towards the open staircase. Then he was weightless, thrown down the basement steps, stomach in his chest as gravity ripped him towards safety. He was faintly aware of his own screams.

The younger boy hit the basement floor hard on his side, his shoulder cracking on the landing. His grandfather tumbled down the stairs next to him, his weathered body snapping and breaking with every impact on the wooden steps. His shoulder was excruciating, but he forced the pain to become a distant ache as he collected himself and scrambled to his grandfather. Keston barely reached his savior before the older man stood and dragged his grandson away from the exposed base of the stairs.

Tucked safely in the arms of his grandfather, the winged boy stared at his small view of the open door at the top of the staircase. He continued to cry as the entrance glowed a terrible orange, and a ripping gust sent debris flying like bullets through the opening. Shaking, he covered his ears against the eerie wind that sent even more death and destruction.

In the awful silence following, shock's painfully cold grip tightened around the boy.

Pépé squeezed his grandson closer. Keston clung to his protector, his scraped and bleeding palms refusing to release his only remaining certainty. Slowly, Keston looked up at his grandfather's face, more terror filling his veins at how broken his grandfather looked. Hair covered in dirt, ears bleeding, and glasses fractured, Pépé seemed half dead.

Keston's chattering teeth slowed just enough for him to whisper, "Pépé, what happened?" He barely managed that before he broke down into more sobs.

For a moment, Pépé was quiet, his breathing hitched and uneven. When he finally spoke, he struggled to look down at his grandson. "I don't know." He sighed. "I don't know."

The pair sat there for what felt like decades, huddled together in silence. Pépé's eyes remained on the ceiling, listening for any sign that could signify hope or certain doom. Keston wasn't sure what to listen for, but he was too terrified to make a sound. Eventually, satisfied with their safety, Pépé stood painfully slow and cautiously lumbered up the stairs. Each step for the man was laborious, and if the boy hadn't been frozen in time, he would have rushed to help his grandfather. But he couldn't move. His limbs refused to listen.

Panic stung in his chest. What happened to his home?

"Keston, we need to move," Pépé croaked from the level above.

The boy shook his head at the demand, the sting in his chest becoming an intense ache. The constant *boom, boom, boom* as his heart thudded against his ribcage. If he focused too hard on the noise, it sounded like the explosion that had ripped his world to shreds.

"*Now, boy!*" Pépé barked again.

The order snapped Keston out of his daze, and he scrambled to his feet. He cried out in pain as he attempted to move his injured shoulder. So much dizzying pain made him want to collapse back to the ground. But Pépé never shouted at him like that, so he couldn't afford to stop.

Keston wasn't prepared for what he saw at the top of the stairs. Spare a few brave remnants of drywall and concrete, the blast had leveled Pépé's home and holistic hospital. The boy's amber eyes settled on the crumpled frame of a former gurney, struggling to imagine what level of force would be needed to bend even the stiffest of metals. Pépé's desk was charred with a few embers scattered across it, still glowing. The sky was ashen and filled with clouds of debris slowly shielding the light of the full moon. Soon, the only light in the town came from the few fires left burning as they fed on the last remnants of houses and buildings.

Then Keston heard the distinct sound of wood splintering and bricks shifting. His ears marked the sound just in time to turn to the remnants of his town's church. The steeple crumbled and groaned under the explosion's damage. He barely had time to commit the town's central landmark to memory before there was one final *crack,* and the steeple's brass bell crashed to the ground. A haunting ringing reverberated throughout the leveled town of Mende.

For the first time, he found a musical note abhorrent.

"Celine," Pépé gasped his daughter's name in terror. The older healer looked down at his grandson. "We need to run," he breathed.

Despite their injuries, adrenaline shielded the pain long enough for the pair to sprint through their town of embers and ruin. Whatever goodness the silver light of the moon once granted that night, the ashes of the fallen town had covered it completely, leaving the frantic pair in demonic darkness. Keston ran next to his grandfather, his young mind finally realizing why Pépé was terrified. Celine's home may be at the edge of the town, but there was no guarantee that the house had dodged the blast. And his family's meager cabin didn't have a basement.

"Mom," Keston breathed, "Gen!"

The boy ran faster, refusing to believe that a simple choice to help his grandfather sort herbs that night was what separated him from the rest of his family's fate. Their home was safe, he promised himself. The blast didn't make it that far.

He was quickly proven wrong.

His family's home. The place where he would practice Chopin with his father, dance the *valse musette* with his sister, and sing forgotten show tunes from before the Great Disaster with his mother. Now, it was nothing more than a pile of scattered wood and stone, torn to shreds by the explosion's decimating waves.

Keston fell to his knees.

Pépé pulled him to his feet, saying something the boy was too stunned to process. Stumbling, Keston ran the last tenth of a mile to his house. Even the forests beyond their cabin, which rested in the grassy meadow, were leveled and flattened. Forests he could thank for his stamina that day; forests he used to spend every moment he could spare inside of.

Ruined.

Keston was little more than a husk as he stared at the house. He was too overwhelmed to help as Pépé began searching the wreckage. "Celine?" the healer cried out. Genevieve? Celine!" Despite his fractured bones, Pépé continued to wade through the rubble, tears streaming down his ash-coated face. "Can you hear me?"

The boy shook his head, watching the scene. Gone. His family was gone. He could feel it deep in his gut. Was his father buried there, too? Had he returned from work yet? Keston was too overwhelmed to give it much thought.

His grandfather's startled cry pierced the ringing in Keston's ears. The winged boy whipped his head up, eyes going to where Pépé knelt in the wreckage. Before Keston knew it, he was running to the site, his gaze focused solely on one thing: a bloodied hand resting in Pépé's palms.

"Mom!" Keston screamed.

Pépé's shoulders shook as he pulled the limp hand of his daughter to his chest. Keston landed next to him, his lips quivering at the sight. Celine rested face down on the charred ground, her head covered in gore and grime almost beyond recognition. Her light blonde hair was astray, with scattered yellow and blue feathers resting next to the straw-colored strands.

"Pépé, do something," the boy whimpered.

As if realizing he wasn't alone, Pépé turned in shock towards his grandson. The man jumped, quickly moving to shield Keston's eyes, "You're too young to see this!"

But it was too late. Buried beneath the home she had worked so hard to build, Keston's mother was seared into his mind like the blast marks on the remaining walls of Mende. The boy stared into his grandfather's palm, the sight of his mother only growing in clarity. Freezing panic smothered him once more, and his breathing slowed. His senses narrowed as his teeth started to clench harder and harder.

And in that heightened moment of fear, as the world slowed around him, his young *Fera* ears picked up on the hitched breathing of a *third* person. As if possessed, the boy shoved his grandfather away, eyes locking on the spot like an eagle honing in on prey. Suddenly, he didn't care that his mother wasn't breathing. In those moments, his only focus was on the person *alive* beneath her. Against Pépé's shouts of warning, Keston jumped forward and yanked the wreckage away from his mother, broken shoulder forgotten.

A fiery strand of hair. Then, two exposed and broken legs. But Keston didn't let hope fill his chest just yet. He kept digging. Pépé joined in, carefully removing his daughter from under the beam that had ultimately claimed her life. And there, unconscious but still breathing, was Genevieve.

Celine had given her life to protect her daughter from the blast. She hadn't shielded the younger girl entirely, but her sacrifice hadn't been in vain. Genevieve's upper body, though covered in soot and her mother's blood, was unharmed. Her lower body had borne the damage, but Keston didn't care. Someone could live without legs.

All that mattered was that his sister would *live*.

Keston fell next to her. His fingers were cracked and bleeding from his manic digging, but he didn't care as he raised a shaking hand to run his fingers through her hair. Closing his eyes, he kissed her on the forehead as sobs wracked his body.

Genevieve's life was their mother's last gift.

At that moment, Keston promised his mother's ghost that no one would *ever* hurt their dear Genevieve again.

Writer's Note
I hope you enjoyed your flight!

At the heart of The Tyrant's Daughter is a story about family. Anyone who knows me personally can detect reflections of myself and my family in the characters within this book. How can I not include them? Every author takes what's familiar when constructing the fictional: intentional or not.

My inclusion was intentional. As a young girl, I saw creating a world where I could be the hero as my form of escapism. Arianne and Keston were made to be subversions of the classical hero genre. I wanted them to struggle, grow, and ultimately feel *real*. Naturally, if I saw myself in Arianne, then who did I see as the story's titular villain, Leon Murray?

My father is someone I could never begin to try to describe on the page. What he means to me and the many remarkable aspects of who he is go beyond what I could begin to depict in one character. Ultimately, parts of him inspired all of the father figures for Arianne in the story: Caesar, Kalfas, and, yes, Leon. Caesar represented the love and protectiveness of my father: wise, caring, and ultimately always looking out for his little girl. Kalfas was the coach: strong, uncompromising, and constantly pushing for improvement.

And Leon Murray, I find, is the greatest compliment of all. My father is brilliant, passionate, driven, ambitious, outspoken, and an unwavering leader. These qualities have made my father a staple in all the communities he is in. And I, a writer who loves to ask questions, said: "But what if he was evil?" Because if anyone knows my father, they know that if he does anything, he does it *right*. And to me, taking someone like my father and twisting his motives into something sinister... that would make a brilliant villain indeed.

Arianne's struggles with being a perfect copy of her father were an interesting side effect of this decision. In real life, many people joke that I am a carbon copy of my father. And this is something I'm immensely proud of. But for Arianne? A hero fighting for good being just like her evil father? This struggle created a dynamic that made me fall in love with her character even more.

This is a very long-winded way of saying: thank you, Dad, and I love and respect you more than you know. Thanks for putting up the endless jokes from our friends and family about being the "Tyrant" in the Tyrant's daughter. Without your inspiration, this series would not exist. I hope everyone who has made it this far will stick around and watch Arianne and Leon juke it out in the series to come.

Lastly, before I go, I want to thank everyone who has supported me in this journey. To my Nana, thank you for everything: whether it was teaching me how to spell, erasing my bad handwriting, writing my first picture book called "Aliens," or staying awake on camping trips to get one more chapter of my book in. To Simon, thank you for reading my books (no matter how terrible) since middle school. To Haniya, thank you for finally pushing me to publish this book and amicably guiding me through every step of the way. To Mr. Stoncius, thank you for lighting a passion for writing that changed my life. And to my friends and family, thank you for your love, support, and patience.

The Legends of Pangaea Series continues with *The Prince of Paradise*, I hope to see all of you there!

www.ingramcontent.com/pod-product-compliance
Lightning Source LLC
Chambersburg PA
CBHW031239310726
48971CB00004B/1097